The
SECRET LIBRARY

CRAIG HALSTEAD

This novel is entirely a work of fiction. The names, characters and incidents portrayed in it are the work of the author's imagination. Any resemblance to actual persons, living or dead, events or localities is entirely coincidental.

ISBN: 1478209399
ISBN-13:978-1478209393

for Aaron

Chapter 1

The professor struggled violently, but it was never going to make any difference. He was in his sixtieth year, and the three black-clad men who had burst into his study were all much younger, a lot stronger, and armed.

Two of the men gripped his arms, forced his hands behind his back and held them there, while the third intruder taped his wrists together.

'What do you want?' he asked. 'I have nothing of value.'

They ignored him.

One of the intruders aimed a black pistol at his head, as a second tore a strip of silver duct tape from a roll, pressed it firmly over his mouth, silencing him.

'Get on the floor – face down.'

Too frightened to disobey, the professor complied.

Rain lashed the study window and, briefly, lightening flashed and lit up the night sky, before one of the intruders pulled the curtains closed. Somewhere not far away thunder rumbled. Thinking about it, the professor realised he hadn't been down to lock his front door yet; occasionally, he totally forgot and left it open all night. Nothing untoward had ever happened. This evening, he had been so engrossed in his work he hadn't given it a thought, but … it didn't matter. A locked door might have delayed the intruders, but he doubted it would have kept them out. He had no idea why he had been targeted.

The intruders wasted no time in setting about their business.

There was a professional, military air about the three men, and it didn't escape the professor's attention they made no effort to hide their faces, or to blindfold him.

He knew that wasn't a good sign.

Head raised, straining his neck to look up, the professor watched two intruders start to fill a large holdall with papers, files and notebooks from his desk, before turning their attention to his filing cabinets and bookshelves. At the same time, the third intruder pulled a small black device from his pocket and inserted it into the PC. The professor wasn't computer literate enough to know exactly what the device was, or what it was called, but he could guess its function: to copy all his files.

Although he still lectured part-time at Cambridge, the professor devoted most of his time to researching what his two daughters referred to as his 'obsession', a forty year passion that had cost him three marriages. But two months ago, on his third visit to Ecuador in as many years, he had made a significant breakthrough, and since then he had been working feverishly to verify what he had been told. In his head, if not on paper, he had already begun planning another expedition, to prove it wasn't just a myth. To find it, share it with the world. But now … somehow, the intruders must have found out, and he was powerless to stop them from stealing his life's work, and profiting from it.

Minutes before the intruders appeared, as he did most nights, the professor had poured himself two fingers of Glenmorangie, his favourite single malt Scotch, and lit a Cuban cigar. His daughters were forever nagging him to quit smoking, and he had cut down to three or four cigarettes a day, but he enjoyed his evening Havana too much to even contemplate giving it up. As he watched, the intruder who appeared to be in charge had the temerity to pick up his cigar, puff life into it, before blowing a grey-blue smoke ring.

The professor knew the intruders planned to kill him.

He'd seen their faces, he could identify them … slowly, nothing to lose, he began inching across the polished wooden floor, toward the study door. The door was ajar. If he could just reach it, take the intruders by surprise, he might –

A black boot stopped him.

'Nice try, old man.'

The intruder knelt down next to the professor, placed his hand on the professor's right shoulder. The professor grimaced, as the intruder's hand gripped his shoulder, steadily increased the pressure … he started to feel dizzy, and increasingly faint.

The intruder didn't want to kill the professor, not yet and not this way. His instructions were clear: it must be made to look like an accident. So, as soon as the professor lost consciousness, he relaxed his grip.

There was an old leather armchair in one corner of the study, old enough to be stuffed with fibres that weren't flame retardant. The intruder half-carried, half-dragged the professor to the chair, dumped him on it.

Less than thirty minutes later, the lead intruder was satisfied they had everything they'd come for. 'Go wait for me in the car,' he instructed. 'This will only take a few minutes.'

The intruder ripped the tape off the professor's mouth, cut the tape from his hands, and rested his hands on his lap. The professor's head lolled on one side, as if he'd fallen asleep.

With a combat knife, the intruder nicked the green leather of one of the chair's broad arms, inserted his right forefinger finger and pulled. The old leather ripped easily. The intruder teased out some of the grey-white stuffing, before puffing on the professor's cigar, and touching the glowing end to the stuffing.

The fibres glowed red, but didn't catch alight.

The intruder tried again. This time, he cupped his free hand over the tear, and gently blew as he touched the glowing end of the cigar to the stuffing.

Suddenly little yellow-orange tongues of flame appeared.

Dropping the cigar in the flames as he stepped back, the intruder watched the blaze steadily increase in intensity. Remarkably quickly, it spread up the chair arm and across the back of the chair, and leapt across to the professor's clothes. The flames turned the professor's white shirt black, and when he detected the acrid stench of burning flesh, the intruder knew it was time to leave.

The intruder closed the study door on the way out, confident by the time a neighbour or passer-by noticed the inferno and alerted the emergency services, the professor would have been cremated.

At the same time
Salt Lake City, USA

'Do you know who they are?' the former priest asked, surprised to learn he wasn't the only one showing an interest in the discredited professor.

'Negative,' his man in England answered.

'I suspect, like us, they are interested in the professor's research materials.' The former priest shifted the cell phone from one ear to the other, as he slid his conservatory door open, stepped inside. His favourite lilac bush, rising majestically from a large, ornately decorated terracotta planter, was coming into bloom and filled the air with its sweet, grape-like aroma. He had been keeping tabs on the professor for more than five years now. Last fall, the professor had spent nearly a month in South America, but at the time it appeared nothing new had been discovered, no new leads uncovered. But perhaps he had been mistaken, and written off the professor's expedition too hastily?

'Would you like me to intervene?'

'No, but I do want you to observe and keep me informed.' He crossed to a high-back, natural wicker chair with two cream cushions on it,

3

paused next to it but didn't take a seat. 'Place a tracker on their vehicle, and follow them when they leave. I want to know who they are.'

'Consider it done.'

'I will speak to you shortly.'

The former priest ended the call, slipped his cell phone into the breast pocket of his black Armani shirt, as he strode into his lounge. Like his father and grandfather before him, he had been born and raised in The Church of Jesus Christ of Latter-day Saints. The Church was established by Joseph Smith, Jr., as the Church of Christ, in 1830, and underwent several names changes during the 1830s. Like all worthy males, the former priest was ordained at the young age of 12, into the Aaronic priesthood; six years later, he was ordained into the Melchizedek priesthood. But two years ago, accused of preaching false doctrine and speaking out publicly, he was called before a disciplinary council. Apparently, it was perfectly acceptable to hold any opinion he wished – in his head. He refused to be silenced and, accused of holding and publicising 'radical views', he was excommunicated from the Church.

Initially, the decision hit him hard: he fervently believed in the Church's theology and teachings, and he had been brought up to observe the Word of Wisdom, a health code that encouraged the use of wholesome herbs and fruits in season, moderate consumption of meat, and the consumption of grains, but which meant no alcohol, coffee, tea or tobacco. Contrary to what many non-adherents believed, the Church promoted monogamy. Indeed, since 1890, polygamy was illegal. He had one wife and together they had raised five children, and he lived by a moral code that prohibited sexual relations outside of heterosexual marriage. He was well aware his views, and the views of the Church, on homosexuality were both offensive and unacceptable to an increasing number of people outside the Church, but …

The former priest was standing in the kitchen, staring out over his one and a half acre garden without really taking in its beauty, when the cell phone in his breast pocket began to vibrate. He set his glass of water on the worktop and his cell phone's ringtone – Carl Orff's *Carmina Burana* – started. He glanced at the caller identity, felt his pulse quicken as he answered it. He listened intently, as his man in England brought him up-to-date.

'Is it possible the professor survived?' he asked.

'Negative.'

The fact the professor had been murdered suggested his killers must be on to something, must have found what they were searching for – almost certainly, the same thing he was determined to find ahead of anyone else.

4

'Do you want me to deal with them?'

'Not yet.' The former priest smiled patiently. 'This could be the breakthrough we've been waiting for. What they seek, our Church has been trying to locate for over eighty years, without success. Find out who they are and shadow them, but keep your head down and let them do the work – then we can reel them in and reap the benefits.'

Chapter 2

'That's her.'

The two men were seated in a dark blue transit van, inconspicuously parked next to a blue Fiat Panda, at the far side of the small car park in front of Monkey Park. Both vehicles bore false number plates. The driver, who had spoken, stubbed out his half-smoked cigarette and flicked the crushed butt through the van's open window.

The second man whistled softly. 'Man, she's one hot bitch!'

The woman – the driver knew her name was Samantha Frewin-Hamilton – was twenty-seven. Her skimpy shorts were lime green, and – the driver had no idea what the silky yellow and green fabric wound across her breasts and up around her neck was called, but it looked very striking, set against her sun-tanned skin and wavy, shoulder length brown hair. But, today, she wasn't their primary target.

Five minutes ago their accomplice, the women who had driven here in the Fiat Panda, entered the small zoo as soon as it opened. By now, she should be in position – ready to act at the first opportunity.

The driver focused his attention on the two kids who clambered out of the taxi after the woman. The older boy, who was eight, wore a Spider-Man T-shirt and red shorts; his four year old brother's T-shirt had Ben 10 splashed across the chest and his shorts were blue. Both kids, in contrast to their mother, had dark skin and short black hair.

'I don't get it – I thought her old man was English.'

'He is,' the driver confirmed.

'So the kids – they can't be his, right?'

'They're not. She has only been married a year.'

'They look like fuckin' Pakis.'

The driver didn't care what the kids looked like, but he did envy the lucky bastard who had spread their mother's legs, and sired them. He watched them run ahead of their mother, clearly eager to get inside the small zoo, explore it. A good sign. He made a quick call on his BlackBerry, saying only, 'They've arrived.' He waited until the kids were a few paces away from the zoo's entrance, before he reached to open the van door.

'Okay, let's do this.'

'Mummy! Look, Mummy!'

'I see it, sweetheart,' said Samantha, smiling at Luke's excitement. Her youngest son was pointing at a long, horizontal jungle mural with 'MONKEY PARK' painted across it. The monkeys on it were expected, but she was more surprised to see the large black cat's head on the right hand side of the mural.

'Is that a black panther?' asked Joshua.

'It sure looks like one, doesn't it?' she agreed. 'Let's go inside and find out, shall we?'

The boys ran ahead of her, and she caught up with them at the admission kiosk, manned by an attractive Spanish woman. As well paying their entrance fees, she bought two bags of food – a mix of cereal, seeds and small chunks of dried bread in a small polythene bag. But not for the monkeys. She had already taken her animal mad sons to Jungle Park and *Loro Parque* but before yesterday, when she had gotten into conversation with a fellow holidaymaker on *Playa de los Cristianos* beach, as her sons played at the water's edge, she wasn't aware Monkey Park existed. The woman told her the park opened at 9:30am, and recommended they get there early, as later it got busy and the monkeys would be asleep. The woman mentioned the monkeys preferred raisins or grapes to the bags of food sold at the park, but she said, 'your sons will enjoy feeding the dried food to the guinea pigs.'

She envisioned Monkey Park to be a small zoo, with the focus on monkeys, and up to a point she was right. Leading into the park, at one side of a short path, down a concrete slope overgrown with vegetation, Luke was excited to spot a small crocodile and several turtles.

She stepped aside, to allow two men in their mid-to-late twenties to pass, as her sons took turns to pose with a cockatoo cradled in their arms as it played dead. Joshua was quick to correct his young brother when Luke called the bird a 'white parrot', and she had to smile when the female photographer explained to Joshua that cockatoos were actually members of the parrot family, so calling her bird a white parrot was okay.

'Mummy, look – those men are going in that cage!'

'Gracias.' She thanked the photographer, before turning to her son and revealing, 'That's what's special about Monkey Park, Josh – we're allowed to enter some of the enclosures.'

'No way!' Joshua's eyes widened. 'Can we, Mummy – can we really?'

'I want to catch a monkey!'

She laughed, and knelt in front of her sons. 'Once we get inside the enclosures, we have to be quiet – we don't want to scare the monkeys, do we? If we're quiet, real quiet, and we show them we have food, the monkeys will come to us.'

Taking her digital camera out of her shoulder bag, she walked close behind her sons as they approached the first, large walk-through enclosure. She noticed the two men who had preceded them had moved on, and were already passing through the second enclosure.

'Look – it says squirrel monkeys!' Joshua pointed to the small plaque on the first of two wire mesh gates set about four feet apart.

Samantha opened the first gate, allowed her sons to enter first, having instructed them not to open the second gate until she'd closed the first. 'We don't want the monkeys to escape, do we?'

There was a lot of leafy tree branches overhead, with a narrow strip of raised ground between them and the mesh of the enclosure to their left, and a much larger space to their right – pale, hard baked earth with rounded boulders and vegetation poking out of it. The concrete path they were standing on led straight ahead, on into another enclosure.

'I can't see any monkeys,' said Luke, frowning as he glanced up and around the enclosure.

'Hold out your hands.' She sprinkled a few plump raisins into each of her sons' palms. 'Stand still and wait.'

Sure enough, the first small, greenish monkey with a dark head and nose, and light markings around its eyes, appeared. Incredibly quick and agile, it darted along a low branch, snatched a raisin from Joshua's hand, and disappeared back up into the foliage.

She stood back, wanting to capture the sheer delight on her sons' faces as more squirrel monkeys appeared, and helped themselves to a juicy breakfast.

The mongoose lemurs in the second enclosure were larger, and bolder, than the monkeys. One of them, to his obvious delight, perched on Joshua's shoulder as it chewed on a raisin.

'Look, Mummy!'

She turned – and reflexively gasped, taking a hasty step back.

Close behind her, crowded up against the enclosure's perimeter, were three huge, scaled lizards with rusty-grey dewlaps hanging below their jaws and a row of spines running down their backs, to their long grey tails.

'Are they iguanas?' asked Joshua.

'I think so,' she replied, pleased the reptiles appeared to be asleep.

The third enclosure, in addition to a giant tortoise and a couple of brown and white guinea pigs, housed just one lemur. A black and white ruffed lemur, according to the name plaque on the gate, and it was easily twice the size of the mongoose lemurs. Incredibly agile, despite its size, it held on to a branch with its rear feet and let itself hang down, low enough to take several raisins from Luke's out-stretched hand.

The ring-tailed lemurs – two cute babies among them – were friendly and mischievous. Seated on a low wall, Samantha could have stayed there all days, watching her sons feeding the animals, which climbed all over the boys, leaving dusty footprints on their clothes. She snapped lots of photographs, and regretted the fact her husband wasn't with her, to capture a few images of her with her sons.

The half term holiday, her sons' first trip abroad, was Richard's idea. A genuine surprise. 'You need a break,' he'd said, 'we all do.' The past few months, following the death of her father in a house fire, had been tough and initially, she had been in two minds about flying to Tenerife. But her sons' excitement was contagious, and she was disappointed when Richard told her he would only be able to spend the first four days of the holiday with them, as he was already committed to attend a two day conference in Cambridge, where he was booked to make an important speech.

Glancing back, as they finally exited the ring-tailed lemur enclosure, she noticed a noisy group of small children, a local nursery class by the look of it, had entered the squirrel monkey enclosure. Pleased she'd headed the advice to arrive early, she led her sons into a stand-alone brick built enclosure. To the right, a row of glass-fronted cages housed tiny marmosets and tamarins, but to their left the enclosure was open. She spotted a mongoose lemur, and several small red-handed tamarins, running free. Inquisitive, but shy, the tamarins kept their distance initially, before one of them approached Joshua and snatched a raisin from his hand.

The rest of Monkey Park, after the magic of the walk-through enclosures, was a bit of a let-down. More, larger monkeys, all caged. Boisterous, noisy chimps housed in a smallish, concrete enclosure. Colourful birds. Three big cats – black jaguars, not panthers; two were sleeping, the third prowled around another small, uninspiring concrete enclosure.

Across from the chimp's enclosure, Samantha sat on a wooden bench, overlooking her sons. Crouched down next to each other, Luke and Joshua chatted animatedly as they poked seeds and dried bread through small wire mesh, into an enclosure housing at least fifty or sixty, mostly black and white guinea pigs. She took the opportunity to review the digital snaps she'd taken. As usual, a few were dreadful or out of focus, most were so-so, and a handful were excellent. There was a good one of

Luke with a ring-tailed lemur on his shoulder; her son was looking up at the lemur and his expression was priceless. Equally good, one of Joshua surrounded by several ring-tailed lemurs, but her favourite was definitely the snap of her two sons standing next to each other, with a ring-tailed lemur straddling their shoulders.

A broad, double-sided path with enclosures on both sides, led down from the guinea pigs, around, and back up towards the jaguars.

'Josh, no!'

Too late.

Her son's fingertips touched the trunk, the like of which she had never seen before. The thick, straight trunk was light grey-brown – and covered all over with lethal looking, inch long spikes.

'Owww!' Joshua withdrew his hand quickly, as if he'd been pricked by red hot needles.

She knelt beside him. 'Let me see.'

'It hurts,' said Joshua, holding up his right hand.

'I did try to warn you.' She held her son's hand, examined it. The tips of two fingers – his forefinger and index finger – were oozing blood, but it could have been a lot worse. If Joshua had put it on the tree trunk with any force, the spikes would have ripped his hand open. She dug out a tissue, dabbed away the spots of blood and wrapped the tissue around her son's fingers, before giving him a hug.

'Better?' she asked, and Joshua nodded.

Standing, she ruffled her son's hair. She noticed the nursery children had nearly caught up with them. The children – about twenty-five of them – were all a year or so younger than Luke ... looking around, she couldn't see him.

Moments ago, Luke had been standing in front of a nearby cage, checking out some birds, but he wasn't there now and she couldn't see him anywhere else.

A cold shiver of panic surged through her chest, but she quickly suppressed it. It was a small zoo, and Luke couldn't have gone far.

'Josh, did you see where your brother went?'

'No, Mummy. I – my fingers hurt.'

Almost subconsciously, she took hold of Joshua's left hand, held it firmly as she looked all around her. She told herself Luke must be close by, right in front of her somewhere, but hidden from view.

'Luke!' She could see other little boys, lots of them. But she couldn't see Luke.

Where can he be?

The nursery class was watching the chimps.

Dragging Joshua behind her, she hurried towards them. She studied the children closely, and then again. One boy was black, but all the others were white. So were all the girls. Luke definitely wasn't among them.

She tried asking one of the teachers if she'd seen Luke, but the woman just smiled apologetically, and shrugged; the woman clearly didn't speak English and she didn't speak more than a few words of Spanish.

'Luke!' Looking wildly around, she raised her voice, shouted her son's name at the top of her lungs. 'Luke!'

No answer – and no sign of Luke.

Joshua started crying.

More terrified than she'd ever been in her life, Samantha hardly noticed her elder son's distress. Close to tears herself, she tried to force herself to think logically – to think like a four year old.

Monkeys and lemurs.

Luke had been absolutely enthralled by the monkeys and lemurs. He might have retraced his footsteps, wanting to see them again. Not seeing him anywhere else, she decided to do the same.

Running now, as fast as she could without letting go of Joshua's hand, she came within inches of knocking one of the nursery children off his feet. Not stopping to apologise, she raced on and on – until a woman blocked her path. The woman was standing in front of the building that housed the tamarins and marmosets. She didn't recognise the woman – then suddenly she did.

'You!'

The long black wig was gone, she was wearing different shades, but she was definitely the same woman she'd spoken to yesterday on *Playa de los Cristianos* beach. The same woman who'd told her all about Monkey Park.

'Mrs Frewin-Hamilton.' The woman smiled.

Her blood froze.

She realised the woman had spoken her surname.

She didn't recall telling the woman her name yesterday, and even if she had, she would have introduced herself as 'Sami'. Not Mrs Frewin-Hamilton. *Never* Mrs Frewin-Hamilton. Somehow, she knew with certainty this woman must be involved with Luke's disappearance.

'Where's my son?' she demanded. 'What have you done to him?'

'Your son is fine.'

'Where is he? If you've hurt him – '

'He's somewhere safe.' A thin smile. 'Would you like to speak to him?'

She snatched the BlackBerry from the woman's hand, pressed it to her ear – heard her baby crying.

'Luke, sweetie, it's – '

'Mummy!'

'Sweetie, I – '

The BlackBerry went dead.

Chapter 3

The following day
Bayswater, London, England

A muffled blast killed their screams.

James Harris woke with a start, bathed in sweat. Breathing hard, through his mouth, he opened his eyes. He saw a nipple, just inches away from his face – a plump, purplish-brown nipple that crowned a firm, ebony breast. It took him a moment or two to remember her name. *Rochay.*

As the nightmare inside his head faded, and his breathing returned to normal, he rested back his head and closed his eyes. He realised he'd been dreaming. It was the same nightmare that had plagued his sleep too many times in recent weeks, since his dishonourable discharge from the Special Air Services.

He opened his eyes.

The bedside alarm read 6:27.

He slipped out of bed, paid a quick visit to the bathroom to take a leak, but he didn't risk a shower. He needed one, badly, but not here. Too much noise might wake Rochay. His clothes were downstairs, scattered across the living room floor, where he'd hastily shed them last night. Briefly, he smiled at the memory, as silently he padded past a closed bedroom door – presumably, her child's bedroom. Child, or children? He didn't find out she was a mother until they arrived back at her apartment late last night, and he hadn't asked how many children she had. It didn't concern him, one way or another. Her babysitter, as she let her out, had winked at Rochay, and he'd heard her whisper, 'He's well fit – have fun!'

They did have fun, plenty of fun, but now it was over and today was another day. His twenty-sixth birthday, as it happened, but he didn't have anything to celebrate or anyone special he wanted to celebrate it with.

Born out of wedlock to an English mother who died when he was four and a Pakistani father, James stood a shade under six feet with bare feet, and a shade over six feet wearing shoes. Athletically built, he crept downstairs, flicked on a table lamp just long enough to find his clothes and get dressed. So early, it was freezing cold outside, and the leaden skies over the capital promised rain. Or more snow. There was already a light dusting of white covering the ground that hadn't been there last night. Nevertheless, as he strode along Bayswater Road, he was looking forward to his daily, half hour run through Hyde Park, which he liked to follow with a martial arts work out, and a cold-hot-cold shower.

Following his discharge from the SAS, barely two months after successfully completing the rigorous selection process and gaining his coveted beige beret with its distinctive winged dagger insignia, he'd rented a one bedroom apartment in Gloucester Terrace, a two minute walk away from Hyde Park. He'd taken out the six month minimum contract, and he had given himself that long to decide what he wanted to do with the rest of his life. Opening a martial arts centre was an appealing option, if he could find suitable premises and raise the necessary capital, as was setting up his own security consultancy.

One thing was certain: no force on Earth would persuade him to drive a taxi for a living again, as he had done before he run away from home and joined the army.

He didn't expect to find a mountain of birthday cards waiting on his doormat, and he didn't. But someone had shoved a large, plain brown envelope through his letterbox. There was no name, no address – clearly, it must have been hand delivered.

By whom?

And for what reason?

There was only one way to find out.

A photograph.

An image he'd seen before.

An image he'd never forget.

An image that ended his army career … somehow, despite the blurriness, blown up to A4 the photograph was even more disturbing.

With a red marker pen, someone had scrawled 'Happy Birthday' above the Iraqi boy's head.

Not funny.

He turned the photograph over, scanned what was written on the back.

Looking for a job?

£5k up-front, £95k on successful completion.

Call ASAP.

A mobile number he didn't recognise.

He tossed the photograph on the breakfast bar, face down, and poured himself a glass of fresh orange juice from the refrigerator. Sitting on a high stool, he sipped his drink and read the message again.

A sick joke?

He half emptied his glass, set it down on the table next to the photograph; he scratched his unshaven cheek, ran his hand back across his short black hair. He stared down at the brief message, read it a third time ... the photograph suggested, somewhere, there was a forces connection. There must be. But, assuming for a moment the message was genuine, '£5k up-front, £95k on successful completion' indicated some kind of mission. An ex-forces mission, with that kind of pay-check on offer. Back on civvy street for the first time in over five years, he couldn't pretend he wasn't tempted – *if* the offer was genuine, and *if* the bastard who'd taken the photograph wasn't involved because if he was ...

Who dares wins

The motto of his former regiment.

Despite niggling reservations, he reached into his jacket pocket for his iPhone. He tapped in the number on the back of the photograph. A male voice he didn't recognise answered, asked him who was calling.

'James Harris. Who am I speaking to?'

'Meet me at the Serpentine Bar at twelve noon if you want in.'

'Want in – '

The line went dead.

James arrived at the Serpentine Bar, located at the south-eastern edge of the Serpentine lake in Hyde Park, at 11:35. A prime spot. Huge windows that looked out over the lake zig-zagged like an oversize concertina, and meant even on an overcast February day the interior was well lit. Chunky wooden tables and chairs stood on a polished floor that mimicked crazy paving. Clean shaven, and wearing black jeans and a plain white shirt under his black fleece lined jacket, he claimed a window seat that gave him a good view of both restaurant's entrance and the path that wound its way between the restaurant and the lake. Hungry, he ordered an English salad with soft-boiled eggs and a bottle of mineral water.

His contact appeared at 12.03.

Around six two or three, well-muscled if a few pounds overweight, dark blond buzz cut – the guy couldn't have been more obvious if he had 'military' branded across his forehead. Sure enough, as soon as the guy spotted him, he made a bee-line for his table.

'Mister Harris?'

He thought he detected a faint German accent. 'That's me,' he confirmed. 'And you are?'

'Dieter Zimmermann – my friends call me Manny.'

The German didn't offer his hand and James didn't get up.

'Pull up a chair.' The German did so. 'So what's the deal?'

'Sorry, Mister Harris, I can't tell you anything. Mister – my boss, he wants to meet you.'

He pushed his plate aside. 'So what are we sitting here for?'

They exited Hyde Park at Aldford Street North Gate, from where Zimmerman drove him to a Mayfair address. He followed the big German into a four storey property with an impressive white façade, up a flight of stairs, along a corridor with cream walls and plush carpeting, to a polished oak door. Zimmerman knocked twice, and he heard a muffled 'Enter'.

There were two men in the room.

Seeing them, he stopped dead.

Anthony Vaughan and Thomas 'Tommo' Martin.

Without saying a word, he turned to leave.

The big German closed the door – blocked his exit.

'Get out of my way.' He spoke quietly, yet firmly.

Zimmerman grinned, and clenched his right fist. 'Make me …'

'I'm leaving, whether you want me to or not. I don't want to hurt you.'

Zimmerman's grin widened. 'I would like to see you try …'

The punch the German unleashed from his waist was long and lazy, and he had plenty of time to anticipate it. He could easily have blocked it, but instead he simply stepped back, out of reach of the intended blow.

He turned to Vaughan. Seated behind a large, polished mahogany desk, the former squaddie he'd served with was clearly the man in charge. 'Tell him to stand down.'

Vaughan smiled thinly, seemingly amused, but before he responded James sensed movement behind him.

He half-turned to see the German coming at him again, with all his bulk and considerable power. This time, if he stayed where he was and failed to defend himself, the incoming fist would strike his head – hard. He couldn't allow that to happen.

Two seconds later, the German was on his knees at his feet, head down, face creased in agony. A quick twist, and he could have snapped the German's arm like it was a dry twig.

'That's enough!'

Vaughan jumped to his feet and he released the German, turned to see Tommo was pointing a black pistol at his chest. He recognised it as a Browning Hi-Power. Personally, he preferred a Beretta 92FS, but the Browning was an excellent choice, too. Leaving the German on his knees, cursing as he rubbed his right arm, James ignored the threat posed by Tommo and approached Vaughan's desk.

'Hello, Harris.' Five ten, with short reddish hair and a clipped moustache that drooped half an inch over the edge of his mouth, Vaughan was wearing a dark grey polo shirt. 'I'm sorry about Manny's, er – welcome. I did warn him you were good, but even I'd forgotten just how good.'

'Cut the crap, Vaughan.' Inches away from the edge of his desk, he stared into the man's pale green eyes. 'I don't know what job you're offering me, and I don't care. I'm not interested.'

'Oh, but I think you will be, once I've explained the situation fully,' said Vaughan, with confidence. 'I'm putting together a small team, and I haven't much time to do it. I'd very much like to have a man with your talents on board.'

'Not a chance.' He took the folded A4 photograph that had brought him here from his jacket pocket, tossed it on the desk in front of Vaughan. 'This is yours, I believe. And if you're thinking you can use it to blackmail me, forget it. You stand to lose as much as I do if this ever gets out, and you know it.'

'You're right, of course, which is why I've taken out, er – a little insurance policy.' Vaughan opened a drawer in front of him, picked out a slim package about six by eight inches. The package was wrapped in glossy green paper decorated with gold stars. 'Happy birthday, by the way.'

Taken by surprise, he made no move to accept the gift.

'No?' Vaughan's moustache twisted as he smiled. 'Then allow me …'

Two photographs in cheap white plastic frames.

James, on seeing the first image, felt his pulse quicken.

Two faces from the past. *His* past. He recognised them instantly, even though he hadn't seen either of them in over five years.

Samantha and Joshua.

Samantha had let her hair grow over her shoulders, coloured it darker brown, and her son had grown into a handsome boy.

Vaughan revealed the second photograph.

Joshua again, but this time he was with a smaller, similar looking boy about half his age. Even before Vaughan spoke, he felt a strange, tingling sensation growing in his chest.

'I rather suspect you didn't know Joshua had a little brother, did you?'

Vaughan was right: he didn't.

'He's only four – but he'll be five in August'

James didn't need to consult a calendar to work out when Joshua's brother must have been conceived.

Chapter 4

Samantha stood by the living room's bay window, staring outside without really seeing anything, as she waited for her husband to arrive home.

The instructions the female kidnapper rattled off were simple enough: spend the rest of the day and tomorrow in her hotel room with Joshua, ring the airline to cancel Luke's flight home, check-out of the hotel on Friday morning and catch her flight back to Gatwick with Joshua. Go straight home, talk to no one and stay there until her husband arrived home.

'If you contact the police, or talk to anyone at all about this, we will know – and your son will die. If you fail to follow any of my instructions, for any reason, your son will die. There will be no second chance. Do you understand me?'

She'd opened her mouth, but closed it again without managing to say, 'Yes.'

The kidnapper, before departing, gave her a plain white envelope with 'Prof. Richard Frewin-Hamilton' printed on it. The envelope was sealed. 'This is for your husband – do not open it. We're aware he is at a conference until Saturday. Give it to him as soon as he arrives home. You may discuss the contents with each other, but if you talk to the police or anybody else, your son will die.'

Boarding a flight home, with only one of her two sons, was the most difficult thing Samantha had ever had to do. She'd done a lot of crying during the night, when Joshua was asleep. She didn't go to bed at all herself, knowing she wouldn't be able to sleep … she couldn't stop thinking about Luke. Why had he been kidnapped? Where had they taken him? How were they treating him? Luke was only four – still her baby, in so many ways. Even if his abductors were treating him well, which she prayed they were, he would still be terribly distressed.

One question haunted her above all others.

Will I ever see Luke again?

Even if she did everything asked of her, there was no guarantee the kidnappers would release her son unharmed, no guarantee they wouldn't kill him anyway.

She was convinced the envelope she had been given, to pass on to her husband, must be a ransom demand. Clearly, the kidnappers were aware Richard came from a wealthy background. Her father-in-law, thanks to a hugely successful property development business, was a multi-millionaire who lived in a twenty-one room mansion located in the Surrey countryside. She would gladly give up everything she possessed, to get Luke back, but even though she stood to inherit half of her late father's estate her bank balance was still insignificant, compared with her husband's side of the family.

If it wasn't for her father, and his and Richard's shared interest in ancient languages and civilisations, she would never have met her husband. Indeed, her father introduced her to Richard, at a mutual colleague's fortieth birthday party. Having just been through a messy divorce, her father had invited her along as his guest, and she happily accepted. Two small children meant opportunities to socialise and engage in lively, intelligent conversation with like-minded people were few and far between. Meeting Richard was a bonus she didn't expect, but she had no hesitation in accepting, when towards the end of the evening he asked her if she fancied going out to see a West End show at the weekend. How he got tickets, at such short notice, she didn't know but he took her to see *Les Misérables* – a fabulous musical, and as the evening progressed, she found herself warming to Richard as well.

Richard drove her home, but increasingly nervous about how he might react, she didn't invite him in. Inside, her babysitter was waiting, and she feared once he found out she was a mother with two young sons, two Anglo-Pakistani boys, Richard would vanish from her life as suddenly as he had appeared. Ever the perfect gentleman, Richard didn't appear offended by her lack of civility. He did ask her if he could see her again. He took her out to dinner twice in the next eight days and on their second date, over dessert, she finally confessed she had two children.

'Yes, I do recall your father mentioning them,' he said, as he scooped up a profiterole on his spoon. 'Two young sons, I think he said.'

'Joshua and Luke,' she confirmed, relieved to learn he already knew she was a mother. But did he also know both her sons were Anglo-Pakistani? There was only one way to find out. She opened her purse, showed him a recent photograph of her sons, taken on a day out to London Zoo.

He popped the profiterole into his mouth, before he accepted the photograph from her, glanced at it while he chewed. She watched him closely but his expression didn't change.

'Handsome little chaps, aren't they,' he commented, after swallowing. He passed the photograph back to her. 'Do they see their father at all?'

'No, I – ' She hesitated, but she couldn't lie. 'They have different fathers, but no – neither of their fathers were still on the scene, when they were born.'

'I'm sorry, Samantha, I didn't mean to pry.'

She smiled warmly, pleased he was taking everything so nonchalantly. She placed her hand over his hand, gently squeezed it. 'Showing an interest isn't prying.'

Over coffee, she told Richard a little about Luke's and Joshua's fathers. 'I was only eighteen when I met Josh's father,' she said. 'I was still in the sixth form, studying for my 'A' levels, and he worked at a newsagent near my school.'

She didn't reveal Joshua's father was more than ten years her senior – as, in fact, was Richard. Malik, as he was called, was a strikingly handsome man with a neat, clipped moustache and a designer beard, and he was friendly and intelligent. Married, too, with three small children and a fourth on the way. Not that any of that mattered. Until he offered her a lift home one rainy afternoon, and her step-mother glimpsed him as she got out of his car, she'd never thought of Malik as anything more than a casual acquaintance, albeit an extremely attractive one.

'Who's that Paki you're seeing?' her step-mother demanded, almost before she closed the front door after her.

'He's just a friend, Norma – and I'm not *seeing* him.'

Her step-mother sneered. 'Don't think I didn't see the way he looked at you – stripping you naked with his filthy eyes, he was.'

'If that's what you think,' she said, tossing her schoolbag on a chair, 'you need to change your glasses!'

'How dare you?!' Her step-mother glared. 'You just wait 'til you father gets home, girl. I –'

'My father isn't racist,' she cut in, but she stopped herself from adding 'like you'.

Norma was her father's third wife, and they'd only been married for two years – the longest, most challenging two years of her, Samantha's, life. She didn't like Norma any more than Norma liked her. Quite what her father saw in the woman, she had no idea, and she was confident if Norma did make false accusations, her father wouldn't give two hoots about the colour of Malik's skin.

Norma accused her of sleeping with 'that Paki', a charge she strenuously denied, and when her step-mother forbade her from seeing 'that Paki' again she did what most teenagers do when faced with authority: she rebelled.

She began going out of her way, to see as much of Malik as she could, and flirting with him. He was quick to respond, take advantage of their growing friendship. After she'd lost her virginity on the back seat of his Ford Mondeo, they started seeing each other regularly, and they had sex as often as they could. In his car mostly, but occasionally, when her folks were out or when he was on his own at the newsagent, she sneaked him up to her bedroom or they made out in the back of the shop. Somehow, the risk of getting caught together only added to the excitement. They'd only been secret lovers for four months when a little blue line on a home pregnancy test kit confirmed her worse fear: she was expecting Malik's child.

His handsome features darkened when she broke the news to him, and 'you stupid white cunt' was one of the kinder insults he hurled at her. He accused her of tricking him, by claiming she was on the pill when she wasn't. How could she be, if she had gotten pregnant? She didn't know how, but she swore on her father's life she hadn't lied to him, or tricked him. She *was* on the pill. He didn't believe her. Before he screamed at her to get out of his car, leaving her standing at the side of the road in tears, he flatly denied the child she was carrying was his. He never called her, he never texted, and she started avoiding going anywhere near the newsagent where he worked. But at least, with Malik, she knew exactly where she stood ... unlike Luke's father, who simply disappeared before she discovered the birth control pills she was taking had failed her again.

Now, Samantha twirled her wedding band around her finger, round and round. Her hand was trembling when she pulled back the curtains, saw the black Range Rover turn into the drive. Joshua was sprawled on the rug in front of the sofa, watching she hadn't noticed what cartoon on TV.

'Richard's home,' she said, turning to her son. 'Go play in your bedroom, please – we have to talk about Luke.'

'Mummy, I want to – '

'Now, Joshua – please.'

Her son scowled, but he knew better than to argue. He flicked the TV off and went upstairs to his bedroom, and moments later she heard the front door click open.

'I'm home, darling!'

She met her husband at the living room door. Six four, and lanky, with thick, unruly brown hair and a scraggly goatee, Richard was wearing light tan slacks, an open neck white shirt and his favourite tweed jacket. Seeing her, he grinned, and she stepped forward and threw her arms around his waist. She hugged him more tightly that she usually did.

'Phew, I'm glad that one is over,' he started, as he broke the embrace. 'You'll never guess what that pompous old fart – '

'Richard, I ...' She felt hot tears welling in her eyes again, and she couldn't stem the flow.

Her husband's grin faded. 'Samantha, what is it – what's upset you like this?'

'It's Luke …'

'Luke?' He stared down at her. 'What about him?'

'He – ' Tears rolled down her cheeks as she forced herself to say it aloud. 'He's been kidnapped.'

'Kidnapped! But – when? How?'

He took her arm, steered her to a sofa, where they sat down. He held her hands in his and, between sobs, she told him about Luke's disappearance at Monkey Park.

'What did the police say – you have reported this to the police, haven't you?'

'No, I – I can't – '

'Well, I most certainly can.' He took out his mobile.

'No, Richard – please.' Fresh tears filled her eyes. 'The woman – she told me they'd kill him, if I went to the police.'

'Yes, well, she would say that, wouldn't she? That doesn't mean – '

'Richard, please – no police. Luke is my son, and I'm not willing to risk his life.'

The words spilled out.

Too late, she realised what she'd said, and she instantly regretted it. Most men wouldn't look twice at a single mum with two young children, especially not a white English single mum with two Anglo-Pakistani sons. Richard genuinely didn't appear to notice or care both her sons were dark skinned, and he was a good role model for them, a valued father figure. She really hadn't meant to draw attention to the fact Luke wasn't his son in the way she had.

He looked at her, a pained expression etched on his craggy features. He fingered his goatee. 'Okay, so what do you want to do? Have the kidnappers contacted you yet, with their demands?'

'The woman,' she said, reaching for the white envelope on the coffee table, 'she told me to give you this.'

'What do they want – cash?' He accepted the envelope from her, glanced across at her when he noticed it was still sealed. 'You haven't opened it?'

'I wanted to,' she admitted, 'but the woman – she told me not to, and …'

Her husband tore the envelope apart, extracted a rectangular piece of white card.

'How much do they want?' she asked the question, dreading the answer.

'They – er, it's not a ransom demand. It's an address – '

'An *address*.' She didn't understand.

'An address in London. They want me to go there, tomorrow at eleven o'clock.'

She spoke her mind. 'I'm coming with you.'

'I – er, the note's only addressed to me, and – '

'I'm coming with you,' she repeated, firmly.

Her husband hesitated. 'What about Joshua?'

Momentarily confused by the switch of focus, she didn't answer.

'We can't take him with us.'

'No, of course not …' She had completely forgotten about her eldest son. Schools, following the Half Term break, would re-open on Monday, but tomorrow was Sunday and …

How am I going to explain Luke's absence to school?

She had no idea. Until now, the question hadn't even occurred to her. But she did know who would mind Joshua for a few hours.

'I'll take him round to Beverley's,' she said. Their neighbour Beverley was Callum's mother, and Callum was Joshua's best friend. Most alternate Saturdays, Joshua and Callum slept over at each other's homes, and on Sunday afternoon Beverley often took Callum and Joshua swimming, while she minded baby Megan. 'Playing with Callum will help to take his mind off what's happened.'

'You do realise, don't you,' he pointed out, 'Beverley is certain ask about Luke?'

She did, as soon as her husband mentioned it. 'Of course, I – I'll tell her Luke fell and broke his arm in Tenerife, and that he's staying with my sister for a few days.' Her sister, who had two children of her own, lived in Oxford. Although they had met, she didn't think her sister and Beverley had each other's contact details, and they were unlikely to bump into each other in the next few days.

Richard fingered his goatee as he slowly nodded. 'Okay, but you do realise you will have to talk to Joshua as well, so he doesn't unwittingly say something you don't want him to?'

'I will,' she said. 'I'll talk to him in the morning.'

Chapter 5

'That's right – the little brat's your son.'

Numb with shock, James studied the photograph more closely. Snapped on a sunny beach somewhere, probably with a telephoto lens, the two boys were sitting on the sand together, with a red and black football. Both wore only swimming shorts. They had the same brown skin, the same black hair, and the same mischievous grins. He'd grown a lot in five years, of course, but James didn't doubt the older boy was Joshua … he focused on Joshua's kid brother.

My son…

A few moments ago he didn't have a son … now, out of nowhere, he did.

Suddenly, he recalled words Vaughan had spoken earlier, something about 'a little insurance policy'. At the time, it was meaningless chatter, but now …

He tore his gaze away from his son, glared at Vaughan. 'Where is he?'

Vaughan smiled. 'In safe hands, I – '

'You bastard, you've taken him, haven't you?' The only thing that stopped him from grabbing hold of Vaughan, yanking him off his feet and beating the crap out of him, was the width of the desk between them. 'Cool it, Harris.' Tommo raised the Browning, aimed it at him again, and stepped closer. Once again, he ignored the threat.

'Thank you, Tommo,' said Vaughan, 'but I really think you can put that away now.' He stared up at James. 'Harris isn't going to do anything stupid, are you?'

He clenched and unclenched his fists, made a conscious effort to control his anger. If Vaughan really had kidnapped the boy – his son, he needed to calm down, start listening – and learning.

'As I was saying,' continued Vaughan, looking smug, 'your son is in safe hands, and I personally guarantee he won't be harmed if certain people – and yes, Harris, you are one of those people – give me their full co-operation.'

'What about Sami and Josh?'

'By Sami, I assume you mean the lovely Samantha Frewin-Hamilton?' Vaughan smirked. 'But, of course, you won't know her by her married name.'

'She's married?' He wasn't sure why, but the news hit him like a kick in the groin.

'To an eminent Cambridge professor, no less – who, like you, will be joining our little expedition if he values the boy's life.' Vaughan's eyes narrowed. 'I'm assuming you will now be joining us …?'

'Like I have a choice?' He didn't, and they both knew it. He asked, again, about Samantha and Joshua.

'They should be flying into Gatwick tomorrow afternoon. I'm pleased to say, so far, Mrs Frewin-Hamilton has done everything we've asked of her.'

So it's just my son the bastard has kidnapped.

'What's this all about, Vaughan?' He placed his right hand on the edge of the desk, but he didn't put the photograph down.

'Patience, patience.' Vaughan stroked his moustache. 'I've organised a briefing on Sunday at 11:00. I expect you to be here at 10:30, or …' He unfolded the A4 photograph on his desk, slid it back across the desk to James. 'We wouldn't want anything like this to happen to your brat, would we?'

He didn't dignify Vaughan with a reply.

Vaughan watched with amusement as Harris and Manny exchanged hostile glances, as Harris departed.

'Worry not, my friend,' he said, with a grin, after the German had closed the door. 'He doesn't know it yet, but Harris will be travelling on a one way ticket.'

The afternoon passed in a blur.

Still trying to get his head around the fact he was the father of a four year old boy, James couldn't stop staring at the photograph he'd brought home with him.

He was only twenty when he and Samantha met. Nearly two years older, she was a university student; he was a taxi driver. A Muslim taxi driver called Mohammed Hassan – the name his father gave him when he took him in, converted him to Islam, after his English mother died of a heroin overdose. Samantha Radcliffe, as he soon learned she was called, was a fare he picked up outside the former UMIST campus. Having driven her to Salford Quays, she carried her young son to her first floor apartment and he followed with her bags. He was on his way back to his taxi when the door behind him burst open again.

He reflexively turned around.

'Please, help – you've got to help me.' One hand raised, she clawed at her spiky brown hair. 'It's my son – I – I don't know what's wrong with him. A minute ago he was fine, but now he's – I don't – something's happened!'

'Show me.' He followed her into the house.

Her son, a mixed race boy aged about three, was sitting on a patterned rug on the living room floor. His crying eyes were bulging and both his hands were clutching his throat, as if –

He's choking!

'Do something, please. I don't – '

'Has he swallowed anything?'

'No, I don't think – oh, my God, he's choking, isn't he?'

'I think so,' he confirmed, kneeling besides the boy. Close-up, he could see the sheer terror in the poor kid's eyes – terror caused by his inability to breathe.

I've got to do something.

'You'd better call an ambulance,' he said.

'I – I've no credit on my mobile, and I don't have a landline – what are you doing?'

No time to run out to his taxi for his own mobile, make the call himself, he lifted the small boy to his feet – slapped him on the back.

Nothing happened.

He slapped the boy again, harder, between the shoulder blades.

Still nothing, except more tears.

'You're hurting him!'

Ignoring her, he put the boy over one of his knees, with his head so low down it was nearly touching the rug.

He slapped the boy's back again.

Once, twice, three times – each slap harder than the previous one.

Nothing.

'Stop it! You're hurting – '

He slapped the boy's back as hard as he dared.

The boy's mouth opened wide – something small and shiny shot out of it like a bullet. He felt, as well as heard, the boy gulp in a mouthful of air, before he suddenly burst into tears.

'It's okay, it's okay,' he said softly, as he lifted the distressed toddler up, held him close to his chest. His words didn't stop the boy's cries from becoming more hysterical. Lifting him up towards his mother, he said, 'He's breathing again now – I think he's okay.'

Her green eyes blazed.

'*Okay!* How can you – just look at him! You hit him too hard!'

What was I supposed to do?

He'd only known what to do because he had attended a First Aid course at his local *dojo*.

She hugged her son tightly and he glanced down – spotted something on the carpet. Reaching down to pick it up, he realised his hands were literally shaking, and he felt a really weird inside, as if he'd just had an electric shock. Moments later, after dry retching twice, the boy sobbed quietly in his mother's arms and he showed her what was in his hand.

'A marble!' She stared at the clear glass marble for a second, before she turned on her son. 'Josh, I thought I told you to throw that away! And what have I told you, about putting things in your mouth – don't you ever listen!'

The boy wailed.

'Go easy on him,' he said. 'He's upset enough already.'

She glared at him. 'And whose fault is that?'

Thinking she might have a point, and suddenly fearing she might be right about him hitting the boy too hard, he suggested, 'Maybe you should take him to A&E, get a doctor to check him over?'

She hesitated, and nodded. 'Call me an ambulance.'

'My taxi's outside. It will be a lot quicker if I run you there?' The nearest hospital was only ten minutes away.

She accepted, and a minute later they were on their way. As he drove, with mother and son behind him on the back seat, he heard the boy retching again. Moments later, a sickly sweet stench filled the car – made him gag.

The little shit's been sick!

'Do you want me to come in with you?' he asked, pulling up outside Hope Hospital's Accident & Emergency department.

The woman opened the car door, glared daggers at him. 'Don't you think you've done enough already?'

Fuck you!

She slammed the door shut, and he watched her hurry into the hospital with her son under her arm, before firing the engine again. He would have waited, driven her and her son home again, but … he didn't expect he would see her again.

Twenty-four hours later, when he was called into the office, he feared he must be in trouble. Deep, deep shit. He learned the woman had contacted the office, left a request urging he visit her at home. He didn't. He feared, if she pressed charges and he was convicted of assaulting a small child … the woman contacted the office again the following day, twice, and this time his boss told him to 'get your ass round there!'

He arrived at seven thirty and, smiling warmly, the woman invited him into her apartment. She introduced herself as Samantha Radcliffe, but she asked him to 'call me Sami'.

'I've bought something for your son,' he said, indicating the Tesco bag he was carrying. 'I hope you don't mind?'

'You shouldn't have … '

'I thought it might cheer him up.'

'I'm sure it will, but he's in bed – I'll give it to him in the morning. And thank you.'

He asked how her son was.

'He's fine, really – his back's still a bit sore, but that's all.'

'I'm sorry I hurt him.'

'Don't be silly,' she said, 'the nurse at A&E said you did everything right – she said you probably saved Josh's life.'

He felt uncomfortable. 'I wouldn't go that far – '

'I would,' she said, firmly, 'and I can't tell you how grateful I am. Joshua is all I have, and if anything happened to him …'

'I'm glad he's okay.'

She nodded. 'Thanks to you, he is, and – I want to apologise for the way I behaved. I – I was out of order. I was a bitch – I'm not normally like that, honest. I just – seeing Josh like that, I – I just panicked. I'm really, really sorry.'

He smiled. 'Apology accepted.'

Before he left, Samantha invited around again, to tea the following evening – so he could say hello to Joshua, and give him his gift personally. He accepted, and when he arrived she surprised him with a present 'from me and Josh'. A polo shirt he declined to try on, saying it was the right size, after he'd glanced at the label.

It happened on his fourth visit.

When she said it was time for her son's bath, not wanting to overstay his welcome, he rose to leave. But she placed her hand on his arm and asked him to stay. 'After Josh has had his supper and I've put him to bed,' she said, 'we can get to know each other better.'

He didn't know what to say, or what to expect, when she joined him on the sofa. But he never imagined she would be so direct, so forward. Certainly, no Muslim woman ever would be.

Sitting so close their legs were almost touching, she looked at him and smiled as she placed her hands on his waist. She leaned forward and kissed his mouth. And again, as she put her hands around the back of his neck, drew him closer. He felt the press of her breasts against his chest. He couldn't believe how good it felt to hold her close, couldn't stop himself from responding, kissing her over and over and over again.

She reached for the top button of his shirt – opened it.

And the next button, and the next, before she slipped her hand inside, stroked his chest with her fingers for a long, sensual moment. Briefly, too briefly, she placed her other hand over his groin, traced the outline of his rapidly expanding hard-on.

Between kisses, she popped another button, and another … she didn't stop at the last button on his shirt. He tensed as she opened his trousers – pulled the zip down.

She kissed him again, whispered, 'Have you ever been with a white woman?'

'Never,' he admitted.

He didn't admit he was scared half to death, didn't admit he was still a virgin – and ten minutes later, he wasn't. Only afterwards did he realise he hadn't used a condom or anything, but she just smiled and put her arms around his waist, pulled him closer and kissed his lips. 'Don't worry, I'm on the pill.'

In the days and weeks that followed, he visited Samantha as often as he could – an hour here, two hours there, longer on Saturday or Sunday when he wasn't working. More than once, as they lay in bed together, she whispered, 'I wish you could stay the night.' It was a desire he shared, but he still lived at home with his father, step-mother and two youngest sisters, and too many questions would be asked if he stayed out all night. Questions he wouldn't dare answer truthfully. Somehow, his father found out about Samantha anyway.

Father, as he often did when he wanted to discuss something, drew him aside after Friday prayers, asked, 'Is what I am hearing true?'

No idea what Father was hearing, he answered cautiously. 'Is what true, *Abba*?'

Father's dark eyes stared. 'You are seeing an English girl.'

'I – ' He didn't dare lie. 'Yes, *Abba* – I – we …'

The back of Father's hand across his face wouldn't have surprised him, unjust though that would have been. He could name three English girls his eldest brother had been linked with in recent years, and if the rumours circulating were true, at least two of them had borne him illegitimate children. Not forgetting the fact he would never have been born if Father hadn't cheated on his own wife with an English girl, all those years ago.

Father did raise his right hand, but only to place it firmly on his shoulder. 'Tell me, what are your intentions?'

'My intentions …?'

'This English girl, I hear she has a son – a half-caste son.'

He silently wished Father wouldn't refer to Samantha's son as 'half-caste', it was a term he despised, but he couldn't deny what Father had heard was true.

'Are you shagging her?'

Shocked by Father's course language, and surprised to be asked so bluntly, he didn't lie. 'Yes, *Abba* ...'

'Good, good.' Father's hand squeezed his shoulder. 'Perhaps,' said Father, winking, 'if Allah wills it, this English girl will bear you a son as well.'

He didn't tell his father Samantha was on the pill.

Back then, James was naïve enough to think the oral contraceptive pill was 100% effective. Now he knew better, and ... the three and a half months he and Samantha were lovers was, by some distance, the longest lasting relationship he had ever enjoyed.

Staring at his photograph, wondering what he was like and wondering how much Samantha had told the boy about him, he realised he didn't even know his son's name.

Chapter 6

'Yes, Manny?'

'He has arrived, boss – but his wife is with him.'

BlackBerry pressed to his ear, Vaughan stroked his moustache with his free hand. He had addressed the 'invite' to the professor, expected him to come alone, but … he glanced at Harris, who was standing on the other side of the conference table, talking to the explosives expert, Berro. He couldn't suppress a smile. He hadn't planned a surprise reunion, but now she was here …

'Boss …?'

'I'll be down in a minute – wait there for me.'

Vaughan slipped his BlackBerry into his pocket, attracted Harris's attention, called him over. 'A word in your ear,' he said, lowering his voice as Harris approached him. 'About your brat – if anyone mentions him or asks about him, you don't know anything. Nothing at all. Got it?'

'Why? I – '

'Just keep it buttoned, Harris, because if you don't …' He smiled. 'You wouldn't want to be responsible for your ex getting her little darling's crown jewels delivered to her in a box, would you?'

Harris didn't answer, but he didn't like the bastard's defiant glare.

'I mean it, Harris – mess with me and the boy suffers.'

'I hear you,' said Harris, quietly.

Satisfied he had asserted his authority, Vaughan turned to face the other men in the room, clapped his hands. 'Gentlemen, take a seat – our guest has arrived, and we'll be getting this show on the road in a few minutes.'

He hurried downstairs, to greet Professor Frewin-Hamilton and his wife. The professor, like many men as tall as six four, stood with a slight stoop. He was wearing a tweed jacket and brown slacks, while his wife was dressed in black trousers and a dark green jacket over a cream blouse. The snapshot in her dossier didn't do Mrs Frewin-Hamilton justice, but it was impossible to miss the redness around her eyes.

She spoke. 'Are you in charge?'

'I'm sorry, my – um, wife insisted on accompanying me …'

'No problem, Professor,' he said, smiling. He turned to the professor's wife. 'Yes, I'm in charge, and – '

She didn't let him finish. 'Where's my son?'

'Somewhere safe.'

'How do I know you're not lying – how do I know he's still alive?'

'You don't – but I assure you, he's perfectly fine.'

'I want to see him,' she demanded.

'That won't be possible, I'm afraid – but, if you and your husband behave, I might allow you to speak to him after the briefing.'

She stared at him, and nodded slowly. 'I'd like that – thank you.'

'I should mention, not everyone at the briefing knows about your son, and I'd like to keep it that way.' He smiled faintly. 'We wouldn't want him to lose one of his fingers, would we?'

She gasped, and the professor frowned as he put his arm across her shoulders. He said, 'We won't say anything to anyone.'

'Good, I'm glad we understand each other.' He indicated the stairs. 'Now, if you'll lead the way …'

This was going to be fun.

James took a seat facing the door Vaughan exited.

He was one of five men in the dining-cum-briefing room. Thomas 'Tommo' Martin he'd become reacquainted with yesterday, and the German Dieter 'Manny' Zimmerman was around somewhere, too. Nathan Gately, like Vaughan and Tommo, he'd served with in Iraq. That left Phillip 'Wilko' Wilkinson and Alexandro Berro. The former was short and wiry, with close-cropped straw blond hair; the latter was taller, more athletic looking and dark-skinned. Both, he guessed, were probably ex-forces. He hadn't met either man before today, but the shaven-headed Berro did have the decency to shake his hand when he introduced himself and told him to call him Alex, and appeared friendly enough. But he wasn't fooled. Berro, like every member of the team, was under Vaughan's command.

Including me.

'Any idea what this is about?' asked Alex, taking the seat next to him.

'You know as much as I do,' he replied.

After discovering he had a son, he'd phoned around to try to discover something, anything, about what Vaughan was hatching. It hadn't taken him long. He didn't have many friends, and since his discharge from the army he had kept himself to himself, wanting to avoid questions he couldn't answer. Not truthfully. He'd spoken to a handful of ex-forces contacts, but drew a blank. No one knew anything or, if they did, they weren't willing to share their knowledge with him. He did discover the rumour mill was in full swing, regarding the reasons behind his sudden discharge from the army. He flatly denied one accusation, which was closer to the truth than he felt comfortable with, but he'd politely declined to say more.

There were four wood back chairs on each long side of the dining table, on which sat two jugs of iced water and two stacks of five half pint glasses. Several buff files were piled up at the head of the table and on the opposite, far side of the table, Tommo was seated with a laptop in front of him. The laptop was linked to the screen at that end of the table. At the moment, a 'WELCOME' screensaver bounced around the screen, giving nothing away.

Vaughan reappeared.

'About bloody time,' muttered Alex.

Vaughan stepped aside and James saw her.

A split second later she spotted him.

She stopped dead, eyes widening, and she raised her hand to her open mouth. The beanpole behind her bumped into her, knocked her forward, and she might have fallen if hands on the end of long arms hadn't steadied her.

She stared at him and he stared back.

Then the beanpole stepped between them … her husband? Tall, lean, with unruly brown hair and an untidy goatee, James judged he was in his mid-to-late thirties. That made him a decade older than Samantha and, sporting an old fashioned tweed jacket, he did have the aura of an academic about him.

Alex nudged his arm. 'What's with you and the broad?'

He didn't answer. He did notice he and Samantha were being watched – closely. And Vaughan had an amused glint in his eyes.

The bastard's set us up.

Clearly, Samantha hadn't expected to see him here, any more than he had anticipated her appearance. Suddenly, he understood why Vaughan wanted him to play dumb about her kidnapped son.

He doesn't want her to know I know.

Which begged another question.

How much does she know?

And what must she be thinking, on seeing him here, and seeming to be part of the team responsible for abducting her son?

'Gentlemen, may I introduce Professor Richard Frewin-Hamilton and his lovely wife, Samantha. As some of you know, Professor Frewin-Hamilton has kindly agreed to join our little expedition.'

Vaughan indicated the two chairs directly opposite James and Alex; without looking at James, Samantha claimed the seat across from Alex, leaving her husband to sit opposite James.

'My good friend Manny you've already met.' Vaughan raised his hand toward the German, who had followed the Frewin-Hamiltons into the room. 'I'm Vaughan, and around the table we have Tommo, Wilko, Gately, Berro and Harris.'

James waited, but Vaughan didn't say anything to indicate he was aware he and Samantha already knew each other. No one else said anything, either. Samantha steadfastly stared at Vaughan, who had taken up position next to the white screen at the head of the table.

'Tommo, I think we're ready ...'

Tommo tapped the laptop, and the 'WELCOME' screensaver was replaced by an image that filled the screen: a head and shoulders portrait of an elderly man with a kindly face, bald on top but with thinning silver grey hair around the sides and a matching wispy beard.

James didn't recognise the old man, but Professor Frewin-Hamilton clearly did.

'This, gentlemen – and lady,' said Vaughan, with a nod in Samantha's direction, 'is – '

'Father Crespi!'

'Indeed, professor, and since you know considerably more about the gentleman than I do, perhaps you would like to share your knowledge with everyone else – but please, keep it brief.'

'Yes, well – um, Father Crespi, Father Carlos Crespi Croci was born in Milan in 1891,' said the professor. 'A Silesian monk, he lived in Ecuador from 1923 until his death in 1982. He – um, he spent his life doing missionary work among the indigenous Indian population, mostly in remote valleys around his adopted city, Cuenca. The local populace adored him – in fact, an impressive sculpture to his memory was erected in Cuenca, following his passing, and – '

'Thank you, professor,' Vaughan interrupted. 'Kindly tell us, if you will, about the artifacts Crespi was given by the local Indians.'

Crespi's photograph was replaced by four images of strange artifacts – including a metal plaque, bronze or possibly gold, with a pyramid motif on it. Curiously, there were what appeared to be stylised cats on either side of the pyramid, with a snake above each cat and a tiny elephant below each cat's tail, at the base of the pyramid.

'Yes, of course. I, um – Father Crespi, over the years, collected numerous local artifacts, many of them believed to have a ritualistic purpose. The best known pieces include tablets made of gold foil, silver and different alloys including bronze, many of them with mysterious symbols and unknown letters. Father Crespi stored the artifacts at the Maria Auxiliadora church. Regrettably, a fire in 1962 destroyed many of the artifacts, and over the years others have been lost or found their way into the possession of treasure hunters.'

'The artifacts,' said Vaughan, 'came from subterranean cave systems in the jungle, did they not?'

The professor nodded. 'It is believed so, yes, but – um, there have been a number of expeditions to the Tayos Cave region over the years, including a Mormon expedition in 1968 and a joint British-Ecuadorian expedition in 1976, but – '

'But contrary to expectations, the Metal Library has never been found, has it?'

The professor and Vaughan looked at each other.

'I, um – how do you know about the Metal Library?'

Vaughan smiled. 'Come now, professor – it's existence is hardly a state secret, is it? As I'm sure you're aware, several online sites even carry a map of its location, with precise GPS co-ordinates.'

James, although he'd always had a passing interest in history, had never heard of the Metal Library.

'Do you believe the Metal Library exists, Professor?' asked Vaughan.

'I – yes, I do. I believe – '

'You believe you know exactly where the Metal Library is really located, don't you?'

'I – ' Professor Frewin-Hamilton shifted uncomfortably in his seat, 'I don't – I'm not certain of anything – '

'Richard, please ...'

She only spoke two words, but hearing Samantha's voice again after so long, James felt – he didn't know what he felt. Strange, certainly, but ... he wished he could have met her again under different, happier circumstances.

'It's true, is it not,' said Vaughan, 'your father-in-law, Professor Edgar Radcliffe, visited Ecuador three times in recent years?'

Samantha visibly stiffened, at the mention of her father – a man she had talked to James about, although the two of them had never met.

'Professor Radcliffe – he, um – '

'My father is dead.'

Four words, bravely spoken.

Samantha was still refusing to acknowledge he existed, so he couldn't see her face, but he did feel her pain.

'So I've heard – a house fire, wasn't it?'

The question went unanswered.

Vaughan turned to Professor Frewin-Hamilton.

'Professor, I sincerely hope you do know where the Metal Library is located, because that's where we are headed.'

Chapter 7

'Are you certain?'

'Of course I'm certain!'

Still reeling from coming face-to-face with the biological father of her kidnapped son, at a meeting with his kidnappers, Samantha couldn't believe her husband doubted her.

'But – what's-his-name, Vaughan.' Her husband, who was driving, didn't take his eyes off the road as he spoke. 'He called him Harris, didn't he? I thought you told me Luke's father was called – Mohammed something-or-other, wasn't it?'

'Hassan, Mohammed Hassan,' she confirmed. 'That's what he was called when I knew him, but his mother was English, and before she died he was called James Harris. He's obviously using that name again.'

She had no idea why Hassan had reverted to using his birth name, and frankly she didn't care. He appeared to have ditched Islam, as well. Although she'd not said a word to him at the briefing, and had avoided making eye contact, she had spotted him tucking into a cheese and ham sandwich at lunch-time. That, and the name change, suggested he was no longer a practicing Muslim. So what? His religious beliefs, or lack of them, interested her as much as his change of identity. All she cared about was getting her son back.

Vaughan had kept his word – let her speak to Luke. Only for a few seconds, but they were precious seconds, and the contact confirmed her son was still alive. She could scarcely believe, already, her son had been missing for over four days.

Heading north-west, towards the Henley-On-Thames home she had moved into last year following her marriage to Richard, her husband sped down the slip road on to the M4.

'This Harris fellow, you don't think he's involved with Luke's abduction, do you?'

'Of course not,' she snapped.

'I was only thinking …'

He fell silent and she apologised. She hadn't meant to snap, but Hassan's sudden reappearance, after more than five years, had thrown her. More than she liked to admit. So many times, before she met Richard, she wondered where Hassan was and what he was up to. Suddenly having him back in her life again was a dream and a nightmare, all rolled into one.

You don't think he's involved with Luke's abduction, do you?

How could Hassan, or whatever he was calling himself these days, be involved with Luke's abduction when he didn't even know he had a son?

Ignorance is no defence.

Looking at it logically, from her perspective, Hassan *was* implicated in the abduction of her son. But that pre-supposed he knew about Luke, which as far as she was aware, he didn't. She didn't find out she was pregnant until after he disappeared. But she couldn't deny, in the few months they were lovers, he had built up an excellent relationship with Joshua. So good, her son had asked her 'Is Hassan my Daddy?' twice, and he had asked Hassan 'Are you my Daddy?' Thankfully, the answers they gave were consistent and truthful: Hassan was her friend, and she was happy Joshua and Hassan were friends, too.

Even if Hassan – James Harris – did know about Luke's abduction, he didn't necessarily know he was the boy's father. But he might. Vaughan did know Luke was her son, but did he also know the identity of Luke's father? And if so, how did he know? More to the point, if Vaughan did know, what if anything had he said to Harris? Vaughan had threatened to harm her son, if she or Richard said anything to anyone about Luke's kidnap. He could easily have threatened Harris as well. She had only been in the same room as Harris and Vaughan for three hours, but even so she had sensed the animosity between the two of them. Even Richard had noticed, and after they were shown out of the meeting he'd commented on how unpopular Harris appeared with the other members of the team. 'He's friendly enough with that black guy, but I don't think anyone else likes him.'

Which begged the question: *why not?*

Conflict between Harris and her son's kidnappers suggested he wasn't on the same wavelength as the others. She liked to think, even if he did know about it, Harris had played no part in her son's kidnap because if he had – at best, he was guilty by association.

At worse … it didn't bear thinking about.

Samantha asked her husband to drop her outside Beverley's three bed detached home on Bradley Road, just a short walk from where she and Richard lived. As well as Callum, Joshua's best friend, Beverley was mum to baby Megan. Walking up the short, flagged path to the white front door, she silently prayed her son hadn't let anything slip about his young brother's abduction.

'How's Josh been?' she asked, wiping her feet on the russet 'welcome' mat behind the front door.

'No trouble – he never is.' Beverley, a short, attractive brunette, closed the front door after her. Her friend was wearing a faded pink T-shirt and grey jogging bottoms. 'He's been a bit subdued, actually. I expect he's still a bit tired, and I think he's missing his brother.'

He isn't the only one.

She made a bee-line for baby Megan, who she was pleased to see was wide awake. 'She gets more gorgeous every day,' she said, lifting the blue eyed, curly haired baby out of her cot and cradling her. 'Every time I hold her, I feel broody.'

Beverley grinned. 'So – you could be nice to Richard!'

She rolled her eyes. 'Or not.'

Joshua's birth delayed the start of her studies at the University of Manchester by two years, but thanks to financial support from her father and childcare, she went on to complete her three year course in Ancient History & Archaeology, gaining her B.A. degree with honours. She was planning to enrol for a part-time postgraduate course when she discovered Luke was on his way, but … broody or not, she didn't plan on having a third child any time soon, if ever. Thankfully, Richard hadn't expressed a desire to add to their family, either.

'Besides,' she said, 'he's hardly ever home these days, and it looks like he'll be jetting off again on Saturday.'

'What, so soon! Where's he off to this time?'

'Ecuador.'

'That's where he went last year, isn't it, with your Dad?'

'It is.' She took the plunge, and lied. 'He's asked me if I'd like to go with him this time, but I told him there's no way.'

'Why not?' asked Beverley.

'Come on, Bev, how can I? We've only just got back from Tenerife, Luke's broken his arm and Josh is back at school tomorrow.'

Truth, lie, truth.

'So?' A measured pause. 'How long is he going to be away?'

'I don't know,' she admitted. 'At least a week, maybe two.'

Right on cue Beverley made her offer.

'I'd love to have Josh stay with us, if you want to go …?'

Samantha did want to go, desperately, but she felt guilty about lying to her best friend. She felt even guiltier, at the thought of jetting off to South America and leaving Joshua behind, especially at a time like this. But she knew she would go crazy, sitting at home, not knowing what was happening when Luke's life depended on the outcome of the Ecuador trip.

'Thanks, Bev, I appreciate your offer,' she said, 'I really do, but … let me talk to Richard again first, okay?'

'Mummy, when is Luke coming home?'

Samantha stopped reading, set the book down beside her, on Joshua's bed. She reached down, gently stroked her son's short black fringe. 'Soon, Josh – I hope he's coming home real soon.'

Joshua frowned. 'I miss him.'

'I miss him, too, sweetheart – very much.' Tears welled in her eyes but she blinked them away, as she leaned down, kissed her son's forehead and hugged him. She didn't want Joshua to see her crying. 'Me and Richard are doing everything we can, to try to get him back, but ...'

She had assumed, once they were married, her sons would start to call her husband 'daddy', but that hadn't happened. Her sons had never asked, and when she raised the subject with her husband, he had told her, 'I really do prefer Richard.'

'Is he still at Monkey Park?'

She found a little smile. 'No, Josh, of course he isn't. He – he's staying with some people. They're taking good care of him, but – me and Richard might have to go away for a few days, to try to find him and bring him home. If we do, how would you like to go stay at Callum's while we're away?'

Joshua didn't answer, but he didn't appear unduly concerned by the suggestion, either. She kissed him again, wished him a goodnight, before turning off his bedside lamp. 'Sleep tight, sweetheart. Mummy loves you very much,' she whispered. 'I'll see you in the morning.'

She crept downstairs, where she joined her husband in the dining room. He was exactly where she had left him: seated at the dining room table, with his laptop open in front of him and his gold-rimmed reading glasses perched on the end of his nose. Numerous documents, notebooks and books were spread untidily across the table's polished surface, almost entirely hiding it. He was so engrossed in what he was doing he didn't hear her approach.

'How it's going?' she asked, halting by his right shoulder.

'What – oh, I'm not sure,' he answered, suddenly turning to face her. He pushed his glasses up his nose, pulled on his goatee. 'I – I've tried to narrow the search parameters as much as I can, but – I won't know anything for certain, until we are actually in Ecuador.'

She knew the 'we' didn't include her.

'Can I get you a drink?'

'Yes, thank you – I'd appreciate a Scotch. Make it a double, please.'

She poured her husband's drink, cleared a space on the dining table to set the glass down. 'Richard, I've been thinking – maybe I should come with you. I – '

'No.'

'What do you mean, no!' His response didn't surprise her, but it did disappoint her. She had hoped he would be more understanding, more supportive. Clearly, her husband was forgetting she had studied the region's history. The Incas, especially, had always fascinated her. As for the Metal Library, thanks to her late father's obsession with proving the damned thing existed, she'd literally grown up with it. That, and a stubborn streak: even as a little girl, if someone told her 'no' she couldn't do something, she went out of her way to prove 'yes' she could.

'Samantha, this isn't a package tour. I don't think you have any idea of the dangers we're going to face in Ecuador. The jungle is – '

'No place for a woman?'

'I – that is not what I was going to say, but – ' He scratched his cheek. 'This discussion is rather academic, don't you think? The decision on who goes to Ecuador, and who doesn't, is not mine to make.'

Chapter 8

Too late to stop him, James watched Alex approach the kitchen table, pick up the framed photograph of his son and Joshua he'd left there. Turning around, raising the snapshot, Alex glanced at him.

'Yours?'

'The older boy isn't, but his little brother is,' he admitted, as he silently wished he hadn't left the photograph in view. But when he stepped out this morning he hadn't anticipated bringing anyone back home with him – and it could have been a lot worse. He could have left Vaughan's 'Happy Birthday' greeting on the table, as well. *That* photograph he really didn't want to have to explain, not to anyone. Never again. He didn't offer any more information about his son and, thankfully, Alex didn't ask.

'He's a cute kid.' Alex put the photo down again, and he dropped the seafood pizza that had just been delivered next to it. 'I didn't know it at the time, but my ex was knocked up when she kicked me out last year. The bitch got a bad migraine, so she came home early from work – she caught me having fun with a fit Italian stud!'

Briefly, James visualised the scene in his mind, but he didn't pass judgment.

Over lunch – bought-in sandwiches and fresh fruit – he'd learned Alex lived south of the Thames, in Croydon, but that he was in the process of re-locating to north London where, after serving nine years in the army, he'd set himself up as a private investigator. Vaughan escorted Samantha and her professor husband out of the briefing turned planning meeting after lunch, but the meeting carried on without them. And on and on and on – until 20:30. Before they finally left, Vaughan said, 'I want everyone back here tomorrow morning, 9:00 sharp.' On the way out, thinking he might appreciate it, he offered Alex his sofa for the night.

Alex hesitated. 'Sounds good, but … there's something you should know before you make an offer like that.'

He already knew. 'You're gay.'

'How the fuck …?' Alex didn't hide his surprise.

'I overheard Wilko talking to Gately earlier.'

Alex nodded faintly. 'Yeah, and I bet he didn't call me gay, did he?'

'If I remember correctly,' he said, smiling, 'the term he used was "fuckin' queer".'

'Yeah, that figures. He's a fuckin' asshole – he's not even right. Just because I like guys, that doesn't mean I don't like chicks, as well.'

'You're bi?'

Alex nodded. 'So …'

'So …' He wasn't sure how Alex expected him to react.

'So – ' Alex raised a hand, ran his fingers over his shaved head. 'I just thought you should know, that's all.'

'Okay, I know – and my offer stands, if you don't want to drive back home tonight?'

'You're cool with that? I mean, I happen to think a lot of straight guys are bi-curious, but they'll never admit it, 'specially not when they're sober, and most straight guys feel threatened if they – '

'I don't feel threatened,' he cut in, 'and I'm not bi-curious. I should warn you, though, Vaughan and I – you probably noticed he's not exactly my number one fan.'

'Yeah, I noticed.' Alex grinned. 'So why are you on board?'

He repeated the question over in his mind.

So why are you on board?

He felt no great desire to join Vaughan's treasure hunt, and he wouldn't, if there was any way he could avoid it. But to do that, he must find out where his son was being held, and free him. He was desperate to know exactly what had happened, and where, and the best person to tell him that was the boy's mother. Alex, he'd learned, had earned a living as a private investigator since quitting the army. It was apparent Alex knew nothing about his son's abduction, but he didn't feel he knew him well enough to share the information.

'I could use the cash,' he replied. It wasn't a lie, it just fell a long way short of the whole truth.

'You and me both,' said Alex. 'If we pull this off, I'm thinking of setting up my own security consultancy.'

No wheels of his own yet, James had taken a cab to the briefing, which was located less than ten minutes away from his Bayswater apartment. He accompanied Alex to his vehicle, a silver Vauxhall Astra SXI.

'The professor's wife,' said Alex, 'you know her, don't you?'

'I used to do,' he admitted, 'before I joined the army.'

'Intimately?'

He nodded. 'Intimately.'

Grinning, Alex slapped the roof of the Astra. 'I knew it!'

They climbed in. As he inserted his key in the ignition, gunned the engine, Alex asked, 'So what happened?'

'I left without saying goodbye.'

Alex whistled. 'No wonder she totally blanked you.'

If only you knew the whole story.

But that was something he didn't want to share with anyone.

Clunking his seatbelt on, he changed the subject, 'How well do you know Vaughan.'

'Only met him once before today.' Alex fired the engine. 'I served with Wilko. He's known him for – I don't know exactly. Two or three years, something like that.'

'What do you think of him?'

'First impressions – he's likes everyone to know who's boss, doesn't he?'

James didn't disagree. He hadn't asked many questions, after Samantha and her husband departed the meeting, but the answers he'd been given didn't inspire confidence this was going to be a well organised, well manned or well equipped expedition. He still couldn't quite believe Vaughan planned on leading a team through tropical jungle, without recruiting someone with a medical background.

'Fuckin' tosser,' muttered Alex, shaking his head.

As Alex drove east, along Bayswater Road, James took out his mobile and ordered a seafood pizza. Alex's choice, but it was one of his favourites, too.

'Don't look over your shoulder,' Alex warned, as they approached his apartment, 'but there's a white Corsa just pulled up fifty yards back. It's been with us all the way.'

Silently, he cursed.

'You reckon it's Vaughan?'

He didn't reckon it was Vaughan; he *knew* it was Vaughan. 'Not in person, but yeah – it's me he doesn't trust.'

Speaking to Samantha about her son's abduction had suddenly gotten a lot more complicated.

Alex cocked an eyebrow. 'Why do I get the feeling I'm missing something here?'

'Because – I'm sorry, Alex, I can't talk about it.'

'Fair enough, but if you need my help ...'

'I'll ask.'

About fifteen minutes after he unlocked his front door, invited Alex inside, the pizza delivery boy arrived. He cut the seafood pizza into slices, grabbed a couple of plates off the rack and told Alex to help himself.

'My ex,' said Alex, after swallowing his first mouthful, 'we didn't hear her come upstairs – the bitch took a photo of us screwin' with her mobile, and another when we turned toward her.' His expression hardened. 'I can understand she was angry, but the fuckin' bitch had no right to out me.'

'She didn't know you were bi?'

'Uh-uh, no way. I'm a bit more open about my sexuality now, but back then – I knew I liked guys, but no one else did. *No one.*' Alex demolished his first slice of pizza, before reaching for another. 'The bitch, she texted one of the photos to everyone we knew – she even posted it on her Facebook page. I don't know how long it was up for, before it got deleted, but ... ' He shook his head slowly. 'We had a blazin' row. We lived in Islington, and I packed my bags and moved to Croydon. I hadn't been there a month when the bitch texted me, to tell me she was expecting my kid. She took great delight in telling me she was gonna get rid of it.'

'She had an abortion?'

'Yeah,' Alex confirmed, putting his pizza down on his plate. 'I tried to stop the bitch – I mean, that kid was as much mine as it was hers, right? But nothing I said to her made any fuckin' difference.'

James hadn't counted how many women he'd slept with, between Samantha and Rochay. But too many, probably. Sometimes, when his conscience got to him, he wondered how women like Rochay reacted when they awoke and realised he was gone. He didn't doubt, if he had roused her instead of slipping out of her bed, a night of passion could easily have turned into a morning of passion. And then ... what? Was Rochay, like him, happy with a one night stand, or was she hoping for more? A long term relationship? A husband? A daddy for her kid? Or kids. And how did finding him gone, with no way of contacting him again, make her feel? Disappointed? Angry? Used? Would she, if he'd stuck around long enough to ask her, have agreed to see him again? He suspected she probably would have, but ... in the army, he'd seen too many men with wives or girlfriends suffer horrific injuries or lose their lives, and he had always shied away from getting too involved with anyone.

I'm not a soldier now ...

He poured two glasses of fresh pineapple juice, as Alex asked, 'You got just the one kid?'

He nodded. 'He lives with his mother.'

When he isn't being held by kidnappers.

'You see him regular?'

'Not as regular as I'd like.'

Not ever.

'Why ain't I surprised.' Alex polished off another slice of pizza. 'Just 'cos they carry 'em for nine months, the bitches think they own 'em.'

After eating his fill, James powered up his laptop. With Alex standing by his right shoulder, he googled 'metal library'. In just 0.17 second, the search engine produced a mind boggling 69.2 million results. Several on the first page immediately caught his eye.

The Quest For The Metal Library.
Tayos Gold Library – The Metal Library.
Does The Metal Library Really Exist?
The Metal Library and the Cueva de los Tayos.

'Does the Metal Library really exist?' Alex read aloud. 'It better fuckin' had do, or we're up gonna be up shit creek.'

He clicked on the link, which took him to a page from the Project Avalon Forum. Scrolling down, he spotted one name neither Vaughan or the professor had mentioned.

'Erich von Däniken,' said Alex. 'Isn't he that crazy dude who's written some crap books about aliens?'

'Not everyone thinks they're crap,' he said, smiling.

Alex raised an eyebrow. 'Don't tell me you believe that shit?'

'I didn't say that.' He could only recall the title of one of von Däniken's books: *Chariot Of The Gods*. He hadn't read it, but he did know how controversial it was … the forum comment that von Däniken's TV series *Ancient Aliens* had made a 'big splash' about the Metal Library didn't exactly inspire confidence.

Apparently, von Däniken visited the Tayos Cave system where the Metal Library was supposedly located in 1972, and wrote about it in another of his books, *The Gold Of The Gods*. However, the guy who supposedly took him to the tunnels subsequently undermined von Däniken's credibility, when he denied ever having been in the caves with von Däniken. Worse, von Däniken himself later admitted to fabricating some of his claims in *The Gold Of The Gods*, to add interest to his book.

Not good, not good at all.

He opened another site.

This one carried the same aerial photograph of the supposed Tayos Cave location that Vaughan had shown them, and gave the same calculated location of the 'treasure cave' – 77° 47' 34" west and 1° 56' 00" south – the professor had rubbished.

Scrolling down the home page of the third site he visited, James paused at a photograph of a man inside the Tayos Cave, a man wearing a miner's lamp and reaching out his right hand to touch a vertical rock formation that resembled a thick, gnarled tree trunk. A man he should have recognised, but didn't.

'Fuck me …'

He couldn't resist. 'I'd rather not, thanks.'

Alex grinned. 'Don't worry, you're not my type – I prefer white guys!'

He nearly said something, but stopped himself. He turned his attention back to the screen. The man pictured was someone else Vaughan and the professor had neglected to mention: Neil Armstrong.

The first man to walk on the moon.

That's one small step for man, one giant leap for mankind.

Alex spoke aloud what he was thinking. 'What the fuck does a famous astronaut have to do with the Metal Library?'

'Aliens, astronauts … '

It wasn't looking promising.

He scrolled down the page, learned Neil Armstrong had been recruited as the honorary figurehead of a 1976 expedition that visited the Tayos Caves. A burial chamber, with a seated body dating to 1500 BC was discovered, plus some four hundred new plant species – but once again, no Metal Library.

Does it exist?

He checked out several more sites … he read incredible claims there were hundreds of miles of tunnels under Ecuador and Peru, which he didn't believe for a second, but not much else he hadn't heard or read before. He googled Father Carlos Crespi instead, but again he didn't learn anything significant that Vaughan and the professor hadn't already briefed them on.

'So, what do you reckon?' asked Alex.

James shook his head. He didn't know what to think and, if he was being honest, he didn't care if the Metal Library existed or not. But even if it did, and by some miracle they located it, there was nothing to stop Vaughan from returning her son to Samantha in a body bag.

And putting a bullet in my head.

Vaughan was many things, but he wasn't stupid. However this panned out, he was unlikely to want to leave any loose ends, and like it or not that is what Samantha's son would become, just as soon as this was over.

He's not the only one.

'Let's hope,' he said, pushing disturbing thoughts to the back of his mind, 'the professor knows what he's talking about.'

There was something he wanted to do, something he couldn't do without help … silently, as he ran one more search, he debated how far he could trust Alex.

He googled Professor Edgar Radcliffe.

He discovered Samantha's father had indeed perished in a house fire, in mid-November. The authorities, reportedly, had concluded there were no suspicious circumstances, but … Alex read his mind.

'I hope you're not thinking what I think you're thinking.'

He asked, 'And what am I thinking?'

'That maybe that fire wasn't an accident.'

'Is that what you think?'

'Uh-uh, it doesn't sound suspicious to me – unless you know something I don't?'

'You know as much as I do, but I … ' It was too late to do anything tonight, and there was something he needed to know first. 'Alex, can I ask you a favour?'

Alex grinned. 'You wanna know if it's true, what they say about black guys, right?'

He had to smile. 'Wrong.'

He told Alex what he wanted.

Chapter 9

Back home after his early morning run through Hyde Park, noticing his guest was still asleep on the sofa, James quietly peeled off his sweat-stained T-shirt, discarded his trainers and socks. He padded barefoot into his bedroom. Small, but uncluttered, and he'd moved the double bed up against the far wall, to leave some open floor space. Not as much as he would have liked, for what he was about to do, but it was adequate.

The apartment had wood flooring throughout and, as he squatted down, he almost unconsciously touched the puckered skin over his left shoulder. He'd fixed a wide, full length mirror on the wall directly opposite him. Although he couldn't see much unless he twisted his torso and raised his left arm, the scarring extended down his left side, and halfway down the left side of his back as well. A few nights ago, Rochay had asked, 'Will it hurt if I touch it?' He'd assured her it wouldn't, and it didn't, but sometimes – especially when the cold got to it, as it had this morning, his shoulder throbbed like a bad toothache.

He closed his eyes, tried to clear his mind, before he performed a few warm up exercises. As well as stretching the muscles in his arms and legs, he did fifty push-ups and fifty squat thrusts. Then, facing the mirror, he stood up straight, in *yoi* – with his arms by his sides, and his fists clenched. He stood in *yoi*, focused and ready for action, for two whole minutes, before he bowed towards the mirror. He spent a good fifteen minutes practicing some of the basics: punches, blocks and kicks. A short breather, as he stood in *yoi* again, composing himself. In his mind, he could see his old Sensei standing before him, saying, 'Announce *kata*', and he replied, '*Pinan Godan*, Sensei.'

A Japanese word, *kata* literally meant 'form'. It described a detailed, specified series of martial arts movements, ideally performed while maintaining perfect form, in which the practitioner visualises enemy attacks and their responses.

Now, he executed *Pinan Godan*, *Pinan Nidan* and *Pinan Sandan* twice, followed by *Sanchin* and *Tensho* – two *kata* he always found particularly challenging, as they must be performed very slowly, and emphasized deep breathing combined with dynamic tension.

Aware he was being watched, he drew himself up to his full height with his hands in front of his chest, held himself still for a moment, before he exhaled and relaxed.

'Not bad – not bad at all.'

He turned to Alex, who was standing in the bedroom doorway in a sleeveless white vest and black Calvin Klein boxer shorts. Last night he had learned, like him, Alex was mixed race. The son of an Anglo-Spanish mother and a black African father he had never met. 'Morning, Alex. Sleep well?'

'Like a baby, thanks – and thanks for letting me crash here.'

'No problem.'

'Let me guess – you're a black belt, right?'

'Third Dan.' He noticed Alex, like most people who saw it exposed, was staring at his left side. 'Iraq,' he said, before he was asked. 'IED.'

Improvised Explosive Device – what the media liked to call a 'roadside bomb'.

'Sounds nasty.' Alex lifted his vest high, showed him a pale, inch and a half scar below his left nipple. 'This is where I got stabbed when I was eighteen.' He let his vest fall, tugged up his boxers on his right thigh, exposed a small scar just below his groin. 'I picked this one up in Helmand. An insurgent shot me, but I got the bastard.' Alex grinned. 'I lived to fight another day. The fucker who got me didn't.'

Alex revealed he'd also attended karate lessons when he was a kid. 'I got my black belt when I when fourteen, but then we moved and I discovered sex, and I lost interest and quit.'

By the time James had showered and dressed, it was a few minutes before eight. He was rustling some scrambled egg and toast, when Alex emerged from the bathroom with a navy towel wrapped around his waist.

'Any chance I can borrow some clean kit?'

'Sure.' He was taller than Alex, but there was less than an inch in it, so he reckoned most of his gear would fit, and pointed Alex in the right direction.

Alex wouldn't have minded if James stayed in the bedroom, and watched him dress, but he didn't.

He's not interested.

Pity, he thought, as he pulled the towel from around his waist and rubbed his groin dry. He hadn't lied when he said he preferred white guys, but he liked variety, too, and there was something about James ... knowing he was bi had a curious effect on most straight men. Many straight chicks, too. But James didn't appear fazed at all. Clearly, he didn't feel threatened by his sexuality. Then again, why should he be? Although they'd only just met, he was in no doubt James was the kind of guy he'd much rather have on his side in a fight, than opposing him.

He pulled on a pair of black jeans, and reached for a dark green polo shirt, with white piping around the collar and sleeves. Born a few miles outside Barcelona, he had spent the first five years of his life in Spain, before his mother split with her Spanish lover and moved back to England, where she had been born and raised, and where her brother, sister and parents still lived. His mother's ex, he realised as he grew older, wasn't his real father. How could he be, when her ex's skin was almost as pale as his mother's and his was as dark as milk chocolate. But all his mother could tell him about his biological father, other than the fact he was long gone by the time he was born, is that he was called Nelson and that he was 'African'. He'd pointed out Africa was a huge continent but whenever he asked her to be more specific, his mother used to say, 'I never asked him – it didn't seem important at the time.'

Between the ages of five and fourteen, Alex lived in a two-up, two-down mid-terraced house in an almost exclusively white area of Canterbury. At school, he was one of only two non-white kids in his class; the other was an Indian girl. Over the years, his mother took in a succession of lovers. Losers, most of them. One bastard, when he'd had a few drinks, used to think it was hilarious to do a monkey impersonation and toss him a banana – until, one day, he caught the banana and hurled it right back. He caught the bastard just under his eye, gave him a black eye, which bought him a beating that left him sore for a week. He was always in trouble at school, too, because all too often he reacted to racist abuse. He was only nine when he was expelled from one primary school, for busting the nose of an older boy who called him 'nigga boy'.

He was only fourteen when it happened.

Once, sometimes twice a week, he went to his friend Dean's house, where they did their homework together. Dean was a stocky, street-wise lad with bleached blond hair and a pierced eyebrow who, like most of the kids in their class, had a PC in his bedroom, with access to the internet – great for researching school work, but most evenings he visited they found time to check out a few porn sites as well. He didn't dare admit he was as excited by big, erect pricks as he was by tits and shaved cunts, couldn't understand why that should be. He told himself, over and over again, he wasn't queer. No way – he couldn't be. It was unthinkable. But one night, scrolling down a page, Dean stopped at '*GAY SEX*'.

10 pics – Horny studs hardcore action.

16 pics – Interracial gay sex action.

12 pics – Crazy bisexual threesome.

The list carried on down the page.

'Wanna look?' asked Dean, grinning.

He did, but he shrugged indifference. 'If you want to …'

Dean clicked on '*16 pics – Interracial gay sex action.*'

Leaning closer, he watched a series of small, thumbnail photographs of a young white guy having sex with a young black guy appear. They were both naked. The white guy was lying on his back, with the black guy straddling him, but facing the opposite way. Seeing them, studying them, he had never felt so aroused in all his life.

'That's called sixty-nine,' said Dean, grinning. 'Wanna try it?'

'What – ' He couldn't believe his friend was suggesting what he appeared to be suggesting.

'Me and you,' confirmed Dean, nodding at the monitor screen.

He looked at the screen, watched as Dean clicked on one of the more explicit thumbs, enlarged it. He liked what he saw, he liked it a lot, but … turning back to his friend, he asked, 'Do you?'

'Sure, why not – it should be a laugh!'

He and Dean had been having sex once, sometimes twice or even three times a week, for nearly six months when his mother's sister fell seriously ill, and they moved down to London, so his mother could be closer to her. They moved into a two bedroom, fifth floor apartment in Islington. Here, for the first time in his life, he found himself living in a neighbourhood where there was a sizeable black community. But his initial delight, at seeing so many faces as dark as or even darker than his own, soon turned to dismay as it became apparent he still didn't fit in.

Within a week of starting at his new school, one of the black kids in his class started to call him 'bounty', after the milk chocolate bar with sweet, white coconut on the inside. 'Admit it, man,' his new friend teased, 'you look black, but you're fuckin' honky on the inside!'

He hated the slur as much as he hated being called nigga or monkey but, especially among his new black friends, the nickname stuck.

Determined to be accepted, to be more black, he began observing his new friends closely. The way they talked, the way they dressed, the way they moved, the music they listened to. Everything about them. Wanting to be like them, he spent hours alone in his bedroom, trying to copy them. He started drinking. He started smoking – dope, as well as tobacco. He started carrying a blade. And he started dating – black chicks, mostly, and he was still only fourteen when an older black girl seduced him. Not that he was complaining. He enjoyed the experience as much as he'd enjoyed having sex with Dean.

Almost without realising it, he became part of a local gang. A black gang known as the Red Dragons. He put what had happened with Dean behind him, told himself over and over again it was all Dean's fault, and that he liked girls, not guys. Definitely, definitely not guys. As if to prove it, he had a succession of girlfriends. Black chicks mostly, but occasionally he got lucky with a white girl.

He was seventeen when Jermaine Dutton moved into the neighbourhood. JD, as he liked to be known, was also mixed race except, in JD's case, his mother was black and his father white. JD, with his cute baby face, looked fifteen or sixteen, but he'd actually just turned nineteen. JD was incredibly handsome – least ways, he thought so, but JD was so overtly homophobic he didn't dare let his true feelings for him be known.

They started hanging around together and once, when they double-dated, he saw JD naked. He couldn't believe how intensely jealous he felt of JD's girlfriend and that night, as he lay in his own bed, he couldn't stop fantasizing – couldn't stop imagining he was having sex with JD, as he jacked-off.

Then, one night, he and JD gate-crashed a party – had too much to drink. It was gone midnight when they got a cab back to JD's apartment, where they had another beer, and shared a joint. Too pissed to undress himself, JD asked him to help him, and he was happy to oblige ... sober, he would have kept his hands to himself, when he tugged JD's jeans down. But he wasn't sober, and when he noticed JD's boxers had slipped down as well, exposing him, he couldn't resist touching him ... minutes later, having hastily shed his own clothes, he and JD were lying close to each other, touching and groping and kissing – having sex.

They fell asleep wrapped in each other's embrace and when they awoke, after promising each other never to tell anyone about their illicit relationship, they had sex again. They were still secret lovers ten months later, when one of JD's girlfriends gave birth to a daughter. They were on their way back from the hospital, keen to get back on home territory and celebrate, when JD suggested they take a short cut. Knowing the area better than JD, he should never have agreed, but he wasn't thinking straight and he did.

The moment they turned the corner, headed down a quiet side street, Alex knew he'd made a mistake. A big mistake. For, not far ahead of them, there was a gang of youths. Seven or eight of them, black youths wearing black bandanas, and laughing and joking. They all looked in their late teens or early twenties.

Panthers.

The atmosphere changed the instant the rival gang spotted the two of them approaching. He swore under his breath and JD said, 'Stay cool – they'll let us pass.'

Silent now, the Panthers turned to face them, and his fear intensified when he realised he had seen at least two of them before. A skirmish, just a week or so ago. No one on their side got hurt, but he'd heard one of the Panthers got knifed. How badly, he had no idea, but ... he wanted to turn around and run but, hearing at least two sets of footsteps closing on them from behind, he knew that was no longer an option.

We're trapped!

The Panthers blocked their path – forced them to stop.

'You with the Dragons ...'

It was more of a statement than a question.

JD lied easily. 'Uh-uh, not us, we're new 'round here.'

'We're not looking for trouble,' he added. 'We just – '

The Panther who'd spoken leapt forward, and unleashed a punch that drove him back on his heels.

'That's for Tito,' his attacker snarled.

The blow took his breath away and, reflexively, he clutched his chest where he'd been struck – felt wetness. Looking down, he was shocked to see deep crimson seeping through his fingers, darkening his shirt.

Blood!

He glanced at his attacker – saw the blade.

I've been stabbed!

Suddenly afraid, he gripped his chest tighter.

He stared and his attacker stared back.

Unable to tear his eyes away from the thin, glistening blade still threatening him, he took one small step back, and another – then, suddenly, JD made a break for it.

Within a matter of seconds, both he and JD were on the ground, as the Panthers laid into them. One of the bastards kicked him in the face. Almost immediately, he tasted blood – *his* blood, filling his mouth as he rolled himself into a ball, tried desperately to protect himself from the vicious blows striking him. Brutal hands and feet punched and kicked his head, his back, his arms, his legs – every part of his body. Then a particularly savage blow whacked the side of his head, and his world turned black.

He regained consciousness two days later in a hospital bed – lucky to be alive, he realised, when a doctor told him he had been stabbed within an inch of his heart. JD, he learned, hadn't been so fortunate: the Panthers had beaten him to death.

It was a life changing experience.

He wanted to make something of his life, he wanted to see the world – maybe even have kids one day, kids he wanted to be around to enjoy and treasure. JD's daughter would grow up not knowing her father. He didn't want something like that to happen to him, and he didn't want to be buried six feet under before he hit twenty-one. No way. But until, propped up in his hospital bed, he saw a TV advertisement for the British army he had no idea how he might escape the low life he was living.

He signed up for nine years, and that's how long he served, rising to the rank of corporal. By the time he got out, just over two years ago now, he had seen front-line action in Iraq and Afghanistan, and he'd served in Germany, Cyprus, Somalia and the Falkland Islands as well.

Even before he quit the army, he had decided what he wanted to do when he was back on civvy street, but his mental image of what being a private investigator entailed proved to be wide of the mark. He'd anticipated days and weeks and months filled with exciting challenges but, more often than not, he was hired for surveillance and matrimonial issues by wives and husbands who suspected their husband or wife was cheating on them, and wanted him to confirm their suspicions. That's why, when Wilko contacted him a couple weeks ago, to ask if he was interested in joining an expedition to South America, he didn't think twice about accepting.

As he sat on the edge of his bed, pulled on a pair of black trousers, Alex wondered why James wanted the professor and his wife's address. That, last night, is what James had asked him if he could find. He could and he did, in less than half an hour, but the question 'Why do you want it?' was answered with, 'It's better you don't know.'

He hoped James wasn't planning anything stupid.

Chapter 10

The scream in Samantha's throat was smothered by a large hand, pressed over her mouth. Reflexively, she struggled to free herself, but whoever was behind her, holding her, was too strong

'Please don't be alarmed, Sami – I just want to talk to you for a few minutes.

Hassan!

He'd spoken in a whisper, but she recognised his voice instantly.

He was behind her, holding her firmly, but she couldn't see him, couldn't imagine what he was doing here – in her kitchen.

'Samantha …'

Her husband called her name.

As footsteps approached, Hassan swiftly released her. Dressed all in black, he raised his forefinger to his lips, as he stepped behind the door that led, via a short hallway, to the dining room.

'Are you okay?' Richard stopped in the doorway, and her heart thump-thump-thumped inside her ribcage. If her husband took one more stride into the kitchen, he was certain to spot Hassan.

'I thought I heard – '

'I'm fine,' she interrupted. Rubbing her right elbow, she forced a weak smile. 'I – I banged my elbow on the kitchen worktop, but I'm okay.'

She had no idea what Hassan wanted, but the fact he had taken the trouble to find out where she lived, and had somehow gained entry to their home without her or Richard hearing a thing, suggested it was important. And clearly, he wanted to talk to her – not her husband.

What does he want?

'I – we haven't enough milk for morning,' she said, taking a couple of steps toward Richard, to discourage him from entering the kitchen. 'I'd better nip to the off-license, before it closes. Josh won't be happy if he can't have his Cheerios for breakfast.'

'I'll go,' he offered, as she was ninety-nine per cent certain he would. 'I'll pick up another bottle of Scotch while I'm there. Do we need anything else?'

'No, I don't think so – and thank you.'

She accompanied her husband to the front door, helped him on with his tweed jacket, but as soon as he was gone she hurried back to the kitchen.

55

'Thank you,' said Hassan, as she reappeared.

'What are you doing here?' she demanded, more aggressively than she intended. 'How did you get in?'

'Josh's bedroom window is open,' he answered. 'He's grown a lot since I last saw him.'

She paled. 'Did he – '

'Relax, Sami – he's asleep. He didn't see me.'

She did relax, but only slightly.

'What do you want, Hass– ' She stopped herself, remembering he wasn't calling himself that anymore.

'Please, call me James.'

'James ...'

Somehow, she couldn't stop thinking of him as Hassan. He certainly looked a lot more Asian than he did English. He looked – she couldn't deny it, he looked pretty damn good. Chest hugging black sweater, black trousers, black footwear. He looked like a gangly teenager with a cute little moustache and wavy, shoulder length hair when she met him. Now, he'd definitely grown into his adult body, and he appeared fit and healthy. He was clean shaven, and he suited his hair cut very short. And his eyes – his deep, chestnut eyes were exactly the same shade as Luke's.

'I know Vaughan's probably warned you not to talk to me,' he said, 'but if I'm going to get your son back unharmed, I need to know what happened.'

'My son ...'

He knows!

He reached inside his sweater, extracted a photograph, which he turned over so that she could see it.

She gasped.

Luke and Joshua – on *Playa de los Cristianos* beach, if she wasn't mistaken. Tears welled in her eyes as she focused on Luke's happy, mischievous face. Already, it seemed like forever since she'd last held him, kissed him, and told him how much she loved him.

'Vaughan gave it to me,' he said, softly.

'Did he ...' Glancing up at him, she couldn't say it.

He nodded slowly. 'He told me when he was born – that was enough.'

She couldn't look him in the eye. 'I'm – I would have told you, but –'

'My fault,' he cut in.

Damn right it was!

But, whatever his motive for walking out on her, that was history now.

Tears spilled from her eyes, wet her cheeks. 'James, I – I'm so scared ...'

He rested his hand on her shoulder and she leaned forward, put her face against his chest for a long moment. He put his arm around her waist, but withdrew it when she raised her head, pulled away.

'I'm sorry, I …' She wiped her eyes with the sleeve of her blouse.

'Don't be – none of this is your fault.'

'I know, but – I want him back. I want him back so much.'

He waited a moment, and asked, 'What's he called?'

'Luke.' She found a brief smile. 'Luke James.'

He smiled, too. 'Good choice.'

'I think so.'

'Have you told him about me?'

'Not much,' she admitted. Not anything, really. 'He's too young to understand, and …'

Her voice trailed off, and he let the subject drop. Instead, he asked her to tell him about Luke's abduction, everything she could remember, and he listened intently as she did so. He appeared surprised to learn her son had been snatched whilst they were on holiday in Tenerife and, although he didn't say anything, she sensed the location wasn't something he had expected to hear or was happy about.

'Have you had a proof of life call since your return to the UK?'

Is that what they call it?

A proof of life call.

She nodded. 'Vaughan let me speak to him after the briefing, but only for a few seconds. Luke sounded – I don't know, sleepy.'

'They've probably sedated him, which is no bad thing,' he observed. 'He'll be less distressed, and – I don't know how yet, Sami, but I'm going to try to find out where your son is being held.'

'Our son,' she corrected, without thinking.

He looked at her, and nodded faintly. 'Right, *our* son.'

Vaughan's warning came back to haunt her.

We wouldn't want him to lose one of his fingers, would we?

Vaughan, clearly, didn't want her or her husband to talk to anyone about Luke, including James. *Especially* James. But James already knew about Luke's kidnap, and – she felt the need to warn him anyway.

'James, please be careful – if anything happens to Luke …'

'I'll find him, Sami. I promise, one way or another, I'll find him and get him back for you, or I'll die trying.'

She desperately wanted to believe him.

'I – I'm sorry you had to find out about him like this,' she said. 'I swear, I would have told you if – '

The burst of a door opening cut her off.

'That'll be Richard,' she said, headed for the back door, which led out on to the patio. 'Quickly, this way.'

James touched her arm. 'We never had this conversation.'

Then he disappeared as suddenly as he'd appeared.

'Mission accomplished.'

James tossed Alex his car keys.

'That's great,' said Alex. 'Give me ten, and I'll be back.'

'Thank, Alex. I couldn't have done it without you.' He placed his hand on Alex's shoulder. 'I owe you one.'

Even as he said it, he realised his choice of words was lousy, and open to misinterpretation. Sure enough, Alex pounced.

'Yeah, right – I should be so lucky!'

It had taken Alex less than an hour to action his first request: Samantha's home address in Henley-on-Thames. An hour's drive away. But, with Vaughan's goons still shadowing him, he couldn't have visited Samantha without subterfuge. And, to accomplish that, he needed to call on Alex again.

Alex, after dropping him off outside his apartment, had driven off. As expected, the white Corsa on their tail parked up down the street. They didn't follow Alex, who drove around the back of the apartment block, where he met him. He drove to Henley-on-Thames, spoke to Samantha, and drove back again. Now, Alex would go collect his Astra, drive around to the front of the apartment block and park up again, as if he'd just returned from wherever.

James powered up his laptop, and he was staring at a map of the Canary Islands and the west coast of North Africa, when Alex re-entered his apartment.

'The Corsa's still there.'

He nodded, but he didn't turn away from the screen and he didn't say anything.

'Wrong continent,' observed Alex, standing by his shoulder.

'That depends what you're looking for.' On the drive back from Henley-on-Thames, he had made an important decision. Glancing up, he asked, 'If I abducted someone on Tenerife, where would I take him?'

Alex raised an eyebrow. 'You thinking of going into the kidnap business?'

'Not exactly.' He took the photograph of his son and Joshua out from inside his sweater. 'Sami, the professor's wife, is their mother – '

'No shit!' Alex grinned broadly. 'I knew I was missing something, but – you certain you're his daddy? '

'Positive,' he answered, 'but I've never met him. I didn't know anything about him until a few days ago.'

Alex's grin faded. 'What – the bitch didn't even tell you?'

'She couldn't – I wasn't around when she found out she was pregnant, and I made sure she had no way of knowing where I was.'

'Yeah, whatever.' Alex didn't sound convinced, but he let it pass.

'The family were on holiday in Tenerife last week. My son – he's called Luke – was snatched on Wednesday morning. He's not been seen since, but Vaughan let Sami speak to him briefly yesterday.'

Alex's expression hardened. 'Vaughan's behind this?'

He nodded. 'That's the real reason I'm on board, and I'm guessing that's why the professor is being so co-operative.'

Alex swore foully. 'I knew Vaughan was a fuckin' tosser, but this – kidnapping little kids. That's just sick.'

He didn't disagree. 'I reckon they probably took him off Tenerife by boat, but where are they holding him?'

The other Canary Islands didn't strike him as a likely safe haven. Madeira and the Azores, due north, appeared equally unlikely. Mainland Spain and Portugal were some distance away. The UK was even further north. That left the west coast of North Africa: Western Sahara to the south-east, Morocco to the north-east. Unless – and it was a real possibility – they were keeping his son aboard a boat somewhere, in which case finding him would be next to impossible.

I wish I knew …

'How about Morocco?' suggested Alex.

He nodded slowly, staring at the map in front of him. Morocco made a lot of sense – and in Morocco, thanks to his skin colour and dark hair, his son would easily pass as a local child … studying the Moroccan coastline, he picked out too many major towns and cities, from Tarfaya in the south to Tangier in the far north.

'That's where I'd have taken him,' said Alex, 'but – it's a big place.'

Too fucking big.

They were silent for a long moment.

'Who else is in on this?' asked Alex.

'Tommo and Manny are definitely involved,' he replied. 'I'm not sure about Wilko and Gately.'

'So what are you planning to do?'

'Find out where he's being held,' he said, with certainty. 'I don't know how yet, but when I do … I'll kill anyone who gets in my way.'

Samantha was wiping her eyes on kitchen roll when her husband came into the kitchen, carrying a carton of milk and a bottle of Scotch.

'Is everything all right?' he asked.

'I can't stop thinking about Luke.' She scrunched up the kitchen roll in her hand and Richard put the milk on the kitchen table.

'Perhaps you should have an early night,' he suggested. 'I can make you some hot chocolate, bring it up to you?'

'Thank you, but – I know I won't be able to sleep.' She hadn't slept more than two or three hours last night, and she wasn't expecting tonight to be any different.

Richard reminded her, yesterday, he had suggested she make an appointment to see her GP, to ask him to prescribe something to help her sleep. She hadn't taken his advice, and she had no intention of taking anything stronger than a headache pill tonight, either.

Her husband disappeared, and she opened the fridge – immediately spotted two cartons of milk, one nearly empty but the other unopened. She considered opening it and pouring the milk away, just in case her husband spotted it, but she hated waste. She lay the full carton down behind a pack of fruit yogurts, out of sight, before she put the new carton in its place.

I'll find him, Sami. I promise, one way or another, I'll find him …

Before yesterday, she hadn't seen James in over five years. Now, suddenly, he was back in her life, and … she was desperate to believe the promise he'd made, desperate to get her son back, but …

She found her husband where he had spent most of the afternoon and evening: sat at the dining room table, with his laptop open in front of him. She halted behind him, placed her hand on his shoulder.

'Richard, I've been thinking …'

Chapter 11

Vaughan smiled to himself, and stroked his moustache as he turned away from the window. He pocketed his BlackBerry, spoke to Tommo. 'Book another ticket, will you – the professor's wife will be travelling with us.' Tommo grinned. 'That should spice things up a bit.'

Vaughan wasn't convinced the decision to allow the professor's wife to join them was wise, but he couldn't deny he was enjoying playing with Harris's head, and having his ex on board was certain to crank up the pressure a few more notches. He was loathe to admit it, but he harboured niggling worries about Harris ... he recalled, quite vividly, how ruthlessly the half-caste Paki had despatched six of the nine insurgents who ambushed their four man patrol in Iraq. He'd nearly shit his pants, certain he was going to die a horrible and painful death, but Harris ... clearly, since being thrown out of the army, the Paki had lost none of his ability or his arrogance. Manny was no push-over but, without apparent effort, Harris had humiliated him. Hopefully, having the mother of his bastard son along for the ride would serve to distract him – remind him what was at stake, if he stepped out of line, or fucked up.

Shame he won't live long enough to watch his brat die.

He lit a cigarette. 'Has Manny reported in yet?'

'He has,' said Tommo. 'Berro spent the night at Harris's again.'

He exhaled slowly, through his nose. He wasn't expecting Harris to do anything stupid, at least not before they landed in South America, but he wanted to keep him under surveillance anyway. Just in case. A task Manny and Wilko, each partnered with a local, small-time crook he had no intention of taking to South America with them, had readily accepted. He felt sure, by now, Harris must have realised he had a tail but so far he'd made no effort to lose it.

'I was talking to Gately last night,' said Tommo. 'According to Wilko, Berro's queer.'

He inhaled deeply, blew a smoke ring. 'According to the intel I have, he swings both ways.'

'What's the difference – he still likes screwing guys, doesn't he. You don't think he and Harris are – you know ...' Tommo grinned, as he clenched his left fist, pumped it up and down suggestively.

A mental image of Harris and Berro together, naked, flashed through Vaughan's mind but he quickly dismissed it. 'Harris is straight,' he said, 'but Berro … ' He smiled faintly. '… let's just say his choice of buddy leaves a lot to be desired.'

It was a mistake as costly as a signed death warrant.

'Fuckin' monkey,' said Tommo. 'He should be at home in the jungle.'

He laughed, and drew on his cigarette again.

'Have you heard anything more from Stone?' asked Tommo.

He exhaled again, before grinding out his half-smoked cigarette and dropping it in a mug. 'This morning.'

Stone had flown to Ecuador over a week ago, tasked with finding a local guard and hiring a river boat, as well as buying all the equipment and supplies they were going to need, and couldn't take with them from the UK.

'He's hired a thirty-three foot boat, and the owner is going to act as our guide.'

'Does he speak English?'

'Enough.'

The professor – and Vaughan was inclined to agree – estimated it would take them at least two and a half to three days to reach their destination, travelling up river by boat. A helicopter would be a lot quicker, and a lot less hassle, but tourists as a rule don't hire helicopters and that is what they were posing as. Photo tourists. Added to which, a helicopter was certain to draw the attention of the Ecuadorian army, who had a base uncomfortably close to where they were headed. If the Latinos got a whiff of where their real interests lie, it could wreck the entire mission.

'What about firearms?' asked Tommo.

Regrettably, taking firearms out of the UK wasn't an option, either. 'Stone's seeing what he can pick up locally,' he said. 'He's not anticipating any problems.'

James picked a full length, black and grey Osprey wetsuit with long sleeves from the rack, handed it to Alex. 'Try this for size.'

'You're winding me up, right?'

'What's the matter, isn't it risqué enough for you?'

Alex grinned. 'If it's risqué you want …'

'I'm serious, Alex,' he said. 'You heard the professor – the entrance to the tunnel system is supposed to be concealed below river level. Someone is going to have to get wet looking for it, and I guarantee that someone isn't going to be Vaughan.'

'Yeah, I guess, but this …' Alex held up the wetsuit. 'Isn't this a bit OTT? We're talking about a fuckin' river, not deep sea diving.'

'We're talking about a river teeming with life – some of it dangerous.'

Alex looked at the neoprene wetsuit. 'This ain't gonna stop no piranha from taking a chunk outta my ass.'

'No, it isn't,' he conceded, with a smile. He considered a moment, before asking, 'Ever heard of the candiru?'

'The can–what?'

'The candiru,' he repeated. 'It's a small, thin fish, about two inches in length. It's also known as the toothpick fish and the vampire catfish.'

Alex's eyes narrowed. 'And this vampire fish – it what? Sucks your blood?'

'In a manner of speaking,' he answered. 'It's fairly common in South American rivers. Normally, it embeds itself in the gills of larger fish, but it would happily swim up your big black dick, spread its gill spines and lodge itself there.'

Alex winced. 'Ouch – that's gotta hurt!'

'It does. The fish blocks your bladder, leaving you in excruciating pain for twenty-four hours, before you die.'

'Can't you get it out?'

'No – the only way to get rid of it is to cut your dick off.'

Alex flinched, and lowered his free hand to his groin.

'The Amazon can be a very dangerous place.'

'Okay, I get the message.' Alex looked at the wetsuit again. 'I'll go see if this fits.'

The second size Alex tried fit; the same size fit James snugly as well.

'It's kinda tight between my legs,' Alex observed, raising his right leg, 'if you know what I mean.'

He smiled. 'So long as it keeps the candiru out.'

'Amen to that.' Alex broke into a grin. 'Anyway, how do you know I've gotta big black dick?'

'Are you telling me what they say about black guys doesn't apply to you?'

'No way, they're spot on but – ' Alex's grin broadened. 'The way I hear it, Asian guys are supposed to be small – smaller than white guys, even.'

'I've never had any complaints.'

Alex laughed. 'No, I bet you haven't.'

Having settled on a wetsuit each, James added black neoprene boots, gloves and hoods to their basket. Last year, he had emerged from a river in the Belize jungle with more than a dozen leeches attached to his chest, arms and legs. Not a pleasant experience, and one he wanted to avoid repeating, if at all possible … time was fast running out and, although he'd originally wanted to avoid it, he was now resigned to joining Alex and the rest of the team, in jetting off in search of a Metal Library he wasn't convinced existed. He was convinced, if he left it up to Vaughan, they would arrive in Ecuador ill-equipped to accomplish anything.

Before heading for the checkout, he picked up three high intensity head lights, plus three compact, waterproof Maglites – one set for him, one for Alex and spares. He tossed several packs of batteries in the basket as well. Nearby, he knew of a popular fishing tackle store that stocked shooting supplies and a wide range of blades as well, including several non-metallic and non-magnetic brands that would easily pass through airport security undetected. He'd love to pack firearms as well, especially as he doubted Vaughan would trust him or Alex with any kind of lethal weapon, but it was too risky.

'Vaughan should be picking this up,' Alex complained, as the cashier rang up their three figure bill.

'Feel free to ask him.'

As agreed, they split the costs fifty-fifty.

'You got anything planned for tomorrow night?' asked Alex, as they exited the store.

'Nothing special.' Tomorrow night would be their last in the UK, before they flew out to Ecuador – via Amsterdam – the following evening. 'Why?'

'You do now,' said Alex, with a grin. 'I'm taking you out for a slap-up meal.'

He shot Alex a quizzical look.

'Hey, come on – it's the least I owe you, after you've let me crash at your place this week.' Alex put his arm across his shoulders. 'We can go to a gay club after we eat, if you're up for it?!'

Alex tapped James on the shoulder.

'Over there.' Alex nodded towards his right, to where snakes of people were waiting to check-in at a KLM desk.

James spotted her immediately.

He tensed, but then he relaxed. 'She's probably seeing the professor off.'

But even as he said it, he knew he was mistaken: there were two bulging suitcases stacked on the luggage trolley the professor was pushing, and one of them was bright cerise, with little white flowers decorating it. He swore under his breath, as he quickly scanned the departure lounge for Vaughan, but the bastard was nowhere to be seen. Either he hadn't arrived yet, or he'd already checked-in.

'Uh-uh, I don't think so,' said Alex. 'I think she – '

'Watch my bags, will you?' he cut in, dropping his hand luggage on top of his holdall.

There were only ten or so people in front of Samantha and the professor in the check-in queue. She didn't see him until he was within touching distance of her. Her eyes widened and her mouth opened, but she closed it again, without saying anything.

'What are you doing here?' he asked, letting his anger show.

She raised her hand, brushed a strand of hair back from her cheek. 'James, I – '

'Excuse me, I – um, I really don't – '

'Shut up, professor.' He glared at the academic for a moment, before turning back to the professor's wife. 'Sami, this is not a good idea.'

'Says who?' Her stare was defiant. 'You? You've no idea why I'm here. You don't – '

'Sami, please – this isn't a package holiday,' he said, moderating his tone. 'The Amazon is a dangerous place. I don't think you realise – '

'I'm not stupid!'

'I didn't say you were.' Their heated exchange, he noticed, had already attracted quite an audience. He carried on, regardless. 'Does Vaughan know you're here?'

'Of course he does.'

The professor found his voice. 'Yes, he – as a matter of fact, he does – I asked him if my wife could accompany us, and he graciously agreed.'

He would, the bastard.

As if he didn't have enough to worry about.

He stared at Samantha and she stared back, almost daring him to continue opposing her, but he realised he would be wasting his breath. Her son's life was at stake and, in her position, he'd want to be in on the action, too. But he had a good idea what to expect. She might think she did as well, but how could she? It didn't matter. The decision had already been taken.

Last night, over dinner, he and Alex had vowed to watch each other's back, and keep an eye on the professor, who like them would become expendable once Vaughan found what he was searching far. Or, more likely, didn't find anything at all and gave up. Now, they were going to have to watch out for Samantha as well.

Before turning to re-join Alex, he said, 'I hope you don't live to regret this.'

Chapter 12

'Hell hath no fury like a woman scorned.'

James ignored Alex and Samantha ignored him as, just two rows ahead, she stashed her hand luggage in the overhead compartment. This was their second flight of the day. The first, KLM's flight from Heathrow to Amsterdam's Schiphol airport, touched down on time at 21:40, after two and a half hours in the air. On that flight, he hadn't been seated anywhere near Samantha and her husband, and she had avoided making eye contact with him when they boarded this, their second KLM flight, which was scheduled to take off at 23:25, destination Simon Bolivar airport in Guayaquil, Ecuador. It was a long haul flight he wasn't looking forward to.

He slammed the overhead compartment shut, before he sat down next to Alex, who had claimed the window seat. Trying to make himself comfortable, he silently wished he had learned of Samantha's desire to join them before Alex spotted her and her husband checking-in at Heathrow. But ... he wished he had more leg room, too. It wasn't that he disliked flying, so much as he found it ... boring. There was precious little to do, the food was lousy, he could never get comfortable and he found it difficult to sleep. Almost anywhere else, no problem; all he had to do was close his eyes. But on a plane ... he rested his head back, but he didn't close his eyes until they were in the air.

'Tired?'

He opened his eyes, half-turned his head. 'Flying always saps my energy.'

'Yeah, right.' A wry grin.

'It's nothing to do with last night.'

'If you say so.' Alex's grin widened. 'That was one helluva night, though, wasn't it?'

'I'm not complaining.'

As the plane rose into the night sky, he closed his eyes again, hoping to sleep at least a couple of the eight or so hours they were in the air.

Last night ...

Last night, Alex had insisted on taking him out for a meal, and asked to choose he'd plumped for Chinese. They went to Soho's Top Of The Town Restaurant, and they both ordered from the seafood menu: steamed fresh scallops to start, followed by baked lobster with ginger and spring onions, accompanied by a bottle of dry white wine. He didn't drink alcohol that often, but last night – against his better judgement, he'd let Alex twist his arm.

After eating their fill they hit a lively nightclub, where they soon attracted the attention of two good looking, busty blondes – Swedish students, they learned. Swedish students with a refreshingly modern attitude to casual sex. Barely two hours after hooking up, the four of them were piling into a black cab, headed for the apartment the two girls shared. One apartment, two bedrooms, but the lounge was larger. That's where, side by side on the floor, they spread two double duvets. It wasn't the first time he'd entertained two girls at the same time, but it was the first time he'd spent the night with two girls and a guy. Waking up with Alex's arm draped across his chest was slightly disconcerting, but he couldn't pretend he hadn't enjoyed his first foursome. And there was time for a leisurely encore, before he and Alex said their goodbyes.

Last night ...

As his mind drifted, blonde morphed into brunette, and he imagined he was pleasuring the spiky haired Samantha he'd met over five years ago and Samantha as she was now, both at the same time. She kept having babies, lots of babies that instantly turned into little boys, dark skinned, black haired little boys that kept disappearing, disappearing, disappearing ... another little boy appeared, an older boy, and he wasn't alone. A young girl was with him, and a young woman. A toddler, too. Then Vaughan appeared, and Tommo, and Stone, and things quickly turned nasty.

He woke suddenly, sweating copiously and breathing hard. His heart was pounding and Alex's hand was on his shoulder. Alex was staring at him, his dark features etched with concern.

'You okay, buddy?'

Sitting up straighter, he rubbed his eyes. 'Bad dream.'

'Must've been a shocker.'

He nodded. 'Iraq.'

'Yeah, I get that sometimes – only it's usually Helmand with me.'

James had done a couple of six month tours of duty in Afghanistan's Helmand Province, as well as serving in Iraq. Glancing at his wristwatch, he was disappointed to learn he had been asleep for less than an hour.

'I got you something to drink,' said Alex, as he passed over a miniature bottle of red wine and a packet of crisps, 'and some munchies.'

He would have preferred mineral water, to combat dehydration, but he thanked Alex anyway. He didn't fancy the crisps right now, but the red wine was gone in two swallows.

Alex broke the silence.

'How did you get into the SAS?'

He answered, 'I was referred.'

'By your CO?' Commanding Officer.

He nodded. 'Once you've served for three years you can apply, but if you do, you have to go through an interview stage first.' His referral, he suspected, owed much to his Asian appearance, his knowledge of Islam and his ability to speak Arabic fluently. Not much use where they were headed now, but all big pluses in a terrorist hot spot like the Middle East – especially if you wanted someone to go undercover and that, he suspected, is what they had in mind for him before his past caught up with him.

'So how does it work – I mean, I've heard talk, but I've never had the lowdown from someone who's been through it?'

'There's a selection process,' he said, silently debating how much to tell Alex. Since his dishonourable discharge, he had avoided talking about his former life, but they were stuck on a plane and he had another seven hours to kill. 'It's designed to be tough mentally, as well as physically,' he said. 'It's split into three phases, and failure at any stage of any phase means a candidate is RTU'd – returned to unit.'

The failure rate was high: only one in ten candidates made the grade. The first phase, the endurance or 'hills' stage, lasted three weeks and took place in the Brecon Beacons and Black Hills of South Wales. Each candidate had to carry an increasingly heavy Bergen – a large rucksack – over a series of long, timed hikes, navigating between checkpoints. In sharp contrast to the norm, the Directing Staff shouted no instructions, gave no abuse and no encouragement; each candidate was expected to be self-motivated. The phase culminated with 'the long drag': a forty mile hike carrying a 55lb Bergen that must be completed in twenty four hours.

Alex prompted, 'Go on then – how long did it take you?'

'Twenty one hours and eight minutes.'

'That's good?' Alex laughed. 'Of course, I could probably do it in under twenty.'

He raised an eyebrow. 'Is that with or without the Bergen?'

The second selection phase, jungle training, was the stage he enjoyed most. The training took place deep in the tropical jungle of Central America, in the former British colony, Belize. As well as learning the basics of surviving and patrolling in harsh conditions, candidates were expected to show discipline, and keep themselves and their kit in good nick whilst on long range patrols – none of which caused him any problems.

'I never got the chance to serve anywhere like that,' said Alex.

'Maybe not, but you do speak Spanish.' As, apparently, did Wilko and Professor Frewin-Hamilton. And that, where they were headed, was a lot more useful than Arabic or Punjabi or French, the only languages he spoke apart from English.

'*Sí, gracias a mi madre* – yes, thanks to my mother.'

Alex attracted the attention of a stewardess, asked for another red wine. He took the opportunity to grab a bottle of mineral water, which was deliciously cool and refreshing.

Only a small number of candidates made it through to the third and final selection phase, which was split into two halves: escape and evasion, followed by tactical questioning. After being briefed on appropriate techniques, he was dressed in vintage World War II gear, and set free in the countryside, with instructions to make his way to a series of waypoints without being captured by a hunter force of other soldiers. He was eventually captured, but not until towards the end of the third and final day – good enough to secure his progress to the final challenge.

During tactical questioning, a candidate was only permitted to give 'the big four': his name, his date of birth, his rank and his serial number. Failure to answer any other question with 'I'm sorry, I cannot answer that question' meant instant failure – and a return to his unit.

He expected to be treated roughly by his interrogators, but common sense told him they weren't going to hurt him, not seriously, and no one was going to slit his throat or put a bullet in his head – which might happen, in the course of a real interrogation.

He was wrong: his interrogators did hurt him, badly.

Before a single question was asked, one of his interrogators kneed him in the groin. Hard. As he doubled over, creased in pain, the interrogator's forearm smashed into his face. Knocked off balance, he hit the floor, writhing in agony and coughing blood. Almost immediately, strong arms yanked him upright again. The lead interrogator glared at him for a full minute – then demanded his name.

Through busted lips, he gave it, and his rank, and his serial number, and when his interrogator asked him how old he was, he gave his date of birth.

'I asked,' the interrogator barked, 'how old are you?'

He repeated his date of birth.

The interrogator made a fist, and planted it deep in his stomach. As he doubled forward again, spitting blood as he gasped for air, his interrogator kicked his legs from under him. Reflexively, he threw his hands down in front of him, to try to break his fall. He still hit the concrete floor heavily. An unseen boot slammed into his ribs. Moments later, dripping blood all over his chest, he was on his feet again, arms gripped tightly by an interrogator on either side of him. The lead interrogator, again, demanded to know how old he was.

'I'm sorry,' he mumbled, 'I cannot answer that question.'

His interrogators dragged him to a small, windowless room, made him stand with his hands on his head for what seemed like hours, while disorientating white noise was blasted at him. When they returned, they stripped him naked, and a female interrogator mocked the size of his manhood. They accused him of fucking pigs. They screamed crude insults about his mother. They made fun of God and Allah. They threatened to rape him with a dog. They denounced him as an Islamic terrorist. They called him a paedophile. He answered all their questions with: 'I'm sorry, I cannot answer that question.'

Two jovial, friendly interrogators appeared next – allowed him to get dressed in clean clothes, offered him a drink of water and a Mars bar, tried to get him chatting by asking trivial questions like 'Where are you from?' and 'Which football team do you support?' When he didn't fall for any of their tricks, his interrogators turned aggressive, and stripped him naked again. They roughed him up. They doused him with ice cold water. They made him stand in stressful positions. They blasted him with white noise. They mocked him. They threatened him. They screamed insults at him … and so it continued.

They didn't feed him.

They didn't take him to the bathroom.

They didn't let him sleep.

He soon lost track of the time, and began to lose all sense of reality, but somehow he kept his focus, kept answering every question he was asked with the only acceptable words: 'I'm sorry, I cannot answer that question.'

Finally, after what seemed like weeks but was actually only thirty-six hours, his ordeal ended – and he was told he had successfully completed the SAS selection course. He spent the next twenty-four hours in a hospital bed, while the medics checked him over, before giving him a clean bill of health.

'Jeez,' said Alex, grimacing. 'I know it's meant to be tough, but – some of the things the bastards did to you …'

'What do you think would have happened,' he asked, 'if I'd been taken prisoner in Iraq, or in Afghanistan?'

'Yeah, well, that's different – that's for real.'

'The missions the SAS undertake are for real.'

'I guess,' Alex conceded, 'but – what I don't get is, why did you put yourself through all that shite, and then quit?'

He hesitated, before admitting, 'I didn't quit.'

'You didn't?' Alex looked puzzled. 'But I thought – so what happened?'

'I was discharged. I – not long after I joined the army, I was in the wrong place at the wrong time, and last November the top brass got wind of what happened. I got hauled in and was accused of something I didn't do, and … here I am.'

Alex scowled. 'Couldn't you have appealed or something?'

'I could have,' he said, 'but if I lost, and the odds were against me, I would have been lucky to get away with twenty-five years in the slammer.'

Alex sucked in a breath and, before he could probe any deeper, James changed the subject. 'Promise not to say anything,' he said, 'and I'll let you in on a secret.'

Alex grinned. 'I'm all ears.'

'Promise?'

'Sure – I promise.'

'Vaughan applied to join the SAS.'

Alex's eyes lit up. 'You're kiddin' me!'

'It's true – he applied before I was referred, but we went through the selection process at the same time.' He paused. 'I made it through, but Vaughan failed tactical questioning.'

Chapter 13

The first thing to hit Samantha was the heat.

The plane was air conditioned, but the moment she stepped outside, started down the steps to the concourse below, she felt like she'd stepped into a hothouse. Her wristwatch, which she had re-set to local time, told her they had touched down at 2.25pm. It didn't tell her that this was the third plane she'd disembarked in a little over twenty-four hours. The Aerogal Aerolineas flight from Guayaquil to Cuenca was only half an hour, but before that there had been a tortuous eleven and a half hour wait at Simon Bolivar airport. She didn't understand why they couldn't have checked into a hotel, to catch a few hours' sleep and freshen up, but Vaughan was in charge and he had instructed everyone to remain the airport.

The plane they had flown in on was, by some margin, the smallest she had ever boarded. Even so, it was more than an hour before she and her husband claimed their baggage, and exited the airport. They were met outside by the German, Manny, who escorted them to the parking lot. She spotted Vaughan, leant against one of two filthy, ancient land rovers, talking to a man she didn't recognise. Vaughan introduced them.

'Stone, this is Professor Frewin-Hamilton and his lovely wife, Samantha.'

'It's a pleasure.' Stone, in his mid-to-late thirties, looked ex-military. No surprise there. About five ten, he had a stocky build with broad shoulders, a thick neck, and light brown hair shaved to stubble on his head. He had at least three days growth of beard as well. He was wearing a khaki outfit, covered with dust, which failed to disguise he was carrying a few extra pounds. He shook hands with her husband but, when he turned to her, a lewd grin twisted his lips. He acknowledged her with a slight nod. 'Mrs Frewin-Hamilton.'

She disliked him instantly.

'We're still waiting on Harris and Berro,' said Vaughan, as he tossed his cigarette butt on the parking lot, crushed it beneath his right boot.

'They – uh, they were right behind us,' said Richard.

'I will find them,' said Manny, as he headed back toward arrivals.

Vaughan turned to her husband. 'Professor, you're with me.'

'Yes, of course.' Richard looked at her. 'What, er – what about my wife?'

'She'll be right behind us,' answered Vaughan, indicating the second land rover with a dismissive wave. 'Wilko, Gately – let's get loaded up!'

Samantha watched Wilko and Gately hoist their bags atop the second land rover, lash them securely in place. Once James and his friend Berro joined them, they would number ten: five to each vehicle. No way did she want to ride up front, no matter who was driving. She was approaching the back of the second land rover when Manny reappeared, with James and Berro trailing a few paces behind him. They didn't appear to be in any hurry.

'Nice of you boys to join us,' said Vaughan, sarcastically, as James and Berro finally reached them. 'Stone, this is Berro.'

Stone and Berro shook hands briefly.

'Hello again, Harris,' said Stone, with a grin.

James glared. 'The pleasure is all yours.'

Stone's grin turned into a scowl. 'Get your fuckin' bags loaded.'

Samantha turned away, not sure what to make of the exchange she'd just witnessed, and climbed in the back of the land rover. Wilko had already made himself comfortable in the driver's seat and, as soon as the last of the baggage was stashed, Gately joined him. Even before Vaughan pointed them in her direction, she guessed who her travelling companions would be.

She looked away, through the window, as James claimed the opposite window seat. She felt, rather than saw, Berro occupy the space between them.

'Well, this is cosy,' he said, as his right leg pressed against her left leg. 'I'm Alexandro Berro, by the way. I know Vaughan likes to call me by my surname, but my friends call me Alex.'

Meaning?

She was slow to respond.

'Suit yourself.'

'I'm sorry,' she apologised, turning to meet his gaze, 'I didn't mean to be rude – it's been a long day, and I'm tired.'

'Hey, no worries – we're all beat.'

'I'm Sami.'

'Yeah, I heard.' He had an easy, genuine smile. 'Pleased to meet you, Sami.'

She found herself wondering what, if anything, Alex knew about her son. The fact he was on friendly terms with James suggested he wasn't one of the kidnappers – that he was on their side. Wilko fired the engine, and moments later they were on their way again.

She leaned her head against the window, and promptly fell asleep.

'What d'you reckon?'

There were two river boats moored along the river bank, bow to stern, with just a few yards separating them. The murky brown river, at this point, was maybe thirty yards wide. On seeing them, James had hoped the larger, more modern craft was theirs, but regrettably he soon learned it had been hired by another group of tourists. Americans, naturally. Their boat, which was moored further upriver, was about thirty-five feet compared with a good fifty plus for the Americans' vessel, and was open to the elements along both sides, whereas the larger boat had two enclosed, white-painted levels with an observation deck atop the higher level. The smaller craft was at least a decade older, and looked a bit like a long, half-finished mud hut dumped on a varnished, dark wood base. River worthy, no doubt, but it was definitely the budget option. Black lettering, flaking in places, proclaimed the boat was called *Amazon Dawn V*. With ten of them on board, plus the boat's owner-cum-guide, it was going to be an uncomfortably cramped jaunt. But that's not what concerned him.

'I reckon,' he said, staring at the larger boat, 'we have some serious competition.'

Alex raised an eyebrow. 'What – the Yanks?'

He nodded. 'I don't see him now, but one of them has been with us since Heathrow.'

Alex swore. 'Now you mention it, those guys don't look much like tourists, do they?'

He agreed: with one exception, the Americans he'd seen were all male, all aged between twenty-five and thirty-five, and they all looked reasonably fit. Most were visibly armed. Ex-military? He wouldn't be surprised. They were definitely not a typical bunch of tourists, by any stretch of the imagination.

The one exception, who he'd glimpsed a few minutes ago, was a short, balding man he guessed was about fifty. Dressed in khaki shorts, a pale green short-sleeved shirt, and carrying a white Panama hat, he'd spotted the man in conversation with a taller, younger and fitter looking blond guy, as they boarded the Americans' boat. He might be wrong, but he reckoned the older guy was probably in charge of the rival expedition. 'Let's take a walk …'

Ten minutes later, James casually strolled toward the larger vessel. Their smaller boat, he'd learned, had just one private cabin towards the stern, which Samantha and her husband had been allocated. The rest of them would sleep in a large common area, under mosquito nets, on roll-out mattresses or in hammocks. There was no electricity and no refrigeration, but for cooking there was a four burner propane gas stove, and he'd noticed a couple of crates filled with live chickens and ducks waiting to be loaded. Fishing gear, too, suggesting they would be catching some of their own meals. The rival American boat looked big enough to be comfortable, but small enough to access smaller tributaries as well. He didn't doubt it was better equipped and packed more horse power than their boat, too.

One of the Americans, a young guy with short brown hair, was standing beside the boarding platform. The American, who had a short-barrelled, pump action shotgun slung over his shoulder, eyed him with suspicion.

'Nice boat,' he said, coming closer. 'I don't suppose you'd consider a swop?'

The American smirked. 'Not a chance.'

'Thought not,' he said, with a laugh. Over the American's shoulder, he watched Alex wander down river, toward the stern of the rival boat. 'Where are you headed?'

'That's not up to me.'

'What, your tour doesn't have an itinerary?'

'Sure we do, but it's flexible.'

Alex reached out, ran his hand over the polished stern, as if admiring the Americans' river boat.

'It a beautiful vessel – big enough for what? Twenty, twenty-five of you?'

'Something like that,' the American replied, guardedly.

'We're going to be packed like sardines, I reckon,' he said, with a smile. Catching a discrete thumbs-up, as Alex strolled away from the rival boat, he wound-up the conversation. 'Have a good trip.'

He was on his way to rendezvous with Alex when Vaughan called him over to their boat, eyed him with suspicion.

'What are you up to, Harris?'

Vaughan, he noticed, had a black pistol stuffed down his belt. He couldn't be certain, from where he was standing, but it looked like a semi-automatic Heckler & Koch P7.

'Just being neighbourly,' he answered, wondering how many other members of the team were now armed. Vaughan must have caught him looking.

'Give me half an excuse, Harris,' he said, placing his hand over the butt of his pistol, 'and I won't hesitate to put a round or three in your gut. Then I'll leave you to bleed to death – if the jungle doesn't claim you first.'

You're all heart.

He didn't say anything.

'We don't have time for chit-chat,' said Vaughan. 'Go find Berro, and help Manny and Gately get our gear on board. I want to be ready to sail in an hour.'

He found Alex, who grinned broadly.

'Piece of cake.'

'Are you okay with this?'

Samantha stared at James, who had posed the question, but before she could respond her husband took her by the arm.

'Of course she is okay,' said Richard, brusquely, 'why wouldn't she be? This vessel is perfectly safe.'

Before she stepped aboard the boat, she glanced down river with envious eyes, at another river boat that was not only a lot bigger than theirs, but appeared a lot newer and safer as well.

The river, though not terribly wide by Amazon basin standards, did appear frighteningly deep and foreboding. She knew, her husband having pointed it out to her on a map, the river meandered south-east from here, where it met other small rivers before it eventually joined the mightiest river on the planet: the Amazon. Stepping aboard the *Amazon Dawn V*, with Richard still holding her arm to steady her, she wished Pedro, the boat's owner and their guide, hadn't revealed the word 'Amazon' originally derived from the native *amazona* – meaning 'destroyer of boats'.

She didn't want to know what happened to *Amazon Dawn* through *Amazon Dawn IV*.

Richard headed toward the narrow bow and, more cautiously, she followed. Her nose wrinkled at the unpleasant, fishy stench, and she had to be careful not to trip over the thick coils of a filthy, oily rope strewn across the deck like a huge black snake. She tried to avoid looking over to her right, where the river lapped gently against the boat, focused straight ahead – where, as her husband stepped to one side, the river suddenly opened up in front of her eyes.

Her heart beat faster.

'Just wait until we get underway,' said Richard, grinning as he turned to face her. 'Up river, the scenery will be quite magnificent.'

She hid her trepidation behind a little smile.

I've only myself to blame.

She had wanted to come, she'd fought tooth-and-nail to be allowed to come – better here, than stuck back in the UK, with no idea what was going on. And now she was here, she was determined to contribute any way and every way she could, to ensure their visit was a success, because if it wasn't … she sensed, despite the high stakes, her husband was looking forward to the expedition. Enjoying it, even. And why wouldn't he be. This, after all, was the fulfilment of his dream – an obsession he had shared with her father, before …

Are you okay with this?

Her husband might have dismissed James's concern out of hand, but he would; he didn't know she suffered from aqua-phobia. A fear of deep water. In the eighteen months they had known each other, no occasion had arisen where she'd felt compelled to divulge anything to Richard. Even in Tenerife, with two small children, she had been able to avoid the hotel's main swimming pools without arousing suspicion, keep to the kiddies pool – freshwater, heated, and pleasantly shallow. That she could handle, no problem, but … she was surprised James remembered her aversion to deep water.

The first day she had spent with Hassan, as he was back then, was a Sunday. After much discussion, they agreed to take Joshua to the zoo. It was Hassan's suggestion, and she recalled leaning forward and kissing him, saying, 'Josh simply adores animals – take him to the zoo, and he'll be your friend for life.'

Her son, not surprising given how hard he'd slapped his back when he was choking, was still a bit wary of Hassan but all that changed at Blackpool Zoo. Being small, Joshua soon complained he couldn't see the animals, and as the morning wore on he complained his legs hurt, meaning he was getting tired. 'I'm not carrying you,' she told him, and when Hassan offered, she warned him, 'He's heavier than he looks.'
Joshua's face lit up when Hassan swung him up on his shoulders, and she and Hassan put an arm around each other's waist, like the lovers they were, as they strolled around the zoo. By afternoon, her son had warmed to Hassan, who rounded off a wonderful day out by insisting he buy Joshua a huge, cuddly tiger – her son's favourite animal. The middle-aged woman behind them in the queue, not unnaturally given their appearance, mistook them for a family.

As winter set in, the weather was invariably cold or wet or both, so at weekends – whichever day Hassan wasn't working – they started going to an out-of-town leisure complex. Teaching Joshua to swim was Hassan's idea, one she readily supported, but she was much less keen to take the plunge herself.

'I wasn't much older than Josh when my step-father took me swimming for the first time,' she confessed, when Hassan tried to change her mind. 'He picked me up and threw me in, literally. He thought it was a good laugh, but I nearly drowned – at least, I thought I was drowning. I was hysterical, and I had nightmares about it for months after.'

She sat out her son's first swimming pool experience and, before she allowed him to take her son into the water, she made Hassan promise to stay with Joshua all the time, and not to take him out of the shallow end of the pool or allow him to take his bright orange armbands off. She needn't have worried. Hassan was a strong swimmer and he was brilliant with her son, and Joshua clearly loved every minute he spent in the water with Hassan.

Although she had, on subsequent visits, joined her son and her lover in the water, she never ventured out of the shallow end of the pool, and over five years on, although she now took both Joshua and Luke for a swimming lesson every week during school term time, she still hadn't conquered her phobia.

Her husband was right.

Shortly after they cast off, chugging up river at a leisurely pace, all signs of civilisation melted away and gave way to jungle on both sides of the river. Thick, dark green jungle – beautiful, but Samantha was under no illusions about how dangerous it could be, especially for a complete novice like her.

The river frightened her more.

Chapter 14

'What's going on?'

'Harris thinks we're being followed.'

Samantha didn't hide her surprise. 'Followed – who by?'

'I don't know,' Richard replied. 'Harris thinks it's the Americans – he claims he caught a glimpse of their boat, but I don't think Vaughan is convinced.'

She couldn't imagine why the Americans would follow them, but if James claimed to have glimpsed their river boat, she was inclined to believe him.

But why?

Having slept late, she had missed breakfast, and when her husband told her Pedro was rustling up fresh piranha for lunch, she thought he was joking. He wasn't. Several of the team – including James and Alex – had spent the morning fishing, and apparently most of the fish they'd caught were red-bellied piranha.

As if I'm not frightened enough of the river already.

She had never been in a tropical jungle before, and she'd been too worried about Luke to do much preparation, but during the twenty-four hours before they departed she had forced herself to scan some of her husband's immense collection of articles and books about the Amazon region. But nothing she read had prepared her for the reality. Within twenty minutes of dressing in cream shorts and a beige blouse, even though she was only sitting around watching the jungle pass by, she was perspiring so copiously dark, ugly patches began forming under her armpits. Her husband had advised her against packing anti-perspirant. Insect repellent, too. 'It's a waste of time,' he'd told her. 'Whatever you put on, your body will sweat off again in a matter of minutes.'

She had packed roll-on insect repellent, but Richard's advice proved correct: the repellent didn't stop flying insects and bugs from dive-bombing her with annoying regularity. She was bitten several times, but she heeded her husband's warnings, and resisted the urge to scratch herself. 'Assassin bugs,' he told her, 'have a nasty habit of biting and defecating at the same time, and scratching the wound only helps to release a potentially lethal protozoa into the bloodstream.'

Richard, when he'd been trying to deter her from wanting to join the expedition, had warned her about sand flies that carried a leprosy-like disease, and blackflies that transmitted worms that caused river blindness. Or was it the other way around? She couldn't remember. Then there was the risk of cholera, typhoid, malaria, yellow fever and a host of other awful diseases, not to mention venomous snakes, spiders and other dangerous animals that inhabited the jungle.

'The jungle is an extremely hazardous place,' her husband stated but, wisely, he'd stopped short of telling her 'it's no place for a woman.'

Samantha loved most kinds of fish – filleted, with the head and tail removed. The tail she wasn't too fussed about, but there was nothing more off-putting than having fish eyes staring up from her plate. That's how a grilled piranha, which was so large it jutted out over the edge of the aluminium dinner plate, arrived. Once Richard had removed the head, however, she found the fish to be surprisingly moist and tasty. She'd nearly eaten her fill when she noticed the commotion towards the stern of the boat.

'What's Vaughan going to do?' she asked.

Richard shrugged. 'I really don't know … he'll have to check it out, I suppose.'

'I'll go with him.'

'No,' said Vaughan, firmly.

'I'll be quicker alone,' said James, not surprised Vaughan wasn't happy at the prospect of Alex accompanying him. He was equally certain Vaughan wouldn't trust him to go recce by himself.

'Yes, I'm sure you will,' said Vaughan, with a mocking smile. He took one last drag on his cigarette, flicked the glowing butt into the river as he exhaled, before he turned and shouted, 'Gately!'

James was squatted near the bow of the boat, between Alex and Vaughan, with a map spread out on the deck between them. Inwardly, he cursed. He still wasn't sure, one way or another, whether Gately was involved with or even knew about his kidnapped son. He would have preferred Manny, or Tommo, or Stone … he didn't say anything as he watched Gately tear himself away from a card game, approach them with a quizzical look.

'Yes, boss?' In his mid-thirties, Gately was wearing light brown shorts, a darker short-sleeved shirt with the top three buttons open, and a white baseball cap with a pale blue NY logo, to protect his head from the blazing sun.

'You and Harris will be taking a dip shortly. Harris thinks we're being followed – I want to know if he's right.'

Gately glanced at him. 'Sure thing.'

'We're here.' Vaughan poked the river they were following on the map with his forefinger. 'We'll drop you here,' he said, sliding his finger to the start of a U bend, and on to the other side of the U, 'and pick you up here.'

The way Vaughan told it, he made it sound like his own idea – not what he, James, had suggested only moments ago. The idea was, at the drop point they would take cover – wait to see if the American boat was cruising up river in their wake. Then they would head through the jungle, to the other side of the U, where the *Amazon Dawn V* would pick them up again.

Having talked it through with Alex, he had decided to pretend he'd glimpsed the American boat, rather than reveal Alex had placed a GPS tracker on the stern of the rival craft. That the Americans were able to shadow them, without ever getting close enough to be spotted, posed its own questions.

Alex suggested, 'They might have put a tracker on our boat.'

'They might,' he agreed, thinking that was probably the most likely explanation, given most of the Americans had evidently arrived in Cuenco ahead of them.

Given no time to change into his wetsuit, even if he had wanted to, James slid over the side of the river boat and let go. He was wearing a dark green T-shirt, black shorts and black sneakers. Briefly, he disappeared under the water, enjoying the sudden cool rush as the river washed over him. The water hadn't appeared to be flowing especially swiftly, but the tug of the current on his body was stronger than he'd anticipated. He surfaced and kicked away from the boat, reaching the river bank in ten or so strokes. Gately wasn't far behind him.

Carefully, watching his footing, he emerged from the river. Following him, Gately slipped on the muddy bank, and swore aloud as he stumbled. He noticed one of Gately's trainers had gouged a deep furrow in the soft mud. It was unlikely any of the Americans would spot it as they cruised past, but he wasn't taking any chances, and hid the mark by bending a long, fern-like leaf over it.

The river bank was a tangled mess of overgrown vegetation – much like he had expected a tropical jungle would be, before he knew better. But he'd learned in Belize that, thanks to the dense canopy of branches overhead, as little as ten percent of the available light reached the forest floor. As a result, the lower levels were surprisingly devoid of vegetation, and the floor was covered with a thick, dark mulch of decaying leaves and branches, where many different species of mould and fungi thrived alongside graceful ferns, fragrant orchids and thick, rope-like vines called lianas.

'Vaughan's not going to like it,' said Gately, as they took cover, 'if you're wrong about this.'

'I'm not wrong.'

Gately shrugged, as if to say, 'Like I care.'

'How well do you know him?' he asked.

'Who, Vaughan?' Gately replied. 'Well enough.'

Gately didn't elaborate and he let the conversation die.

There was a small, green waterproof pouch attached to James's belt. He opened it, took out the military-style binoculars he'd picked up in London, and raised them to his eyes. Aware the rival boat was unlikely to appear before their boat was out of sight, which might take another twenty minutes, he turned the binoculars up river and focussed on the *Amazon Dawn V*. Samantha was standing beside her husband, looking in his general direction, but he doubted she could still see him. She looked … vulnerable.

I wish she wasn't here.

At the same time, he admired her determination to be where the action was. Her husband, he guessed, hadn't been given much of a choice but she had, and the choice she'd made took guts. He asked himself, as he waited for the *Amazon Dawn V* to disappear from view, what he would have done, had he learned Samantha was expecting his child before his father let it be known he was planning to take him to Pakistan for an arranged marriage.

It was a tough one.

He liked to think he would have done the right thing, but would he? He liked to think he would, but … probably not. His father would never have permitted it. His father would have insisted his wedding go ahead as planned and, if what had happened with his two older brothers was any guide, he wouldn't have been allowed to return to the UK until his bride was pregnant. His father might have agreed he could carry on seeing Samantha, on his eventual return, but she would never have been anything more than a second, common-law wife. Such an arrangement did occasionally work, but he doubted Samantha would have accepted it, and he wouldn't have been happy with it either … he couldn't deny, if he had found out about her pregnancy and if his father had given his consent, he would have asked Samantha to be his wife. She was his first love – his only love …

Twenty minutes passed.

Gately asked, 'So where are they, the fucking Yanks?'

The *Amazon Dawn V* was still visible, but only just. Another minute or so, and the boat would reach the bend of the 'U', and start to turn. He answered, 'Be patient.'

Gately muttered something unintelligible under his breath.

Sure enough, inside two minutes of the *Amazon Dawn V* disappearing from sight, another vessel appeared, down river. Even before he raised his binoculars, focussed them, he knew he was seeing the American boat – knew the Americans must be tracking them, just as he and Alex were tracking them.

'Looks like you were right,' said Gately, grudgingly.

As the rival boat chugged nearer, James searched for the old guy he believed was in charge, but he couldn't spot him.

'I count seventeen on the observation deck,' he said, lowering the binoculars and passing them to Gately.

'Yeah, I make it seventeen as well.' Gately passed the binoculars back. 'I don't get it, why are they following us?'

'Why do you think?'

Gately considered for a moment. 'The Metal Library ...' He shook his head. 'Vaughan's not gonna like it.'

Vaughan's not the only one.

They crouched low, out of sight, as the rival boat passed within twenty feet of them. As it cruised up river, after the *Amazon Dawn V*, James noticed there was a small motor launch trailing the American boat. *Interesting.*

He waited ten minutes, before he raised his head – spotted long hairy legs, poking out from a bromeliad a foot above Gately's head.

'Don't move,' he started, as Gately rose, 'there's a – '.

Too late.

'What?' asked Gately, as his head bumped the bromeliad.

The spider tumbled out and landed on Gately's head.

Seeing it, recognising it, he urged, 'Don't move.'

'What the fuck!'

Ignoring his advice, Gately raised his hand to his close-cropped hair, and as he did so the spider slid off his head, bounced off his right ear, and landed on his neck.

James moved swiftly – pressed his hand firmly over Gately's mouth, just in time to supress his scream.

Chapter 15

Samantha asked, 'Mind if I join you?'

Turning around, looking up, Alex appeared surprised to see her. 'Be my guest.'

He was sitting on the left side of the boat – the port side, she reminded herself. His white sleeveless vest and pale blue shorts accentuated his dark skin, and he had a large, elaborate dragon tattoo on his right shoulder. His legs were dangling over the edge of the boat. She wasn't that brave, especially as there was no barrier of any description, to stop her from falling into the river. She sat to his right, a safe distance from the boat's edge, and he swivelled around to face her.

'I never imagined it would be so beautiful,' she said, staring at the seemingly impenetrable jungle less than ten yards in front of her. Already today, she had spotted several monkeys foraging in the treetops, and birds abounded. A harpy eagle and three large red, blue and green parrots, especially, had imprinted themselves on her memory. So had a huge black caiman, a good fifteen feet long, that hadn't so much as twitched as their boat cruised past the sandbar it was basking on.

'Yeah, I guess it is,' he said.

She noticed he hadn't shaved today, not his face or his head. The resultant dark shadow suited him as, she had to admit, did a shaven head. Funny, baldness didn't suit most young white guys – somehow, it hardened their features, and made them appear older than their years. In contrast, most young black guys did look good with little or no hair, to her eyes anyway, but then she had always found dark-skinned guys more attractive than white guys. Alex, she judged, was still the right side of thirty by two or three years.

'Did you see the Americans' boat?' she asked.

'Uh-uh – but I know it's there.' He sounded certain.

'How can you be sure, if you didn't see it?'

'James saw it – that's good enough for me.'

And me.

She couldn't think of any reason James would lie about it. She asked, 'How long have you been friends?'

'Not long,' he answered. 'I met him maybe thirty minutes before you and your husband were shown into the first briefing.'

Her eyes widened. 'But I thought – you get along so well, I thought you must have known him for years.'

'No such luck,' he said, with a grin. 'You, on the other hand …'

She felt her cheeks burn. 'How did you – he's told you about us.'

She didn't mean it to sound like an accusation, but it did.

'Hey, he's mentioned he knew you before he joined the army, that's all.'

'I'm sorry, I didn't mean …' Her voice trailed off.

'No sweat.'

A large bird she didn't recognise flew across the river, not far behind them, and from somewhere in the jungle she heard a series of loud, deep guttural sounds. Even before her husband had confirmed it, when she'd heard similar noises earlier, she guessed she was hearing howler monkeys.

He asked, 'How long have you and the professor been married?'

'A year – thirteen months tomorrow, to be precise.'

'Unlucky for some.' He grinned again. 'Any kids?'

'Two boys,' she replied, trying not to let any emotion show, 'but they're not Richard's.'

He didn't look surprised, and she couldn't shake the feeling she wasn't telling Alex anything he didn't already know.

How much has James told him?

James, surely, wouldn't have told someone he had just met about Luke's abduction, would he? She started to say something, to change the subject, but stopped when she noticed Alex suddenly tense. He was looking up river. She followed his gaze, but she couldn't see anything unusual.

'James is back,' he said, rising to his feet. 'Go tell Vaughan to stop the boat – it looks like something bad has happened.'

Standing now, she spotted James on the river bank, almost camouflaged by rampant vegetation. It was a moment or two before she realised he was carrying Gately over his shoulder.

Quickly, heart pumping fast, she hurried to find Vaughan – told him what she had seen. Then she ran back to where she'd left Alex, just in time to see him dive into the river. He surfaced almost immediately, and began swimming toward James with fast, strong strokes.

James, with Gately over his shoulder, waded into the river. The water quickly reached his chest. He halted, eased Gately off his shoulder and supported the motionless body in the water, before he put one hand under Gately chin. Then he began swimming on his side, keeping his fingers under Gately's chin as he pulled him through the water, until Alex reached them. Together, they supported Gately in the water, brought him to the side of the boat.

Looking down, Samantha spotted an ugly swelling on Gately's neck.

'One, two, three ...'

James and Alex hoisted Gately out of the water, high enough for Wilko and Manny to grasp him under his arms. As they pulled Gately out of the river, up on to the deck of the *Amazon Dawn V*, James turned to Alex and thanked him.

'No problem.' They trod water for a moment, catching their breath. 'What happened?'

'He's been bitten.'

'Snake?'

He shook his head. 'Spider.'

Alex swore, but he didn't go into any detail, as they clambered aboard the boat. Gately was laid flat on his back, unconscious, with Wilko knelt beside him. The rest of the team had gathered around. Even before he found his feet, Vaughan confronted him.

'This had better be good, Harris.'

'He's been bitten,' he repeated, dripping water as he rose to his full height. 'I tried to warn him, but – he's been bitten on the neck by a spider. I'm not certain, but it looked like a wandering spider.'

'Did you see it?'

He and Vaughan turned to the professor.

'I saw it,' he confirmed. 'It was large, light brown in colour and hairy. It had a one and a half inch body, with red eyes, and a leg span of at least five inches.'

'The genus *Phoneutria*,' said the professor, nodding. 'It's Greek for murderess. There are eight known species, and – '

'How venomous is it?' Vaughan cut in.

'Extremely – it, um, it's highly aggressive and it's one of the most venomous arachnids in the world. Its venom contains a potent neurotoxin that causes a loss of muscle control and breathing problems, which results in paralysis and – '

Samantha interrupted her husband. 'Is there any anti-venom?'

Vaughan hesitated, clearly unsure.

'There is,' the professor said, nodding, 'but I rather suspect no one thought it necessary to pack any ...?'

Vaughan confirmed no one had.

There was no medic on board, either – an omission James had brought to Vaughan's attention at their first briefing but which, like much of his input, was ignored.

'Then we need to get help,' said Samantha, 'or take him back down river to – '

'No,' Vaughan said, firmly.

'But – his neck's already badly inflamed,' she persisted. 'If it keeps swelling, it's going to affect his breathing. We can't just do nothing.'

'Asphyxiation is the primary danger,' the professor agreed, 'but without any anti-venom …'

'Hey, professor,' said Tommo, 'what's with the hard-on?'

Stone and Manny laughed.

Glancing down at the prone body, James noticed the firm outline of Gately's erection, pressing up against the wet cotton fabric of his shorts.

'Ah, yes – that, er, the venom can cause priapism in humans,' said the professor. 'The resultant erections are extremely painful and can last for hours, and can lead to impotence.'

Assuming he survives.

James thought it, but it was Vaughan who asked the obvious question. 'What are his chances?'

'Without treatment …' The professor shook his head slowly. 'I honestly don't know.'

Vaughan glared at James, leaving him in no doubt who he blamed for what had happened. But, sorry as he was for Gately's condition, he didn't feel responsible.

If he'd stayed still …

'We have another problem,' he said, quietly. 'The Americans are – '

Vaughan snapped, 'Fuck the Americans!'

'They're definitely tracking us,' he said. 'With your permission, I'd like to search the boat, see if I can find a GPS tracker?'

There was a long silence before Vaughan answered.

'Do it – get Berro and Manny to help you.'

Fifteen minutes later, with no warning, the heavens opened.

James, flanked by Alex and Manny, was inspecting the starboard side of the boat. Manny swore, and dashed undercover, but he and Alex would have stayed put if Vaughan hadn't called them over, instructed them to help Pedro to unroll the heavy duty plastic sheeting from along the sides and front of the roofing.

'Do this, do that,' muttered Alex. 'I swear, if he gives us the graveyard shift again tonight … '

He smiled, as he unfurled one of the sheets, all the way to the deck. It was an effective, if not terribly high-tech, way of keeping the rain out. Last night, a decision he approved, Vaughan had decided to post an all-night watch. Alex had been allotted 22:00 to 2:00, then he had taken over for the next four hours. They had all slept on the boat, which had been moored along the river bank, with mosquito netting dangling where the plastic sheeting was now. But, even though both he and Alex had asked, Vaughan refused to issue either of them with a firearm.

The rain became increasingly torrential, but he welcomed it like a shower after a hard, martial arts work-out. It was a big improvement on the boat's outhouse, with its bucket shower, and soon washed all the dirt and grime from the river and jungle off his body and out of his clothing. More importantly, it gave him and Alex the opportunity to talk, without being overheard. As they moved along the starboard side of the boat, searching towards the bow, he brought Alex up to speed with what he and Gately had seen.

'They out-number us by two-to-one, maybe more – and they're all armed.'

'Yeah, that figures,' said Alex. 'We're fucked, if they mount an attack.'

'They won't – not before we find something.'

'*If* we find something.'

He had to agree, right now, that was a big 'if'.

Alex asked, 'You decided what you're going to do yet?'

'I'm still working on it.' He was confident he could make Stone, Manny or Tommo talk, given ten minutes alone with either of them. That was the easy part. But somehow he needed to conjure the time it would take him to get back to Europe or North Africa, find and rescue his son, without Vaughan realising he was gone – because, as soon as he was missed, the bastard was certain order the boy's execution. Unless …

An idea began forming in his mind.

The rain pelted him and Alex, as they reached the bow without finding anything suspicious. But then, stuck on the underside of the outside of the bow, where it curved to the port side, he found it. His fingers closed over it, plucked it off.

'Bingo!' Alex grinned, as he showed him the small black device.

Chapter 16

William Clayton stood at the prow of the *Rey de la Selva*.

Silent and unmoving, he stared straight ahead, thinking. Short in stature, but solidly built, he was wearing a white safari shirt and beige shorts, and a straw Panama hat with a black band around the rim sat atop his short, steel-grey hair. The river boat was moored, as it had been for two hours and counting. Not far ahead, the course of the river veered away to the right, as he viewed at it. Around the corner, just two hundred yards up river, was the boat carrying the English professor and his mercenary band of treasure hunters … or was it?

The skies had cleared as quickly as the tropical rainstorm struck, more than twenty minutes ago. Clayton couldn't think of any good reason why the English boat would have stopped during the downpour, or why it was still stationary, but their GPS tracking device was telling him it was.

Abruptly, he turned on his heels, strode through the dining room and kitchen, past two cabins, the shower room and flush toilets. On his way, he took out his Motorola VHF two-way radio, summoned his right hand man to meet him at the boat's stern.

'Mr Clayton.' Hank Sanderson stood head and shoulders over his boss. Slim, with short blond hair, he was wearing a sleeveless red vest and black shorts.

'Hank, I want you to take the motor launch up river,' he said. 'I want to know if the English boat is where our tracker is telling us it is.'

Sanderson cocked an eyebrow. 'You think the limeys are on to us?'

'Too much is at stake to try to second guess them – I want to know.'

Sanderson inclined his head. 'Of course.'

'And Hank,' he added, as Sanderson started to turn away, 'Contact me as soon as you know anything – and don't worry if you can't avoid being seen. Finding out what the opposition is up to, and exactly where their boat is, is more important than maintaining the element of surprise.'

He watched Sanderson fire life into the outboard engine, turn the motor launch around, leaving a curved arc of rippling white water in his wake as he headed up river at speed … according to his faith Joseph Smith, Jr., who founded the Church of Jesus Chris of Latter-day Saints in 1830, discovered the gold plates which, when translated, gave rise to the Book of Mormon. Since that revelation, rumours claiming other caches of gold plates awaited discovery somewhere in the Americas persisted, but to date only fakes and forgeries had surfaced.

Clayton was a believer, and his research led him to believe the gold plates – possibly in the form of gold books – were here, in Ecuador, stashed in the long lost Metal Library. Having come this far, after waiting so long, he wasn't prepared to let this opportunity elude him. Failure wasn't an option. Not when he was so close to achieving his goal. And when he did, the Church that had thrown him out would beg him to return and return he would, but only if one condition was met. He wanted a seat on the Church's presiding body, the Quorum of the Twelve, and long term he had his sights set on the Presidency itself.

He wasn't, by nature, a violent man and he would happily spare the lives of the English professor and band of his mercenaries, if they surrendered and co-operated with him. But if they didn't ... he knew, thanks to the advance party he had sent to Ecuador, there were just eleven bodies aboard the English boat, and that included one local and one woman. Quite what the professor had been thinking, when he agreed to his wife joining his expedition, he didn't begin to understand. Nor was it his problem. He had assembled a team of twenty-three, all male and all ex-military or ex-law enforcement, and even without the element of surprise he was confident they would quickly neutralise any threat the opposition posed.

'Mr Clayton, the limeys have dumped the tracker and taken off.'

He clutched the two-way radio tightly, anger flaring.

'Do you want me to head up river, see if I can catch up with them?'

'Do it, but keep your distance – we'll be on our way shortly.'

'How's Gately?'

It was just after 7.30am and Samantha, having been awake for only a few minutes, was still in her sleeping bag. Even before he replied, her husband's expression told her the news wasn't good.

'He, er – he died during the night.' Richard fingered his goatee. 'Vaughan has asked Harris and Berro to take his body ashore. He's given them twenty minutes to bury him.'

Propped up on her elbows, she felt the blood drain from her cheeks.

He died during the night.

This time yesterday, Gately was alive and well ... she couldn't pretend she'd liked the man, and she had no idea if he'd been involved with or knew about her son's abduction, but – it was a horrible way to die, and served to reinforce how dangerous the jungle could be. How unpredictable. Who would have thought a spider could kill a man? A venomous snake, yes, but a spider ...

I shouldn't be here.

Once again, she found herself questioning what she was doing in Ecuador, as she slipped on the same pair of cream shorts she had worn yesterday. The honest answer was not very much. The river terrified her and, so far, she had made no meaningful contribution to the expedition. None at all. And given Vaughan treated her as if she didn't exist most of the time, she couldn't imagine that would change any time soon. Her husband, on the other hand, was spending more and more time with Vaughan. Sometimes, he appeared so wrapped up in locating the fabled Metal Library, it was as if he'd forgotten all about the real reason they were both here.

The only reason I'm here.

She slipped out of her sleeping bag, threw on a pale green T-shirt, and padded barefoot to the outhouse that served as a bathroom – except there was no bath, no flush toilet, and no proper shower. She emerged from the outhouse just in time to see James and Alex lift Gately's body out of the river, on to the bank. The corpse was wrapped in a filthy, white cotton sheet. Although she wasn't particularly religious, and she had no idea if Gately had been or if he had any family, she still felt uncomfortable, knowing his body was going to be dumped in a shallow grave with no service whatsoever.

She noticed Vaughan, with most of the other men including her husband, had gathered towards the stern of the boat. Vaughan, naturally, was doing most of the talking. She didn't know what was being discussed, but she could guess.

The Americans.

Yesterday, not long after James and Alex found the tracking device and Vaughan tossed it on the river bank, a motor launch had been spotted down river. She hadn't seen it herself, but apparently there was only one man in it, and as soon as he spotted them he turned around and headed back the way he'd come.

During the afternoon, Vaughan had posted a watch and she had glimpsed the motor launch three times, as it re-appeared every so often to check on their progress. Any doubt the Americans were following them quickly evaporated, and Vaughan responded by calling a meeting, but she was one of only two people on the boat – Pedro was the other – who wasn't invited.

Last night, clearly spooked, Vaughan had doubled the guard. James and Alex, with Wilko and Tommo, respectively, had been given the same late night/early morning slots they had worked the night before. It was noticeable Vaughan was giving them all the jobs no one else wanted, and she'd overheard Alex muttering obscenities under his breath, but James appeared happy enough to do what was asked of him. That's how it worked in the army, she supposed: whether you liked it or not, you did as you were told.

Especially when your son's life is at stake.

'You wanted us?'

Vaughan was discussing options with Stone when Harris and Berro approached, shortly after he'd sent Wilko to rouse them. It was early afternoon, and they had been getting some shut eye, after he'd placed them on night duty two nights running. Harris was wearing shorts and a white T-shirt, Berro shorts only. They didn't know it yet, but they wouldn't be getting much sleep tonight, either.

'We're on schedule to arrive at the search site early tomorrow morning,' he informed them. 'We need to deal with the Americans before then.'

'So what are you proposing?' asked Harris.

Berro chipped in, 'We have enough C4 on board to blow them out of the water.'

'That's not an option,' he said, firmly. 'There's an army base a couple miles away – I don't want to risk alerting them to our presence.'

'We make our move after dark,' said Stone. 'Our mission is to sink the launch or set it adrift, and disable their boat.'

'Piece of cake,' said Berro, sarcastically.

'I'm glad you think so,' said Vaughan, with a nasty grin. 'You have two hours to come up with a plan I'm happy with.'

Chapter 17

'Get down!'

James, Alex and Stone hit the soft, wet ground.

The roar grew steadily louder as the motor launch powered up river. Crouched low, James peered through the dense foliage on the river bank as the launch rushed toward them. He and Alex had donned the wetsuits they picked up in London, but Stone was wearing a black T-shirt and black shorts. All three of them had daubed camouflage paint on exposed skin, including their faces. He and Alex were naturally dark-skinned, but the moon tonight would be fuller than was ideal, and he didn't want to jeopardise the mission with avoidable reflections. There was only one American on board the motor launch, the same athletic looking guy with short blond hair who had already checked on their progress several times today.

They stayed down as the launch motored by. James, although Vaughan had put Stone in charge of the mission, was the only one of the trio with jungle experience and, as soon as the launch had passed their position, he took the initiative. Keeping low, he crawled away from the river, scanning ahead for any sign of danger. They had already lost one man, and he didn't want anyone else getting hurt tonight. Not even Stone. Alex and Stone followed him, as he took up position beside a huge tree, from where they still had a reasonably good view of the river.

'Now we wait,' he said, quietly.

Initially, Vaughan had wanted them to wait until darkness fell before they made their move, but to him it made more sense to get into position before dusk, and let the Americans come to them. For once, Vaughan saw the logic in what he proposed, and he had given the go ahead.

Thanks to the GPS tracker, he and Alex knew their rivals were nearly a quarter mile down river of the *Amazon Dawn V*. After studying the course of the river, he'd suggested to Vaughan that their boat be moored at the end of a relatively straight section. He assumed the Americans would want to maintain their distance, and moor their boat out of sight, somewhere on the previous bend – which is where they were waiting.

Night falls quickly close to the equator.

Soon after the motor launch reappeared, travelling back down river, the light began to fade. The incessant chatter of birds gradually lessened, as darkness began to throw a shroud over the jungle, but the cacophony of noise didn't cease. Frogs croaked incessantly, and night flying bugs emerged from their hiding places. James didn't move when a small moth alighted on his cheek, where it stayed for several seconds before fluttering away.

As the American boat cruised into view, Stone whispered, 'Here they come …'

James counted fifteen Americans on the observation deck, as the boat glided ever closer, and the brash laughter grew louder, more boisterous. He focussed on the stern, as the boat sailed past them, dragging the empty motor launch after it. Silently, he willed the boat to stop and finally it did, but not until it was a good fifty yards up river. Further than he had judged, but the distance wasn't a problem.

They settled down to wait.

Stone extracted night vision binoculars from his backpack, but he didn't switch them on. Not yet. For now the moon, shining brilliantly in the clear, rapidly darkening sky, gave them more than enough illumination to observe the Americans.

The unmistakable, guttural *cough-cough-cough* of the Amazon's top predator broke their vigil.

'What the fuck was that?!' Alex wanted to know.

'Jaguar.' It was a sound he'd heard only once before.

'Shit!' Alex cursed and Stone gripped the old, but still highly effective, AK-47 assault rifle slung over his shoulder.

'Relax,' he said, 'even if it picks up our scent, it's unlikely to come anywhere near us.'

'Yeah, well – this place gives me the fuckin' creeps.'

'Shut the fuck up,' hissed Stone. 'Do you want the Yanks to hear us?'

James hadn't spoken above normal conversation level; neither had Alex. There was no chance the Americans could have heard them, but he exchanged a knowing glance with Alex, and they fell silent anyway.

Hours ticked by and, as they did so, the noise and activity on the American boat gradually started to wind down, as men began to retire to their sleeping quarters for the night. Stone switched on his night vision binoculars, raised them to his eyes, and focussed on the rival boat.

'See anything?' he asked, keeping his voice to a whisper.

'Take a look.'

The binoculars he accepted from Stone picked out the Americans and their boat in ghostly shades of green. He counted five – no, six Americans still on the observation deck. He liked to think they would be cocky enough to think they could get away without posting a guard, but he wasn't counting on it. Lowering the binoculars, he turned to Stone.

'We should get into position.'

'I wonder what happened to Harris's shoulder?'

'Pardon?' Richard, pouring over one of his notebooks by the light of a lantern, clearly hadn't been paying attention.

'I was just wondering,' said Samantha, as her husband looked up, 'what happened to Harris's shoulder. You did notice he's badly scarred, didn't you?'

Richard pushed his glasses up his nose. 'I, um – yes, I noticed.'

They were sitting, side by side, on the deck of the *Amazon Dawn V*, towards the bow of the boat. Earlier, as the only woman on board, she had felt embarrassed when James and Alex began to strip off. She averted her eyes, but she couldn't resist a surreptitious glance, as they dropped their shorts. They were, after all, two attractive and fit young men. Then, as they donned their black and grey wetsuits James turned around, and she noticed the scarring on his left shoulder, which extended down his side and back as well. The injury wasn't there when she and James were lovers, so whatever caused it must have occurred in the past five years. A fire, or even an explosion, struck her as the most likely causes, especially as James had served in the army. The injury didn't appear to bother him now, but she could only imagine how terribly painful it must have been, when it happened.

'Harris is trouble,' said Richard, 'and his friend Berro ...'

She asked, 'What about him?'

Her husband shook his head, and lowered his gaze to his notebook. 'It doesn't matter.'

'Richard!' It always infuriated her when her husband started to tell her something, only to stop short, and say 'it doesn't matter'. If it really didn't matter, she wished he would just keep his mouth shut.

'It's just – um, I heard Stone and Wilko talking earlier, and – the language they used was a bit course, but it is clear from what they were saying that Berro is gay.'

'You're kidding!' The revelation stunned her.

'Apparently, he's been staying at Harris's place and Stone and Wilko were – um, they were speculating he and Harris are lovers.'

'No way!' That she didn't believe.

Richard pointed out, 'They do spend rather a lot of time together.'

'Yes, but – James isn't gay.'

No way, no how – he can't be, he just can't!

Her husband didn't notice she'd said James, not Harris.

'Isn't he?' Richard sighed, and pulled on his goatee. 'Frankly, Samantha, I have no idea if he is gay or not, and nor do I care. I'm just passing on what I heard.'

Her husband turned his attention back to his notes and, for several minutes, she sat motionless, numb to the core. She couldn't refute the fact James and Alex spent a lot of time together, but James was hardly likely to be on friendly terms with Vaughan and whoever else had snatched their son, was he? Neither James nor Alex looked gay, but then how many gay men did? It was impossible to judge anyone's sexuality, just by looking at them, but … she was willing to accept Alex might be gay, but James? He wouldn't be the first gay man to father a child, but – no. No way. He was, he'd admitted, a virgin before they met and become lovers. And yes, she had definitely made the first move, but James had been quick to respond to her advances – was keen to see her again, and the three and a half months they spent together were among the happiest of her life. So unless James had 'found himself' in the past five years …

It occurred to her James might be bisexual.

Richard was so engrossed with the notes he was studying, he didn't glance up or speak, when she stood up and slowly walked toward the boat's stern. The light was fading fast, but the course of the river was still clearly visible, as its dappled surface reflected the moonlight. Somewhere out there, with Alex and Stone, James was risking his life – for what? She knew, as early as tomorrow morning, the search for the Metal Library would begin in earnest. While she was willing to acknowledge such a discovery would be a momentous event, her focus was elsewhere: on her missing son.

She detested Vaughan, and she didn't trust him to keep his word – which left her with just one hope. She had never been particularly religious but now, as she gazed down river, she found herself praying for James's safe return, because if he didn't return …

James slipped into the water, closely followed by Alex, leaving Stone hidden beneath the foliage on the river bank, to provide covering fire if they were spotted and needed to make a quick getaway. He took a deep breath, before he submerged and struck out, kicking his legs as he swam underwater against the current toward the American boat.

He and Alex surfaced twice, just long enough to gulp a lungful of air, before they reached the stern of the boat. Treading water as Alex surfaced beside him, senses on full alert, he listened intently for any hint that their approach had been heard or seen. Nothing. They were in the clear.

The Americans, as expected, had posted a guard. Just one. When they entered the dark water down river from the boat, the guard was seated at the bow, smoking a cigarette. No doubt, anticipating any trouble was likely to come from that direction, the guard was focussing his attention up river.

Still cautious, he turned to Alex, who had already eased the waterproof holdall from his back. Alex extracted two small incendiary devices and, after accepting one of them, he let the current float him toward the motor launch. As he drifted backward along one side of the launch, he scanned the stern of the river boat for any sign of the guard, as Alex set to work.

So far, so good.

On reaching the back of the launch, he eased his way around to the outboard motor; it didn't take him more than a minute to attach the incendiary device. It was only a small charge, but Alex had assured Vaughan it was enough to damage the motor launch beyond repair and take the outboard motor to the bottom of the river.

A pity.

He had been thinking, once he discovered where his son was being held, he might be able to 'borrow' the launch to make good his escape. He hadn't, as yet, come up with a workable Plan B. He gave Alex the thumbs-up, and in unison they activated the two devices. The timers were pre-set for five minutes.

Before he could sink below the water, he heard footsteps. Instantly, he signalled Alex, who silently acknowledged he had heard someone on the boat approaching as well. He glided behind the motor launch, out of sight, but Alex's position was more exposed.

He risked a quick look-see: the guard was standing at the stern, gazing down river, as he smoked his cigarette.

If he looks down ...

Alex would have slipped under the water, but he could only hold his breath for so long ... there was also the small matter of two incendiary devices, slowly but inexorably ticking down toward detonation.

He counted down the seconds and minutes in his head.

Four minutes ...

Three minutes ...

Alex must have surfaced by now, for air, but he hadn't heard anything and neither, judging by his lack of action, had the guard.

He heard a flick, then a little plop and sizzle. The guard must have finished his cigarette, discarded it.

Then a shot rang out and the guard toppled head first into the river.

Chapter 18

Dripping water, James glared at Stone as he clambered out of the river, but he held his anger in check as he accepted two pairs of night vision goggles.

'Let's go,' he said, as he switched them both on. He watched the display's initial flare fade, before he turned to hand one of them to Alex – spotted the red dot flitting over the chest of his friend's wetsuit.

Reflexively, he hurled himself at Alex, knocked him off his feet and into the undergrowth.

'What the – '

A bullet zipped through the foliage where Alex had been stood a moment ago.

Quickly, no time to do anything with the goggles, he hauled Alex up again. Following Stone, who had already bolted, they scrabbled through the dense vegetation growing along the river bank, as a second bullet fizzed somewhere behind them.

Away from the river, the lush plant growth thinned rapidly, and as soon as he felt sure they were out of sight and out of range of the Americans, James called a halt. He handed one pair of goggles to Alex, donned the other, and suddenly the jungle around them became several times brighter, albeit in eerie shades of green.

'Thank, buddy,' said Alex, as he donned his goggles, 'that was damn close.'

'Too close,' he agreed. 'I – '

Two muted explosions, in quick succession, silenced him.

'That should keep the Yanks busy for a while,' said Stone, smugly.

'No thanks to you, you fuckin' tosser.' Alex rounded on Stone, pushed his chest. 'Why the fuck did you take out the guard?'

'He saw you. He – '

'He didn't see me.'

'He looked down and – '

'You got it wrong, you trigger happy bastard, you – '

'That's enough!' James stepped between them. 'We can apportion blame later. Right now, we need to get back to our own boat, and quickly.'

There was a good chance, if Stone hadn't panicked, they might have gotten clean away before the charges blew. But now … he led the way through the jungle, giving the river where the American boat was moored a wide berth, as he scanned the vista ahead.

He moved as briskly as he dared, and they made good time, making it back to the section of river where the *Amazon Dawn V* was waiting for them without further incident. He took out his flashlight, pointed it at the boat and flicked it on and off twice to announce their arrival, before taking off his goggles and handing them to Stone. He gave his eyes a minute to adjust to the darkness, before he waded into the river and started swimming.

He noticed, as he hauled himself on to the deck, no one – not even Samantha, her husband or Pedro – had turned in for the night.

Vaughan was waiting for him, face like a marble statue. 'We heard three shots.'

'Don't look at me,' he said, turning toward Stone, who Manny was helping out of the river. 'I – '

'It was Stone, the fuckin' tosser,' Alex cut in. 'He nearly got us killed.'

'He's dead, Mr Clayton.'

Clayton's expression hardened.

He stared up river, into the clear, moonlit night, for a few seconds longer before he turned to face Hank.

'And thine eye shall not pity; but life shall go for life, eye for eye, tooth for tooth, hand for hand, foot for foot.'

He paused, and looked at Hank.

'Deuteronomy 19:21 is often misquoted,' he said, in a low voice, 'but its message is clear.'

'Yes, Mr Clayton.'

'Vernon was a good man, Hank – a family man, with a wife and three young children.'

'His death will be avenged, Mr Clayton.'

He nodded agreement.

'I was prepared to be magnanimous in victory, but now ...' Inside, he seethed, furious the initiative had been snatched away from him and furious he hadn't anticipated how ruthless the English mercenaries might become, once they neared their objective. 'They must be close, Hank – very close.'

'I agree, Mr Clayton.'

He asked for a damage report.

'We've lost the motor launch,' said Hank, 'but we do have an inflatable zodiac on board, with a small outboard motor. It's not as fast or powerful as the launch, but I can use it to keep track of the English boat.'

'Excellent,' he said. 'How badly damaged is our boat?'

'Wayne and Kurtis are checking it out now. Wayne reckons the charge used was only small, but it was well positioned and the damage it's caused is substantial.'

He winced. 'How substantial?'

'The engine's completely shot, but we do carry a spare motor,' said Hank. 'Wayne reckons, if he and Kurtis work through the night, we should be good to go by first light.'

'What happened?' Vaughan demanded.

Stone swore foully, as his torch highlighted numerous black leeches dangling from his arms; there were at least five or six more attached to his legs.

James couldn't see any leeches on Alex, but there was one near his own right ankle, just below the rim of his wetsuit.

'He happened!' Alex pointed at Stone. 'Everything was going according to plan, before he took out the fuckin' guard.'

Stone blustered, 'He'd spotted you! He – '

'No fuckin' way!'

James kept silent as Alex told Vaughan, and everyone else who had gathered round, what happened.

Vaughan stared at Alex. 'Did you set the charges?'

'Yeah, we set them and they both went off, but thanks to Stone we didn't stick around long enough to see if they had the desired effect.'

'We should head up river,' he said. 'Even if we have disabled the American boat, they might send a team after us on foot.'

Vaughan fell silent for a moment, then nodded and called, 'Pedro!'

The boat owner-cum-guide stepped forward. '*Sí, señor* Vaughan.'

'Pedro, I want you to take us up river, as fast you can without endangering the boat.'

Pedro didn't look happy. 'But – '

'No buts, Pedro – if we're not underway in five minutes, I'll want to know why.'

'*Sí, señor* Vaughan.' Pedro hurried away.

Stone struck a match, puffed life into a cigarette. 'This will get rid of the little fuckers.'

'I wouldn't do that, if I were you,' he said.

Stone exhaled smoke. 'Why the fuck not?'

Before he replied, Professor Frewin-Hamilton said, 'I – er, Harris is right. If you remove a leech with heat, the shock will make it regurgitate

100

the contents of its stomach into your bloodstream – including any parasites or diseases it is carrying.'

Stone glared at the professor. 'So how the fuck do I get 'em off?'

'They'll drop-off, once they eaten their fill,' said James, 'or you can remove them like this.'

He raised his right leg, put his foot up on the side of the boat. Reaching down, using his forefinger, he slid his fingernail under the smaller, thinner end of the leech near his ankle. That broke the seal. He slid his fingernail around to the fatter end of the leech, to break the seal there as well, and flicked the leech into the river when its jaws detached. The small round wound immediately filled with blood.

He turned to Samantha. 'Can you get us a First Aid kit, please?'

She nodded. 'Of course.'

When she returned a few minutes later, he had already removed four leeches from Stone's arm. Initially, the four little wounds bled copiously, thanks to an anti-coagulant secreted by the leeches. He knew blood would continue to ooze for a few hours, until the effects of the anti-coagulant wore off.

He helped Stone to remove another nine leeches from his arms and legs, before he set about cleaning his own wound and putting a small adhesive dressing over it, to soak up the blood and keep it clean.

Leaving Stone to attend his own wounds, he went to join Alex, who was on his own, squatted at the boat's stern and staring down river. As he sat down beside him, Alex turned toward him, and spoke in a low voice.

'I have a bad feeling about tomorrow.'

He concurred. 'Tonight, thanks to Stone,' he said, 'we've as good as declared war on the Americans.'

They fell silent.

Alex said, 'There's always Plan D …'

He nodded, thinking along the same lines. Back at his Bayswater apartment, he and Alex had discussed as many possible scenarios they could think of, before dismissing most of them – including Plan D, where D might have stood for desperate. But that was before they arrived in South America, learned they had serious rivals. Vaughan and company he was reasonably confident he could take care of, especially with Alex on his side, but the Americans …

'It's risky,' he said, 'and if we go ahead, you need to make contact tonight.'

'That shouldn't be a problem,' Alex responded, with a half-smile. 'Last night, Tommo was sleeping like a baby before midnight.'

'I don't like it,' he said, 'but …'   He found himself nodding. 'Let's do it.'

Chapter 19

The visibility was lousy.

Underwater, as well as above it, the river bank was matted in thick vegetation. James, between Alex and Manny, poked and prodded the dense growth with a three foot pole he had cut from a sapling. He didn't see the snake he'd disturbed until it lunged at him – struck at the pole he was searching with.

Reflexively, he released the pole and swam backwards, and the five foot serpent disappeared as swiftly as it had appeared. He had no idea what species it was, didn't know if it was venomous or not, but he was relieved it had attacked his pole and not his arm. Using his waterproof Maglite, he signalled Alex and Manny, to let them know he wanted to take a break.

The search had begun shortly after dawn, and it had only taken him a few minutes in the river to realise they weren't going to see or find anything, without assistance. An underwater passage, if it did exist, was certain to be overgrown, and using their hands to search for it didn't strike him as a smart move – hence the sapling he'd cut on the river bank, and split into three equal lengths. It was, he reflected as he hauled himself out of the water, a decision that might just have saved his life.

'Have you found anything?' asked Professor Frewin-Hamilton, towering over him as him sat on the deck and raised his dive mask on top of his head.

'Sorry, professor,' he answered, looking up. 'Not unless you like snakes.'

Disappointed, the professor drifted away, headed toward Vaughan.

'Please tell me that was a joke,' said Alex, as he flopped down beside him.

'No joke,' he said, and he told Alex what had just happened.

Alex swore, and rolled his eyes. 'I hate fuckin' snakes.'

He couldn't resist. 'I know – you prefer white guys.'

Alex laughed. 'Do I detect a twinge of jealousy?!'

'You wish!'

Overhead, the mid-morning sky was azure, with not a cloud in sight. The *Amazon Dawn V* was moored about twenty yards north-east of a lazy, thirty degree bend in the river. Looking down river, the right bank was relatively flat and covered with rampant vegetation. In sharp contrast, the left bank rose steeply above the river, and there was a small, sparkling waterfall with a drop of at least thirty feet. Logic dictated it must be here, below the left bank, where any underwater passage or tunnel must be located. If it existed. The professor was convinced they were searching in the right place but, after over two hours in the river, he beginning to think they were wasting their time.

After consuming an energy bar and a fresh mango, washed down with bottled water, he felt good to go again. Briefly, he discussed strategy with Alex, and as they rose to their feet Alex nudged his shoulder and whispered, 'Looks like we've got ourselves a new chaperone.'

He turned his head, and saw Tommo approaching, wearing black shorts and a sleeveless grey vest, and carrying swim goggles. Five ten, with broad shoulders, a thick neck and wavy dark brown hair, Tommo was bare-footed.

'The boss wants you back in the river.'

'You joining us?' asked Alex.

Tommo nodded. 'Manny's not feeling too well,' he said. 'The boss's told him to rest.'

He and Alex looked at each other, and he silently thanked Alex for supressing whatever wisecrack he was thinking of making. He, like Alex, was wearing his Osprey wetsuit, plus black neoprene boots, gloves and a hood, and a dive mask – and, in the river, he still felt vulnerable.

Rising, he suggested, 'You might want to put something on your feet.'

Tommo sneered. 'I'm not a fuckin' wimp.'

Like you and Berro.

Tommo didn't say it, but the inference was definitely there.

He let it pass.

Before resuming the search, he cut another, larger sapling, trimmed off the side branches and leaves with a machete. Then, remembering the snake, he sliced the resultant pole into three lengths of four to five feet.
The three of them had only been in the river about thirty minutes when it happened.

With Alex to his right and Tommo on his left, James thrust his pole into a mangled mass of roots.

Suddenly, something huge lunged out of the murk, between him and Tommo. Reflexively, he twisted to one side, as the monster shot past him at lightning speed. Its muscular tail brushed his arm, and he felt an uncomfortable tingle pass through him, as the monster spun away from him – slammed into Tommo's chest.

The tingle intensified and Tommo's face contorted in pain.

He recovered quickly.

Inwardly, he swore.

At least six feet in length, and thicker than his arm, he'd initially feared the monster must be another, larger snake. It wasn't. It was a fish, a special kind of fish capable of generating powerful electric shocks.

An electric eel.

He had experienced a minor shock, but Tommo – clearly, as it hit his chest full on, the huge fish must have discharged a strong, incapacitating bolt of electricity. The eel disappeared into the river but, seeing his facial features relax and air bubbles leaking from his open mouth, he was more concerned about Tommo.

He's unconscious.

With his peripheral vision, he saw Alex raise his Maglite, to signal he'd witnessed the attack. He reached Tommo a moment later, grasped him under his arms, as the current threatened to carry the sinking body down river.

A steady stream of bubbles rose from Tommo's mouth, as he kicked upward, toward the surface. Alex joined him, taking hold of Tommo's left arm, just before they surfaced.

Alex broke the surface. 'What the fuck was that?'

'An eel,' he answered, as he raised Tommo's head out of the water, 'an electric eel.'

Alex swore. 'I thought fuckin' snakes were bad …'

'We need to get him out of the water, and quickly.'

He couldn't be certain, but he had a horrible feeling Tommo had stopped breathing.

Five minutes later, Tommo was lying flat on his back on the foredeck of the *Amazon Dawn V*, surrounded by everyone on board.

'… a big one – the fucker swam into his chest,' Alex was saying, as James knelt beside Tommo and placed his fingertips on the unconscious man's thick neck, felt for his carotid pulse.

Weak, and racing.

'He's alive,' he said, 'but he's – '

Vaughan cut in.

'Manny, Berro – take over here,' he instructed. 'You,' he said, glaring down at James, 'with me – now.'

James, only too aware where the axe was going to fall, followed Vaughan toward the stern of the boat. Behind the solitary cabin, out of sight of the others, Vaughan rounded on him.

'What the fuck are you playing at, Harris?!'

'I'm not – '

'Is this your idea of a joke?'

'You think I wanted this to happen?' he asked, meeting Vaughan's stare. 'That eel could just as easily have come at me, or at Alex.'

Vaughan sneered. 'But it didn't, did it?'

'No, it didn't – but I don't see how that's my fault,' he said, with a calmness he didn't feel. 'Visibility in the river is a few feet at best. If you think you can do any better – '

'Don't get clever with me, Harris.' Vaughan prodded his chest. 'Do I need to remind you what's at stake here?'

'I haven't forgotten,' he said, somehow keeping his rising anger in check.

'Good – because if you fuck up again that little brat you sired – '

He didn't let him finish.

'If anything bad happens to my son,' he said, in a deceptively low voice, 'you are a dead man.'

He caught a flicker of fear in the bastard's eyes, before Vaughan forced a smile – and placed his right hand over the Heckler and Koch P7 stuffed inside his belt.

'Are you threatening me, Harris, because if you – '

'I don't make threats,' he cut in, 'just promises.'

He met Vaughan's glare.

So close, he was confident he could take the bastard, if Vaughan moved to draw the Heckler and Koch – and Vaughan must have realised it, too, for his hand slowly dropped away from his waist.

'I'm warning you, Harris, if you – '

Stone suddenly appeared.

'Boss, I'm sorry to butt in – it's Tommo, he's having a seizure.'

'Coming.' Vaughan turned to James, and snarled, 'I want you and Berro back in the river – and this time you'd better pray you find something.'

He kept his thoughts to himself as he followed Vaughan and Stone to the bow of the boat where, as the bodies parted to let Vaughan through, he saw Alex and Manny crouched over Tommo, impotent to do anything as his body convulsed and thrashed involuntarily on the deck.

Then, moments after he halted behind Samantha's right shoulder, Tommo's back arched violently, before he exhaled noisily and suddenly collapsed. It didn't take Alex more than a few seconds to establish Tommo had stopped breathing.

Cardiac arrest?

That was his guess, and Professor Frewin-Hamilton said much the same thing aloud, as Alex and Manny performed CRP on Tommo ... better equipped, with a defibrillator, Tommo might have stood a fighting chance, but with no specialised equipment or drugs, and no medic on board …

He feared the worse.

Chapter 20

The day wore on.

After burying Tommo, James cut another sapling, slashed it in half and fashioned a couple of sturdy six foot poles. Alex wiped the back of his hand across beads of sweat glistening on his brow, and slung the spades they had used to dig a shallow grave over his shoulder.

'Are you thinking what I'm thinking,' asked Alex, as they headed back to the river.

'We're wasting our time?'

'Yeah – that, too.' Alex halted, and looked at him. 'Tommo's gone, and we lost Gately yesterday.' A pause. 'I'm starting to like the odds.'

'They're improving,' he agreed.

Vaughan, Stone, Manny and Wilko.

Four versus two – and that was without counting Samantha and the professor on their side. He had faced far greater odds, and lived to fight another day. Wilko, he was reasonably certain, didn't know anything about his son's abduction, but the other three ... given half a chance, he was confident he could make any one of them talk.

'You reckon we can take them?'

'They're armed and we aren't, but ... I'm sure we can.'

'Any time you're ready,' said Alex, 'just say the word ...'

He placed his hand on his friend's arm. 'I appreciate your support, Alex, but – let's see how this afternoon goes.'

He didn't say so, as they waded into the river, but he was more concerned about what happened when the Americans caught up with them, than any threat Vaughan and his goons posed.

But if they don't show before tonight, and we don't find anything ...

He knew he might not get a better opportunity.

Wanting to avoid another run-in with Vaughan, he waited close to the bank, as Alex swam out to the *Amazon Dawn V* and tossed the spades on the deck. Then, with Alex in his wake, he let the current take hold of him, carry him down river a short distance to the search zone, before he struck out for the far bank, where he handed one of the six foot poles to Alex. He lowered his dive mask over his eyes, sucked in a lungful of air, and dived.

They found nothing.

After lunch – grilled fish and an exotic assortment of fresh fruit – Vaughan, following a private consultation with the professor, decided to move the search up river, to the next bend. Broader and longer but, like the first stretch, the geology rose steeply from the river on one side to over thirty feet. A surprising amount of vegetation clung tenaciously to the cliff face and, within a few yards of each other, three small waterfalls glistened as they trickled down to the river.

James didn't expect to find anything interesting on this stretch of the river, either, and he didn't – but Alex did.

The river, where they were searching, was only seven or eight feet deep. Barely a yard apart, he and Alex attacked the matted vegetation and gnarled roots under water with their poles, wary of disturbing another, potentially harmful monster. His pole, as it had done before Tommo's fatal encounter with an electric eel, hit solid geology wherever he jabbed the dense growth and so did Alex's – until, on their umpteenth dive, his pole drilled through the vegetation and kept on going. Without apparent effort, Alex shoved his pole five feet into the river bank, before he halted.

They looked at each other.

Alex withdrew the pole, stabbed the bank again, a foot closer to James. He met resistance. He tried again, a foot the other way – and, once again, the pole disappeared into the river bank with ease.

They surfaced together.

'What d'you reckon?' asked Alex.

'I'm not sure,' he admitted.

They agreed whatever Alex had discovered merited further investigation.

It took them several dives to establish, shielded from view by poor visibility and thick vegetation, the anomaly was a good five feet wide and about two, two and a half feet deep. Located three to four feet under the river's surface, it might be nothing more than an underwater cave – but it might be what they were searching for.

A secret passage.

Alex asked, 'Do you wanna tell Vaughan?'

'Not yet,' he answered, treading water. He glanced up river, toward the *Amazon Dawn V.* Only Samantha and her husband were visible on deck. The professor's gaze was firmly buried in a book, but Samantha was watching them. 'Let's clear away some of the vegetation,' he suggested, 'and take it from there.'

They've found something.

No desire to breathe the same air as Vaughan and the others, who were enjoying a siesta on the foredeck, Samantha had plonked herself down near her husband at the stern of the boat. She was wearing a muted, light green crop top and darker green shorts. Her hair was tied back in a ponytail, and she wore a white baseball cap, to keep the blazing sun out of her eyes. Richard, in a cream, short-sleeved shirt and khaki shorts, was flicking through one of his notebooks, and glanced down river only occasionally. But, nothing else to do to pass the time, she had spent much of the day watching James and Alex searching first one, and then this second bend in the river her husband had identified as the location of the secret entrance to the Metal Library. Manny and Tommo, too, before Manny was reprieved and Tommo …

First Gately, and now Tommo.

Two deaths in as many days.

The Amazon is a dangerous place.

They were James's words, spoken at Heathrow when he learned she was joining the expedition, but her husband had told her much the same thing. Her husband went further, tried to put her off by detailing some of the dangers … Richard hadn't mentioned killer spiders or electric eels.

Now, she estimated James and Alex had spent at least ten minutes in more or less the same position, a few feet down river of one of the tiny waterfalls that trickled down the steep, rugged limestone cliff that rose high above the river. They surfaced every minute or two, before disappearing again – but they didn't move on. They didn't, as they had earlier, methodically work their way around the sweeping bend in the river.

Why not?

The obvious answer – they must have found something – excited her, but it scared her, too.

If they have found something …

It was easy to lose track of the days in the jungle, and it took her a few moments to work out what day it was … they had arrived in Ecuador on Sunday, and today was … Thursday. That meant her son had been missing for fifteen days. And it was eleven days since Vaughan had allowed her the 'proof-of-life' call. Fast approaching two weeks since she'd heard her baby son's voice. For a split second, when she tried to picture Luke, she couldn't see his face. Then relief flooded her, as an image of her son's dark, mischievous grin filled her mind.

God, I hope he's still alive.

She had no way of knowing, one way or another, if Luke was alive or dead. Gately and Tommo were dead and, on Vaughan's instruction, both had been buried close to where they died. In unmarked graves. Their deaths, she knew, would go unreported – their disappearance, if anyone missed them, forever unexplained.

She might not know as much as her husband or James about the dangers the jungle posed, but she wasn't stupid. She knew, if he achieved his objective, Vaughan was ruthless enough to kill her and Richard, and probably James and Alex as well, and dispose of their bodies in much the same way as he had done with Gately and Tommo.

Realising James and Alex hadn't surfaced for at least four or five minutes, Samantha turned to her husband.

'Richard, I think they've found something ...'

'Oh, crap!'

James was still debating the threat level, when Alex surfaced close beside him – spotted the anaconda. Its coils were as thick as a man's thigh, thicker where what must be a recent meal bloated it, not far along its body from its head, which was rested on one of its dark green, spotted coils. Black, beady eyes stared straight at them. He estimated it must be at least twenty foot long but, other than raising its head slightly, the serpent didn't react to their sudden appearance.

'I hate fuckin' snakes,' said Alex, treading water beside him.

He grinned. 'This one's big enough to fuck you.'

'Ha-ha – you're so funny.'

'You should hook up with Indiana Jones – he loves snakes as much as you do.'

Alex glared at him, but for once he didn't come back at him with a witty response.

'Relax,' he said, 'I think this one's harmless enough.'

'It's fuckin' massive!'

He didn't disagree. 'We're okay – it looks like it's just eaten.'

Having cleared away two square foot of vegetation, he and Alex had made three dives into the horizontal tunnel Alex had found. Visibility was poor, and he had to feel his way along the tunnel, as he kicked his legs. The passage, after about nine or ten feet, angled sharply upwards. After surfacing and discussing their options, they had decided to risk exploring it before reporting to Vaughan. But neither of them had anticipated coming face-to-face with the biggest snake he had ever seen.

A few inches of water covered the floor of the cavern they had surfaced in – ideal, as a place for the anaconda to rest up, digest whatever it had consumed. The snake was large enough to take a young child, maybe even a small adult, but as a species the anaconda more commonly preyed on fish, river fowl, capybara, forest deer and other mammals. Really big specimens, like this one, were known to devour the occasional caiman and jaguar as well. Hollywood liked to portray the snake as lightning fast but the truth was, out of water, it was heavy and ponderous – and posed no real threat.

'Yeah, well,' said Alex, 'I don't – oh, fuck!'

Slowly the anaconda's head rose, as it uncoiled itself, and James and Alex reflexively parted, pressed themselves to opposite sides of the submerged shaft they had just swam up. The snake, head first, came toward them, and slid into the black water between them. James felt its muscular body brush against his legs, as it disappeared into the depths, headed toward the river.

Alex let out an audible sign. 'I think I just wet myself.'

He laughed, as he heaved himself out of the deep water, on to the stone floor. The air inside the cavern was a bit stale and dank, but it was perfectly breathable. Looking around, unable to see much detail by the head lights he and Alex were wearing, he reached for the Maglite strapped to his waist.

'Whoa!' Alex slapped him on the back. 'Looks like we hit the jackpot!'

He was less impressed by what the high intensity light beam revealed. Less impressed, but still surprised. The cavern they were standing in was about eight feet square, and the straight walls, which appeared to have been hewn out of bedrock, rose to seven feet. No archaeologist, he had no idea how old the cavern might be, or who might be responsible for excavating it, but it was definitely man-made. In the far corner, his Maglite highlighted a series of small, hand-size niches that had been cut into the wall. They led up to a semi-circular gap in the ceiling.

'Hey, wait up,' said Alex, as he sloshed across to the far corner of the cavern, and shone the flashlight up. 'Shouldn't we go tell Vaughan we found something.'

He couldn't see much. 'We will, just as soon as we know what we've found.'

'Yeah, well – be careful, this place might by booby trapped.'

He smiled. 'Yes, Indy.'

Cautiously, he climbed the stone ladder, one niche at a time. A couple of the niches crumbled slightly, under his touch, but there were no unpleasant surprises. Moments later, he was standing in a second, slightly bigger cavern. Ten by ten. No water on the floor, but this cavern had dead straight, glassy walls. Wet looking, but dry to the touch. It was as if the rock had been glazed, after being chiselled and smoothed.

'This is fuckin' weird,' Alex observed, running his fingertips over the wall, 'and all the corners – they look like perfect right angles.'

He concurred.

In fact, the cavern itself appeared to be a perfect cube.

How is that possible?

Once again, in the far corner, a series of small niches led up to a gap in the ceiling like a ladder. This time, Alex followed him up without comment.

A tunnel.

It widened on both sides to about six feet, and rose to around seven feet. The walls, as in the upper cavern, were amazingly straight, smooth and glassy, as was the ceiling. The tunnel led directly ahead, away from the river, rising for the first dozen or so paces, before it gradually began to decline. There was no telling how long the tunnel was, or where it led – or what secrets it might hold.

Secrets like a Metal Library?

'We found it, buddy,' said Alex, resting a hand on his shoulder as he halted. 'We actually found it!'

He wasn't sure how he felt.

If this was the tunnel system Vaughan was searching for, and he didn't doubt it must be, whether or not it led to a Metal Library or something else, things were set to move on to a whole new level ... he didn't trust Vaughan to keep his word.

'If this is what Vaughan's looking for,' he said, as they turned around and headed back down to the first cavern, 'we need to start watching our backs.'

And Samantha's.

And the professor's.

Pedro's, too, probably.

And, somehow, he needed to find out where his son was being held, because he had an awful feeling if it were left up to Vaughan, the boy would never see his mother again.

'Got'cha.' Alex eyed the black, water filled shaft that led back to the river with suspicion. 'You don't think that fuckin' snake is still around, do you?'

Chapter 21

'No, Richard.'

'Don't be silly, Samantha,' her husband said, eyes sparkling. 'Aren't you excited? We could be this close – ' He held his thumb and forefinger less than an inch apart. ' – to making a momentous discovery. I – '

'That's *not* why I'm here,' she snapped. 'You go ahead, but I'm staying put.'

'Samantha, your father – '

'Do we have a problem here?'

She and Richard turned to Vaughan.

'It's – um, my wife. I don't understand why, but she – er, she doesn't want to come with us.'

'I'm staying here,' she said, before Vaughan could speak in support of her husband. She noticed James, who had been talking to Vaughan, was taking an interest in their exchange, but he kept his distance and he didn't say anything.

'I really don't think that's wise, Samantha,' said Richard, 'and certainly not on your own.'

'Pedro's not going with you,' she pointed out. 'I can – '

'Pedro's going to take the boat up river, beyond the next bend,' Vaughan cut in, 'to draw the Americans away, should they manage to repair their boat and come looking for us.'

'Fine,' she said, 'I'll go with him.'

'No,' said Richard, firmly. 'I won't – '

'You won't what?' she challenged, not allowing her husband to finish. She hated being told what she could and couldn't do, almost as much as the river terrified her. As for the prospect of diving under the deep, murky waters, to swim through a dark, long forgotten tunnel ...

I can't, I just can't!

'Let her stay, professor.'

In unison she, Richard and Vaughan all turned to James, who had stepped closer to them.

'What did you say?' Her husband stared hard at James, as if to tell him 'this is none of your business', but James wasn't fazed.

'Let her stay on the boat,' he repeated, calmly.

Richard started to object, but Vaughan placed a hand on his shoulder. 'Actually professor – a word in your ear ...'

As Vaughan led her husband out of ear-shot, she turned to James. 'Thank you.'

'No problem,' he said, with a faint smile.

'Richard doesn't know I suffer from aqua-phobia,' she said, feeling the need to defend her husband's apparent lack of sensitivity and understanding.

He nodded. 'I guessed as much.'

An awkward silence.

'I – I don't see what the fuss is about,' she said. 'I'll be fine, if I stay on the boat with Pedro.'

'Not if the Americans show, you won't. They're going to want to know where everyone is and, after what happened last night, I can't see them asking politely.'

Reminded a man had been shot last night, and probably killed, she fell silent. First Gately, then the American, and just a few hours ago Tommo … suddenly, remaining on the boat with only their local guide as protection, didn't strike her as such a sensible idea, after all.

Shortly, Vaughan re-joined them. Addressing James, he said, 'You and Wilko are staying on the boat with Mrs Frewin-Hamilton.'

James didn't look happy, but he didn't object. 'If that's what you want.'

'It is,' said Vaughan, firmly.

'What if the Americans show?'

'Use your fucking initiative.' Vaughan's grin as sardonic.

James kept his cool. 'I'm not armed.'

'No, but Wilko is – and since you won't be needing it, I trust you've no objection to loaning me your wetsuit.'

It was more of a command than a request.

Samantha turned her back, focussed on a small flock of colourful birds flitting back and forth across the river, as James and Vaughan stripped off. But she was close enough to catch the words Vaughan spoke to James in a low, smug voice.

'Just in case you're wondering, Harris, Wilko doesn't know a damn thing about the half-caste brat you sired.'

'Here is good, Pedro.'

'Sí, Señor Harris.'

Leaving their guide to moor his boat, James cast his gaze down river, but the location of the submerged passage wasn't visible. By now, the five man team led by Vaughan and the professor would already disappeared beneath the river. There was no sign of the Americans, either. Not yet. But he didn't doubt, sooner or later, they would be on their way.

Samantha was standing by his left shoulder. 'Do you think they'll find the Metal Library?'

'I don't know,' he answered, truthfully.

'If they do – do you think Vaughan will keep his word?'

She didn't spell it out, but he knew what she was asking.

Will Vaughan release my son?

He saw the pain in her eyes, knew how much she must be hurting inside, but he didn't lie. 'I hope so, Sami. I hope so.'

'But you don't trust him, do you?'

'No more than he trusts me.'

Minutes earlier, as they cruised up river, Wilko had headed toward the bow of the boat, saying he was 'gonna get me some shut eye'. As soon as the boat was safely moored, Pedro took to his hammock, to resume his afternoon siesta. No desire to join them, despite having shared the 2:00 to 6:00 watch with Wilko, he replayed Vaughan's words over in his mind.

Wilko doesn't know a damn thing about the half-caste brat you sired.

For once, having long suspected Wilko wasn't part of the inner circle, he believed Vaughan was telling the truth. And Vaughan had been quick to seize the opportunity, to reduce the threat level even further, by splitting him and Alex up. That made him feel … uncomfortable. Vulnerable. He was confident he could disarm Wilko, any time he wanted to, but – then what? He would love to be to be in a position to follow the five man team into the tunnel, pick off Stone or Manny or even Vaughan and make him talk, but abandoning Samantha wasn't an option.

There is another option.

Shaded by the boat's roof, and more comfortable in the khaki shorts and pale blue T-shirt he had changed into, James leaned against the port side of the cabin. Samantha stood beside him. Hair tied back in a ponytail that poked out through the back of her baseball cap, she was wearing green shorts and a light green top with thin shoulder straps, that didn't quite reach her navel. No bra. This, he realised as he averted his eyes from her breasts, was the first time they had been on their own since he'd surprised her in her kitchen, and he felt … he wasn't sure what he felt. Awkward, somehow, yet … she was the woman who had taken his virginity, the only woman he had enjoyed anything like a long term relationship with, and over five years on she was still an incredibly attractive, desirable woman.

The woman who bore my son.

A boy he'd never met, and might never meet unless … he didn't know how yet but, silently, he reaffirmed his vow to do everything within his power to reunite her with her son. But first …

He waited until her was certain Wilko and Pedro were asleep, before turning to Samantha. 'I need to use the radio,' he said. 'Do me a favour, and keep your eye on those two.'

Her expression was quizzical, but she nodded, 'Of course.'

He returned ten minutes later, half-expecting her to ask for an explanation, but when he thanked her she didn't say anything. She did follow him around the cabin, toward the boat's stern, and when he sat on the wooden deck she sat down beside him, no more than a foot away.

He turned to her.

'James, I – '

'Tell me – '

She smiled and so did he. 'I'm sorry.'

'Ladies first,' he said.

She hesitated. 'I was just going to ask – you're not angry with me, are you?'

He didn't follow. 'Angry about what?'

'About Luke.'

He still didn't get it.

Why would I be angry about Luke?

'Luke … ?'

'I – remember, the first time we – I told you I was on the pill.'

Now she mentioned it, he did remember.

How could I forget?

There was only one first time for everyone, and he felt certain most men remembered theirs. Most women, too.

'I didn't lie, James, but I didn't tell you the whole truth, either,' she said, lowering her gaze. 'I was on the pill when Joshua was conceived as well.'

Not sure how she expected him to respond, he didn't say anything.

She raised her head. 'You are angry …'

'No, I'm not,' he said. 'I just wish … I meant what I said, Sami, about finding Luke and getting him back.'

'I know, and I'm grateful.' She hesitated. 'I – can I ask you something? Something personal …'

'Of course,' he replied, suddenly nervous.

'You don't have to tell me, if you don't want to, but – why did you run away from home? It wasn't anything to do with me, was it?'

'Definitely not,' he answered. 'I – I got scared.'

She smiled faintly. 'I find that difficult to believe.'

'It's true. I …' He paused, before continuing. 'My father told me we were going to Pakistan. He showed me a photograph of one of my cousins over there, one of his sister's daughters. She'd just turned sixteen. She was very pretty, but – even before my father confirmed it, I knew he was planning our wedding.' He was aware Samantha knew, as well as he did, arranged marriages were an integral part of Islamic culture. 'Apparently, I'd met the girl briefly when I was in Pakistan for my brother's wedding, but I didn't really know her and the thought of marrying her …'

'I'm sorry, James. I had no idea.' Briefly, she touched his arm with her hand. 'I don't suppose you could have refused?'

'Not without bringing dishonour on my family,' he said, 'and I knew if I boarded a flight to Pakistan, I would be forced to marry.'

'So you ran away.'

He nodded. 'I waited until morning, and I started taxiing as normal, but at lunchtime I radioed in and said I wasn't feeling well. I drove to a second hand car dealership just outside the city centre. I sold my taxi, and an hour later I was on a train, headed for London Euston.'

She asked, 'When did you change your name back to James Harris?'

'The same day,' he answered. 'I had no idea what I wanted to do with my life when I arrived in London, but I did know I didn't want an arranged marriage – not then, and not ever. I wasn't born Muslim. I wasn't Muslim for the first four years of my life and – Islam is a way of life, but it's a way of life I never felt comfortable with. My step-mother never really accepted me – why should she, when I was a constant reminder her husband had cheated on her with an infidel?

'Growing up, even after my father converted me to Islam, I always felt more English than Pakistani, and when my older brothers were married off I kept telling myself when it was my turn, I'd run away and that's what I did. I needed to get away, make a clean break, and ditching religion and changing my name was the best way I could think of to do that. Joining the army was something I did on impulse, but I never regretted it.'

Samantha was silent as his confession sank in.

'I know it's a bit late to apologise, Sami,' he said, looking into her eyes, 'but I'm sorry I didn't tell you anything, or contact you. Please believe me, I wanted to, but I was scared if I did my father would pressure you into telling him where I'd gone.'

'He did try,' she said, quietly.

His heart lurched. 'He did?'

'Your father, your uncle, and your brothers.'

'I'm sorry, Sami. I – they didn't hurt you or anything, did they?'

'A little,' she admitted. 'They shouted a lot, and made threats. Your father slapped me across the face a few times, made my nose and mouth bleed, and one of your brothers threated to rape me. But what frightened me most was when your uncle threatened to break every bone in Joshua's body, if I didn't tell them where you were.'

Shocked to learn how badly she had suffered, at the hands of his angry relatives, he didn't know what to say. He didn't say anything.

'I couldn't tell them anything, of course, and after they'd gone I called the police,' she went on. 'I didn't want to, but the police insisted I go to hospital, for a check-up, and ...'

'I'm sorry, I had no idea.' It was a hopelessly inadequate response, given more than five years too late, but he couldn't think of anything else to say.

'That's when I found out I was pregnant.'

'I'm sorry, Sami – if I'd known ...'

'I know, but you didn't, and now ... '

They fell silent.

'Why didn't you tell me?' she asked, at length.

'About?'

'About what your father was planning.'

'I – I don't – I didn't think ...'

I panicked.

'If I'd known,' she said, with a smile, 'we could have run away together.'

He stared at her, uncertain how serious she was. 'You would have done that – for me?'

'I loved you, James,' she said. 'I wanted to be with you.'

He found himself nodding. 'I wanted to be with you, too. But ...'

Telling her, and asking her to run away with him, never occurred to him at the time ... how different his life might have turn out, if only he had stopped to think. But he didn't, and however much he might want to, there was no turning back the clock.

'Josh still asks about you sometimes,' she said.

'He does?' He was surprised her first son remembered him.

'You were like a father to him, a good father. You've no idea how much he missed you when you disappeared. We both did – very much.'

She was right: he had no idea.

118

He did know he had missed her and Joshua, far more than he imagined he would. If only circumstances were different, and he'd been around when she learned she was carrying his child, he would have happily taken on responsibility for Joshua as well.

But they weren't different, and I wasn't around.

And now she was married and Joshua had a different father.

And so does Luke.

'What about you?' she asked. 'You're not wearing a wedding band …'

He smiled. 'I'm not married, and I don't have any kids – apart from Luke.'

Her eyes flickered, at the mention of her missing son, but she recovered quickly. 'Do you have a girlfriend?'

'Uh-uh – not at the moment.'

A little, knowing smile. 'I'm sure there must have been girls …'

'A few,' he admitted, 'but I've not met anyone special … no one like you.'

'Thank you.'

'I mean it, Sami.'

'I know you do.'

He looked in her green eyes and she looked at him. Before he could stop himself, he leaned forward and kissed her, lightly on the mouth.

A second passed, and another, as he gazed at her.

Her eyes twinkled.

He placed his hand around her waist, drew her closer.

He kissed her again …

'James, we shouldn't …'

… and again. 'I want to …'

'James, I – what if someone sees us?'

'Wilko and Pedro are taking a nap,' he said, as he moved against her, 'and the others could be gone for hours.'

He took her in his arms and, as they moved even closer together, she folded her arms around him and he slid his hand up inside her top. She murmured pleasurably when his fingers fondled one of her firm, round breasts, and twirled her nipple between his forefinger and thumb. He couldn't stop himself from becoming aroused.

The kisses started off soft and gentle, and he felt a shiver of excitement when her hand caressed his thigh, and her fingers crept up inside his shorts, found him. His heart thudded wildly in his chest, and he felt himself becoming more and more excited, as their kisses became deeper and more passionate.

119

Chapter 22

'This is amazing – absolutely amazing'

'You ain't seen nothing yet, professor.' Alex swung the beam of his Maglite around, to highlight the stone niches in the far corner. 'The second cavern is up there.'

'After you, Berro,' said Vaughan.

The professor got there first, and he didn't hesitate to climb the rock ladder. Alex followed him up. 'Pretty impressive, huh?'

'This is …' The professor ran his palm over the glazed wall. 'I've never seen anything like this – look how straight and glassy the walls are, and the angles – they appear perfectly square … astonishing, simply astonishing.'

Vaughan joined them, but Stone and Manny were still on the way up as the professor pressed on, mounting the second set of niches.

'Not so fast,' said Vaughan, but the professor was like a small child let loose in Willy Wonka's chocolate factory, and paid no heed.

Alex hurried after the professor, with Vaughan close behind him.

'We've found it,' the professor said, aiming the beam of his torch down the tunnel. 'It *does* exist, and we've found it …'

That must be the royal 'we', he thought sourly, well aware he and James were unlikely to be given the credit they deserved for discovering the tunnel. Regrettably, he wasn't expecting to be paid the £s Vaughan had promised him, either. He was planning on staying alive.

'We haven't found anything yet, professor.' Vaughan turned to him.

'This is as far as we went,' he said, anticipating Vaughan's next question.

Vaughan nodded. 'Professor, I suggest you let Berro lead from here – it might not be safe.'

Thanks a bundle, you fuckin' tosser.

If he hadn't already known he was expendable, he did now.

He proceeded with caution, the high intensity beam of his Maglite penetrating the blackness only ten or so yards ahead. The ground beneath his feet was smooth, level and firm – natural bedrock, he was guessing. The tunnel itself appeared to have been carved out of bedrock, too, and although it gradually narrowed to about five feet, it remained remarkably straight and uniform.

The tunnel went on and on.

He judged they were at least a hundred yards in before the beam of his torch drew his attention to a dark shadow up ahead. Approaching it, on his left, he realised it was a side tunnel. It was narrower than the main tunnel, only three feet wide, and it appeared to curve away to the right, headed in the same general direction as the main tunnel.

He turned to Vaughan. 'Want me to check it out?'

'I'll go with him,' said the professor, before Vaughan replied.

'Be careful,' said Vaughan, 'and don't go too far. I want you back here in ten minutes, tops.'

He nodded. 'No worries.'

He led the way, with the professor on his shoulder; the tunnel wasn't wide enough for them to walk side-by-side. Less than thirty seconds in, opposite each other, they came upon the first pair of recesses: two feet high and wide, and cut maybe six feet into the bedrock. Both were empty, but that didn't stop the professor from labelling them as 'burial chambers'. They came across several more pairs, all identical and all empty, before he called a halt.

'Time to go back, professor,' he said.

'But, please – just a little further. We might find – '

'We're gonna get our asses kicked,' he cut in, 'if we don't turn around now.'

They re-joined the others, and he left it to the professor, to tell Vaughan what they had found. Or not found. Nothing of value, certainly – and no hint of a Metal Library.

Head rested on his naked chest, Samantha felt the steady thump, thump, thump of James's heart, as she snuggled closer for a long moment. It felt right. Comfortable. Like she belonged. Eyes closed, she could easily have fallen asleep, if he hadn't whispered in her ear.

'We should get dressed.'

He was right, of course, but she'd not felt like this in a long time and she didn't want to break their intimate embrace a second before she had to.

'Sami ...'

She raised her head off his chest, and opened her eyes, as the strong arms around her loosened. He reached for her shorts, handed them to her, and she reluctantly sat up and wiggled into them. Moments later, they were both decent again, although he was still holding his T-shirt in his hand. When he looked at her, she sensed awkwardness between them, as if he wasn't quite sure how she was going to react, now their passionate encounter was over. Smiling, she leaned toward him, to give him a peck on the cheek.

He shot her a quizzical look.

'I just wanted you to know I don't regret – you know,' she said, with a playful smile. 'Do you?'

'Definitely not,' he said, matching her expression.

He brushed the backs of his fingers across her cheek, a fleeting gesture that made her want more. As they leaned toward each other, and their lips met again, the words he had spoken earlier echoed in her head.

I've not met anyone special ... no one like you.

She couldn't deny she felt the same way about him. But she felt guilty, too.

I'm married to Richard.

They had only been married a year and she'd never cheated on her husband before, never even considered it, but ... even before Luke was abducted, she had begun to question her husband's commitment to their marriage. Something didn't feel right. It was almost as if, once the thrill of the chase was over and they were husband and wife, Richard no longer felt the need to make an effort anymore. Before they were married, he was the perfect gentleman. Affable. Attentive. And not only to her. To her sons as well. But more recently ... even when they had sex, which wasn't as often as she would like, sometimes she felt as if Richard was going through the motions. And since their arrival in Ecuador, his sole focus was on locating the Metal Library, and her kidnapped son didn't appear to matter to him anymore.

James was different in so many ways and, as they embraced and kissed again, she couldn't help wondering what the future held when they all returned to the UK.

Will he want to carry on seeing me?

The thought excited her, but it frightened her, too.

If Richard finds out ...

As he raised his T-shirt over his head, to put it on, she touched his left shoulder. She traced the discoloured, puckered skin downward with her fingertips. Gently, she asked, 'What happened?'

'I got lucky,' he said, as he pulled his T-shirt down over his torso.

She raised an eyebrow. 'You call that lucky?'

'When I joined the army, my first overseas posting was Iraq.' He hesitated, and she guessed the cause of his terrible scarring wasn't something he liked to talk about. Understandable. However it had happened, the memories it evoked were never likely to be pleasant ones. 'I'd only been there a couple months when – we were on patrol, four of us, when an IED – an Improvised Explosive Device – exploded beneath our vehicle. Two of the guys with me died instantly, and Dunn – he died of his injuries five days later.'

Inwardly, she cringed. 'That's awful.'

In recent years, like most people, she'd read and listened to so many news reports about soldiers being killed or maimed in Iraq and Afghanistan especially, she had become almost immune. But James wasn't a stranger, and learning what happened to him and the soldiers serving with him really brought home just how terrible war could be.

'I probably wouldn't have survived, either,' he said, 'if I hadn't been thrown clear. I vaguely remember the actual blast, but I don't remember anything of what happened after it. I woke up in a field hospital, badly burned but alive. I was flown back to the UK the following day for treatment. I had to have two skin graft operations on my shoulder but – as I said, I was lucky. I survived, and I was passed fit to re-join my unit.'

'I'm surprised you wanted to,' she said. 'I don't think I would have, if something like that happened to me.'

'I'm not a quitter,' he said, with a forced smile.

'So when did you leave the army?' she asked.

'In December.'

'It must have been a tough decision to take, after what – five years?'

It was an innocuous enough question, or so she thought, until she noticed how uncomfortable he looked. There was a lengthy pause before he answered.

'I didn't – it wasn't my decision,' he admitted. 'I was discharged.'

'Discharged!' She was more shocked than surprised. 'But – why?'

He hesitated again, and shook his head slowly. 'You don't want to know.'

A pause like that … whatever the reason, it was tearing at him. Badly. And the more she heard about what he'd been through – was still going through – the more it tore at her as well.

'Yes, I do,' she said, softly. 'Please, James …'

Hank Sanderson leered.

'Nice, very nice,' he murmured, as he zoomed in on the woman's naked chest. He glimpsed her dark pussy, too, before she put her shorts and top on. Shame. She was a real beauty, but he'd only arrived on the scene in time to catch a few minutes of hard core action ... what did the professor's wife think she was doing, screwing around with the dark-skinned, Indian-looking guy?

And where is the good professor?

A hundred yards down river from the *Amazon Dawn V*, Sanderson was squatted in a black, one man inflatable zodiac, hidden behind some over-hanging vegetation. Careful to avoid giveaway reflections, he adjusted his binoculars, scanned the river boat's deck slowly. He picked out a guy in a hammock and, possibly, one man asleep on the deck. His low vantage point made it impossible to be certain if it was a man or just a mound of baggage. But, probably, a man. No one else was visible, but part of the deck was obscured from his view. Given the close proximity of the illicit lovers, he doubted anyone was in the boat's small cabin. He reached for his two-way radio, flicked it on.

'Yes, Hank?'

'I've found them, Mr Clayton. The boat is moored, but there appears to be only four hostiles on board, maximum.'

'Four,' Clayton repeated. 'Where are the others?'

'I can't see them – they're not in the river and I can't see anyone on the river bank, either.'

A pause. 'Has anyone spotted you?'

'Negative,' he replied. 'Now I know where they are, I'm going to head back down river and wait for you, then we can decide how we're going to proceed.'

'Excellent – we should be with you shortly.'

Chapter 23

Samantha kissed his lips. 'Sometimes it helps to talk …'

James hesitated.

He had never spoken of what happened, not until he was compelled to defend himself at his disciplinary hearing – after which, the nightmares he thought he had conquered returned with a vengeance. But … Samantha wasn't just anyone. She was the first woman he'd slept with, the only woman he'd ever fallen in love with, even if he was too stupid to realise it at the time.

The mother of my son.

A child he knew nothing about two weeks ago.

I loved you, James … I wanted to be with you.

Past tense, but – she still had feelings for him. Strong feelings. She must have, or the intimacy they'd just shared would never have happened. He wanted her back in his life so badly it hurt. He wanted to get to know his son – and if he could get Luke back, unharmed, maybe, just maybe …

'What happened, it wasn't – it was … nothing much happened the first couple weeks I was in Iraq,' he started, 'but then – we were on foot patrol, seven of us. We were passing through a small village south of Baghdad when we came under fire.'

He closed his eyes, remembering it like it was yesterday.

Bullets raked the ground in front of him, kicking up sprays of orange-brown dust, as he dived for cover behind a small, mud-brick wall. Suddenly, an armed insurgent ran out from the dwelling to his right. Reflexively, he did what he'd been trained to do: he raised his assault rifle, took aim and squeezed the trigger.

The insurgent stopped, wide eyed, as his chest turned crimson. The young man – he couldn't have been more than seventeen or eighteen – dropped his weapon, staggered back two steps with his hands clutching his bloody chest, before he keeled over in the dirt.

'I knew he was dead,' he said, quietly. 'I'd never killed anyone before, but … we waited, but no more insurgents fired on us.'

She didn't say anything, as she waited for him to continue.

'Corporal Smythe ordered us to check one of the dwellings,' he said. 'I went in first, with Butler, but we didn't find anyone else – not until we discovered there was a basement.'

125

Nearly shitting himself, he was so scared, he clutched his assault rifle tightly, poised to squeeze the trigger again at the first sign of danger, as one step at a time he and Butler descended the stone steps … he was relieved to find only a woman and two children, huddled together in the far corner, crouched at the side of a long, L-shaped sofa. The woman was dressed all in black, with a full *burka* over her head. The two kids, a boy who looked about ten and a girl a year or two older, both wore *shalwar kameez*. Clearly petrified, the trio didn't appear to be armed and they posed no threat.

'I would have left them alone, but Butler – he called the others …'

Corporal Smythe, Vaughan, Stone and Tommo appeared.

'Corporal Smythe, he ripped the woman's *burka* off her head, and when she spat on him he slapped her across the face … '

The woman didn't appear old enough to be the children's mother; more likely, she was their sister, sister-in-law or aunt. Blood trickled from her mouth as Smythe and Butler and Tommo grabbed her. Laughing as she resisted, wriggling and striking out, they ripped the clothes from her body, and she screamed obscenities at them when they exposed and groped her small, round breasts.

'Butler and Tommo threw her on the sofa, held her down, and Corporal Smythe – he reached for his belt and unbuckled it. I knew what was going to happen, I knew it was wrong, but I …'

Stone grabbed the young girl, snatched a handful of her *shalwar kameez* – tore it from her, revealing her boyishly flat chest. Undeterred, Stone and Vaughan quickly stripped her naked and tossed her on the sofa, next to the woman Smythe was screwing.

He spied a third child, a sobbing boy aged only two or three who had been hidden behind the other, older children, a split second before the elder boy jumped up, shouted something unintelligible as he came at Vaughan with a long, thin-bladed knife.

The poor kid didn't stand a chance.

Vaughan saw him coming, casually knocked him to the floor with his forearm, before he brought his right foot down on the scrawny wrist holding the blade – hard.

Bone cracked and the boy screamed.

Vaughan snatched up the blade – held it to the kid's throat. 'You're gonna regret that, you stinkin' little cockroach!'

He just stood there, numbly, seeing but not wanting to see, as Smythe and Butler and Tommo and Stone and Vaughan took turns at the woman and the girl. Vaughan, having forced himself on the girl, raped the boy as well – brutally.

'Anyone else wanna dip their pecker?' Vaughan turned to him as he zipped his fly. 'What about you, Harris?'

He stared down at the naked Iraqi boy at Vaughan's feet, felt decidedly queasy as creamy-white cum streaked with blood oozed from between small, pale brown buttocks.

'Suit yourself.' Fly zipped, belt buckled, Vaughan stood over the sobbing boy, gripped his arm, dragged him off the short end of the sofa and flipped him over on his back. He grabbed the kid's hairless genitals with his left hand, pulled viciously upwards, so that the kid's skin was unnaturally taut. Grinning, he let the kid see the weapon in his right hand – the kid's own knife.

The boy's dark eyes widened, and he started to babble incoherently as he twisted and thrashed and kicked, desperate to escape Vaughan's grip. But, without apparent effort, Vaughan held him firm.

Finally, he found his voice. 'Vaughan, no … '

Too little, too late.

The blade slashed taut skin and, as Vaughan triumphantly raised a handful of bloody flesh over the boy's heaving chest, dripping blood, a crimson fountain bloomed between the boy's legs. The boy screamed hysterically and Vaughan stuffed his bloody prize into the boy's mouth.

'Shut the fuck up, won't you!' Vaughan laughed. 'You scream louder than a fuckin' girl!'

He turned away and fled up the basement steps, into the kitchen, through the living area. He didn't quite make it to the front door, where Irvine was stationed, before he heaved once, twice – then he spewed his guts.

Listening to his confession, Samantha didn't say a word, but her horrified expression spoke volumes.

'After they were through, Corporal Smythe ordered Vaughan and Stone to torch the place,' he revealed, in a low voice. 'I thought they must have killed the woman and kids first, but they didn't … I'll never forget their screams.'

Screams silenced by a muffled blast.

A grenade, he later learned, lobbed into the basement by Vaughan.

'It wasn't your fault, James,' she said, her voice little more than a whisper. She placed her hand on his arm. 'You didn't do anything.'

'No, I didn't,' he agreed, meeting her stare. 'I did nothing, nothing at all – but I should have. I should have – I don't know what I should have done, but I should have done something. What they did, what Vaughan did … I can't believe I just stood there and watched it happen.'

She squeezed his arm. 'You were young, and you were scared – anyone would have been, in the same situation.'

He couldn't deny what she said was true: he was young, and he was scared ... a young woman and two kids, brutally violated. Not forgetting the toddler, who witnessed atrocities no kid of any age should see, before his short life was snuffed out in a most terrible way.

Their screams still haunted him.

'I didn't know it at the time,' he said, 'but Vaughan must have taken a photograph of the mutilated Iraqi boy on his mobile. Last November, after he'd quit the army, he sent the photograph to the top brass at the Special Air Service HQ in Hereford – with a date, a location and one name.'

She guessed, 'Your name?'

He nodded, but he didn't say anything.

'But – why? I don't understand ...'

'I ...' He had given it a lot of thought, since his dishonourable discharge, and only one explanation made any sense. 'I think he was jealous.'

'Jealous! Of what – of you?'

'Of me – of what I'd achieved,' he replied. 'We never really got on and last year, he applied to join the SAS. He failed the final selection phase. He took it badly, and quit the army. When he found out I'd been successful – '

'You were in the SAS?' Her eyes widened.

He nodded again. 'Briefly, but – I made it through selection, and I was placed on probation, as all new recruits are. I was waiting for my first posting when I was hauled before my CO. I had no idea what I'd done, but I soon learned I was in deep, deep shit.'

The top brass, he told her, already knew the names of the seven soldiers who had made up the Iraqi patrol. More than four years on, two were dead, and himself apart the only man still serving was Irvine – the squaddie who had stood guard in the house, without ever stepping foot in the basement and seeing the atrocities he witnessed.

'That left four of us: Vaughan, Stone, Tommo and me,' he said. 'There was a hearing ... I told the truth, but the others – Vaughan admitted taking the photograph, but he claimed it was me who sodomised and mutilated the Iraqi boy. Stone and Tommo backed him up, so ... I think my CO believed my version of events, but the top brass couldn't afford to take any risks. If something like that ever got out, and one of the soldiers involved was serving with the SAS ... no charges were brought against me, but I was dishonourably discharged from the army.'

Her eyes blazed. 'That's so unfair!'

He found a smile.

'Life is, sometimes,' he said. 'If I hadn't been discharged, I'd probably be in Afghanistan today, not here – and I wouldn't know I have a son.'

Chapter 24

James tensed.

Cawing noisily, the birds flapped their wings frantically as they burst above the treetops, then as one dark mass they darted this way and that, before they soared high over the river and disappeared into the jungle on the opposite side. At least twenty, twenty-five of them. Species unknown. Clearly, something had startled them – caused them to take flight.

'What is it?' asked Samantha.

'I'm not sure,' he replied, suddenly alert.

He focussed his gaze on the jungle where the birds had taken to the air, but the green wall of vegetation was impenetrable and he couldn't see anything. But he knew the birds wouldn't have taken flight like that, so suddenly, without good reason. Something – or someone – had disturbed them.

'I can't see anything,' she said, her eyes following his gaze down river.

'That makes two of us.' And that is what concerned him.

They fell silent.

He watched and he waited …

Five minutes passed.

Then he saw it – away to the right, close to the river bank, barely fifty yards away. A metallic glint. A split second glimpse, but it was enough.

Inwardly, he swore.

The Americans.

'We have company,' he said, answering her questioning glance.

'Company …?'

'The Americans, probably.'

'Oh, God – you don't think …' Her voice trailed off.

He didn't know what to think. He did know, irrespective of how many hostiles were closing on them, his options were limited. He wasn't even armed. Alone, he would have headed for the bow, slipped over the side of the *Amazon Dawn V* and taken his chance in the jungle. But Samantha hated water, she couldn't swim, and he couldn't just abandon her. Last night, he feared, one of the Americans had died and the dead man's buddies were unlikely to be in a charitable mood.

'Follow me,' he said, quietly.

Casually, aware they were almost certainly under observation, James rose to his feet and strolled toward the bow of the *Amazon Dawn V*.

And thine eye shall not pity; but life shall go for life, eye for eye ...

Having closed to within thirty yards of where the rival boat was moored, Sanderson replayed Mr Clayton's words over in his mind, as he watched the woman and her illicit lover rouse another limey. He didn't know how, given how silent and stealthy his eight man advance party had been, but it appeared lover boy had rumbled them – not that it was going to make any difference.

Hidden in the dense undergrowth along the river bank, mindful of where the sun was, Sanderson raised his binoculars to his eyes and zoomed in on the woman again, and smiled. Shapely figure, nice tits – she was definitely a looker, but not so long ago she had proved she was no better than a common whore.

Thou shalt not commit adultery.

He hadn't told Mr Clayton about the promiscuity he'd witnessed. But, early this morning after they buried Vernon, Mr Clayton had come round to his way of thinking: no loose ends.

No survivors.

He doubted Mr Clayton would have been so agreeable, before the limeys mounted a surprise attack that took Vernon out, but the death had enraged Mr Clayton and ... it was the right decision. The only decision, and he was more than happy to action it, just as soon as the limeys led them to what Mr Clayton was paying him mega-bucks to find and secure. But, before he slit her throat and tossed her body in the river, he had plans of his own for the pretty whore.

Without giving his position away, he backed into the jungle and re-joined his men. Had the terrain being more to his liking, he would have split his eight man team in two, four men on either side of the river. High, craggy cliffs on one side of the river made that impossible. Instead, he instructed two men to stay put, and led the rest of the team up river, until they were directly opposite where the rival boat was moored. Here, he sent two men further up river, so between them they could cover the *Amazon Dawn V* from three different angles.

As his men got into position, he took the M24 Sniper Weapon System – the military and police version of the Remington 700 rifle – from his shoulder. With its detachable telescopic sight, the M24 had an effective range of over 800 yards – many, many times greater than the distance between him and his targets. Edging forward, but careful to keep himself concealed, he was keen to formally announce their presence – find out where the professor and the rest of the limeys were holed up, take control of the situation before he called Mr Clayton.

Sanderson had lover boy's forehead in his sights, with his finger on the trigger, when the woman suddenly filled the crosshairs of his scope. Silently cursing her, he waited a moment, controlled his breathing and took aim again ... so close, he couldn't miss.

He squeezed the trigger.

Samantha screamed.

Red mist splattered her face and James grabbed her arm.

'Get down!' he hissed, as he yanked her down on the deck. He spread-eagled himself over her and Wilko's lifeless body hit the deck beside them. She found herself staring at the fist-sized crater blasted out of the dead man's head, oozing blood and gore.

'Oh, God,' she moaned, 'Ooohh, God ...'

James shifted position, just enough to shield her from Wilko's head, but the macabre image remained firmly imprinted in her mind. Blood, *Wilko's* blood, trickled down her cheeks but she was too scared to move, to wipe it away. She remained motionless beneath James, breathing through her mouth, half-expecting whoever had killed Wilko to open fire again at any moment.

'Stand up and put your hands on your head.'

A loud male voice, the accent unmistakably American.

'You have five seconds.'

'Do as he says,' whispered James, as she felt his weight lift off her. He grasped her hand, helped her to her feet. The American, who was standing on the river bank no more than twenty-five feet away, was an athletic six footer with close-cropped blond hair who looked about thirty. She recognised him as the same guy she had seen in the motor launch yesterday.

The American wasn't alone.

He was flanked by three other men, and she noticed another four more men – two down river and two up river – as well. All eight Americans brandished guns – rifles or sub-machine guns? James probably knew exactly what make the weapons were, and what they were capable of, but she had no idea. But she didn't doubt the weapons were loaded, or that the men brandishing them knew how to use them. She noticed, too, the Americans appeared to be wearing something under their T-shirts. Bullet-proof vests? She exchanged a brief, knowing look with James. An unspoken acknowledgement that, for the moment, the smart thing to do was exactly as they were told.

She put her hands up, on her head, and James did the same. So too, a short distance away, did Pedro. Their poor guide, having tumbled out of his hammock, looked as terrified as she felt.

Five minutes later, as four of the Americans covered them, four more boarded the *Amazon Dawn V*. Including the tall blond American, who dripped water all over the deck, as he approached her and James.

'Today must be your lucky day.' The American stared to James, and grinned. 'First you get laid ...' He glanced at Samantha, and she felt her cheeks burn.

Oh, God, he saw us ...

'... then your mistress gets in the way at the last second – stops me from blowing your brains out.'

Her embarrassment quickly faded as the words sank in, and she realised it could easily have been James who was lying dead, with a gaping hole in his head.

James didn't say anything.

The American's expression hardened. 'Your luck just ran dry.'

She held her breath, as the American told his friends to cover him, while he frisked James. He did it quickly, yet efficiently. The American smiled, on finding a concealed knife, which he tossed in the river. Then it was her turn. The American's hands were large and strong, but she didn't flinch when he touched her – not until he slid his hands up inside her crop top, fondled her breasts.

'Get your filthy hands off – ' She lowered her hands, gripped the American's wrists, but she wasn't strong enough to remove his groping hands.

She glared at the American and the American turned to James, almost inviting him to react, but she shook her head faintly and, thankfully, James kept his emotions under control. Finally, the creepy American withdrew his hands.

'Thank you, Randy.' The American accepted his rifle back, used it to indicate Wilko's lifeless body. 'That there's payback for Vernon ...'

She guessed Vernon must be the American who Stone had shot, and presumably killed, last night.

'... and this is for messing with our boat.'

Giving him no time to defend himself, the American planted the butt of his rifle in James's belly. Deep. She sucked in a sharp breath and James's face creased in pain, as he lowered his hands and doubled forward, clutching him chest.

'Please,' she started, aghast, 'you – '

The American struck James again.

James sank to his knees.

'Get up, and get your fuckin' hands up – both of you!'

She raised her hands, placed them on her head.

More slowly, James did the same. Clearly hurting, he didn't take his eyes off the American.

She waited, dreading what might happen next.

The American instructed two of his minions to 'get rid of that', indicating Wilko's corpse, before he turned to her.

'Where's your husband?'

'I, er – he went hunting with the others,' she replied, making it up as she went along. It was a plausible enough explanation, but the American wasn't fooled.

'Wrong answer.'

She watched, with a growing sense of dread, as the American exchanged his rifle for a stubby black pistol. Taking his time, the American fitted a sleek black extension – a silencer, before he raised the elongated weapon, pressed it against James's temple.

Despite the sweltering heat, Samantha felt a cold sweat break out across the back of her neck. The American's cold, blue eyes were devoid of emotion. Suddenly, she realised this was no bluff.

He's going to kill him.

Chapter 25

'What do you think, professor?'

The red flare died, but not before it lit up a vast subterranean cavern, the like of which Alex hadn't seen before … high as a cathedral, with fantastic formations of stalagmites rising from the floor like a petrified forest, and stalactites hanging from the ceiling like gigantic icicles. A good twenty yards across, from left to right, but the flare wasn't bright enough to reveal how far ahead the suffocating darkness extended.

'I – um, I think,' the professor started, clearly thrown by the tunnel's abrupt end. 'I wasn't expecting the tunnel to – '

'We go on,' said Vaughan.

'Of course,' the professor agreed, nodding vigorously. 'We go on, definitely. This, clearly, is a natural formation but it doesn't mean the tunnel system doesn't resume somewhere ahead of us.'

Alex cautiously led the way deeper into the bowels of the Earth. Initially, the moist ground beneath his feet sloped gently downward, but it gradually levelled off. The air was surprisingly fresh, yet increasingly chilly, and the plop-plop-plop of water echoed eerily in the darkness. He crept onward, veered left to avoid a stalagmite with a trunk as thick as a century old oak, and felt the first calcium-laden drop splatter on his shaven head.

No idea how large the subterranean cavern was, and aware how easy it would be to become disoriented in the heavy darkness, he swung his Maglite to his left every few paces, wanting to keep that side of the cavern in sight. Behind him, the professor and Vaughan speculated where the cavern might lead, and what they might find. He was more interested in what happened when they did find something – and what happened if the cavern proved to be a dead end.

Now Vaughan had split him and James up, the odds weren't so good: three armed men versus one unarmed man, with the professor thrown in as a joker.

He knew James was right, in believing if they were to discover anything of value, Vaughan planned on sharing the spoils with Manny and Stone. No one else. And Vaughan didn't strike him as the kind of guy who liked to leave loose ends, which meant … he hated to even think it, but he feared James and Samantha's young son had already been murdered.

Deeper inside the cavern it was raining, or so it appeared, as drops the size of glass marbles fell silently from the cavern's ceiling. He sloshed through several large puddles, no more than an inch or two deep, before the ground started to fall away again and the beam of his Maglite highlighted a flat black surface, dotted with thousands of small ripples, dead ahead.

An underground lake.

The dark surface extended beyond the reach of his Maglite and it was impossible to judge, just by looking at it, how deep the expanse of water was. He wasn't keen to find out, either, so without turning around and consulting Vaughan, he began to follow the curve of water around, to the left. He was relieved to discover the lake didn't extend as far as the side of the cavern. There was a ribbon of bedrock, no more than two feet wide, between the water's edge and the wall of the cavern.

He led the others, in single file, around the lake which he judged was at least forty-five yards long. He sensed it was deep, too. There was only one way to find out how deep, but even in a wetsuit he didn't fancy taking a dip.

Briefly, he traced of edge of the lake away to the right with his Maglite, but the beam wasn't powerful enough to cut through the blackness, to the far side of the cavern. Keeping to the left, he moved on, noticing a veritable forest of stalagmites rising over to his right. No sign of anything else. Nothing interesting. Silently, he wondered how far underground Vaughan and the professor were prepared to go, before they called it a day and accepted the fabled Metal Library didn't exist.

Then, as he swung his Maglite straight ahead, Alex saw it.

'No, wait – please! I'm sorry – I'll tell you!'

The black, carbon fibre suppressor indenting James's temple, close to his right ear, was attached to a Walther P5, a 9mm semi-automatic pistol developed in the 1970s by the German small arms manufacturer, Carl Walther GmbH Sportwaffen. His stomach, where the bastard holding the Walther had hit him twice, was ablaze but he didn't waver as Samantha pleaded with the American.

He spoke first.

'We found an underwater passage,' he said, meeting the American's icy stare. 'It leads to a small man-made cavern, which in turn leads up to a second, slightly larger cavern.'

The suppressor prodded his temple. 'Go on …'

'The second cavern leads up to a tunnel.'

The American's eyes glinted with excitement. 'Now we're getting somewhere. Go on …'

'That's it – that's as far as I went.'

The American stared at him, and gripped his arm, harshly. He felt the black suppressor indent his temple again. 'You've been there?'

'Yes.'

'If you're lying …'

'I'm not lying,' he said, keeping his voice level.

'You'd better not be, because if you are …' The American glanced at Samantha, and smiled. 'Before I blow your brains out, I promise you'll get a front row seat while me and the boys have some fun. And when it's over … *Bang! Bang!* I feed you and Miss Infidelity to the fishes.'

Samantha gasped but he didn't react, not outwardly, but inside …

'The professor,' the American said, lifting the Walther an inch away from his head, 'he's already exploring the tunnel, right?'

He nodded. 'Yes.'

'The rest of your team is with him – all six of them?'

'Not six – four.'

The American's eyes narrowed. 'And the other two?'

'They're both dead.'

The American was skeptical. 'How?'

He answered truthfully.

'Sounds nasty.' The American grinned. 'Like I said, if you're lying …'

'I can show you where Tommo is buried.'

'Thanks, but no thanks. I'll take your word for it – for now.'

The American stepped away from him, lowered his Walther to chest height, but with three M-16's trained on him there was no way he could risk tackling the American.

'What's your name?'

'James Harris.'

'Okay, James Harris, I'm Hank Sanderson.' The American indicated the deck with his Walther. 'Take a seat – you as well.' He motioned toward Samantha, then Pedro. 'And you.'

'*Señor*, please. I is not – '

'Get down – now!'

At gunpoint James, Samantha and Pedro sat on the deck with their backs forming a triangle, and with their legs stretched out in front of them. Instructed to do so, they put their hands behind their backs. James winced, as a black plastic tie bit into his right wrist – secured it to Pedro's left wrist. Moments later, his left wrist was attached to Samantha's right wrist, and her left wrist was attached to Pedro's right wrist.

'Watch them – especially him.' Hank indicated James, and unclipped a two-way radio from his belt, as he walked toward the boat's stern.

Samantha leaned back against him, whispered in his ear, 'Who do you think he's calling?'

He guessed, 'His boss, probably.'

'I – I thought he was going to kill you.'

'He won't – not while I'm still useful to them.'

Not until I've shown them where the tunnel is.

She hesitated, and asked, 'Do you think we'll find the Metal Library?'

'I didn't, before we found the underwater passage,' he admitted, 'but now, I'm not so – '

'That's enough chit-chat.' Pocketing his two way radio, as he returned, Sanderson stopped in front of them. 'Mr Clayton will be with us shortly.'

Not one, not two – *three* tunnels.

The subterranean cavern was over one hundred and fifty yards long and, as the professor had hypothesized, the tunnel system did resume. But, as Alex stood in the opening of the first tunnel, noting it veered away to the left, Stone's flashlight revealed a second tunnel. This one appeared to run straight ahead, but the third tunnel they discovered veered away to the right. Only six feet separated the first tunnel from the second, with another six feet separating the second from the third, and all three entrances appeared identical: around six feet high and four feet wide, forming a rectangular opening with unerringly straight, glassy walls.

Now what?

Glad the decision wasn't his, Alex stood a few feet away from the middle tunnel, and ran his hand over his shaven head. He felt cold water trickle down his neck, and seep inside his wetsuit. He turned to Vaughan and the others.

'Take your pick, professor.'

'I, er – I think we should – I'm not sure.' The professor's eyes flitted between the three dark openings. 'The tunnels all appear to lead in the same general direction, but if we're not going to miss anything important, we must explore each one – '

'We'll be quicker if we split up,' Vaughan cut in. 'Stone, Manny – you take this one.' He highlighted the tunnel on the left with his torch. 'Berro, that one is yours.' The tunnel on the right. 'Professor, you're with me – we'll take the middle one. I suggest we meet back here in – let's say twenty minutes, tops.'

'Of course,' said the professor, nodding, 'but please, I implore all of you, don't touch anything you find – not until I have had the chance to see it *in situ.*'

'You heard the professor,' said Vaughan, turning to Alex, and then Stone and Manny, before he turned back to the professor. 'Okay, let's go.'

He watched Vaughan and the professor head into one tunnel, and Stone and Manny disappear into another, before he stepped inside the third tunnel. He couldn't make up his mind if being singled out, and instructed to explore on his own, was to his advantage or not.

What the fuck do I do if I find something?

Chapter 26

Half an hour after they were boarded, the American boat cruised into view. Samantha watched it chug up river, fixed her gaze on the short, portly man dressed in a white shirt, brown shorts, and wearing a straw Panama hat, who was standing at the bow of the *Rey de la Selva*. Clayton, and she was in no doubt the man was Mr Clayton, looked in his early fifties.

There was a slight bump, as the two river boats came together, and moments later Clayton stepped aboard the *Amazon Dawn V*. The tall American called Sanderson went to meet him. Still staring down the barrels of three rifles, and secured to James and Pedro with uncomfortably tight plastic ties, the only thing the three of them could do is watch and listen.

'Nice work, Hank.' Smiling, Clayton tipped his Panama to the blond American. Balding on top, Clayton's short hair was steel-grey.

'It's a pleasure, Mr Clayton.'

Clayton gave her a cursory glance, before halting in front of James.

'Hank tells me you have found a submerged tunnel.'

James didn't say anything.

'Yes? No?'

'No,' said James. 'We found an underwater passage – the tunnel it leads to isn't submerged.'

Clayton's expression hardened. 'Don't get pedantic with me.' A brief pause. 'This tunnel, you have seen it?'

'Yes.'

'Describe it.'

Keeping it short, James did so.

Clayton demanded, 'Where's the entrance?'

'Down river.'

'How far down river?'

'Release me and I'll show you.'

Clayton strode away and conferred with Sanderson. Samantha strained to hear the exchange, but the Americans kept their voices low, and she only caught the odd word. Agreement must have been reached as, when Sanderson approached them again, he took out a black-handled knife from his belt.

'I should warn you,' said Clayton, as Sanderson proceeded to cut the ties securing her to James and Pedro, 'my men have orders to shoot first and ask questions later.' He looked at James as he delivered the warning. She rubbed her smarting wrists and Sanderson called one of the other Americans. 'Dillon, take the local to the cabin, tie him up and lock him in.'

James showed no obvious discomfort, following his mistreatment by Sanderson, as he helped her to her feet.

Clayton enquired about specialist equipment.

'We didn't take anything, apart from Maglites and head lights,' James answered, 'but we didn't explore the tunnel.'

Sanderson wanted to know, 'Who's we?'

'Me and Alex,' James replied.

'He's the black dude,' Sanderson guessed, 'right?'

James nodded, and hesitated before he continued. 'Professor Frewin-Hamilton identified the location of the underwater passage, but Alex found it and we – you should know, before we go any further, our team isn't as united as you might think.'

Silence.

Clayton spoke. 'And this concerns me how?'

James glanced at her, as if asking her permission to divulge more, but before she could respond in any way he broke eye contact.

'Anthony Vaughan is in charge,' he said. 'Stone and Manny are in Vaughan's pocket, but ... I'm sure you know Sami is married to the professor, but I've known her a lot longer. We have a child, a four year old son who Vaughan abducted two weeks ago. That's the reason I'm here – the only reason.'

Clayton turned to her. 'Is this true?'

'Yes, I – my son, *our* son ...' Reminded of Luke, and how long he had been missing, she couldn't stop tears welling in her eyes. 'Please, I don't give a damn about the tunnel or the Metal Library or any treasure, I just want my son back. Vaughan's threatened to kill him if ...'

Tears flowed down her cheeks and, when he put his arm around her, no one stopped her from burying her face against James's shoulder.

'Vaughan, Stone and Manny are armed,' revealed James. 'Alex isn't – he's on our side, and Vaughan knows it.'

'What about the professor?'

'The professor – ' James hesitated, and glanced at her again. 'I think the professor would have jumped at the opportunity to mount an expedition to locate the Metal Library, whatever the circumstances. He's aware of the situation regarding our son, of course, but right now his focus is on proving the Metal Library exists.'

It pained her to admit it, even to herself, but she knew James spoke the truth.

'I can show you where the tunnel is,' he said, 'but I've no idea where it leads and I don't care. All I want is ten minutes alone with Vaughan, Stone or Manny. They know where the boy is being held, and I'll do whatever is necessary to make one of them talk.'

No one spoke for several seconds.

Then, lightly, Clayton placed a hand on her shoulder. 'I'm sorry about your son, I didn't know he'd been taken.'

She nodded, and wiped the back of her hand across her glistening cheek. 'Thank you.'

'I realised Vaughan was a nasty piece of work when he stole your father's research,' said Clayton, 'but I never imagined he was ruthless enough to target a small child.'

What?!

'My father ...' She felt an icy fist grip her heart.

Oh, God – no! He can't mean ...

'What do you mean, he stole my father's research ...?'

James confirmed it.

'He means,' he said quietly, 'your father was murdered.'

For the first twenty or so yards the tunnel headed right, away from the central tunnel they had discovered at a thirty degree angle, and Alex found nothing. Then, abruptly, the tunnel changed direction. A thirty degree left turn. The tunnel continued on, unerringly straight – on a parallel course with the central tunnel.

Shoulders hunched and head down, to avoid banging his head on the low ceiling, he shivered, feeling the cold as he slowly advanced. The bedrock beneath his feet was smooth and dry. Every pace or two, he swung his Maglite from left to right, determined not to miss anything. He was equally determined not to lose his bearings. Getting lost, this far underground, was not an appealing notion.

As he advanced, he silently speculated on who might be responsible for excavating the tunnel system, and when. The obvious candidates were the Incas. He had briefly researched the local area, with James, before they departed – learned there was evidence of human culture in the region dating back thousands of years. However, it wasn't until the 1460s that the region was conquered, and assimilated into the Incan Empire. More recently, when the Spanish conquistadors arrived from the north, the empire was ruled by a guy called Huayna Capac, and upon his death in 1525 the empire was divided between his two sons, Atahualpa and Huáscar. The former took charge of the northern part of the empire, the latter the south, including the Incan capital, Cusco. Seven years on, Atahualpa went to war with his own brother, defeated him and claimed control of the empire. It was a short-lived victory: the following year, the Spanish conquistadors captured Atahualpa.

The Spanish, of course, believed the Incas possessed many treasures – including gold. When he was imprisoned him, the conquistador Francisco Pizarro promised Atahualpa his life and freedom, if he filled two-thirds of a room measuring twenty-three by sixteen feet by ten feet deep with gold. Foolishly, Atahualpa took Pizarro at his word, but as soon as the Incas had filled the room to the required depth with gold, Pizarro broke his promise and ordered Atahualpa's execution, on the grounds he had murdered his brother.

The Incas were famous for their architecture, from the capital city Cusco to a hidden gem not discovered by the outside world until 1911. Machu Picchu. Stone temples were built without the use of mortar yet, remarkably, the huge stone blocks knitted together so well a knife blade couldn't be pushed between the stonework. It was a method of construction that led to incredible stability and, even with the aid of modern technology, engineers would struggle to replicate any of the Incan structures with the same kind of precision.

Did the Incas build tunnels as well?

Alex didn't know the answer, but if they did, he couldn't think of anywhere safer to hide their precious treasures from the Spanish invaders. It was exciting to think, somewhere close, a hoard of Inca gold and other treasures might be waiting to be discovered.

He checked his watch. Another two or three more minutes, and he would have to turn around and head back, if he didn't want to exceed the twenty minutes Vaughan had specified. Resigned to returning with nothing to report, he played the beam of his Maglite over the walls ahead of him, left then right – so quickly, he almost missed it.

A dark shadow.

Up ahead, on his right, two foot or so below eye level ... the niche cut into the wall was eighteen inches square but only half as deep. Nestling inside it, there was a statue. Carved stone, not gold. It depicted – a man? The lack of breasts definitely suggested the statue was male, but the clothes he was wearing were strange, and his arms were unnaturally chubby. There was a decorative belt around his waist and what appeared to be some kind of weird headdress around his head.

Alex left the statue *in situ*, but he couldn't resist heading a little deeper into the tunnel – where, just a few paces on, he made a startling discovery.

Chapter 27

'James, I can't do this. I can't – '

'Yes, you can,' he said, gently yet firmly.

'I can't – I won't – '

'Sami, you don't have a choice – you have to.'

Sitting beside her at the port side of the *Amazon Dawn V*, covered by two Americans with M-16s, James knew Clayton's team was more or less ready to move out. He couldn't be sure, until they actually set out, but it appeared they would be accompanied by Clayton himself, his sidekick Sanderson and at least seven or eight other Americans – easily out-numbering, and out-gunning, Vaughan's team. The Americans, as he had known they would be, were much better equipped to explore underground, too.

Telling Clayton about his son's abduction was a calculated gamble, one he knew might come back to haunt him, but he wanted the Americans to know he wasn't interested in the Metal Library or whatever else awaited discovery underground. He did want to stay alive long enough to find out where his son was being held … if he wasn't already too late. Vaughan, he'd learned, hadn't offered any proof of life since he allowed Samantha to hear Luke's voice on the day he'd met her again, for the first time in over five years. That was nearly two weeks ago – a long, long time for a small child to be missing.

Clayton, after confirming his suspicions about the death of Samantha's father, had told her she would be accompanying them as he, James, showed the Americans to the tunnel he and Alex had located. He knew, like Vaughan, Clayton was using Samantha as a way of keeping him in line. It wasn't a decision he approved, but no one had asked his opinion and she hadn't been given any say in the matter, either. He didn't trust the Americans, any more than he trusted Vaughan, and he viewed the ruthless way in which Sanderson had despatched Wilko as a bad omen. Samantha was a distraction he could do without, but the decision had been taken, and telling Clayton that she couldn't swim hadn't bought her any sympathy.

'Remember the first time we took Josh swimming,' he said, knowing he didn't have long, to try to allay some of her fear.

'Of course, but I don't see what that's got to do with …' She glanced over the side of the boat, at the river, and there was no mistaking the sheer terror in her eyes.

'He was only three at the time,' he reminded her.

Her expression said, *'So what?'*

'The first time we went to the leisure centre, you sat and watched me and Josh in the pool – the second time, too. Even after I persuaded you to join us in the water, you refused to leave the shallow end of the pool. But even though he couldn't swim, you let Josh ride on my back all the way to the deep end.'

'I – you were a good swimmer,' she said, 'and – I trusted you.'

'So trust me now,' he said, softly. 'Believe me, I'm a far better swimmer now than I was five years ago, and I promise I won't let anything bad happen to you. I know you're scared, Sami, but we can do this.'

She didn't look convinced.

He picked up the black dive mask one of the Americans had tossed him, for her to wear. 'This,' he said, 'will prevent water getting in your eyes or up your nose. I know it won't be easy, but when we're in the river I want you to try to relax, and let me guide you. Can you do that for me?'

She closed her eyes tightly for a moment, but when she opened them again, she nodded faintly. 'Just promise you won't let me drown.'

'Find anything?'

'Uh-uh, nothing,' Alex lied, having just emerged from his tunnel to find Manny and Stone loitering in entrance of the middle tunnel. 'You guys?'

'Nothing,' Stone answered.

'Where's Vaughan and the professor?' Having used his twenty minutes and a few more on top, he had expected to be the last one to show at the rendezvous point.

'Not back yet.'

'I hope they found something,' added Manny.

He had found something, but he was inclined to think it was in his best interest to keep it to himself, because once they started finding things – valuable things – certain people might have outlived their usefulness.

People like me and the professor.

They waited five minutes, ten minutes …

Stone wanted to know, 'Where the fuck are they?'

'We could go look for them,' Manny suggested.

'I'm easy,' he said, interested to see if Stone was capable of making a decision on his own. Stone was – sort of.

'Let's give it another few minutes.'

145

They gave it another five minutes.

Vaughan and the professor failed to show.

He played out a number of scenarios in his mind – like trying to calculate his chances of success, if he surprised Stone and Manny. Tried to take them out. One of them, anyway. The other one he, or rather James, needed alive. Dead men don't talk. For him, this was no longer about lost treasure or some mythical library, and it hadn't been since learned Vaughan had abducted James and Samantha's son. A young kid James had never met – hadn't even known about until a couple weeks ago.

How does a guy handle crap like that?

Manny, according to James, definitely knew where the boy was being held. James was convinced Stone must know, too. As did Vaughan, of course … at least while he was underground, the bastard wouldn't be able to get a signal – wouldn't be able to order the boy's execution.

Assuming the poor kid's still alive.

It was a mighty big assumption.

'We should go – something might have happened.' Stone flashed his torch at Manny, then Alex. 'I'll take point. Manny, you watch our backs.'

And I'll be the fuckin' monkey in the sandwich.

Saying nothing, he followed Stone into the middle tunnel, which ran dead ahead. Straight as a die, but no higher than the tunnel he had explored on his own, which meant he had to be careful not to bang his head on the ceiling. He was five eleven and a quarter. Incas, or whoever had built the tunnels, must have been a few inches shorter.

Stone set a decent pace, aiming his torch ahead of him, rarely deviating to check right or left. He didn't bother playing the beam of his Maglite over the walls, either, figuring the professor wouldn't have missed anything worth seeing. They must have been at least fifty yards in when, a long way ahead of them, he spotted a faint white glow.

'Kill your lights,' hissed Stone, and for ten seconds they waited in complete darkness, as the ghostly white luminescence bobbed closer. Stone shouted, 'Identify yourself.'

'It's me, you fuckin' idiot.'

Vaughan.

Alex flicked his head light and Maglite back on, and Stone and Manny did the same with theirs. They went to meet Vaughan, who was alone.

'Sorry, boss, I – '

'Who the fuck did you think I was?'

'I don't know, I couldn't see you and – '

Vaughan didn't let him finish. 'Any of you guys find anything?'

'Nothing,' Stone replied.

Alex asked, 'Where's the professor?'

Vaughan turned, and glared at him for a moment. Then the bastard's face cracked in a grin, and he said, 'In seventh heaven.'

'Oh, God …'

'Let go, Sami – I'll catch you.'

Samantha's knuckles were white, her grip on the boat either side of her was so tenacious. James was already in the river, the dirty brown water swirling around him, turning his pale T-shirt dark blue. At James's suggestion, she had been granted permission to exchange her crop top for a T-shirt, but she was still wearing shorts. Her hair was tied back in a ponytail. On both sides of her, the Americans who would be accompanying them were geared up and ready to go. They were all dressed alike, with plain black T-shirts over what James had called body armour – what she would have called bullet-proof vests.

Still reeling from the revelation the house fire that claimed her father's life wasn't accidental, not to mention witnessing Wilko's brutal murder, her head was pounding like there were a thousand brass bands playing badly inside it. She couldn't concentrate, she couldn't focus, but … slowly, biting her top lip, she began to lower herself. One inch, three inches, six inches … she hesitated, when the toes of her trainers broke the water's surface, but James told her she was doing great and encouraged her to continue. She tried not to think of drowning and blood thirsty piranhas and drowning and electric eels and drowning and venomous snakes and drowning and drowning and drowning … the river slowly crept as high as her knees.

'Oh, God, I can't do this …' Paralyzed with fear, she stopped her descent.

'Yes, you can.' James placed his hands on her calves, held her steady. 'You're doing fine.'

'I can't, James. I can't – '

Suddenly, an unseen hand pushed her between her shoulder blades and she lost her grip – tumbled into the river.

She screamed and James caught her, but he couldn't stop her head from plunging into the river. Her wide open mouth filled with water and she panicked, overcome with a petrifying sensation of drowning, drowning, drowning … her head broke the surface, and she spat river water. She gulped in a lungful of air.

'I've got you, Sami – you're okay.'

147

Coughing and spluttering, arms flailing wildly, she realised James's arm was around her waist and, scared she might slip out of his grasp, she wrapped her right arm around his shoulders and clung to him for dear life. He was talking to her but his words didn't register. The river was up to her chin, her feet couldn't touch the bottom, and …

Someone pushed me in!

Not James, he wasn't on the boat; one of the Americans, then.

Glancing up, she saw three of them – all laughing.

Bastards!

'You're doing fine,' said James. 'Don't fight the current and don't fight me, okay?'

'Okay,' she spluttered, but she didn't feel okay. Her pulse was racing madly and her heart was hammering inside her ribcage. She tried taking a few deep breaths, to calm herself, but she was in fast, dangerous water and the last thing she felt was calm. She was alarmed to notice she was drifting further and further away from the boat. Her life was in James's hands now, literally, because if they became separated …

Don't even go there.

The water was cooler than she expected, quite refreshing actually, but she was too terrified to appreciate it. The current tugged at her legs, tried to pull her away from James, but she fastened on to him like a limpet attaches itself to a rock.

Oh, God, what am I doing here?

The location of the submerged entrance grew closer and closer.

I can't do this …

James started swimming toward the craggy limestone cliff rising out of the river with his free arm, long and deceptively lazy strokes, and beneath the water she could feel his legs kicking. Her fear intensified with each stroke. This was the part she was absolutely dreading, the part where she had to …

Oh, God – I can't, I can't, I can't!

She'd forgotten all about the dive mask, until James plucked it from his waist, and helped her to put it on. Black-rimmed, with huge goggle eyes, the mask was a tight fit. That's how it should be, she supposed, otherwise it wouldn't keep the water out.

The tall American, Sanderson, dived first.

'Close your eyes if you get scared,' advised James, as the American disappeared into the murky depths. 'You'll have to hold your breath for about forty seconds, that's all – try to relax, hold on tight, and you'll be fine.'

If you get scared …

And I'm not scared now?!

Try to relax ...
Relax!

One after the other, two more Americans dived. Then it was Clayton's turn. A short, chubby man who must be nearly twice her age – more like a fat whale than a sleek dolphin.

If he can do it ...

'We're next,' said James. 'Trust me, Sami, you can do this.'

She wrapped her arms around him from behind, so tight her breasts crushed against his back. She took a deep breath when he told her to, and another – then he dived, taking her with him. Her first instinct, when her face hit the water, plunged beneath it, was to struggle, lash out, but she consciously suppressed the urge and focused on repeating three words in her mind, over and over again.

I trust James ...

Her shoulder, and then her foot, brushed against something solid.

I trust James, I trust James ...

She remembered to keep her mouth closed, hold her breath.

I trust James, I trust James, I trust James ...

She felt the hands gripping her shift position, sensed a change of direction.

I trust James, I trust James, I trust James ...

Her shoulder struck something, not hard – then, suddenly, water churned in her ears and, faintly, she heard James's voice.

'You can open your eyes and breathe now, Sami – we're there.'

She opened her eyes, ripped the dive mask off her face. She gasped, gulping air through her mouth. She felt nauseous, but –

I did it!

Relief overwhelmed her and tears flooded her cheeks.

She couldn't believe she'd done it. She'd actually done it! She'd dived in the river, swam through the submerged passage – not swam, exactly. James had done all the swimming, all the diving, too. But she'd made it, and she was here ...

Here was a small cavern totally devoid of any natural light. The beam of Sanderson's torch picked her out, as James took her arms and lifted her out of the water – the deep water, as the floor of the cavern was covered with two or three inches of water as well. Her wet T-shirt clung to her chest, dripping wet. Sanderson was wearing a head light. So was Clayton; he was over in the far corner, pointing his torch up a hole carved in the ceiling.

'You okay?' asked James, with a grin.

'I – I think so – ' She swallowed hard, and again, but she couldn't stop her lunch from rising in her throat, couldn't stop herself from vomiting.

Chapter 28

'Seventh heaven' proved to be a replica of what Alex had discovered in his tunnel.

First, a small niche with a stone statue in it. It wasn't identical to the statue he'd found, but it was the same size, and very similar. A little less ugly, maybe. And then, a few yards on, there was a much bigger recess cut into the side of the tunnel – with human remains in it. The bones were stacked in a neat pyramid, with the skull nesting on top like an oversized egg with two gaping eye sockets in it.

No remnants of clothing.

No treasure.

No sign of the professor, either.

'I told him to wait here,' said Vaughan, clearly annoyed. 'Let's go – he can't have gone far.'

Another statue … more bones … another statue … more bones. So it continued. Perfect, small niches and large recesses cut into both sides of the tunnel … they finally caught up with the professor, by Alex's count, at statue number fifteen.

'Ah, there you are – I was just – '

'I asked you to wait.'

'Yes, I – um, this is a remarkable find, quite remarkable, and – '

'This isn't what we're looking for.'

'No, quite right,' the professor agreed, 'but each of these little effigies does have a value, a quite considerable value, actually. Nothing like this tunnel system has ever been found before, not in this part of the world and certainly not in such a wonderful state of preservation.'

'Give it a rest, professor,' Stone grumbled.

Alex suppressed a smile.

They moved on.

The little effigies and piles of bones kept on coming.

They came to a T-junction.

Left or right?

Straight on was no longer an option.

This should be interesting.

Silently, he urged Vaughan to split the team again, but he didn't. Without consulting anyone, not even the professor, Vaughan chose to turn right. No obvious reason why. But no one argued. Vaughan marked the tunnel they were leaving, at head height on both sides, with blue chalk. The tunnel they were entering, as well. A sensible precaution. He could find his way back to the river easily enough from here, but the tunnel system was fast become like a maze, and he didn't fancy taking a wrong turn if he had to make a hasty exit.

It didn't take Alex long to realise this tunnel wasn't straight: it curved away to the left, albeit very gently. Silently, he speculated if the other tunnel curved to the right, the two tunnels might actually meet and form a huge circle. He wondered how Vaughan would react, if they ended up back where they started.

But that didn't happen.

James followed Samantha up the rock ladder cut into the wall, from the first to the second cavern, where the Americans had already set up a couple of high intensity halogen lights that illuminated the cavern. One of the Americans handed him two dry black T-shirts, told him, 'Change into these.'

A couple of the Americans had already changed, and others were doing so. Dry T-shirts, but no dry shorts. No body armour, either. Samantha was the only woman present. He took her elbow, led her to a vacant corner of the cavern and held up one of the black T-shirts while she changed into the other, to protect her from prying eyes. He glimpsed her firm, round breasts as she struggled out of her wet T-shirt, pulled the dry one on. Breasts, not so long ago, he had been touching and fondling and kissing. It was the first time, in too many years, he had made love with her. He didn't want it to be the last time.

'You okay?' he asked, as he switched T-shirts.

She nodded, and found a smile. 'I'm sorry I puked.'

'Don't be – you were amazing.'

'I was terrified,' she said. 'You're the one who's amazing. I didn't think I could do it, I really didn't, but – thank you.'

He didn't think now was a good time to remind her she was going to have to do it all again, but in reverse. Americans permitting, of course. He figured, irrespective of where the tunnel led or what they discovered, the end game was fast approaching. He didn't know how long it would take them to catch up with Vaughan, but when they did things were certain to get interesting. And dangerous. He wasn't armed but, if the opportunity arose, he wouldn't hesitate to take out a hostile or two. Permanently. No hesitation. No guilt. No remorse. But he needed Vaughan, Stone or Manny alive. Manny or Stone, preferably. Just long enough to loosen their tongue. Then, with Samantha, Alex and the professor, he was gone.

He counted eight Americans in the cavern. Not including Clayton and Sanderson, who had already ascended to recce the tunnel above. So ten in all. A nice round number. But fewer would have suited him better. Sanderson, he'd noted earlier, had donned what at first glance appeared to be night vision goggles. But night vision goggles depended on a light source, and there was no natural light down here. That meant the goggles must be fitted with thermal infa-red imaging, designed to pick out heat signatures. Not something Vaughan had thought of, but then Vaughan hadn't known he had serious competition.

'This is as far as me and Alex went,' he whispered, as he walked close behind Samantha. Sanderson was on point, with Clayton and two Americans next in line. Four ahead, six behind. Spot on, apart from the fact Sanderson hadn't posted a sentry in the upper cavern. Over confidence? It was an oversight he liked to think might work to his advantage.

'Do you think we'll find anything?' asked Samantha.

'I didn't think we'd find this tunnel,' he admitted, 'so who knows.'
She lowered her voice. 'What happens when we – you know, catch up with the others?'

People die.

Not the answer he wanted she to hear. 'Nothing bad, I hope.'

Clayton called a halt, briefly, when a narrow side tunnel was discovered, but after consulting Sanderson he decided to ignore it, and move on. James felt certain Vaughan's team *would* have stopped, for at least ten minutes and possibly longer, to recce the side tunnel.

It wasn't long before Clayton called a halt again, and Sanderson asked for 'lights out'. The darkness in the tunnel was so complete, so absolute, he couldn't see anything. Not Samantha, not even his own body. Nothing. He could hear the *plop plop plop* of dripping water.

'What's happening?' she whispered.

'I'm not sure.' Before blackness enveloped them, he'd glimpsed what appeared to be the end of the tunnel.

So what lies ahead?

He didn't know … he listened. He heard movement. He heard voices, low voices. Behind him, as well as ahead. Clayton demanded quiet. They waited in silence. Samantha's shoulder touched his, and without thinking he put his arm around her. She leaned in and he drew her closer. So close her body pressed against his. It felt good. Still they waited … he heard movement somewhere ahead, and Sanderson's drawl.

'There's a lake up ahead, but I think we can go round it.'

Clayton asked, 'What about the professor's team?'

Vaughan's team, actually.

'Uh-uh – there's no sign of them.'

No heat signatures.

Head lights and Maglites back on, he kept his arm around Samantha's waist as they entered a subterranean cavern. She didn't object. Stalagmites and stalactites – he could never remember which were which – abounded. Huge things, taller and thicker than a century old oak. They glistened like diamonds in sunlight when the beam of his Maglite hit them. The beam wasn't powerful enough to reach the cavern's ceiling, from where water pelted them like rain, quickly soaked his and Samantha's T-shirts. She didn't complain. She did start to shiver, and not only because it was growing colder, when she saw the black expanse of water ahead of them. The path around the lake was too narrow to walk side-by-side. Samantha went first, but she gripped his hand tightly, as she hurried on.

'I swear,' she muttered, as the path widened again, 'when I get out of here I'm never going near deep water again.'

Three new tunnels.

James couldn't second guess Vaughan, but he was interested to see what Clayton and Sanderson decided to do. Split the team, he hoped – which is exactly what happened. Sanderson sent two of his men into the first tunnel, another two into the third tunnel, and he left two men at the entrance. Six hostiles temporarily out of the picture, four remaining: Clayton, Sanderson and two unnamed Americans.

Game on.

Alex, close behind Vaughan and the professor, descended eight broad steps cut into the bedrock. He found himself standing between two stone column plinths. The plinths came up to his waist, but the stylised animal statues atop each towered over his head. One was definitely feline, possibly a jaguar, but he had no idea what animal the other represented.

He didn't know where they were or if they'd stumbled on anything significant, but it quickly became apparent they were no longer in a tunnel. Here, thankfully, the ceiling was higher and he didn't have to stoop. He rubbed his neck, as the five of them fanned out slightly, and he swung his Maglite from side-to-side. Five beams of light explored the darkness … revealing not much.

Vaughan fired another red flare.

The projectile flew dead ahead, at a sixty degree angle – hit the fifteen foot ceiling almost immediately. The flare disintegrated, but not before the bright red light it cast unveiled a long avenue about six feet wide, which was lined on both sides with tall statues on stone plinths, situated in pairs every five or six feet. Animals mostly, but a few appeared human. A dozen pairs at least, all leading – where?

'This is it,' said the professor, excitedly, 'this *must* be it …'

The flare died and darkness returned.

Sensing an opportunity, as animated chatter broke out, Alex hung back as the others surged forward. Torches waving, led by Vaughan and the professor, the others hurried from one plinth to the next, leaving him behind. He reached up and flicked his head light off.

Slowly, noiselessly, he retreated until he was within striking distance of the steps they had just descended. He killed his Maglite and ducked behind a plinth. Melted into the darkness. And waited …

No one noticed he was gone.

Chapter 29

Oh, God – what's he going to do?

Samantha didn't know what James was planning, but when he surreptitiously thrust his torch into her hand and gently pushed her away, she knew he was planning something. Something dangerous. They were crowded around a large recess cut into the tunnel wall, as Clayton and Sanderson examined the old, disjointed brown skeleton inside it. James was standing behind them, and the two anonymous Americans were stood behind James, one on either side of him. Hardly daring to breath, she slowly edged further away from them.

She didn't have long to wait.

Without warning, without turning around, James rammed his elbows back. He caught the two nameless Americans completely unawares. They dropped their torches, went down clutching their chests, struggling to breathe. In the same fluid movement, James kneed Clayton in the buttocks and threw his right arm around Sanderson's neck, put him in a powerful arm lock. Propelled forward, Clayton crashed head first into the recess, scattering the neat pile of bones.

Suddenly, viciously, James twisted Sanderson's neck.

She flinched, as she heard the sickening scrunch of tearing ligaments and snapping cartilage. She knew, even before James released him and he crumpled to the ground, the American's neck was broken.

The two nameless Americans were recovering.

James spun on his heels. At lightning speed, he delivered a powerful karate chop to the side of one neck, and smashed his forearm into the other's face. Blood spurted from the second man's busted nose. This time, when they hit the ground, the two Americans didn't get up.

Hearing the rattle of old bones, seeing Clayton trying to scrabble out of the rock recess with a gun in his hand, she whacked him on the head – as hard as she could, with James's torch.

The American sagged, and toppled to the ground at her feet.

James put his hand on her arm. 'Thank you.'

She opened her mouth, and closed it again, too shocked by what had happened to speak. She'd never seen anything like it. James had taken on four armed men and destroyed them in – what? Five seconds? Seven or eight, maximum. And, incredibly, he didn't even appear short of breath.

He picked up the pistol Clayton had dropped, raised it to the American's head.

My God, he's going to –

'No!' She grabbed his forearm. 'James, please …'

He turned to her. 'He's calling the shots.'

'I know, but – please don't …' She didn't spell it out, but he knew exactly what she meant. They looked at one another for a long moment, before he nodded faintly, and lowered the pistol.

'Thank you,' she said, breathing easier.

He didn't say anything.

Knelt beside him, he placed two fingers on Clayton's neck. 'He's alive.'

She was relieved to hear it.

I could have killed him!

James would have, if she hadn't stopped him.

One of the nameless Americans was alive as well, but the other one was dead. James didn't bother to check the last American, Sanderson.

So … two dead, two unconscious.

'I'm sorry you had to witness that,' he said, quietly.

She was sorry, too, and she started to tremble as the enormity of what she'd seen hit her. Too stunned for words she could only watch as, quickly and efficiently, James frisked the prone Americans and searched their backpacks. He found several pistols, spare ammunition, three knives, bottled water, energy bars and what looked like a two-way radio. As he re-packed one of the backpacks, she reminded herself he had served in the army. He had served in Iraq and Afghanistan, and he'd told her he had killed one man … how many more, she dreaded to think. He had been recruited into the SAS, and it wasn't difficult to understand why. He was ruthless, utterly ruthless.

She remembered what was at stake.

If anyone can get Luke back, alive and well …

She remembered something else, too.

Vaughan killed my father.

'You okay?' he asked, as he used one of the knives to slash the collar of Clayton's T-shirt, before he ripped the garment wide open, exposing a black padded vest.

'I – I think so,' she managed. 'Are you?'

'Better than I was five minutes ago.' He removed Clayton's body armour and handed it to her. 'Quickly, take your shirt off and put this on.'

She didn't argue.

He helped himself to the second survivor's body armour.

She made no attempt to hide her nakedness from him, as they changed. He checked two of the pistols, appeared satisfied.

157

'Have you ever used a firearm?' he asked.

She shook her head. 'Never.'

'No problem,' he said. 'Hopefully there won't be any shooting, but if there is I want you to hit the deck and keep your head down, okay?'

'Okay.'

He removed the strange looking goggles from Sanderson's head, and slung the backpack he'd re-packed over his shoulder. Stood up. Then he put his hands on her waist, drew her closer – leaned forward and kissed her mouth.

'Let's go find the others.'

'Where's Berro?'

'He was here a minute ago.' Briefly, Manny glanced over his shoulder, as if the missing nigger would magically reappear.

'Well, he isn't here now, is he?!' Vaughan glared at Manny, and at Stone. 'You were supposed to be watching him.'

'We were,' said Stone, 'but he – he must have slipped away.'

'You don't say!' Vaughan shook his head, angry Berro had managed to give them the slip. It was as much his fault, as it was Stone's or Manny's, but he didn't plan to apologise for having a go at them.

Manny said, 'He was with us when we came down the steps – '

'Er …' The professor cleared his throat. 'If I may interrupt, does it matter where Berro's gone? He isn't armed and he can't have gone far, anyway, and we really do have more important matters to attend to.'

'The professor's right,' he agreed. 'Forget Berro – let's move on.'

They had passed twenty-four statues – twelve pairs – before he noticed the nigger was no longer with them. Manny was right, Berro had definitely been with them when they came down the steps; now, he was probably high-tailing it back to Harris. No matter. Harris, Berro and the mother of Harris's brat were all living on borrowed time – and the little brat was as good as dead.

Eight pairs of statues on, they came to an arched doorway. Passed through it. He raised his torch, moved it around in a wide arc. Over to the far right, at the very edge of the beam, he spied something that made his pulse race.

The glint of gold.

Stone saw it, too, and shouted, 'Look, over there!'

He got there ahead of Stone and the professor, and at first sight it appeared as if the shelving was made of solid gold. He hoped so, for the shelving extended as far as his torch could illuminate, and rose to nearly five feet. Four rows, each sloping forward, about a foot apart and all stacked with – he didn't know what they were stacked with. Smallish tablets of some description. They looked plastic, but couldn't possibly be, not if they had been down here for hundreds of years.

He took out his combat knife, ignored the professor's protestations and cut into one of the golden uprights, removed a sliver of ... wood, covered with gold leaf.

Cursing under his breath, he picked up one of the tablets. It was hard, smooth and translucent, with parallel grooves running across it. There must be hundreds – no, thousands, of the damn things on the shelves. He turned to the professor. 'What the fuck is this?'

'I, er ...' The professor accepted the tablet, placed it on his palm, turned it over and examined it closely. 'Fascinating, quite fascinating. It appears to be made of crystal, but I've never seen anything like it before, and I wouldn't like to speculate what its function might be – if indeed it has a function.'

'Is it worth anything?' asked Stone.

The professor shrugged. 'I – your guess is as good as mine. I – '

'We're wasting time,' Vaughan cut in. 'Let's see what else we can find.'

Clayton groaned.

'He's coming round ...'

Clayton opened his eyes. His head hurt. Someone, he couldn't immediately see who it was, was patting his forehead. It was dark, except for a beam of white light ... Ross. It was Ross's voice he had heard. It was Ross, knelt beside him, but Gavin was holding the flashlight.   He tried to sit up, couldn't.

'Hey, take it easy, Mr Clayton – you've had a nasty clout on the head.'

'What – happened?'

'Looks like you were attacked.'

It took him a few moments, but he remembered.

The Asian – and the woman.

The woman had hit him over the head with – he didn't know what. Something hard. But the Asian ... Ross helped him to sit up.

He touched his forehead, winced as he felt stickiness he realised must be blood. His blood. Ross had been tending the wound. He asked, 'Where's Hank.'

Silence.

'He's dead, Mr Clayton.' Ross spoke quietly, reverently. 'So is Bobby, and Randy's in a pretty bad way.'

He closed his eyes again, whispered a silent prayer. It didn't stop the anger from bubbling inside him. 'The Asian – he surprised us ... everything happened so quickly.'

He couldn't believe it. He didn't want to believe it. How could something like this have happened? Hank was supposed to be good, very good. Ex-military, as was Randy. Bobby had served with the NYPD. Anti-terrorism. They were good men. Members of the Church, Hank and most of his men. Family men, Hank and Bobby ... silently, he vowed their deaths would be avenged.

'How long have I been out?' he asked, as Ross dressed his head wound.

'I'm not sure, Mr Clayton – about twenty, twenty-five minutes, I think. Landon's taken Randy to the others, he should be back soon. I've asked him to post Alan and Reece at the tunnel entrance.'

He approved. 'Has anyone exited the tunnel?'

'Definitely not, not unless they've found another way out.'

Not likely, not in less than half an hour.

'In that case,' he said, thinking aloud, 'they're still in there.'

'I'm positive they are, Mr Clayton.'

'I want them dead, Ross – I want them all dead.'

Chapter 30

James swore under his breath.

He and Samantha were headed deeper into the tunnel system when the heat signature appeared. He immediately killed his Maglite, and his and Samantha's head lights. He whispered, 'Someone's coming.'

Blackness swallowed them.

She spoke in a whisper. 'I can't see anything.'

Let's hope they can't see us.

No one with Vaughan possessed thermal infa-red imaging, but – they were in a tunnel. Sitting ducks, if someone started shooting. There was nowhere to hide.

Yes, there is!

He grabbed Samantha's arm, guided her back toward to the large recess they'd just passed. Felt along the tunnel wall with his fingertips for it. Found it. 'Get in here, quickly.'

A few seconds later, she was concealed inside one recess, and he was crouched among human remains in the opposite recess, waiting …

Vaughan, Stone, Manny, Alex or the professor?

Not one of the Americans, not unless they had found a way to bypass this tunnel. Unlikely, but not impossible. He peeked out of the recess, silently raised the Beretta 92F semi-automatic pistol he'd taken off the Americans, and watched the twin pools of light grow steadily larger. A head light and a torch. One heat signature. One man, not two …

He waited until the footsteps were three paces away.

'Take one more step and I'll – '

'James!'

He recognised the voice instantly. 'Alex.'

'Fuck me, buddy, what are you trying to do – turn me white?!'

He smiled as he dropped out of the recess, flicked on his Maglite and let Alex see him. 'Black suits you better, especially down here.'

'Yeah, well, I – 'Alex turned around as Samantha popped out of the recess behind him. 'Sami!'

'Alex.'

'What the – ' Alex turned back to him. 'What the fuck are you two doing here?'

'We got a special invite,' he said, 'from the Americans.'

Alex frowned. 'The Yanks are here – in the tunnels?'

'Somewhere not far behind us,' he confirmed.

'How many?'

'Ten, originally,' he answered, 'but two are down – permanently. Number three is no threat, and Clayton's nursing a mighty headache.'

Alex grinned. 'Sounds like you've been busy.'

'Sami chipped in as well – I'm not responsible for Clayton's head.'

Samantha changed the subject. 'How come you're not with the others?'

'All I have to do is turn my lights off and I'm invisible!' Alex laughed at his own joke. 'Seriously, we found some big statues, but I slipped away just as things were starting to get interesting.' He addressed James. 'I was coming back for you,' he said. 'I figured we could take care of Wilko, then come back and deal with Vaughan, Stone and Manny.'

He said, 'Wilko's dead.'

Alex didn't appear surprised. 'You or the Yanks?'

'Not guilty.'

No time to waste, he asked what lie ahead of them, and as he listened to Alex's answer he swung the backpack he had taken from the Americans off his shoulder, unzipped it. Passed a water bottle around and offered high energy bars. Only Alex accepted. He offered Alex something else, too. 'Which do you prefer – a Beretta 92F or a Glock 17?'

Alex's eyes gleamed white in the darkness. 'I'll take a Beretta.'

He approved. Fashioned from steel and black polycarbonate, the Glock 17 was a fine weapon. With seventeen round to a magazine, hence the name, it was light, accurate and powerful. The Beretta 92F was slightly larger, half a pound heavier, and carried two less rounds in a magazine. But it packed more of a punch than the Glock 17 and that, for him, was the deciding factor.

Alex spent a few seconds examining the weapon, before he attached the suppressor he handed him. 'You got anything else in that goody bag of yours?'

'Plenty of spare ammo, plus a couple of Glocks, if we need them.'

Alex grinned. 'Sounds like we're in business!'

'We should go,' he said, aware it wouldn't take the Americans long to regroup, not with Clayton at the helm. He hoped giving in to Samantha, and sparing the American, didn't prove costly. As they headed back the way Alex had come, toward the T-junction he had mentioned, he brought Alex up to speed with what happened when the Americans appeared. He didn't mention the intimacy he'd shared with Samantha on board the *Amazon Dawn V*. That was private. No one else's business. Samantha still loved him, he was certain she did ... he couldn't deny it, he still loved her. They had a son, a young son who had been abducted. A young son he desperately wanted to meet, and get to know – and now, more than ever, he was prepared to do everything within his power to make that happen.

It didn't take them long to retrace Alex's footsteps. He took point, as they approached the steps leading down to the avenue of statues. He crept forward, checked for heat signatures. Nothing. He signalled all clear, and Alex and Samantha joined him. By the light cast by two Maglites, they silently descended the steps.

The large stone statues guarding the path ahead were impressive. Of great interest to the professor, no doubt, but Vaughan was unlikely to have given them more than a passing glance. Valuable? Yes, undoubtedly, but they were far too heavy to move without specialist lifting equipment, and there was no way even twenty men would be able to extract one of the statues from the tunnel system via the route they'd entered it. The statues were simply too big.

They passed through an open doorway framed by ornately carved stone. Samantha was the only one among them with any knowledge of archaeology, but she couldn't identify the small, strange tablets neatly stacked on the gilded shelving.

'I wish my father could have lived to see this,' she said, quietly. 'He was obsessed with proving the Metal Library existed, and finding it, but … I always doubted him. I humoured him, so did my sister, but we always thought the Metal Library was just a myth, like Atlantis and El Dorado.'

James said, 'I didn't believe it existed, either.'

'Or me,' added Alex.

'Looks like we were all wrong.'

Stone discovered the golden skeleton.

Vaughan wanted to know, 'Is it solid gold?'

The skeleton was lying in a large, translucent sarcophagus – hard, perfectly smooth, and intricately sculptured around the edges. Reflective of light, like glass, but not as transparent. Possibly crystal, like the small, flat tablets they had found in their thousands. The sarcophagus dominated a modest sunken vault, in a room adjacent to the library with gilded shelving. There was a three foot wide path all the way around the sarcophagus and, at the skeleton's feet, four steps led up out of the vault. The steps were three feet wide, as was the drop into the vault, on either side of the steps.

'No, I doubt it,' the professor answered, running his hand over the short edge of the sarcophagus. 'I'm inclined to think the skeleton is real but, like the shelving, it has been gilded.'

'Why would someone do that?' asked Manny.

'That is an excellent question, and frankly I have no answer, but that doesn't detract from the fact this is a priceless artefact – absolutely priceless. This gilded skeleton and crystal sarcophagus are, to the best of my knowledge, unique. There isn't a museum in the world that wouldn't jump at the chance to add them to their collection, and they would be willing to pay handsomely to do so.'

'Yeah – and how do you propose we get the damn thing out of here?' asked Stone.

That, Vaughan was beginning to realise, was a challenge he had given far too little thought to, prior to their arrival in South America. But everything they had discovered in the tunnel system must have been brought in from outside, so logic dictated there must be at least one other way out of the tunnels, other than via the river. All they had to do was find it. So far, they had failed to locate another exit but then again, they had only just started to explore, and so far they hadn't found anything that fitted the 'metal library' tag yet, either.

Around the corner from the sunken vault they discovered two – doors?

Set about ten feet apart, they were the right shape and dimensions to be doors, but he had never seen a door encrusted with – what? Precious stones? Semi-precious stones? He played his torch over the surface of the first door, and then his hand. The jewels were huge, bigger than his thumb nail. Some with sharp edges, some smooth. Some coloured, some clear. They reflected the beam of his torch in a dazzling rainbow. The purple stones he guessed must be amethysts, but he couldn't identify most of the others and the clear ones ... he dared to hope they might be diamonds. There was only one way to find out. He shielded himself from the professor, who he knew wouldn't approve, and nicked the surface of one of the clear gems with his combat knife. It scratched easily. Silently, he swore. Quartz, possibly, but definitely not diamond. A pity. Diamonds were relatively small, easily portable, and extremely valuable. Just a pocketful of diamonds, and he would be able to live the life he aspired to become accustomed to.

The professor was in his element. Loving every second of it. Ecstatic. Vaughan doubted he would be any happier in the company of a harem of nubile virgins. But even the professor couldn't say for certain if the doors were what they appeared to be.

'There are no handles, and no hinges are visible,' the professor observed, 'but yes – I do believe they are doors, *sealed* doors.'

'Leading where?' he asked.

'Sealed doors invariably lead into tombs,' the professor replied. 'The fact the doors are still sealed suggests the tombs must be intact – and that is an incredibly exciting prospect.'

Vaughan leaned against the encrusted surface, pushed hard, but he felt no give. Manny joined him, and together they tried again. Nothing. The door, if it was a door, was solid as a brick wall ... but tombs? Maybe, maybe not. They had already found numerous recesses filled with old bones, plus the gilded skeleton – someone of much higher status, obviously. A king, perhaps – so why sealed tombs as well?

'We could blast our way in,' suggested Stone.

Manny grinned. 'Where's the cock-sucking monkey when you want him?'

'Running back to his boyfriend for a quickie!'

Reminded Berro had given them the slip, Vaughan nevertheless found a smile. He didn't believe the nigger and Paki were lovers but the image conjured by Stone's quip still amused him. Losing Berro didn't. There was, in Stone's backpack, a brick of C4 and a box of blasting caps, and he had drafted Berro on team because of his knowledge of explosives. If he did decide to blast one of the tomb doors open, Berro would know exactly how much C4 to use, and where best to plant the charge. He could guess, but if he guessed wrong and used too much ...

Less than ten minutes later, they made another stunning discovery – one that had the professor in absolute raptures.

'This is it – this is it ...' Almost reverently, the professor ran his hand over one of the huge metal books resting on the gilded shelving. 'No one believed me, no one believed the Metal Library existed but it does, it really does exist and we've found it. We've actually found it ...'

Vaughan followed two lines of gilded shelving with his torch, thrilled to see the dazzling frames extended into the blackness. Three rows on each side, and each shelve was a couple of inches higher at the back than the front, where there was a decorated lip to stop the large metal books from sliding off. The books, which lay flat, measured about two by two and a half feet, and were several inches thick. Side-by-side, beautiful and ornate, the majority of the volumes were silvery-black in colour. Tarnished silver? He was more interested in the unmistakable gleam of gold.

He examined the front cover of one of the golden tomes, studied geometric designs and ideographs reminiscent of Egyptian hieroglyphs, but different. He lifted the cover as far as the shelf above allowed, shone his torch inside, saw more ideographs and written inscriptions he couldn't comprehend on the first page. Other pages he checked, too. He closed it, set his torch down on the adjoining volume, and gently lifted the book off the shelf. It was heavy. Forty, forty-five pounds, he judged. This one volume alone must be worth ... he didn't know. But a small fortune, however much a small fortune is. And they had discovered – what? Dozens of metal books, at the very least. More likely, hundreds, or even thousands. A whole damn library.

Vaughan didn't realise they had company until it was too late.

Chapter 31

'Freeze – or I'll shoot!'

James's tone was coldly matter-of-fact, and Samantha stayed well back when he and Alex stepped forward – flicked on their torches. The men they had crept up on did freeze, momentarily, like four rabbits caught in the glare of a car's headlights at midnight.

'Get your hands up,' James ordered, 'where I can see them.'

The four men, as they turned toward James and Alex, started to raise their hands – then, suddenly, Stone reached for the pistol tucked into his belt.

She watched what happened next in terrible slow motion.

The pistol in James's hand was aimed at Vaughan, who was standing between her husband and Stone. Manny was next to Stone, furthest away. Stone's hand grabbed hold of his pistol, yanked it out of his belt. James's aim shifted from Vaughan to Stone. Stone started to raise his pistol ... a deadly race Stone lost.

James didn't hesitate.

The elongated pistol in his hand coughed.

She gasped, as a deep crimson stain suddenly appeared on Stone's T-shirt. It spread quickly as, reflexively, he clutched at his chest. Blood seeped through his fingers. Hands bloody, he staggered, took a step backward ... he stared at James ... at Alex ... at James again ... unable to hold his own weight, his legs started to buckle under him.

The pistol in James's hand coughed again.

Propelled backward, Stone crashed into the golden shelving behind him, as the second bullet tore into his upper chest. Still clutching himself, he raised his head, eyes wide open. He glared at James ... opened his mouth, tried to speak, but only blood bubbled out ... he toppled forward, and his body twitched once. Then he lay still.

James looked at Vaughan and Manny, 'Anyone else fancy their chances?'

No one moved.

No one spoke.

She closed her eyes and buried her face in her hands. Images of Stone's execution didn't go away. She told herself, over and over again, it was Stone's own stupid fault. If he hadn't gone for his gun, James wouldn't have shot him and ...

That's three men he's killed!

And it would have been five, if she hadn't stopped him.

'Frisk them, Alex,' said James, calmly. 'I'll cover you.'

Alex grinned. 'My pleasure.'

She opened her eyes again as Alex approached Vaughan. Before frisking him, Alex glanced at her husband, Richard.

'You can relax, professor – it's these two bastards we want, not you.'

'Yes, yes – of course.' Richard slowly lowered his hands. 'Thank you, I … ' He turned to her, as if noticing her for the first time, and asked, 'Um, may I join my wife?'

'You may,' said James, as Alex frisked Vaughan, 'but please stay out of my line of fire.'

Richard repeated, 'Yes, yes – of course.'

Alex ejected the magazine from Vaughan's pistol, before he tossed it and the magazine into the darkness. They raced across the stone floor with a metallic clatter. Alex found a knife, got rid of that as well.

'Samantha, darling,' said Richard, speaking in a low voice as he took a circuitous route toward her, 'what on earth are you doing here? I thought you said you couldn't swim?'

'I can't, but James – the Americans took us prisoner.' She couldn't bring herself to meet her husband's gaze, scared he might read her infidelity in her eyes. But that, she told herself, was absurd. Absolutely ludicrous. Even in bright sunlight, no man could read her or anyone else's mind, just by looking at them. Down here, so far underground … she forced herself to meet Richard's gaze. 'The Americans, they shot Wilko and threatened to kill me if James didn't show them where the secret entrance was.'

The whites of her husband's eyes grew. 'The Americans are here, in the tunnels?'

She nodded. 'Somewhere – seven or eight of them, at least. The rest are outside. They've taken over our boat and …'

As she leaned into him, to hug him, she felt her husband's left arm snake around her back. He held her loosely for a moment, before he shifted position – stepped behind her. Suddenly, his arm whipped around her chest, just beneath her breasts, and her back was touching his chest. He tightened his grip and his arm pressed into her ribs, so much it hurt. She couldn't breathe properly. She didn't realise what her husband was doing until it was too late to stop him.

'Richard, I – ' She saw the small pistol in his right hand.

Oh, God …

Her husband raised the pistol – pressed the muzzle against her temple.

'Richard, what – '

'Shut up, bitch!'

She barely recognised her husband's voice, it was so harsh. 'Richard, I don't – I thought – '

'You thought what I wanted you to think,' he snarled. 'Drop your gun, Harris – or the mother of your bastard son dies.'

'Take it easy, professor.'

James took in the situation at a glance, instantly realised he had misread the professor – badly. But the professor had positioned himself behind Samantha, shielded from him and Alex, and he was holding a stubby, compact pistol to her head. A SIG Sauer P238. Single action, .380 calibre, with a six round box magazine. Small, but as lethal as any other pistol at point blank range. There was nothing he or Alex could do, without endangering Samantha's life.

'You heard the professor,' said Vaughan, with a smirk. 'Drop your weapon, Harris – now! You as well, Berro.'

He spent a second or two weighing his options. Silently assessing, evaluating … he was within striking distance of the professor, but Samantha was in the way and the professor was holding a lethal weapon to her head. Vaughan and Manny were out of range, but only by a few feet. Alex was closer to them, but …

It's too risky.

The professor squeezed Samantha's arm, caused her to yelp. 'Harris, I'm warning you … '

'Relax, professor.' He showed the professor the butt of his Beretta, before he bent down and placed the semi-automatic pistol on the ground about six inches in front of him. Alex followed his lead, and did the same with his weapon.

'Kick – ' Vaughan started to speak, but Samantha got in first.

'Richard, please – I don't understand. I – '

'Do I have to spell it out for you,' the professor barked, 'you stupid bitch?!'

Thank you, Sami.

He didn't kick his Beretta anywhere. Nor did Alex. He did shift his weight to the balls of his feet, poised, just waiting for an opening.

Samantha twisted her head, tried to look at her husband. Couldn't quite manage it, he was grasping her so firmly against his chest. 'Richard, I – I don't understand – '

'I don't love you, bitch – I never have.'

She sounded increasingly desperate. 'But – I'm your wife – '

'Not for much longer,' the professor declared. His face contorted with loathing. 'Why do you think I let you talk me into allowing you to accompany us? I'll tell you why. The jungle is an extremely dangerous

169

place, that's why. I *wanted* you here. Here, now we have found the Metal Library, I can easily get rid of you – without having to divorce you.'

Tears welled in her eyes. 'But ... why ...?'

'Why?' The professor growled, 'You ask me why?'

'He used you like the whore you are.' Vaughan was wearing a smug grin. 'I mean, come on, two half-caste brats by two different Pakis ...' His grin widened. 'A pretty thing like you, I expect spreading your legs was quite lucrative – '

'How dare you!' she blasted, struggling to escape her husband's grip, but he held her firm. 'How dare you, you – you – '

James suppressed his rising anger, forced himself to ignore the accusation, ignore the racist slurs. Stay calm, keep his breathing and heartbeat steady. Stay focussed. Ready for action.

The professor pressed the SIG Sauer into Samantha's ear. 'You can blame your father, if it makes you feel better to have someone to blame. He was the world's foremost authority on the Metal Library, but he refused to share his knowledge with anyone. I thought if I could get close to you he would start to trust me, but he didn't – not even after I married you. He graciously let me fund our joint visit to Cuenco last year, but I knew the sly bastard was holding out on me – I suspected he possessed information he wasn't sharing with me and I was right!'

Suddenly everything made sense.

The professor and Vaughan are working together.

James didn't know when or how the pair had met, but how else would have Vaughan have learned he had a son before he did, if the professor didn't tell him? Samantha certainly hadn't. But the identity of the fathers of her two sons, surely, was something Samantha must have discussed with her husband at some point. Of course she would. And how else did Vaughan get hold of a recent photograph of Luke and Joshua, if not via the professor? Snapped, he figured, on a beach in Tenerife just a day or two before his son was abducted.

There was something he needed to know, but he was almost too afraid to ask. 'What about Luke?'

He addressed his question to the professor, but Vaughan answered. 'What about him?'

He faced Vaughan. 'Is he still alive?'

'He is,' said Vaughan, with a grin, 'but don't get too excited. I assure you, the little brat's days are numbered – as are yours.'

Relief surged through him like a stimulant.

My son is alive!

Not only that, Samantha's marriage was as good as over – a total sham. It wasn't going to be easy for her, coming to terms with living a lie for the past year or more, but …

If I can get Luke back …

Tears streamed down Samantha's cheeks. The professor was still holding her close, so tight she wasn't strong enough to escape his grip, but he noticed the SIG Sauer had drifted a few inches away from her head. Not ideal, not by a long way. But, he judged, as good as it was going to get.

He glanced at Alex, surreptitiously used his index finger to indicate himself, and then the professor. Alex's nod was so faint he would have missed it, if he hadn't been watching for it. No chance anyone else had noticed, not under such poor lighting.

Manny spoke. 'We should kill them now.'

'I agree,' said Vaughan. 'We've wasted enough time. Harris, kick your weapon toward me. Berro, kick yours toward Manny – and no funny business.'

He nodded compliance.

He used his right foot to kick his Beretta – hard.

Alex did the same to his – equally hard.

The two weapons skidded across the stone floor, flashed passed Vaughan and Manny, and on into the darkness. As they did so, while his attention was momentarily distracted, he launched himself at the professor. Simultaneously, Alex attacked Vaughan and Manny – kicked Vaughan in the groin and smashed Manny across the chest with his forearm.

He snatched at the wrist gripping the SIG Sauer – too late to stop the professor squeezing the trigger. But, in his haste, the professor missed Samantha's head by two inches. The unsuppressed retort rang in his ears. Samantha stamped on the professor's foot, managed to wriggle out of his deadly embrace, and he lunged for the professor's wrist again. Caught it. He tightened his grip, yanked the professor's arm down, away from Samantha. The professor was stronger than he looked, and he didn't release the SIG Sauer.

The professor did squeeze the trigger again.

Chapter 32

Clayton froze as a shot rang out.

He held up his hand, to silently call a halt. There were four of his men with him. All alert, all armed. No one spoke. Everyone waited …

They were in a library of sorts, but not the Metal Library that he was so desperate to locate. He'd never seen anything like the strange, flat tablets filling the gilded shelves before. They reminded him, in terms of their size, of cuneiform tablets, but the latter were made of clay and had pictographs impressed into them, and were more than two thousand years old. These tablets were smooth as glass, and translucent; his best guess was rock crystal. The tablets did have some markings on them, but no pictographs or anything that resembled writing, and it was impossible to ascertain their age. His gut instinct told him they were old. Very old. They must be, given how long this tunnel system had remained a secret. So who had made them? The Incas? Most unlikely. An older, lost civilisation? It was an intriguing possibility, but there was no firm evidence, either way. Nothing to suggest what function, if any, the tablets performed.

He leaned toward Ross, spoke in a low voice. 'How far ahead of us do you reckon the shooter is?'

'It's difficult to tell, Mr Clayton. The acoustics down here are really weird, and – '

A second shot rang out.

Then silence.

'What d'you reckon they shooting at?' whispered Landon.

What – or who?

Ross said, 'I wish I knew.'

Clayton silently echoed Ross's sentiments, thinking it would help his cause greatly if the English mercenaries had fallen out, and were shooting at each other. Killing each other … over the kidnapped boy? The shots had definitely originated somewhere ahead of them, not behind. That meant it had to be the professor's team. By his reckoning, assuming the Asian and the professor's wife had caught up with the others, their rivals now out-numbered his advance party by six to five. But, as the Asian had revealed, the six were *not* united. And they included the professor and his wife, who shouldn't pose too much of a threat. On the other hand, the six also included the Asian, who had already proven how lethal he could be, given half a chance.

Losing Hank was a massive blow. He missed the big man's presence almost as much as he missed his advice, which invariably proved spot on. Briefly, he considered his options.

The professor and his mercenaries were ahead of them, and to the best of his knowledge there was only one way out of the tunnel system. The same way they had all entered. Keen as he was to press on, catch up with the opposition, wipe them out and explore further, he decided to send Landon back to where Alan, Reece and the injured Randy were stationed, with instructions that Reece go back to the boat for reinforcements.

Something this important couldn't be rushed.

Vaughan and Manny scarpered.

On the floor, breathing hard and hurting where the German had landed a vicious blow to his kidneys, Alex couldn't stop them fleeing into the blackness. Reaching for his Maglite, which he had dropped when he and the German wrestled each other to the ground, he was more worried about James and Samantha. He knew the professor's first round had gone astray, hit no one, but the second shot …

He turned toward James, Samantha and the professor, shone his Maglite at them. Saw James was holding on to the professor, as he gently lowered him to the ground. The professor's eyes were wide and staring. Samantha was standing close by, leaning over her husband, with her hand over her mouth, muttering, 'Oh, God … oh, God …'

He's been shot!

Not James – the professor.

The pistol, he recognised it as a compact SIG Sauer, slipped out of the professor's out-stretched right hand as James laid him down. It dropped harmlessly to the ground by his side. James was blocking his view of the professor's upper torso, so he couldn't see where the professor had been hit until he stepped closer … he saw it was a chest wound. A bad one. A sucking wound, by the look of it. Briefly, he and James exchanged glances, but James didn't say anything. He didn't have to. They both knew, even if they could summon immediate emergency medical assistance, the professor's chances weren't good. So far underground, so far from civilisation, the treacherous bastard was as good as dead.

James left the professor's side, came over and placed a hand of his shoulder. 'I'm going after Vaughan and Manny,' he said quietly, as he shrugged off his backpack. 'Take care of Sami for me.'

James took off without waiting for a reply.

He drew in a deep breath, before he approached Samantha, and knelt beside her. She didn't acknowledge his presence. Tears flowing freely,

173

she stared at her dying husband, as he tried to raise his head. The professor opened his mouth, tried to talk, but no sound came out. Blood frothed between his lips, trickled into his goatee. He coughed violently, several times, spitting blood. Face creased with pain, he tried again. More blood bubbled from his mouth and nose. He managed, 'I'm … s-sorr …'

Then he died.

I'm sorry, my ass.

Sorry it had ended like this, maybe, but sorry for using Samantha? He didn't believe the bastard, not for a moment. He put his arm around Samantha's shoulder. She turned toward him, grasped him, and he held her close as racking sobs shook her. She cried for several minutes, before she became quiet and still in his arms. It was another minute or so before she raised her head off his chest. She wiped her eyes with the back of her hand and he hesitated.

What do you say, to the widow of a man who's not only used and betrayed you, but has murdered your father and threatened to kill you as well?

And, he reckoned, the professor must have played a pivotal role in the abduction of her and James's son as well. He might have been able to tell them where the kid was being held, if he was still alive. Quietly, he asked, 'You okay?'

'No, not really,' she answered. 'I – I'm sorry. I …'

'Nothing to be sorry for,' he said. 'This isn't your fault.'

'I know, but – I can't believe Richard – I didn't know, I swear I didn't know.'

'No one said you did,' he assured her. 'He used you and he fooled us – big time.'

She looked around. 'Where's James?'

'Gone looking for answers.' Seeing her worried expression, he added, 'Don't worry, he can take care of himself.'

She didn't say anything.

He unzipped the backpack James had left behind, had a quick look-see and selected a Glock 17 he'd rejected earlier. He spent necessary seconds checking the pistol, pleased to discover it was in good nick, with a full magazine.

'The Yanks will have heard the shots,' he said, as he zipped the backpack and slung it over his shoulder. 'We can't stay here.'

She nodded faintly, and let him help her to her feet. She asked, 'Where are we going?'

Good question.

The Yanks were behind them, and Vaughan and Manny had taken off somewhere, too, with James hot on their trail. Ahead – he had no idea what lie ahead, and he wasn't terribly interested in finding out. Not anymore. This had started out as an adventure, a treasure hunt, but his priorities changed when James told him about his abducted son. Now, they had found priceless treasures and, although he wasn't dumb enough to speak his mind in Samantha's presence, he had a bad, bad feeling about the kid.

'I reckon,' he said, 'we should keep a low profile. If we can sneak past the Yanks, we can head back to the river and – '

'No, not the river,' she cut in. 'I can't – not again.'

'Sami, it might be the only way out of here.'

Chapter 33

The heat signature was twenty yards away, crouched low – hiding.

James halted, trying to fathom the lie of the ground between him and his bright orange-red target ... Vaughan or Manny? He had no way of knowing the identity of the signature. But, clearly, the pair must have split up. Not the smartest move, on their part, but he wasn't complaining. Vaughan, unless he'd taken a firearm off Manny, was unarmed. Alex hadn't had time to frisk the German, disarm him, before the professor demonstrated where his true loyalties lie. He doubted Manny had been carrying more than one piece. So, Vaughan might be armed, and he might not. Same went for the German. One, but probably not both. Fifty-fifty. Not bad odds, especially since he had been so focused on chasing after them, he hadn't stopped to take a Glock out of the backpack before he left it with Alex, hadn't thought to grab the professor's SIG Sauer before he took off.

The signature was a good three feet lower than the ground he was standing on. Steps leading down, maybe. Or another sunken vault, similar to the one they had discovered with the golden skeleton nestled in a translucent sarcophagus. Trouble was, he couldn't see a damn thing through the thermal infa-red imager except body heat ... slowly, cautiously, he edged forward. A few inches at a time, testing the ground ahead of him with his toes, keen to avoid any nasty surprises. He had closed the distance between him and his target by five yards when he reached a decision.

As noiselessly as he could, never taking his eyes off the huddled heat signature, he sank to his knees. Then he leaned forward, slowly lowered himself to the ground, until he was lying flat on his stomach. A much smaller target now, he started to shimmy forward, but he'd only gained a foot or two when whoever it was heard him or sensed his presence.

'Boss, is that you?'

A low, anxious voice.

Manny.

He waited a moment, let the tension build, then said, 'Put your – '

'*You!*'

'Put your hands up – *now!*' he growled.

Two ghostly red limbs slowly rose.

So far, so good.

Manny was assuming he was armed.

He needed to get closer, but he couldn't see where he was going, not through the goggles. What he needed now was his Maglite. But if he killed the infa-red imager and flicked his Maglite on, the sudden brightness would blind him. It would blind the German, too, especially if he aimed the beam directly at him. Low on options, and gambling he would recover at least as fast as Manny, he quickly made the switch.

His head, literally, was inches away from the edge of a sunken vault – empty, apart from the German, who was crouched on the far side near some steps. No time to waste, he leapt into the vault, but he was still ten yards away when the German raised his pistol – got off a wild shot.

He cursed under his breath, but instead of pressing home his advantage, the German scrabbled up the steps and fled. He raced after him, leapt out of the vault – dived for his legs and took him down. Manny hit the ground hard. Before he could recover, he snatched hold of his wrist, twisted it savagely. The pistol, a Heckler & Koch P7, clattered harmlessly to the ground. Giving him no time to resist, he flipped the German over and straddled his chest, pinning his thick arms down with his knees. Breathing hard, adrenalin pumping, he thumbed his head light on. He glared at the German and spoke in a low, threatening tone.

'I want to know where the boy is, and I want to know now.'

'What boy, I don't – '

'Samantha's son.' *My* son. 'I want to know where he's being held – and you're going to tell me.'

'Fuck you!' Manny spat on his cheek, and struggled to free himself, but he tightened his grip and held him down. 'I don't know anything about her fuckin' son.'

'I think you do.'

Time to get nasty.

He let the German see the Blackie Collins CIA Folder in his right hand – a spring assisted, folding lock knife with a razor sharp, partially serrated blade made of thirty-three per cent glass fibre Nylon 66.

Manny's eyes widened with fright as he lowered the Blackie, held it to his throat. The German tried wriggling free, but to no avail.

'If I had more time, I might borrow one of Vaughan's favourite tricks,' he said, 'and castrate you – force you to eat your own balls.'

The German's eyes bulged in their sockets.

'Lucky for you, I'm in a hurry, so here's how we're going to play this.' He increased the pressure on the Blackie, just enough to draw blood. 'I'm going to count to three – then, if you haven't told me what I want to know, I'm going to slit your throat.'

He waited a moment.

'One ...'

The German squirmed, but there was no way he could free himself – no way he could escape the blade threatening his life.

'Please, I – Vaughan will kill me if I tell you.'

'And I'll kill you if you don't – and guess who's holding a Blackie to your throat.' He pressed the serrated blade into his throat again, drew more blood, which trickled down the German's thick neck.

Manny's eyes were wild. 'You will kill me anyway, if I tell – '

'No, I won't,' he cut in. 'I'm not like Vaughan. Tell me what I want to know, and I swear on my mother's grave I'll let you live.'

He didn't let it show, but he was sweating almost as much as the German. If he reached 'three' and Manny didn't crumble, he didn't know what he was going to do.

'Two …'

Showing no sign of weakness, he increased the pressure on the Blackie again, cut deeper. Caused blood to flow more freely. He waited a long moment, before opening his mouth to say, 'Three.'

'No, please – I will tell you,' said Manny, frantically, 'but please, you must promise you won't kill me.'

'I promise,' he said, keeping his tone neutral.

Tears spilled down the German's cheeks.

'I'm waiting …'

'Morocco – the boy is in Morocco.'

Nice guess, Alex.

'Whereabouts in Morocco?'

'Casablanca – at the harbour, on a boat.'

Manny told him the name of the boat.

'How many are holding him?'

'Three – two men, one woman.'

He guessed they were probably the same trio who had abducted his son in Tenerife. He was confident he could handle them – if he got there in time.

If it isn't already too late.

Vaughan had claimed his son was still alive.

The little brat's days are numbered – as are yours.

Again, he asked, 'Is the boy still alive?'

'*Ja* – yes.' The German nodded slightly. 'He is alive, but Vaughan – he has already sent a message.'

'A message – to the kidnappers?'

Another nod.

Fearing the worse, James forced himself to ask, 'What did the message say?'

'It was to tell them when to get rid of the boy.'

*

'I can't believe he killed my father.'

Stunned by her husband's betrayal and his violent death, Samantha was standing behind Alex, so close she could feel his body heat. She still felt cold. Very cold. Alex shone his torch into a small room they had stumbled across, along one side of the Metal Library ... still reeling, she couldn't comprehend how she had been so gullible, for so long. Now Richard had spelled it out, it was so obvious she must have been blind not to see it happening, but she hadn't.

She loved him, and he'd told her he loved her.

It was a lie.

All this time, she had believed he was interested in her and so he was – but only as a way of getting closer to her father, winning his trust, so he would share his research about the Metal Library. But her father never really took to Richard, never really ... she'd been living a lie for the past year. Longer, if she counted their courtship and the months leading up to their wedding. She felt stupid. She felt sick. Angry, too. Angry and scared. Scared because she was trapped far underground with no easy way out, scared because people were dying ... scared because she hadn't seen her four year old son for fifteen days, and she might never see him again.

She had accepted her father's death for what it appeared to be: a tragic accident. That is what the police concluded, and it hadn't occurred to her they might be making a serious error.

But now she knew the house fire that claimed her father's life was no accident, now she knew ...

Richard killed him!

Alex shifted slightly, and turned to face her. Having told her that he only had one spare set of batteries, they had agreed to turn off their head lights, and use Alex's torch. His Maglite, as he called it. Even though they were only inches apart, she couldn't see his dark face, not clearly.

'Sami, I – he probably didn't do it himself, not personally.'

'But he arranged it.'

He didn't deny it.

'Looks that way,' he agreed. 'Best guess is Vaughan, maybe with one or two of the others, carried it out – made it look like an accident.'

She didn't say anything.

'I'm sorry, Sami – I'm really sorry.'

She didn't say anything.

My father is dead – murdered!

Her husband was dead, too.

So was Stone, and Wilko, and Tommo, and Gately, and two nameless Americans – but Vaughan was still alive, and so was Manny. And James.

If anything happens to him ...

'James called it,' he said, 'when we were back in London, but I wasn't convinced.'

She didn't hide her shock. 'James *knew!*'

'Uh-uh, he didn't know anything,' he replied, 'but he had his suspicions – about Vaughan, not your husband. The professor fooled us all.'

Silence.

Alex shifted again, and swept the beam of his torch into the small side room, stepped into it. She followed. As he played his torch around, she saw the room was rectangular, about four by six yards. The walls were bare, but glassy and perfectly vertical and square, like the tunnel walls. There was a stone shelf along each long side, waist high and two feet deep. The shelves were bare, as was the room itself, apart from a four foot high hexagonal pedestal carved out of the bedrock, located centrally at the far end of the room. Atop the pedestal was a tall, stylised statue of a cat – almost certainly a jaguar – sitting on its haunches. Black, beautifully carved and highly polished. Granite, maybe, and the eyes – when the white beam of Alex's torch reached them, the cat's eyes came alive, glowing fiery red.

'Nice cat,' he said, halting in front of the statue.

An understatement, but she didn't say anything.

He shrugged the backpack off his shoulder, on to the stone shelf to his left. A moment later he found her hand, pressed a plastic bottle into it. 'Here, you need to keep your fluids topped up.'

She wasn't thirsty, but he insisted, so she raised the bottle to her lips and took a sip. The water was tepid, but she took another sip, and another; she could easily have drained the whole bottle if she hadn't stopped herself. So much for not being thirsty. She passed the bottle back to him, said, 'You should have a drink.'

'I'm fine.' She heard him twist the cap back on the bottle. 'Sami, when you were on the boat with James, before the Yanks turned up ...'

She held her breath.

'... James didn't happen to use the radio, did he?'

She breathed, and looked at him. 'As a matter of fact, he did.'

'Excellent.'

'How did you know – '

A shot rang out.

Chapter 34

'I don't know, I don't know – I swear I don't know!' cried Manny, sweating under the harsh white glow of the Paki's head light. Tears blurred his vision. He felt the hot flush of urine between his legs, as he lost control of his bladder. 'Please,' he begged, 'Vaughan didn't tell me – he didn't tell anyone!'

The Paki glared down at him for a long moment, with dark, unfathomable eyes that scared the hell out of him. But he wasn't lying. He really didn't know what date Vaughan had specified for the boy's execution, but he knew it must be any day now, if the boy hadn't already been killed. It was too late for the Paki to save the boy, he felt sure of that, and he was glad. He knew the cock-sucking son-of-a-whore was going to slit his throat anyway, despite having promised to let him live, now he had told him where the boy was. It is what he would do, if their positions were reversed.

It didn't happen.

His relief was palpable, as he felt the blade lift away from his throat. Casual as you like, the Paki wiped it on his sleeve, and slipped the knife back into a leather sheath strapped to his thigh.

'I'm going to let you up now – nice and easy.'

He couldn't believe his good fortune. The crazy Paki bastard was going to keep his word, and let him live … he bided his time, waited until he felt the Paki's weight start to lift off his arms and chest – then he struck, raising his hips suddenly, as powerfully and as high as he could.

His move took the Paki by surprise, knocked him off balance, and before the Paki could recover he quickly rolled to his left. The Paki hit the ground and, as he did so, he swung his leg – kicked the Paki on the head, dislodging his fancy goggles. The Paki dropped his flashlight. He pressed home his advantage, kicking the Paki again, and again, and again, as his eyes frantically searched the ground for his pistol.

He couldn't see it anywhere, spun around just in time to block a punch the Paki aimed at his head. And another, thrown to his chest. Back in London, the Paki had gotten lucky, taken him by surprise and humiliated him. Not this time. This time he was going to teach the Paki a lesson he wouldn't forget. Pumped up, confidence soaring, he followed through with a punch of his own, slammed his meaty fist into the Paki's shoulder. Hit him hard. Sent the mother-fucker reeling. Before he could recover he hit the Paki again, harder, and when the Paki tried to get up he kicked his legs from under him.

He roared like a lion as he dived on top of the Paki – pummelled him with his fists. Then, suddenly, the Paki grasped his wrists. Yanked him forward, pulled him down and over his head, as the Paki squirmed from beneath him and pushed him on the ground. Cursing in German, he was poised to launch himself at the Paki again when he spotted his pistol, at the edge of the beam of light cast by the Paki's flashlight.

The Paki followed his gaze, saw the pistol a split second after he did. The weapon was only three feet away from him, six or seven feet away from the Paki. There was no way the Paki could reach it first and they both knew it. As he dived for the pistol, the Paki scrambled to his feet and turned to flee.

The Paki wasn't quick enough.

He snatched the pistol up, swung it around and squeezed the trigger.

His first shot missed, but he fired again, and again.

The force of the bullets ripping into his back propelled the Paki forward, and the Paki was already going down, when he shot him again.

The Paki disappeared.

Quickly, he retrieved the Paki's flashlight, shone the beam where he'd last seen him. Nothing. But his puzzlement faded, as white light picked out the sharp, gently curved edge of the sunken vault he had taken refuge in, after he'd become separated from Vaughan. The Paki must have fallen into it. He listened intently, for any sign of life, but all he heard was the sound of his own heavy breathing.

Cautiously, with his pistol raised and his forefinger on the trigger, he approached the vault and glanced over the edge. He couldn't see anything. Flashlight in his left hand, pistol in his right, he took another small pace forward, and another … the Paki was in the vault, close to the side, lying on his back. His arms and legs were spread untidily, his eyes were closed, and his face was a bloody mask. He looked dead.

Like a corpse in a grave.

A broad grin creased his face.

'That's what you get, you cock-sucking faggot,' he muttered in German, 'if you mess with Dieter Zimmerman.'

Wallowing in his triumph, he couldn't resist a little target practice. At close range, with a static target, he couldn't miss.

One, two, three …

The Paki's corpse jerked slightly, as each bullet tore into it.

… four, five …

Shame he didn't have some gold paint and a glass cage to toss the Paki in.

… six, seven …

The pistol clicked.

He was out of ammo.

He grinned again, as he stuffed the pistol down the front of his shorts. If he wasn't dead when he fell into the vault, the mother-fucker definitely was now. He couldn't wait to catch up with Vaughan again – tell him that he, Manny, had taken care of the troublesome Paki.

The shot made them both jump.

Stepping back, Alex immediately clicked his Maglite off, plunged the side room into darkness. Samantha, standing close beside him, audibly gasped. He held his breath for a long moment. The retort was so loud, and sounded so close, he was desperate to know who the shooter was, and who or what they were shooting at.

Silence.

The darkness was absolute.

He waited, listening … heard nothing.

Samantha's arm brushed against his, and she whispered, 'Sorry.'

'No worries,' he whispered back.

But he was worried, and not just about the shot they had heard. He liked Samantha, but he really didn't need the responsibility of having to babysit her, not now. But even if James hadn't asked him to take care of her, he couldn't have left her on her own, not down here with so many armed hostiles wandering about. He wished he knew the outcome of James's radio contact, but he didn't.

Quietly, he asked her if James had said anything about the call, but her answer was negative. So, until he learned different, he had to assume he, Samantha and James were on their own. Vaughan and Manny were still a threat, but he was far more concerned about the Yanks, who out-numbered them in the tunnel system and had taken control of their river boat – and the river was the only way out of this hell hole.

Aiming it at his feet, where it was less likely to reveal their presence, he flicked on his Maglite – immediately killed it again as another shot rang out.

And another, and another, and another.

What the fuck?!

Samantha leaned closer, gripped his arm. He could feel her trembling. A chill ran up his spine. The Glock 17 in his hand didn't have a conventional safety catch. Instead, on the trigger, there was an extractor with an elevated flat that is obvious visually in good light. Reflexively, he caressed it with his fingertip, and waited. He didn't know who the trigger happy shooter was, but he couldn't shake a bad, bad feeling in the pit of his stomach.

Silence.

Still he waited, torn between staying put for a few minutes to see how things panned out, and making a move. Samantha was still holding his arm. He couldn't see her, but he automatically turned toward her. 'Sami, I think – '

Another shot silenced him.

It was followed, in quick succession, by six more.

He swore under his breath and she grasped his arm tighter. He didn't like it, he didn't like it one bit.

A single shot, four shots, seven shots.

The sequence didn't make any sense.

Chapter 35

Clayton paced.

He halted briefly, when he heard four shots, and exchanged glances with Ross. The shooter was somewhere ahead of them – how far, it was impossible to judge. It had to be one of the English mercenaries, but why? What were they shooting at? He wondered, again, if they were fighting amongst themselves. Or had they run into some kind of trouble? If so, what kind of trouble? Five shots had been fired in a matter of minutes. He didn't like not knowing why. He didn't like the threat the mercenaries posed. Until re-enforcements arrived, the professor's team out-numbered them, and the Asian among them had already demonstrated they were highly trained – and willing to kill.

'Landon should be back by now,' he said.

Ross nodded. 'I was thinking the same thing.'

'So where is he?'

Ross shrugged, but he didn't appear concerned. 'He must have been delayed,' he replied. 'Don't worry, Mr Clayton, I'm sure he'll be – '

Another shot silenced him.

It was followed by six more.

He looked at Ross, but neither of them spoke. His head was alive with unanswered questions. One way or another, the English professor and his mercenaries must be in serious trouble … he was close, so close, and no one was going to stand in his way of achieving his dream. The Metal Library was down here somewhere, he could feel it, and he was determined to find it. Only then could he make those who excommunicated him from the Church grovel, before he laid out the terms for his return. Number one on the list: a place on the Church's presiding body, the Quorum of the Twelve.

The Church, in common with many so-called Christian institutions, had gone soft in recent years, shackled by the increasingly outspoken and influential 'PC' brigade. Whoever heard such nonsense as one man being permitted to marry another man, or two women marrying each other? And yet, astonishingly, the way things were headed same gender marriage would become perfectly legal across the States within the next few years. Just one example, but it was symptomatic of the country's – the *world's* – moral decline. He firmly believed the average American was crying out for someone to stand up and shout 'enough is enough!'

Someone to lead the fight back. He could do it, he was confident he could do it, but first …

'Let's go,' he said, addressing the men with him. 'We're going back.'

Ross asked, 'To the boat?'

'To where Alan and Reece are waiting with Randy,' he clarified. 'Landon should be with them, if he's not already on his way back.'

'And then?'

'Then we wait for re-enforcements.'

'Shit!'

Even as he hissed the expletive, darkness enveloped them again, as Alex switched off his torch. Samantha was so close behind him, she couldn't stop herself, before she bumped into his backpack.

'Someone's coming,' he whispered, as she steadied herself.

They were only a foot or two from exiting the side room, home to the magnificent black jaguar, after she'd reluctantly agreed they should try to head back the same way they had come. The alternative – to head even deeper into the unknown – frightened her more. But she knew the Americans stood between them and the river, and feared they would be inclined to shoot first and ask questions later, following their brutal encounter with James.

The river …

Just thinking about it gave her the jitters.

Sami, it might be the only way out of here.

Alex's words came back to haunt her.

There must be another way out, or there must have been once, as it would be impossible to bring anything as large and heavy as a polished granite statue into the tunnel system via the submerged river entrance. But that was – what? Five hundred years ago? At least that, and possibly longer. In all that time, no one had stumbled across another way into the Metal Library complex, but that didn't mean no other way existed. In dense jungle, an entrance could easily become overgrown and escape detection, and of course whoever built the complex might have deliberately blocked all entrances for some reason. Whatever, they hadn't glimpsed anything that looked like an exit, and she felt no desire to explore any more tunnels or secret libraries.

Silent and motionless at Alex's shoulder, she held her breath, waited … she didn't see anything for a moment or two, and then she did. A faint white light, bobbing up and down, growing steadily brighter as it approached from the right … she silently hoped it was James. James had gotten her into the tunnel system, and he was the only man she trusted to get her out again. Alex – he was a fit, handsome guy, and if Richard hadn't hinted at some of the names Vaughan and his men called him behind his back, she would never have guessed he was gay. Not that that mattered to her, either way. Until James returned, he was her best hope of seeing daylight again. She just wanted the nightmare to end, wanted to go home, before anyone else got killed.

They waited, and waited, and the beam of light grew ever stronger, more intense. Getting closer. She heard laboured breathing, then the hand holding the torch jerked into view and Alex pounced.

'Identify yourself!'

She stayed back, out of the way, and it was too dark for her to make out what was happening. She did hear someone curse in what sounded like German. There was only one German with them, and she recognised his voice instantly.

Manny.

Manny's torch escaped his grasp, dropped to the floor with a thud. Glass shattered and everything went black. But, almost immediately, Alex flicked his torch on and she was relieved to see he was in control. He was holding his elongated pistol a few inches from the German's chest.

'Put your hands on your head,' he snarled, 'and keep them there.'

Manny complied.

She couldn't understand why, despite his capture, the German was grinning like a circus clown.

'What's so fuckin' funny?' Alex demanded.

'Your boyfriend,' sniggered Manny, 'has gone to meet his Paki maker.'

Her heart skipped a beat.

Alex pushed his silenced pistol into the German's chest. 'Say again …'

'Your Paki boyfriend is dead.'

Alex hesitated, and spoke in a low voice. 'You'd better be lyin' …'

'He's dead,' Manny repeated. His grin widened. 'I killed him. I put three bullets in him – and another seven, to make sure.'

Hearing the German's proud boast, Samantha felt physically sick.

'No,' she whispered, shaking her head, as inside her head, she re-lived again the shots heard a short time ago.

A single shot, then four more, closely followed by another seven.

I put three bullets in him – and another seven, to make sure.

'Dear God, no …' A sob burst from her throat and tears welled in her eyes. '*Noooooooo …*'

'You fuckin' Nazi!' The pistol in Alex's hand spat once, twice.

Manny's grin faded and his eyes widened. He lowered his hands, grasped his chest. He stared at Alex, who pushed him back harshly. Pushed him again, and again, making the German lost his balance and topple backward. Even before he hit the ground, Alex kicked him, and stamped on him. Then, from little more than two feet away, he blasted the top of Manny's head off.

She turned away, but not quickly enough to avoid seeing a bloody crater erupt out of the German's forehead, above his left eye. She burst into tears and, when she felt his hand on her arm, she looked at Alex – saw a tear roll down his cheek. He drew her closer and she threw her arms around him, buried her face against his shoulder. He was literally shaking with rage. She couldn't stop the sobs from racking her body.

'I'm sorry, Sami,' he said quietly, when finally her grief subsided and they drew apart. 'I'm sorry about James and …' He shook his head slowly. '… I'm sorry I lost it. I should have asked the Nazi bastard about your son, but … I'm sorry.'

A huge grin split Vaughan's face.

Not for the first time, he had seriously under-estimated Harris. Stone should have known better, than to take on the half-caste Paki, and he had paid with his life. The professor was a goner, too, he reckoned – although, having been disarmed, he hadn't been dumb enough to stick around when Harris and his sidekick went on the offensive. He had become separated from Manny in the dark, but lady luck had smiled on him: he found himself in a stone annex at the far side of the Metal Library. Clearly a workshop-cum-storeroom, the floor and shelves were stacked high with a wealth of priceless artifacts, finished and unfinished. Tools and raw materials, too. He was admiring a solid gold statuette, about six inches tall, when he heard raised voices. He immediately killed his Maglite, and listened. That is when he heard the words that filled him with a sense of euphoria.

Your boyfriend has gone to meet his Paki maker.

It got better.

Your Paki boyfriend is dead …

And better.

He's dead. I killed him. I put three bullets in him – and another seven, to make sure.

Moments later, standing in complete darkness and straining to hear, he detected the unmistakable cough of a supressed firearm. There was little doubt in his mind who was on the receiving end, or who the shooter was. The pistol coughed again, and after a few more seconds it coughed again, a third time. Then all he heard was near hysterical sobbing.

Bye-bye, Manny.

He pitied his stupid German friend, but he envied him, too. He would have paid good money to trade places with Manny, just long enough to squeeze the trigger, as ten rounds drilled bloody holes in his nemesis. He didn't think the German had it in him, guessed he must have caught Harris unarmed and napping, otherwise there was no way he would have emerged victorious. Manny triumphed, but his joy was short-lived – thanks to Harris's sidekick.

Vaughan's groin was still pulsing madly, where he had been kicked – for which the cock-sucking nigger responsible was going to pay a heavy price. Perhaps not here, not now; not with the Americans breathing down their necks. And the nigger was armed; he wasn't. But, assuming the Americans didn't take the fucker down first, he was looking forward to avenging Manny. Not forgetting the Paki-loving bitch who had dropped Harris's brat, or her second, older bastard.

He smiled, imagining the fun he could have with the boy – with his mother watching. Maybe, first, he would use the boy as leverage, to encourage the bitch to be nice to him. *Real* nice. As for Manny's killer, he would dream up something special for him. But not rape. The queer fucker would probably enjoy that. A long, spiky pole rammed up his glory hole? Something like that. And before he killed him, he would take great pleasure in emasculating the nigger – forcing him to eat his own balls.

In complete darkness, Vaughan waited ... five minutes. Ten minutes. He heard nothing. He thumbed on his Maglite and, alert for the slightest sound, resumed his exploration of the priceless treasures he had found.

Chapter 36

Casablanca.

Now a sprawling metropolis, and home to a rapidly growing population, the city immortalised by the 1942 film starring Humphrey Bogart and Ingrid Bergman had humble beginnings. It was originally settled by the Berbers in the seventh century BC, and was named *Casa Branca* – 'White House' – by the Portuguese in the sixteenth century. The town passed through Arabic and Spanish hands, becoming *Casa Blanca*, before the French took control in 1907. Forty-nine years later Morocco gained independence, and Casablanca became the economic and business centre of the country, and one of the largest artificial ports in the world.

Standing at the starboard side of the *Joie de Vie*, Sabine Arnaud drew deeply on her cigarette as she looked out across the Atlantic Ocean, watching the dying sun turn the sky blood red. They were about a mile off shore, and had been at anchor for over three hours. Behind her, the boat's skipper and her English lover were fishing and playing blackjack at the same time. They hadn't caught anything all day. Exhaling through her nose, she crushed the butt between her forefinger and thumb, and flicked it into the water. Another hour, perhaps two to be safe, and it would be dark enough.

'*C'est presque le temps*,' she said, turning to the men.

It's nearly time.

David and Bruno kept their heads down, pretended they hadn't heard. David, her lover, was twenty-eight but his boyish good looks and wavy, shoulder length blond hair made him appear younger. He was wearing black shorts and a pale cream sleeveless vest that accentuated his tanned, muscular arms. Bruno, the boat's skipper and owner, was a year younger but looked older. He was darker, more heavily built and hirsute, with unruly black hair and a thick black moustache. His black T-shirt had a scantily clad woman emblazoned across the chest.

'Another beer?' asked Bruno, looking up as she stepped closer.

'This is stupid,' she snapped, letting her frustration show. 'We all knew it might come to this when we accepted the job.'

No one disputed her statement. No one spoke.

It had been a long, difficult two weeks. Abducting the kid, the part of the job that concerned her most at the outset, had proved relatively easy. Far easier than what followed. She didn't have any children of her own, and if they all cried as much as this one had … it was David who hit on the idea of crushing a sleeping tablet, and mixing it in the kid's milk. It worked a treat. The kid quietened down, sleeping most of the time, but it didn't stop him peeing or shitting his pants.

Eight days ago, she had received a message on her BlackBerry. It was short and to the point. A date. A time. Instructions to dispose of the 'faulty package' if the stated deadline wasn't met. At the time, all three of them had expected to hear from their employer again, before the deadline was upon them. It was a noon deadline. Noon *today*. And they had heard nothing.

Yesterday, in exchange for just a few US dollars, Bruno had picked up an old stockless anchor. Half a metre tall, solid metal, once galvanized but badly rusted now. Sabine, when she tested its weight, found she could lift the anchor but she couldn't have carried it any distance. It weighed considerably more than the kid, was plenty heavy enough to take him to the bottom of the ocean and keep him there. Give it a few weeks, and there would be nothing left apart from a few scattered bones.

'I'm not doing it,' said Bruno, firmly.

She frowned, and turned to her boyfriend. David avoided her gaze, and she guessed he was thinking along the same lines as Bruno. She hadn't wanted it to come to this, either, and much as she despised him she knew taking the kid's life was going to play on her conscience for a long time. But it was worth it. Even split three ways, the price they had negotiated was a good one, and they had already been paid the first two instalments; the first, on agreeing to accept the job, and the second after they successfully abducted the kid. Only the final payment was outstanding.

'Look, we have to do this,' she insisted, 'we all agreed.'

Silence, apart from the faint squawk of a distant gull. Overhead, the sky was darkening, turning day into night, and she could feel the air temperature beginning to drop.

'We don't have to strangle him or slit his throat first,' she pointed out, thinking David and Bruno might be a bit squeamish because of the kid's age. She knew for a fact both men had killed before, so it wasn't as if this was a new experience for either of them. Or her, for that matter. 'We can chain him to the anchor and throw him over the side. He'll drown before he hits the bottom, and the anchor will ensure the currents don't wash his body ashore.'

Bruno hesitated, and nodded slowly. 'Okay, count me in – but we do it together, all three of us.'

'Agreed.' She shifted her focus to her lover, who hadn't said a word yet. 'David …'

He met her gaze. 'Sounds easy enough, but …'

'But what?' she asked.

'I've been thinking …'

James groaned softly.

He moved – wished he hadn't. He winced, lay still and caught his breath. The pain didn't go away. His chest hurt, like a percussion grenade had exploded inside his rib-cage, ripped it apart. He opened his eyes – couldn't see anything … he started to remember where he was, what had happened.

Manny.

The German had shot him – how many times?

Throwing the fight, without making it obvious, hadn't been easy. Manny was slow and cumbersome and predictable, but he was big and powerful. The blows the German landed hurt. Bust his nose and split his lips. He'd felt reasonably confident, when he turned to flee, the German wouldn't hesitate to shoot him. In the back. And that is exactly what happened. But two 9x19mm Parabellums travelling at over 1,150 feet per second propelled him forward with more force than he was anticipating, and he'd tumbled into the stone vault more heavily than he planned to. But not fast enough to avoid a third round, which caught him in the small of his back.

Winded, but still conscious, he'd closed his eyes and played dead when the German came to check on him. His nose and mouth were oozing blood, and he could feel rivulets trickling across his cheeks, down his chin and neck. He had ditched religion before he joined the army, but he still found himself reciting a silent prayer, as he lay waiting. Four unsuppressed rounds, fired in quick succession, meant his ears didn't detect his footfalls approaching, but he knew the German was coming. No question, a professional would have finished him with a head shot, but Manny wasn't thinking or acting like a professional.

The German did celebrate his kill.

Lying prone in the vault, with his back flush against unyielding stone, his chest took the full, devastating force of five rounds from close range before he lost consciousness. The Heckler & Koch P7 chambered anything from eight to thirteen rounds. He didn't know how many times Manny had squeezed the trigger, but he did know without the body armour he'd taken from one of the Americans, his internal organs would have been turned to mincemeat.

Who dares wins.

He needed to know how long he'd been out … slowly, he raised his right hand to his face. Flinched, as he felt a severe pull on his ribs. He ignored the pain. The blood around his nose and mouth was still wet, still oozing. So he couldn't have been out long. A few minutes, maybe. Less than ten minutes, certainly. That was the good news. That, and the fact he was still alive – and he now knew exactly where his son was being held.

The clock is ticking.

He believed the German – believed Vaughan had already sent a message to the kidnappers.

It was to tell them when to get rid of the boy.

Gritting his teeth, he pressed his left hand firmly against his chest, and used his right hand to lever himself to a sitting position. He reckoned, beneath the Kevlar that had kept him alive, at least three or four ribs must be cracked. He knew, from experience, the pain wouldn't go away any time soon, and the discomfort would last for months. He didn't have months. He didn't have weeks. He doubted he had days.

I have to get to Morocco – fast.

He wished he knew when the deadline was. Or, perhaps, it was better he didn't know. Yesterday might not have been soon enough to rescue his son, and even if everything went to plan and there were no delays, Casablanca was at least two days. By the time he touched down, located the kidnappers' boat, Vaughan's deadline might already have passed and his son might be dead.

If I'm too late five people will die.

No ifs, no buts. No mercy.

Four men and one woman.

Vaughan, Manny and three kidnappers.

No matter how long it took, if the bastards had murdered his son, he silently vowed he would hunt all five of them down like the vermin they were – and eradicate them.

He hauled himself up, perched on the edge of the vault and wiped the back of his hand across his bloody mouth. No time to waste, he swung his legs up and crept forward on his hands and knees, fingers searching the ground for his Maglite or the goggles … it took him precious minutes, but he located a torch. Not his. Manny's, presumably. The German must have taken his Maglite. No matter. He listened intently for a moment, before he risked thumbing the torch on. It wasn't as powerful as his Maglite, but it worked, casting a weak yellow-white beam. Good enough. He half-expected Manny would have helped himself to the goggles he'd kicked off his head as well, but his luck held. He found them just a few feet away, and they appeared undamaged. He put them on his head and flicked on the thermal infa-red imager, to confirm it still worked.

Holding his chest, grimacing with each jarring step, he jogged back to a tunnel entrance he had passed when he was pursuing Manny and Vaughan. He hesitated, then entered it, discovered after heading straight ahead for ten or so yards it began to curve gently to his left ... toward the T-junction where, incoming, they had gone right?

This, he surmised, could be the tunnel they would eventually have emerged from, had they gone left instead. It certainly appeared to be headed in the general direction of the T-junction, but ... he was in no fit state to take on the Americans again, and if he simply back-tracked he was certain to run into them. He liked to think the back-up he had called, if it hadn't already arrived, was on its way but ... decision time.

Chapter 37

James was mistaken.

The tunnel didn't take him back to the T-junction, it took him all the way back to the subterranean cavern, where they had taken the centre tunnel of three. This was one of the outer tunnels, the first one they'd discovered. The one Manny and Stone explored, without finding anything interesting. Early on, however, he passed numerous large recesses and small niches containing old bones and stone statues, respectively, similar to those he'd found in the tunnel he explored, but he didn't stop to investigate any of them. He made excellent progress, halting every few minutes, to kill his torch and let his eyes adjust the darkness. Press his hand over his chest and catch his breath, before using the thermal imager on his goggles to check ahead. He saw no heat signatures. He'd already sighted the tunnel's exit when he heard muted voices, and quickly swung his torch behind him, thumbed it off. The tunnel turned pitch black. He paused, breathing hard. With each lungful of air, a spasm of pain gripped his chest like a steel claw.

Clayton, he recalled, had sent two men into each of the outer tunnels and deployed another two men outside the tunnels. He hadn't run into anyone on the way back, so either the Americans who had been sent into this tunnel had made their way deeper inside the underground complex, or they had returned here – making four hostiles. More, if others had returned as well. There was only one way to find out.

Even with the thermal imager switched on he couldn't see anything but, by trailing his fingers along the wall to his left, he advanced slowly and soundlessly toward the mouth of the tunnel. He halted, hearing the low hub of conversation, but he wasn't close enough to make out full sentences. The acrid tang of burning tobacco told him at least one of the Americans was smoking.

He risked a quick look-see – spied one horizontal and three standing heat signatures; one of the latter had an arm raised, and appeared to be pointing into the middle tunnel. Ducking back into his own tunnel, he considered his options. The horizontal signature, he reckoned, must be the American he'd taken down but not neutralised; he wasn't a significant threat. But the other three, he assumed, were armed and dangerous. He wasn't armed, and he was in no fit state to take on three men.

His train of thought was interrupted by a commanding voice he recognised: Clayton. Again, he caught only the odd word, but ... he risked another look-see. The horizontal signature hadn't moved, but two of the standing signatures had disappeared – into the middle tunnel, presumably. The third signature was half-in, half-out the mouth of the same tunnel.

He didn't hesitate.

Silently, he slipped out of his tunnel and turned right, following the natural curve of subterranean cavern around. He wouldn't have been surprised to hear a shout behind him, to signal he'd been spotted, but he heard nothing. He didn't relax until he reached the lake. He skirted around it and, on reaching the far shore, he risked thumbing his torch back on. His nose had stopped bleeding, but his face and shirt were bloody. He knelt beside the water, winced as he leaned forward, splashed water on his face. He was aware the piranha's ferocious reputation as a fearless fish attracted by the scent of blood wasn't entirely accurate, but even so –

The water started to boil.

He quickly withdrew his hands as the lake in front of him came alive with – it took a second or two, before he realised the frenzy was caused by fish. Tiny fish, less than an inch long, but there were hundreds of them – attracted by his blood? No idea what species they were, or how dangerous they might be, he gave up on washing his face.

He didn't know why Clayton had retreated to the trio of tunnels, but it was good news for Samantha and Alex; it would buy them some time. He'd hated abandoning them, but he trusted Alex to take care of Samantha, and he couldn't allow Manny and Vaughan get away. Now, at last, he knew where his son was being held, and Manny believed he was dead. Vaughan, too, with a bit of luck. That should buy *him* some time. He realised Samantha and Alex might hear of his demise, too, but ... if he didn't get to Casablanca in time to find and rescue their son, he would never be able to face Samantha again.

By now, night would have fallen over the jungle, and he knew he had to make the darkness work to his advantage. But how? Assuming he made it to the river, he reckoned he could swim far enough down river to avoid detection, but ... he needed transport. The inflatable zodiac the American Hank had used to keep tabs on them would do nicely, and if he travelled through the night ... all he needed to do was 'borrow' it.

Easier said than done.

Seeing a white glow ahead of him, he proceeded with caution ... the high intensity halogen lights the Americans had set up in the upper cavern were still on, but the cavern itself was empty. So far as he was aware, the Americans hadn't left anyone in the lower cavern, either, but he spent a long moment listening for any sign of occupation. Hearing nothing, he climbed down into the brightly lit cavern, checked the lower cavern. No Americans. No sign of the big anaconda, either.

He was halfway down the second rock ladder when it crumbled beneath his foot, and he slipped. He fell the last three feet, but it felt more like thirty feet. He splashed in a few inches of water, swore aloud as he jarred his ribcage. He grasped his chest as the pain intensified, like he was trapped in the merciless coils of a hungry serpent. He couldn't breathe. But, slowly, the agony subsided and he was able to crawl across the floor to the submerged passage. He paused, holding his chest and breathing deeply. He rinsed his face, and winced when he raised his arms to remove his bloody T-shirt. He didn't shed the body armour that had saved his life – just in case.

He didn't fight the flow of the river, swimming underwater until his lungs were bursting. He surfaced briefly, gulped air and dove again, before striking out for the river bank. A few minutes later, he was crouched directly opposite where the *Amazon Dawn V* and *Rey de la Selva* were moored. It didn't take him long to establish the Americans were no longer in control of their own boat: men dressed in army fatigues were.

'*Señor* Harris?'

The soldier who posed the question was short and dark, with a clipped black moustache. Clearly the officer-in-charge, he looked about thirty-five. Two young soldiers armed with Heckler & Koch HK33 rifles stood either side of him. Both rifles were levelled at James.

They were on the deck of the *Rey de la Selva*. The night sky was black, but he was standing in the glare of two powerful flashlights, leant back against one of the cabins with his hands on his head. 'I'm Harris,' he confirmed, 'and you are …?'

'I am *Capitán* Esteban Mendoza.'

He was relieved to hear it. Surrendering to armed militia without confirming their identity first was a calculated gamble, but it looked like it had paid off. 'We spoke earlier,' he said, 'and my good friend *Señor* Berro – '

'You claim you have discovered a metal library,' *Capitán* Mendoza cut in. His English was good, but heavily accented. 'I have heard talk of this library, but I have always believed it to be – how do you say, a myth.'

'It's no myth, *Capitán* – I've seen it with my own eyes.' He lowered his right arm slowly, placed his hand on his chest where the pain burned brightest. No one objected.

The swarthy Captain inclined his head. 'You have proof?'

'The library exists, *Capitán* – and a lot more besides.' The Captain's eyes grew wider as he revealed some of the things he had seen. 'The treasures we found belong to the people of Ecuador,' he said, playing on the Captain's patriotism, 'but if you don't stop them, the men who brought me and my friends here, and the Americans who followed us, will loot everything.'

'I assure you, *Señor* Harris, no one is going to loot what belongs to my people – I will not allow it.'

He told the Captain how many armed Americans there were in the underground complex, and who else was there. 'The woman and *Señor* Berro – he's the only black man – are friendly,' he stressed, 'but everyone else is hostile.'

Capitán Mendoza nodded. 'At first light, you will show – '

'I can show you where the entrance is now,' he interrupted. First light was hours away, and he didn't want to be detained one minute longer than was necessary.

'Now,' repeated *Capitán* Mendoza, with an indulgent smile. He shook his head slowly. '*Señor* Harris, as I am sure you know, the river is a very dangerous place to be at night.'

'I agree, but – '

'We will wait until first light,' said *Capitán* Mendoza, with finality.

He hesitated, but he wasn't in a position to argue or dictate terms. 'Okay,' he conceded, 'at first light, but – the men who brought me here think I'm dead. I'd like to keep it that way.'

Capitán Mendoza's expression was quizzical.

'It's important,' he added.

'I think,' said *Capitán* Mendoza, without answering his request, 'you need medical attention, no?'

He couldn't deny it. '*Gracias.*'

Capitán Mendoza spoke rapidly in Spanish to the uniforms holding the Heckler & Koch rifles, which they lowered. One of the uniforms took off, and the second listened attentively to further instructions, the gist of which was easy to follow.

Keep a close eye on him.

'Ramos will show you to a cabin,' said *Capitán* Mendoza. 'Our medic will join you shortly.'

The Captain turned to leave.

'Wait,' he said, and *Capitán* Mendoza turned back to him. 'How did you and your men get here?'

No answer.

'By helicopter?' he guessed, having seen no sign of another river boat – and if they had come by river, the locals wouldn't have shown up so quickly.

Capitán Mendoza neither confirmed nor denied it.

He told the Captain what he wanted.

Capitán Mendoza eyed him with suspicion. 'Why do you want to go Quito?'

'That's my business – but I assure you it's important.'

A matter of life and death.

'If you are telling the truth, I can arrange it,' said *Capitán* Mendoza, after a moment's hesitation. His face hardened. 'If, however, you are wasting my time … I do not think you will find the prisons in my country to your liking.'

Chapter 38

'He's dead, isn't he?'

To conserve batteries they were sitting, side-by-side, in absolute darkness. It had taken Alex over an hour to escort Samantha safely back to the first library they had discovered, the one with row upon row of gilded shelving filled with thousands of strange, small flat tablets. In that time they had heard nothing, seen no one. Not Vaughan, not any of the Americans ... not James's bullet-ridden corpse.

The library was a lot bigger than initial impressions suggested, and he had led Samantha around to the far side, a good forty yards away from open doorway that led to the avenue of statues. Here, they had found a small, rectangular alcove with a square plinth. The polished black statue atop the plinth was reminiscent of the jaguar they had seen earlier, but it was only half the size and bird-like. Nestled down next to the plinth, invisible to the thermal infa-red imagers he knew some, if not all of, the Americans were equipped with, they had shared the last of the energy bars. They were down to their last half-bottle of water.

He knew instantly who Samantha meant, but said, 'Your son?'

'Luke,' she confirmed.

'You don't know that,' he said, gently, 'not for definite.'

Even as he spoke, Alex knew he was promoting false hope. With any abduction, the first three days were critical. After the first three days, a kidnap victim was as likely to turn up dead as alive. Fifty-fifty. Dead or alive. Another three days, and the chances of a happy outcome lengthened to one in four. And so it continued, with the odds against recovering a kidnap victim alive doubling every three days. Samantha's son had been missing for – what? Fifteen, pushing sixteen days. But call it fifteen. Fifteen was divisible by three. So ... one in thirty-two. One chance the kid was alive versus thirty-one he was dead. He wasn't a gambler, but he doubted anyone backed a horse with odds as long as like that, and expected it to romp to victory.

The kid is dead.

He knew it, and she feared it.

'Do you think he's alive?' she asked.

He wanted to say 'yes', but he couldn't lie. 'I don't know, Sami. There's a slim chance, but ...'

He didn't finish the sentence.

He felt her shiver, and when she started crying he put his arm around her and drew her closer, acutely aware of the inadequacy of the gesture. She leaned against him, rested her head against his shoulder and sobbed. He felt bad for her, but there were no words he could speak, to ease her suffering.

First her son gets abducted, then she discovers her marriage is a sham and her husband is responsible for her father's death. Now, she's was a widow and the father of her missing son is dead.

He hadn't noticed before, and he didn't notice now, not at first – then he did. There was something beneath her T-shirt, something that felt like ...

'Are you wearing body armour?'

'Yes,' she answered, shifting position. He sensed she was looking at him, as she told him how James had taken the body armour off Clayton and given it to her. She told him James was wearing body armour, as well. Her tone brightened. 'You don't think ...'

For an instant, hope flared ... just as quickly, it died.

I put three bullets in him – and another seven, to make sure.

'Not a chance,' he said, flatly. 'Body armour offers some protection, but it doesn't turn a guy into Superman.'

I put three bullets in him ...

He recalled the Nazi had actually fired four rounds. One miss, then, but three rounds were usually more than adequate to take a guy down. A brief silence ... as the Nazi closed on James?

... and another seven, to make sure.

He'd taken the Nazi down with two body shots, and finished him with a head shot. Just one. The way he visualised it, the Nazi bastard must have been standing over him, when he pumped seven rounds into James.

No way anyone survives that.

A single head shot would do it, and the Nazi's bullish demeanour confirmed he'd made a kill.

Time passed.

He was thinking Samantha must have cried herself to sleep when she broke the silence. Said, 'I want him back.'

Who do you want back?

'Even if he is ... I want him back.'

She's talking about her son.

'I know,' he said, softly. And he did.

No body meant no closure – not ever.

Not knowing is a killer.

He knew, without a body to bury and a grave to visit, she would cling to the hope, however faint, that somewhere her son was still alive. Any mother would, in the same situation. Any father, too. They had never met in life, and he didn't believe in reincarnation, but if he was wrong, if there was something more than burial or cremation after death, he liked to think James would get to know his son.

Eventually, she did drift off to sleep. He felt tired, too. Tired and cold and hungry. But alive, and he was determined to stay that way, determined to keep Samantha safe as well. He would never forgive himself if he let James down.

Take care of Sami for me.

Those were the last six words he heard James speak ... he found himself thinking, again, about the radio call James had made from the *Amazon Dawn V*. Did he get through, or didn't he? And if he did, did he get to speak to *Capitán* Mendoza or not? Alerting the locals to their visit was James's idea, back in London, but as he spoke Spanish and James didn't, he had been the one who made all the calls, to set things up. He had no way of knowing if the locals were aware of the current situation or not, or if James had passed on their precise location. If he hadn't ...

We're fucked.

He closed his eyes – not that it made any difference. He couldn't see anything with them wide open. But, much as he would love to grab forty winks, he knew he had to stay awake. Stay alert ... he couldn't supress a smile, as he remembered his last night in London, with James and two busty Swedish students. It was a good night, an *excellent* night, a memory he would treasure. He replayed it over in his mind. Seeing James naked, seeing him in action, gave him such a thrill ... the blondes faded away, leaving him alone with James. James was smiling. He was smiling. James was naked. Looking good. He was naked. Feeling good. And excited. So very excited. Standing close together, he placed his hands on James's waist, drew him even closer. They started touching, kissing ... rubbing and sucking and tasting. Then James was lying on his back, and he was knelt over him, holding his legs up as he penetrated him. Gripping James's calves, he began to thrust slowly, slowly ...

He awoke.

Reflexively, breathing hard, he lowered his hand to his crotch and touched himself ... he opened his eyes – realised he'd been dreaming.

You fuckin' wanker!

Falling asleep was bad enough, but dreaming he was screwing ... he shook his head, angry with himself. James was as straight as he was dead, and to even dream the two of them were lovers – it was an unforgivable violation of his friend's memory.

Silently, he vowed it wouldn't happen again. Vowed it, but just as soon realised he had no control over what he did and didn't dream. He would never suffer nightmares about the two buddies he'd seen blown apart by a mortar attack in Helmand four years ago, if he did. Or another buddy, who he had been standing next to when his head literally exploded, splattering his face with blood and brain and bits of skull. But he did. Not as regular as he used to, but still too regular for his liking. Nothing he could do to stop the nightmares. So, whether he wanted to or not, chances are he *would* dream about James again.

Beside him, thankfully, Samantha was still asleep. He checked his watch. He had been out for nearly an hour.

Samantha slept on.

James prowled the deck of the *Rey de la Selva*, near the bow, liked a caged animal. He scanned the clear blue sky to the north-east when he heard the faint whomp-whomp-whomp of a helicopter.

Last night, when he removed his body armour, he'd been shocked to see his chest was one huge, ugly purple-black bruise. It was impossible to ascertain how many rounds he had stopped, but the medic who examined him confirmed he had three nasty contusions on his back as well. Tender, but not nearly as brutal as his cracked ribs. The medic gave him some painkillers, and strapped his chest with an elastic bandage, to restrict movement without impairing his breathing. The medic recommended hospital or complete bed rest for a week, but neither was an option, not while there was still a chance he could get to Casablanca in time to rescue his son.

After seeing the medic, he'd drawn a detailed map of the subterranean complex they had discovered for *Capitán* Mendoza, and answered all his questions, keeping it brief and factual. Not sure how the Captain would react, and not wanting to find he was under arrest, he neglected to mention Stone and the Americans he'd taken out. He did mention Professor Frewin-Hamilton's demise, claiming the academic had accidentally shot himself, but leaving it to others to tell the full story. He managed to grab a couple hours shut-eye, but he was up and dressed again before the sun rose.

At first light nothing much happened, and the longer he was made to wait for *Capitán* Mendoza to be ready, the more frustrated he became. But, finally, everyone was good to go and he led the Captain and his men as far as the subterranean lake. Here, he was granted permission to exit the tunnels, but he had only taken a dozen or so strides when the first shots were fired. He hesitated, automatically glanced over his shoulder, but he was desperate to be on his way and when his escort nudged him, he carried on walking.

Now it was mid-morning, and if what was being reported back was accurate, the Americans had surrendered to *Capitán* Mendoza. There had, apparently, been casualties on both sides. No mention of Samantha and Alex yet. Or Vaughan. Or Manny. But *Capitán* Mendoza had assured him, as soon as they were taken into custody, Vaughan and Manny would be thoroughly searched and any means of communication confiscated.

He was wearing a short-sleeved white shirt and light brown cotton trousers. Already, as the temperature soared, the elastic bandage beneath his shirt felt uncomfortably tight and sweaty, and his trousers were sticking to his legs. He ignored the discomfort, focused on the two black dots growing in the sky … as they flew closer, he identified them as military Dhurv ALHs – Advanced Light Helicopters. Four bladed rotors, 12 seats each, manufactured by the Indians. There was nowhere for the Dhurvs to land, but a small stretch of river bank had been cleared of vegetation, and within a matter of minutes the first combat troops rappelled to the ground.

Soon after, face creased in pain, he was buffeted by one of the Dhurv's downdraft, as he swung at the end of a wire below the chopper.

'*Gracias*,' he shouted, through clenched teeth, as he was hauled aboard by two young uniforms. One of them noticed his discomfort, but he didn't say anything until he had helped him to his seat, strapped him in and handed him a headset.

'You is okay, *señor*?'

He forced a smile. 'I'm fine.'

The uniform didn't look convinced. 'You go Quito?'

'Quito airport,' he confirmed, 'and quickly, *por favor*.'

The capital's airport, he figured, should provide his speediest route out of South America – and into North Africa.

The uniform nodded, and spoke rapidly into his headset. The only word he caught was *rápidamente*. Holding his chest, he settled in his seat as the chopper executed a ninety degree turn, before it took off. He couldn't be sure, but before the Dhurv sped away from the river, he thought he caught a glimpse of Samantha clinging to Alex in the brown water below.

Chapter 39

'I can't wait to see Joshua.'

Having declined his offer to take it, Alex was reclining in the window seat; a few minutes ago, when Samantha opened her eyes and yawned, he was staring out the airplane window. There wasn't much to see. It was early morning and, outside the plane, the sun's dazzling rays reflected off the carpet of white clouds below them like they were mounds of fresh, crisp snow.

She loved travelling, seeing different places and experiencing different cultures, but she hated the actual getting from A to B, especially when it meant three planes in twenty-seven hours. Four, if she included the helicopter that flew them from the Metal Library site to Cuenco. A scary experience, but not nearly as harrowing as exiting the underground complex, via the submerged passage and river. If it hadn't been for Alex ... thankfully, this was their last flight. Cuenco to Guayaquil. Guayaquil to Amsterdam. Amsterdam to Heathrow. The little screen on the seat in front of her was black, but Alex's monitor was on, and showed their progress over the Atlantic. The little plane on the map was nudging the UK now, and the up-date on the next page told her she had been asleep for nearly four hours. There was, the same screen informed her, a strong tail wind. The latest estimate claimed they would arrive at their destination ten minutes ahead of schedule.

Alex turned to her. 'He's your other son, right?'

She nodded. 'He's older than Luke – he was eight in December.'

He shifted in his seat, trying to find a more comfortable position. 'Does he see his Dad?'

She didn't answer immediately ... there was a time, when they were lovers, she wished Hassan – as James was called at the time – was Joshua's father. He wasn't, but seeing the three of them out and about together, it was only natural people should think they were a family. Despite the fact she'd been married to Richard for over a year, and the two of them had only been lovers for a few months, James was the closest thing to a father Joshua had ever had. A *real* father. 'Is Hassan my daddy?' he'd asked her. 'Are you my daddy?' he'd asked Hassan. Secretly, back then, she liked to think one day she might hear her son calling Hassan 'daddy', but ... Alex misread her silence.

'Sorry, I didn't mean to pry.'

'No, I'm sorry – I was just thinking.' She smiled faintly. 'Joshua doesn't have a Dad,' she said. 'His father – his biological father, was my first boyfriend. He was a lot older than me, but when I told him I was pregnant he didn't want to know.'

'Sorry,' he said, again.

'Don't be – he's the one who's lost out, not me.'

'Yeah, I guess …'

The plane droned on.

She willed it to go faster. She'd only just awoken, but she still felt shattered, like she could close her eyes again and sleep for a week. The last eighteen days had taken their toll, and … even after the soldiers appeared, and escorted her and Alex out of the underground complex, the nightmare didn't end. That is when the questions started. They were interrogated for what seemed like days, but was actually only eight or nine hours, before they were granted permission to leave. Alex spoke Spanish fluently, so he had done most of the talking. He claimed her husband had accidentally shot himself, which wasn't a lie. She didn't believe James had intended to kill Richard. He had been trying to protect her, trying to take the gun from Richard – stop him from killing her.

He saved my life.

It wasn't James's fault the gun went off.

She felt no sympathy for her late husband, not after the way he had played her for a fool – arranged to have her father killed and her son abducted. She was equally determined Richard wasn't going to be credited with discovering the Metal Library. No way. The lying, scheming murderer didn't deserve it. And what she'd told the Ecuadorians was the truth: Alex and James, aided by her late father's research, were the ones who found the secret entrance to the tunnels that led to the Metal Library.

Now, she just wanted to get home – see Joshua, and sleep in her own bed … except it wasn't really her bed. It wasn't her home, either. Richard owned it, or he had before …

I'm a widow.

She had no idea where she stood, legally. Had Richard even made a will? If he had, she'd never had sight of it. Having met him a couple times, she knew Richard's father was still alive, but as far as she was aware he had no other living relatives. Certainly, none had attended their wedding, a small registry office affair.

'Sami – I know it's none of my business,' said Alex, quietly, 'but when we get back, I think you should go straight to the police.'

She remembered, word perfect, the warning she'd been given.

If you contact the police, or talk to anyone at all about this, we will know – and your son will die. If you fail to follow any of my instructions, for any reason, your son will die. There will be no second chance. Do you understand me?

She understood, and she'd done everything the woman demanded of her. But that was eighteen days ago. A long, long time. She was desperate to believe Luke was still alive, but she'd had no 'proof of life' recently and ... she found herself nodding, couldn't stop tears welling in her eyes. Every time she thought about her missing son ...

'You're right,' she managed, 'I should – I will, as soon as I get back.'

He asked, 'Want me to come with you?'

'Will you?' She wanted him to, she *needed* him to. She was scared she wasn't strong enough to handle this on her own.

'Sure, if you want me to,' he said. 'I'm used to dealing with the police, and I know the kinda questions they're gonna ask.'

'Thank you.' She felt a tears roll down her cheek. 'I'm sorry ...'

'For what?' He smiled, reached out and gently wiped the tear away with the back of his index finger. 'You're doing great.'

She didn't feel like she was doing great, quite the opposite, but she appreciated his kind words. He lowered his hand, placed it over hers. She grasped him, held on to him for a long moment. He smiled again.

'I'm here as long as you need me.'

'*Assalamu 'alaykum.*' Peace be upon you.

The fisherman, who had deeply tanned features and a grizzled beard, accepted James's hand. The fisherman's grip wasn't firm, but it wasn't limp, either. With a toothy grin, the fisherman shook his hand and gave the universal response.

'*Wa alaikum assalam.*' And on you be peace.

James was standing only three or four feet from the water's edge, with two fishing boats dead ahead, so close together he couldn't see a name on the side of either of them. The sky overhead was azure, with a few fluffy white clouds, and the temperature was pleasant, with a light sea breeze. He was wearing an anonymous, long-sleeved white shirt and brown trousers. To his right, on a black plastic sheet, several different species of fish were laid out in neat rows. He recognised plump, uniquely patterned mackerel, but nothing else. In Arabic, he made small talk with the fisherman for a few minutes, before getting to the point.

'I wonder if you can help me,' he said. 'I'm supposed to be meeting some friends for a fishing trip, but I can't find their boat. It's called the *Joie de Vie* ...'

He drew a blank – another one.

Two days ago, when he had finally arrived at Quito's Mariscal Sucre airport, he was dismayed to discover there was no quick or easy way to get from there to Casablanca. Short on options, he'd had to wait until 6:00 the following morning, for a flight to the Bolivian capital, Bogotá. Time enough to buy fresh clothes and toiletries, book into a cheap hotel, get cleaned up, grab a bite to eat and try to get some sleep. It was a short flight, only ninety minutes, but then he had nearly twelve hours to kill before his Air France flight to Paris departed. He'd arrived at Charles de Gaulle airport at 11:05 this morning, waited two hours for another Air France flight, this one to Casablanca's Mohammed V International Airport.

The plane touched down just after 15:00 local time and as soon as he cleared customs, he visited a *Bureau de Change*, withdrew a small amount of local currency and rather more in US dollars – the preferred currency, in many countries. Next, having spent some time studying Casablanca's layout in a travel guide he picked up in Paris, he visited the Avis desk and rented a small economy vehicle. A Peugeot 206, silver in colour, which he drove south and parked up close to the Hassan II Mosque.

The mosque, which stood on a promontory looking out over the Atlantic, was the biggest in Morocco and the fifth largest in the world. Its minaret, rising to 689', was the world's tallest. It was an impressive edifice but, no longer Muslim and more important things than worship on his mind, he paid it scant attention.

Looking west and then east, along the waterfront, he realised in his haste he had neglected to ask Manny pertinent questions about the boat he was desperate to locate. The *Joie de Vie* – the *Joy of Life*. A cruelly ironic moniker. Up the coast especially, as far as the eye could see, there were boats – big boats, small boats, new boats, old boats. Fishing boats mostly, but the odd yacht, too. Numerous boats were moored away from the waterfront as well, many of them too far out to make out their names without binoculars, which he didn't possess.

He had no idea what type of boat he was searching for, and according to his travel guide a new marina was under construction further up the coast. Given the guide had been published two years ago, the marina might have been completed and be in use now, but he hoped not … if anyone could help him locate a boat, local fishermen could, and figuring they were more likely to talk to a fellow Muslim than an English speaking tourist, that is what he posed as.

He worked his way along the waterfront slowly, covertly scanning the names of as many boats as he could see as he passed by, and stopping to make conversation with every second or third person he met – fishermen, mostly. He must have spoken to more than two dozen men before, at last, he saw a flicker of recognition in the eyes of a clean-cut Moroccan man in his early twenties, when he mentioned the *Joie de Vie.*

But the young man shook his head. 'I'm sorry,' he said in Arabic, 'I'd like to help you but I don't know a boat with that name.'

He reached into his pocket, extracted a $10 bill, which he slipped into the Moroccan's palm. 'Please, I have some important news to share with my friends ...'

It took another $10 to loosen the young man's tongue.

'I saw her go out early this morning – I noticed because she hasn't been out much recently. I haven't seen her return, but I've been into town ...'

James learned where the *Joie de Vie* normally berthed, and asked for and got a description: a small, predominantly white fishing boat with a broad red stripe along the length of the hull. As he shook hands with the Moroccan, thanked him and exchanged parting words, he couldn't rid himself of the feeling that he had arrived too late to save his son.

He could think of only one reason why his son's kidnappers would have set sail this morning, after not taking their boat out much recently. He was assuming his son had been kept on the boat since his abduction, sedated probably, but this morning something had changed – and what that something might be filled him with dread.

The *Joie de Vie* was nowhere to be found – presumably, the boat was still out at sea. Briefly, he considered hiring a boat himself, heading out to sea to search for it, but the Atlantic was a mighty big ocean ... he couldn't think of an easier, more convenient place to dispose of a body. Simply attach a weight and toss it over the side. Ultimately, it wouldn't make any difference if his son was dead or alive when he hit the water.

I have to know.

And so, no doubt, did Samantha.

And if the bastards have killed him ...

He settled down to wait.

Chapter 40

'I have read your statements,' said DI Keith McMillan, 'and I must admit to being somewhat at a loss where to start.'

It was a typical interview room. Small, square, with a mirror taking up one wall. Alex knew, on the other side of the mirror, there would be another small room, where several people could watch an interview in progress without the interviewee seeing them. No windows. One harsh, fluorescent strip light. The only furniture was a square table and three hard back chairs. Digital tape recorder on the table, green light on. He was seated on one side of the table, next to Samantha, with DI McMillan standing directly opposite them, a sheaf of papers in his left hand. Their written statements, presumably, which they'd given individually earlier. The DI was fortyish, about five ten, with short black hair greying at the temples and arched black eyebrows. He was wearing an off-the-peg dark grey suit, with the jacket buttoned over a white shirt. Striped tie. Alex had quit smoking three years ago and, even before they were introduced, he detected an unpleasant whiff that told him the DI was a thirty-a-day man, at least.

'I have contacted the Ecuadorian Embassy,' DI McMillan went on, 'but apparently they have no knowledge of your visit to their country, or the underground complex you claim to have discovered there.'

'Give it time,' he said. 'The authorities will – '

'Please, that's not why I'm here,' Samantha interrupted. 'I came to report my son is missing.'

On the plane, Alex had advised Samantha what they should tell the police – and, equally important, what they should leave out. He had considered insisting on making a joint statement, but as he wasn't present when Samantha's son was abducted and that had to be the main focus now, that wasn't possible. He had advised her to tell the truth, the whole truth, about what happened in Tenerife. But South America was different. In South America people died, and he'd killed one of them – in cold blood. An act he didn't regret, but he wasn't stupid enough to confess, either. Instead, he and Samantha had agreed to be as vague as possible about what happened underground, playing on the fact it was pitch black, and claiming the two of them and James were unarmed, which initially they were. He did reveal there had been a lot a shooting, even before the local militia appeared and took control of the situation, but he spoke of only two deaths. Professor Frewin-Hamilton, both he and

Samantha claimed, had 'accidentally' shot himself, and James had been murdered by one of the kidnappers.

'Of course,' agreed DI McMillan, taking a seat, 'and it's as good a starting point as any.' He consulted the papers in front of him. 'Luke James Radcliffe, age four years, mixed ethnicity …' He turned to Samantha. 'According to your statement, Mrs Frewin-Hamilton, your son – '

'Please, don't call me that,' she interrupted, 'call me Miss Radcliffe.'

DI McMillan inclined his head. 'Miss Radcliffe,' he repeated. 'According to your statement your son was abducted on the morning of Wednesday the third of February. At the time, you were on a family holiday to Tenerife with your husband and two young sons. Correct so far?'

'Yes,' she confirmed, 'but Richard wasn't with us when Luke was snatched, he'd returned to the UK for a conference. I had no idea he was involved with my son's abduction at the time, but when we were in Ecuador, when we found the Metal Library …'

'The bastard held a SIG Sauer to Sami's head and threatened to kill her,' he finished.

DI McMillan shot him a glance, and turned back to Samantha. 'Do you have any evidence your late husband was involved with your son's abduction?'

'He told me – he told me he used me to try to get close to my father,' she answered. 'My father was obsessed with finding the Metal Library, and so was Richard. He used me to try to get on good terms with my father so he would share his research, but my father didn't trust him.'

'That's something else you should investigate,' he chipped in. 'The house fire that killed Sami's father was no accident – it was murder.'

'That, Mr Berro,' said DI McMillan, 'is an extremely serious accusation.'

He met the DI's stare. 'Murder is an extremely serious crime.'

The questioning continued.

Without being too obvious, Alex tried to steer the conversation away from South America, and focus on Samantha's missing son. It hadn't escaped his attention today was day eighteen. One in thirty-two after fifteen days doubled to one in sixty-four after eighteen days. The odds were lengthening fast now. Too damn fast. He wasn't wrong, in thinking it was only a matter of time before James's name was dragged into play.

DI McMillan focussed on Samantha. 'Tell me about your son's father.'

'What about him?' she asked.

'What he wants to know,' he said, 'is what makes you think James wasn't one of the kidnappers?'

Whenever a child goes missing, the child's father – especially if he is an estranged husband or a former boyfriend – is always a primary suspect, and rightly so. But in this case, the DI was way off the mark.

He stared at McMillan, challenged, 'Tell me I'm wrong …'

'I'm just covering all angles, Mr Berro.' DI McMillan glanced at Samantha, and his tone softened. 'I don't mean to make a difficult situation even tougher, but at this stage of the investigation we can't exclude any possibilities.'

'Yeah, well you can exclude James – he didn't even know he had a son, until after the kid had been abducted. Tell him, Sami.'

'Alex is right,' she confirmed. 'James didn't – when we split up, I didn't know I was pregnant and when I found out, I had no idea where James was and I had no way of contacting him. I didn't know it at the time, but he'd joined the army and – he didn't know anything about Luke until after he'd been kidnapped. I'm certain he didn't.'

'James was being blackmailed.'

'Blackmailed?'

'Before he was discharged from the army,' he said, 'he was in the SAS. He was a damn good soldier and, having served with him, Vaughan must have known he could use a man like that in South America. I don't know how Vaughan and the professor met, but I figure the professor must have told Vaughan about Sami's boys, and when Vaughan heard who Luke's father was …'

'Aw, mum – I'm winning!'

'You're too good for me!' Alex laughed, and ruffled the boy's short black hair. 'I quit – your mum's right, it's time for your bath.'

'But I need – '

'You need a bath, young man,' Samantha cut in, firmly. 'It's school tomorrow, and you have to be up early.'

Joshua didn't protest further as he gave up his remote, and Alex switched the Nintendo Wii and TV off. It was just gone seven fifteen and, despite having been swimming this afternoon, her son wasn't a bit tired and was eager to play on. Sometimes, she wondered where he got his energy from. She was shattered. After the long journey home, she would have liked nothing better than to hit her bed, but reporting Luke's abduction came first. She'd never been to a police station before, to report any sort of crime, but Alex warned her it was going to be tough and he was right.

In giving her statement she'd heeded Alex's advice and focused on Luke. Of course, there was a strong, inescapable connection between her son's abduction and what happened in Ecuador, and she didn't hesitate to name those she believed were part of the kidnap gang – including her late husband. And Vaughan. Anthony Vaughan. Neither she nor Alex knew the full names of any of the other kidnappers, with the exception of Phillip 'Wilko' Wilkinson, who Alex had served with in his army days. But neither of them knew, with any certainty, if Wilko was one of the kidnap gang or not, and now he was dead it no longer seemed important.

They grabbed a quick bite to eat, after giving their statements, and she took the opportunity to call her friend Beverley again, desperate to hear Joshua's cheery voice. Beverley reminded her she normally took her own son, Callum, swimming on Sunday afternoon. Usually, Beverley took Joshua as well, while she stayed home with Luke and Beverley's baby daughter, Megan. Luke had only just started his swimming lessons and he hadn't learned to swim without foam arm discs yet, whereas Joshua had been having lessons for nearly five years, and was a good, confident swimmer. Joshua pleaded with her, keen to go to the leisure centre with his best friend, and no idea how much longer she was going to be tied up at the police station, she gave her consent.

Giving a statement was tough, but it was nothing compared to the grilling that followed. Without Alex sitting beside her, supporting her and shielding her from difficult questions about what happened in Ecuador, she would have struggled to hold it together as well as she did. Tears flowed, of course they did, but … when DI McMillan pointed out how long her son had been missing, as if blaming her for not reporting his abduction sooner …

'What would you have done?' Alex demanded. 'The bastards threatened to kill her son, if she went to the police. Would you have risked it, if he was your kid?'

Alex drove her from the police station to Henley Leisure Centre, and before they arrived she sounded him out, about how much she should tell Beverley. She'd promised herself, before she travelled to Ecuador, she would tell her best friend everything when she returned. That was no longer an option, and she agreed with Alex, that she shouldn't reveal anything they hadn't told the police. Their luggage, what little they had brought back with them, was still in the boot of Alex's Astra. He dug out a pair of shorts and joined Joshua and Callum in the pool, and it wasn't until she sat down beside Beverley and baby Megan, that she noticed her friend was ogling him.

'He's well fit,' whispered Beverley, leaning closer.

She found a faint smile. 'He's also gay.'

'He's not!' Beverley looked shocked.

'He is.'

'With a body like that – that's so not fair!'

There was no denying Alex was in great shape, but … she took the plunge. 'Bev, when I told you Luke had broken his arm – I lied.'

Her friend soon forgot all about Alex, and the injustices of a gay man being hot, as she revealed what had really happened to her son, and what had happened in Ecuador.

When Callum asked his mum if they could go to Burger King for tea, Samantha stepped in and said she would treat everyone. It was, she felt, the least she owed Beverley, and besides she was in no mood to go home and start cooking a meal. After they had eaten, Alex drove her home and she invited him in, and it wasn't long before he and Joshua were playing games on her son's Nintendo Wii. Kart racing, golf, indoor bowing … at first, she noticed, Alex held back and let her son win. But, when he realised how good Joshua was, he became more competitive. They were an evenly matched pair and it made her feel good, to watch her son enjoying himself in a way he never had with Richard.

'I'd better be off,' said Alex, as he followed her and her son through the living room door, as they headed for the stairs.

She didn't want him to go.

Without him, over the past three days … she didn't want to be on her own, not tonight. They paused at the bottom of the stairs.

'Can we go swimming again tomorrow?' asked Joshua.

'No, Josh – you've got school tomorrow, and I – '

'We can go after school. Please, Mum …'

'No, Josh,' she repeated, 'not tomorrow – it's your lesson on Tuesday, don't forget.' She hesitated, and faced Alex. 'You're welcome to stay the night, if you want. It's been a long day and – I can make up the bed in the spare room?' she added quickly, not wanting to offend him by …

By what?

By coming on to a gay man?

She felt herself blushing, but if he noticed he was polite enough to pretend he hadn't, and he accepted her offer with a grin. Then, as she trailed him upstairs, her son turned to her and said, 'I like Alex.'

So do I, Josh. So do I.

Chapter 41

The light was fading.

James tensed, as another small boat appeared on the horizon, to the north-east of the setting sun … it was definitely white, but head-on he couldn't see if there was a broad red stripe painted along the hull.

He waited.

Several times already, he'd been disappointed … not this time.

As the boat swung around, headed for the waterfront just yards away from where he was pretending to read a local newspaper, he saw the red stripe. He saw something else, too: the boat's name.

Joie de Vie.

His heart pounded against his ribcage as the boat glided into its berth. Almost subconsciously, he placed his hand on his chest, pressed firmly where the pain burned fiercest. It didn't help much. The two painkillers he'd taken early this afternoon were his last, and once their effect had worn off, the pain returned with a vengeance.

He watched a man in his mid-to-late twenties, with tanned skin and wavy, dark blond hair, and wearing a faded black T-shirt, shorts and a baseball cap, jump on to the waterfront and secure the boat.

One of the kidnappers?

Shortly, the man was joined by a woman – younger, with short brown hair. She was wearing shades. She fitted the description Samantha had given him, but it was Manny who had named her. Sabine. The man returned to the boat briefly, before he reappeared with a black Adidas holdall slung over his shoulder.

He buried his head in his newspaper as the couple walked past him, arm-in-arm, speaking French. In the army, he'd been encouraged to brush-up on his schoolboy French, and he caught enough of the conversation to learn the couple were discussing where to dine. They sounded in good spirits, and he suspected they had been drinking.

Celebrating the completion of a lucrative job?

Resisting an urge to follow, he watched the couple head inland until they disappeared from his view, before turning his attention back to the *Joie de Vie*. According to both Samantha and Manny, there were three kidnappers, a woman and two men.

That left one male.

There was no guarantee the man was on board the *Joie de Vie*, but even if he wasn't, he felt certain the couple planned to return … his gut instinct told him his son wasn't still on the boat.

He waited five minutes, ten minutes … nothing happened.

He folded his newspaper.

Then he hesitated, suddenly scared to learn the truth. On his flight across the Atlantic, he had run through countless scenarios in his mind, but now he was actually here …

'Hello!'

The *Joie de Vie* was about twenty-five foot, with a raised cabin at the bow and a small, open cockpit at the stern – so designed, he assumed, for convenient fishing. It was a leisure, rather than commercial, vessel. Stepping aboard, avoiding an oil spillage no one had bothered to mop up, he walked around the outside of the cabin, to the open cockpit. On the far side, there were several rods, and two large tackle boxes.

His call went unanswered.

The cabin extended below deck. Standing at the open doorway, glancing down the wooden steps, he called 'hello' again. No answer. Either no one was home, or … crouching down, he clicked one of the tackle boxes open. Ten seconds later, he was armed with a red-handled Swiss army knife. He extended the blade. It was shorter, and more innocuous looking than a Blackie, but it was good enough. As he crept down the steps, keeping to one side where the tread was likely to be firmer, the stench of stale cigarette smoke and strong liquor assaulted his senses.

Reflexively, when the penultimate step creaked, he halted and listened. Heard breathing, heavy breathing. He took the last step … the missing kidnapper was sprawled on his front, on a narrow bunk to his left. The man was naked from the waist up, and appeared to be asleep.

James's eyes were drawn to the far, right hand corner, where a dirty, rumpled blanket was spread on the floor. On it, lying on its side, there was a yellow plastic infant's cup with two handles and a bright, lime green lid with a drinking lip.

There was no sign of Luke.

It only took Alex a few minutes on Samantha's laptop to confirm what he'd already guessed. He was still checking and comparing airports, times and prices when she came back downstairs, after putting her son to bed.

'Sami, I've been thinking,' he said, as she flopped down on the sofa beside him.

'About?' she asked.

'About Luke,' he replied. 'I know the police and Interpol are searching for him now, but if I catch an early morning flight, I can be in Tenerife by lunchtime tomorrow. I speak Spanish and – I'm not saying I can find Luke, but – I don't know if James mentioned anything, but I've been working as a private investigator since quitting the army. Your son won't be the first missing person I've tried to locate, and I'm willing to give it my best shot.'

He saw the pain in her eyes. 'Do you think he's still alive?'

It wasn't the first time she'd asked the question and, like him, she must know the odds were stacked heavily against her son's survival after he had been missing so long. But that is not the answer she wanted to hear.

'I wish I knew,' he said, softly. 'But if he is – James wouldn't just sit here, doing nothing, and I'm not going to either.'

And if he is dead, I'll track down his killers.

She closed the distance between them – kissed his cheek.

'Thank you, Alex. I appreciate it,' she said. 'I'd go with you, but – '

'Josh needs you here,' he finished. 'I'll keep in regular contact, and we can keep each other up-dated.'

He booked one of the early morning flights he'd found – insisted on paying for it himself, even though she offered.

'I'm glad you're here,' she said, as he logged off. 'I'd never have made it through today without you, and you've been brilliant with Josh.'

'He's a good kid – but yeah, it's been a tough day,' he agreed.

'You're good with children – you'd make a great father.'

'You think?' He had his doubts.

'Definitely,' she answered. 'Wouldn't you like a family?'

'I guess,' he admitted, 'but I'm gonna be thirty in July.' He shook his head, reminded of the pregnancy his ex had terminated. 'Some things aren't meant to be.'

'Thirty isn't old,' she said, with a faint smile. 'You're a handsome guy. I'm sure you'll meet someone special one day, and when you do – I don't suppose it's easy, but gay couples can adopt nowadays, if you really do want children.'

He stared at her. 'Who told you I'm gay?'

But even as he spoke, a dead man's words came back to haunt him.

Your boyfriend has gone to meet his Paki maker.

And then ...

Your Paki boyfriend is dead.

'Look, Sami,' he said, 'what that fuckin' Nazi said ...'

'It wasn't just him. I – ' Her eyes flickered with uncertainty. 'No one said anything to me, not directly, but when we were on the river boat Richard heard some of the others talking about you. They said – '

'They said what – I was queer? A faggot? A cock-suckin' monkey?'

She lowered her eyes briefly, an unspoken acknowledgement he wasn't far wrong.

'They said – apparently, they were laughing and joking and making crude remarks about you and – '

'Me and James.' He closed the laptop and placed it on the pedestal table beside his end of the sofa. 'Sami, let me make this clear,' he said, turning back to her. 'James let me crash at his place a few nights. I slept on the sofa and he slept in his bed. James is – ' He corrected himself. 'James was as straight as any guy I know.'

'I know he liked girls,' she said, 'but I thought – I thought maybe he liked guys as well.'

The irony made him laugh. 'You thought James was bi? Sami, that's priceless!'

She stared at him. 'He wasn't …?'

'Uh-uh – he was straight,' he said. 'I'm the one who's bi.'

She studied him for a long moment, and he sensed the dynamic between them had changed, but he wasn't sure how.

'I've not had that many girlfriends,' he admitted, 'but early last year I moved in with a girl, and I got her pregnant.'

She didn't hide her surprise. 'What happened?'

'I fucked up.' He hesitated, before confessing, 'She caught me with my pants down, with a guy I'd hooked up with over the internet.'

If she was shocked, she kept her feelings well hidden.

'What about the baby?' she asked.

'There is no baby – the bitch had an abortion. I tried to stop her, but …' He shook his head. 'Like I said, I fucked up – big time. I wanted that kid and – the bitch had no right to do what she did.' He looked deep into her eyes. 'I won't make the same mistake again, if I'm lucky enough to meet someone else.'

They stared at each other for a long moment.

Her expression softened, and she smiled. 'I'm a girl.'

'Yeah, I noticed.'

'Do you like me?'

'Oh, yeah …'

He resisted a sudden, compelling urge, to kiss her.

'I like you, too,' she whispered. 'I like you a lot …'

She didn't object when he placed his hand on her shoulder, slid it around the back of her neck, beneath her hair. 'So …'

'So,' she repeated.

They looked into each other's eyes.

He placed his free hand on her waist, drew her closer. So close her body touched against his. He folded his arms around her, and he felt her arms tighten around him, as she melted against his chest. She felt warm and soft and vulnerable and alive, and he couldn't stop the excitement building inside him as they held each other in a long, loving embrace. He felt something else, too, something more urgent, more intense. More carnal.

As they drew a few inches apart, she reached for the shirt button over his naval and popped it open.

'What I said earlier,' she said, as she slid her hand inside his shirt and spread her hand over his naked skin, 'about making up the bed in the spare room …'

'What about it?' he asked, but he already knew the answer.

Her smile was wicked. 'I don't think we're going to need it.'

Then he kissed her.

Chapter 42

'Where's the boy?'

James closed his legs, pressing them against the kidnapper's waist, as he twisted the bastard's left arm behind his back and held it firmly. The kidnapper, who was pushing thirty, had black hair, a thick black moustache, and at least a couple days growth of stubble. Suddenly awake, the bastard squirmed and wriggled and twisted his head sideways, as he desperately tried to see who was straddling him, holding him down.

'Ce qui – qui sont vous?'

'Someone who's looking for answers.' He planted his elbow on the bastard's nose. Hard. Cartilage crunched and, as he pressed his hand firmly over the bastard's mouth to muffle his cry, blood spurted from his busted nose. 'I suggest you keep the noise level down, if you want to live to see the sun rise again– and let's stick to English, okay?'

The man's nod was frantic. As soon as he removed his hand, the kidnapper coughed blood. He let the bastard see the Swiss Army knife.

'That is my – '

'I borrowed it,' he cut in, touching the point of the blade to the bastard's neck. 'I know the boy was here – I want to know what you've done with him.'

'What boy – I don't know about – '

He silenced him by pressing the knife point into the bastard's neck, deep enough to draw blood. The stainless steel blade wasn't long, only about three inches, but it was plenty sharp enough to slash a man's jugular.

'I'm not in the mood to fuck about,' he warned, in a deceptively soft tone. 'Either you tell me what I want to know, or I'll slit your throat.'

The kidnapper's eyes widened.

'Where's the boy?'

'What boy – I don't – '

'Don't fuckin' lie!'

He cut the bastard's neck, opened up a deep, inch long wound.

'No, please – stop! I – I'll tell you, I'll tell you!'

He lifted the blade, but only a fraction of an inch. 'I'm listening.'

'The boy was here, but he – we didn't hurt him, I swear we didn't hurt him, but ...'

'Go on ...'

'Sabine – last week she got a message.'

'A deadline.'

'*Qui* – a deadline.'

'When?'

The bastard looked confused. 'When?'

'The deadline – when was the fuckin' deadline?'

'Friday – the deadline was Friday at noon.'

Cold fear iced James's spine.

Today was a Sunday, which meant …

I'm two days too late.

Samantha pressed her head into the niche formed by Alex's neck and shoulder. Utterly spent, she clung to him as they lay side-by-side on the bed, bathed in the hot, sweaty glow of their love making.

Slowly, her breathing returned to normal, and so did his. Still she didn't move, but she felt him relax his grip on her, and he kissed her brow. Smiling, she raised her head, and as she did so he kissed her lips. She returned his kiss.

'I'm glad you're here,' she whispered.

'Yeah,' he replied, with a lewd grin, 'me, too.'

She kissed him again. 'Thank you for going to Tenerife.'

'It's the least I can do,' he said. 'It's what James would have done, and I – eighteen days is a long time for a child to be missing, but – '

She put her finger on his lips. 'I know – you'll do everything you can, but no promises.'

'If Luke's alive, I'll find him.'

And if he isn't …

She wasn't stupid.

She knew, with each passing day, the chances of finding her son alive and well diminished, especially now they were back in the UK and Vaughan – she still didn't know if the man she believed had planned her son's kidnap with her husband was alive or dead. She did remember, as clearly as if it were yesterday, the promise James had made when he surprised her in her own kitchen.

One way or another, I'll find him and get him back for you, or I'll die trying.

At the time, they were just words – kind, comforting words, but just words nonetheless. Never did it occur to her he meant it literally, and he probably didn't, but their son's abduction had cost him his life anyway. Alex had avenged his death, but … it was hard to believe, just three days ago, she had been lying in James's arms. She was the first woman he'd slept with, and she was also the last. Now, like her late husband, he was gone and she was determined his body would be flown back home, just as soon as it was recovered by the authorities in Ecuador.

Alex rolled on his back, and she sat up slightly, put her arm around him. Her breasts pressed against his dark, glistening chest, as she leaned against him. Neither of them spoke for several minutes.

'Where do you think James would want to be buried?'

He raised an eyebrow. 'You're asking me?'

'You spent a lot of time with him before – '

'Yeah, but you knew him – I mean, *really* knew him.'

'He was Muslim when we – ' Something occurred to her. 'I wonder if his father's still alive?'

'His father is Pakistani, right?'

She nodded. 'He was born and raised in Salford, and I know he had two brothers – two half-brothers and three half-sisters. I know the address where his family used to live, but …'

'But what?'

'He ran away from home and he turned his back on Islam,' she said. 'I wouldn't be surprised if his father disowned him after he left, but I still feel obliged to try to contact his family, to let them know he's …'

She couldn't bring herself to say the word aloud.

'I think James would prefer a secular burial.'

'Or cremation,' she added, thinking that might be the best option. Then James's ashes could be scattered … she didn't know where.

'Cremation sounds good,' he agreed. 'That's what I want, when my time's up.'

She hadn't given any thought to kind of send-off she wanted, when it was her turn to go, as one day she must. That was one certainty in life. Everyone is born, and everyone dies. Some were luckier than others, and lived a long time … she hoped she would live long enough to enjoy her grandchildren – great-grandchildren, if she was really fortunate.

But … she changed the subject.

'What time are you leaving?' she asked.

'About four, four fifteen – it shouldn't take me more than an hour to drive to Gatwick.'

She glanced at the bedside alarm. The red LED display read 10:03. Leaning across him, she set the alarm to wake them at three thirty. As she came back to her side of the bed, he placed his hand on her waist, and stopped her. Without apparent effort, he lifted her, and as she came down on him he spread his legs apart, just far enough to make space for hers. Lying on top of him, with his arms parallel to her sides and his hands on her buttocks, she felt his genitals press into her groin.

She leaned down and kissed him. 'Have you any idea how long you're going to be away?'

He sighed. 'As long as it takes, I guess – I'll play it by ear.'

It was the answer she expected.

There was something else she wanted to know, but she hesitated for a long moment, before asking.

'And when you do get back …?'

Now he smiled, and he reached up and gently stroked her cheek with his fingertips. 'I live in Croydon, but my office is in Haringey so I'm looking to move north of the river.'

She smiled. 'I can recommend Henley …'

'Yeah, from what I've seen it's a nice place.' His smile broadened. 'The locals are friendly and as luck would have it, I happen to know someone who lives there. She's a single mum, but I've been told I'm good with kids and I was kinda hoping, if things work out the way I want them to …'

His voice trailed off and, as they gazed into each other's eyes, she was almost overcome by the strength of her feelings for him. They had only known each other a relatively short time, but the last three days had been so difficult, so intense, and without him … she needed, desperately, to get Richard out of her system. Forget he'd ever existed. She found herself daring to hope, that out of tragedy, something beautiful might arise. Something genuine, something long lasting. He might have read her mind.

'I'm serious, Sami,' he said, in a low voice. 'I don't want this to be a one nighter … do you?'

She answered him with a deep, passionate kiss.

Chapter 43

The nightclub opened at eleven.

James, having checked the layout from outside and observed the establishment for several hours without seeing anything out of the ordinary, waited until 23:15 before entering. Morocco was a predominantly Muslim country, where the drinking of alcohol was generally frowned on, but in tourist magnets like Casablanca alcohol was readily available at most hotels and supermarkets. Many nightclubs, too, this one included. The front windows were shuttered, to prevent people seeing in, and the lighting inside was muted. It was a gloomy, male-dominated domain, where the only females were prostitutes ... probably a few of the young men, too.

Dressed in black Levis and a shiny black leather jacket over a bright cerise shirt, open at the neck, he'd splashed cheap cologne on his face and rinsed his mouth with strong liquor. He got halfway to the bar before an attractive, scantily dressed young woman with long, silky black hair approached him. She asked if he'd like to buy her a drink. Another time, he might have been interested, aware she was hoping he was seeking more than a drink. A lot more. She was right, he was, but he wasn't interested in what she was hoping to sell. Not tonight. Tonight he was playing a different role, even if he hadn't decided, yet, exactly what role that might be.

Hearing confirmation he'd missed Vaughan's deadline by two days, he'd felt physically sick. But hope was quickly re-ignited, when he learned the kidnappers hadn't carried through the task they had been recruited to undertake.

None of us wanted to do it, he was only a kid ... we decided to take him out to sea, do it there, but then David had a better idea.

The bastards didn't kill his son. Instead, they sold him to a wealthy nightclub owner, with a lucrative side-line in prostitution – including child prostitution.

Having learned David Shaw and Sabine Arnaud had rented an apartment in Casablanca, where they stayed overnight, he gagged the third kidnapper, lashed his arms and legs together, and left him trussed on his bunk while he carried out a quick search of the boat. He found Bruno Fournier's French passport and driving licence, and established the identity of his two accomplices. Then, before he knocked Bruno unconscious, he told him, 'If anything bad has happened to the boy I'll be back, and if you're not here I'll hunt you down and kill you – all three of you.'

It wasn't an idle threat.

The barman was a clean cut young man with gelled black hair. Putting on his best American accent, James ordered for a Bourbon, and when the barman brought his drink he leaned toward him, confidential-like, and in a low voice he asked if Mr Mujahid was around. The barman said hadn't seen him tonight, but when he slipped a $10 bill across the bar, he said he would go check. The barman returned a few minutes later with two other men. One short, one tall. Five six and six four, maybe six five. The big guy was more than twice as broad as the little guy, with biceps thicker than most men's thighs. Hired muscle. The small guy was definitely in charge, but he had no way of knowing if he was Mr Mujahid, so he let him speak first.

'Ali tells me you are looking for Mr Mujahid?'

'That's right,' he said, nodding. He silently urged his boss to reveal his identity, and eyed the gorilla nervously. 'I don't want any trouble ...'

About thirty, with dark olive skin and shoulder length black hair slicked back over his forehead, the small man was wearing a dapper blue suit, with lots of gold around his neck and on his fingers. He smiled, asked, 'American?'

'Guilty as charged,' he answered, winging it. 'I know I don't look it, but my daddy's folks came over from India in the seventies. They settled in Chicago – that's where I was born and raised.' Guessing the small man was probably Muslim, he extended his hand. 'The name's Jackson, Dwaine Jackson.'

The small man accepted his hand, shook it briefly. 'I'm Sulaiman,' he said. 'I regret to inform you Mr Mujahid is a busy man, and he is here only rarely. Perhaps I can be of service?'

He hesitated, feigned embarrassment. 'I – I don't know. It's kinda personal and ...'

'You are looking for a girl?' asked Sulaiman, with a knowing smile.

He really didn't want to do this, but ...

'Not exactly ...' He leaned in closer, lowered his voice. 'The thing is, I prefer boys. Young boys ...'

I can't believe I just said that.

Alex would split his sides laughing.

Sulaiman's smile gave nothing away. 'And you think we have boys here?'

'I know you do,' he said, more confident now. 'When I was here last, Mr Mujahid, he was here and he sorted me out. Right hospitable, he was.

He said I was welcome back anytime. Anytime you're in town and you wanna have some fun, he said, you come and see Mr Mujahid.'

'There are no boys here,' said Sulaiman, and smiled again. 'But – I think Mr Mujahid would not want us to disappoint you. Please forgive my caution, Mr Jackson. We have had some trouble with the police recently, so we have moved the boys to a safer location.'

'That's damn smart,' he said, relieved not to have drawn a blank. 'Cops are like fuckin' pigs – always stickin' their snouts in where they're not wanted.'

He laughed and Sulaiman laughed and the gorilla laughed, though he suspected the gorilla hadn't really understood his joke.

'Your boys, I hope they're all clean and healthy,' he said. 'I've got protection, but I'll be pissed off if I catch anything nasty.'

'They are clean and healthy,' Sulaiman confirmed, 'and eager to please.'

'And young, I hope,' he said, winking. 'I like older boys, but the younger they are the more I love 'em!'

'All our boys are underage, Mr Jackson. The youngest, he is eleven years, but already he knows how to please a man.'

He hid his disgust behind a big grin. 'Then let's do business!'

He was relieved his son wasn't one of the boys on offer, but a little disappointed, too: it meant Luke was being held apart from the other boys. He couldn't believe he was standing here, discussing paying for sex with young boys, as easily as he might snap up a vehicle from a second hand dealer.

Put on the spot, he said he wanted two boys for two hours, and Sulaiman named his price. He hesitated, sucked in a breath, and slowly nodded as he let it out again. 'That's kinda steep, but what the heck, I can afford it!' He tapped the bulge in his jacket pocket, where his wallet was. 'I'm flyin' back to the States tomorrow, so tonight I wanna have me some fun!'

They sealed the deal with a handshake.

Five minutes after he was escorted out of the nightclub by a back entrance, Sulaiman and the gorilla were ushering James into what appeared, from the outside, to be a nondescript two storey family home.

Two heavies, sat either side of a backgammon board, acknowledged Sulaiman and one of them told him, in Arabic, one of the bedrooms was in use. The heavies paid him, James, scant attention. His visit, clearly, was nothing unusual. Sulaiman waved him on. 'The boys are upstairs.'

At the top of the stairs there was a long, narrow landing with two doors on each side. Sulaiman ignored the first bedroom he came to, but pushed the first door on the opposite side open.

'You will use this bedroom.'

As soon as Sulaiman opened the third bedroom, the acrid stink of cigarette smoke assaulted James, and his nostrils detected something else, too. Something illicit. There were six boys and two single beds in the room; three boys on one bed, two on the other, with the smallest boy seated on the rug between the two beds. All six boys were wearing white or light coloured *shalwar kameez*. He judged four of the boys were aged fourteen to sixteen, one was a year or two younger, and although he appeared younger he guessed the small boy on his own must be the eleven year old. Three of the boys were sharing a joint, two others were smoking cigarettes, but the boys made no move to hide anything when he and Sulaiman came into the room.

The five older boys looked spaced out.

'I'm sorry, Mr Jackson,' said Sulaiman, 'I'd forgotten Ibrahim was still here, I was going to take him – '

Going to take him – where?

'Which one is Ibrahim?' he asked, guessing anyway.

'The little one – he is only here a few days.'

The little one, Ibrahim, was the only boy who wasn't smoking. His skin had a healthy, deep bronze hue, his short black hair was tightly curled, and he was the only one of the six boys who appeared lucid and naïve enough to tell anyone anything. And if Ibrahim had only been here for a few days, he dared to hope he might have seen Luke.

'He's well cute – I like him!'

'I'm sorry, Mr Jackson,' said Sulaiman, with an apologetic smile. 'He is only eight – '

'Aw, c'mon, Mr Sulaiman! I told you, I like 'em young!' he said, with a big, pleading grin. 'I'll take him and the eleven year old!'

The older boy, one of the three who were sharing a joint, looked pleased to have been chosen but Ibrahim didn't react. Either the young boy didn't understand the significance of what was happening, or he didn't speak English.

'Please, Mr Jackson, Ibrahim has no experience – '

'He will do, after he's spent a coupla hours with me!'

'Mr Jackson, I – '

He took his wallet out again, saw the greed in Sulaiman's eyes.

The bargaining started.

He opened with an offer of $50 – too high, he quickly realised, when Sulaiman immediately demanded $150. He put on a show, tried to haggle and talk Sulaiman down, before agreeing the young, inexperienced boy was worth an extra $120.

'Naabih will show him how to suck you,' said Sulaiman, after he'd handed over a wad of $10 bills, 'but please, you must not be too rough with him or damage him.'

'Aw, come on – I'm not a monster!' he said, pretending to be offended. 'I don't wanna hurt the kid. I promise I'll be gentle with him.'

Naabih kicked his sandals off, then grabbed the younger boy's arm and yanked him to his feet. Ibrahim started crying. Then, as Naabih struck the boy across the face, Sulaiman spoke rapidly to Naabih in Arabic – told him to call Dahi and Za'ir if the American went too far with the little one.

He gave no indication he had understood every word, and silently guessed Dahi and Za'ir must be the two heavies downstairs – not a pair he wanted to tangle with, so soon after Manny had used his chest for target practice.

He didn't like the way Naabih dragged the sobbing Ibrahim by his arm, but he didn't dare say anything or intervene. Somehow, he kept a smile on his face as well when, as they entered their allotted bedroom, Naabih gave him a cheeky grin – grabbed a handful of his crotch.

'I don't wanna be disturbed,' he said, as Sulaiman exited the bedroom.

'Of course not, Mr Jackson, I understand – I will lock the door for you.'

Chapter 44

Ignoring the two young boys, James scanned the ceiling and walls of the bedroom for hidden cameras or microphones, as he walked around the double bed to the window. He didn't spot anything suspicious.

He tweaked the curtains, saw there were no window locks, and learned the bedroom was located at the rear of the house. There was another building directly opposite, seven or eight yards away, but the bedroom wasn't overlooked and the space between the two buildings was poorly lit. Left was clear, but to the right he could see two huge metal containers, one lidded, the other piled high with garbage. A foot or two beyond the trash containers, there was a twelve foot wall that spanned the alleyway between the two buildings.

He turned around to see both boys were on the bed. Naabih had already shed his *shalwar kameez* and, in Arabic, he was urging Ibrahim to do the same. The younger boy's crying intensified and, as he approached the bed, the boy shied away from him. He didn't know what the other, older boys had told Ibrahim about the men who visited this house, but ...

He thinks I'm going to hurt him.

He judged Ibrahim was actually a year or two older than eight, but even so ... like most people, over the years, he had read too many newspaper reports, watched too many horror stories on TV about child prostitution, and it had always disgusted him to think there were depraved individuals who actively sought out young children for sex. But, before tonight, he had never imagined how easy it could be.

Just flash the cash ...

It occurred to him, if there was a police raid and he was caught in a bedroom with two seriously underage boys, he was in deep, deep shit.

As he reached the bed, Ibrahim shrank further away from him, and sobbed uncontrollably.

He sat on the edge of the bed, positioning himself between Naabih and the ornate, wrought iron headboard. On his side of the bed, fixed to the wall adjacent to the headboard, there was a small white box with a red button in the centre. He suspected, if pressed, the red button would activate an alarm – bring the two heavies running. Naabih gave up on trying to undress the younger boy, and sidled closer to him. A mischievous grin creased the boy's pale features.

'Your cock is big?'

Shocked by the boy's boldness, he neglected to answer with an American accent, but Naabih didn't appear to notice.

'Big enough.'

Up close and naked, the boy was painfully skinny, his cheeks were sunken and the whites of his eyes were bloodshot. The poor kid didn't look old enough to be a regular drug user, but evidently he was ... regrettably, he knew it was only a matter of time before Ibrahim was on the same, slippery slope to an early grave.

Still sobbing, Ibrahim had curled himself into a foetal position, and buried his face under his arms. Why did small children appear to think, if they couldn't see you, you mustn't be able to see them? He reached out, gently touched the young boy's shoulder – felt him flinch.

'Do you speak English?'

'He know some words,' answered Naabih, and grinned again. 'He still virgin.'

He spoke his mind. 'Most eight year olds are.'

'I suck first cock when I six,' Naabih boasted. 'He my father friend – he give me candy.' The boy edged closer, so that his knees indented James's leg. Glancing at Ibrahim, he said, 'You give twenty dollar, I not tell Mr Sulaiman you fuck him.'

He glared at the boy. 'I promised Mr Sulaiman I wouldn't hurt him.'

A shrug, as Naabih reached for James's belt. 'If you want later, you change mind.'

'I'll think about it.' He gripped the boy's skinny wrists, stopped him from unbuckling his belt. 'But first, I want to show you something – both of you.'

Naabih shrugged again, as if to say 'whatever'.

'Ibrahim, I'm not going to hurt you,' he said softly, as he reached to touch the young boy's shoulder again. The boy was too frightened to face him. 'I know you're scared, but I'm not going to hurt you,' he repeated, as he lifted the boy toward him. Ibrahim shrieked hysterically, as he put his arm around him, restrained him from crawling away again. 'I'm not going to hurt you. I promise, I'm not going to hurt you ...'

'He cry like baby,' said Naabih, scowling at the younger boy's distress.

He waited a couple of minutes, for the boy's anguished cries to lessen, before he reached into his pocket.

'I'm looking for a little boy,' he said, showing the two boys a photograph of his son. 'He's only four – '

'We no see him!'

Naabih's denial was too quick, too loud.

His pulse quickened. 'What about you, Ibrahim?'

'He no see him!' Naabih didn't let the young boy speak.

'I think he has – I think you both have,' he said, his excitement growing. 'I know he was here – '

'We no see him,' repeated Naabih, defiantly, before turning to Ibrahim and switching to Arabic. 'Don't tell him anything – he's going to get us into trouble!'

He dropped his fake American accent, and addressed the boys in their native tongue. 'I know the boy was here. I know – I don't think so!'

Suddenly, hearing him speak Arabic, Naabih launched himself toward the red panic button. Reflexively, he caught the boy by the arm – then, with the edge of his right hand, he struck the boy just below his occipital ridge.

Naabih collapsed on the bed.

'Is he dead?'

James leaned over Naabih's prone form, checked his carotid pulse on the right side of his scrawny neck, before relaxing and smiling at Ibrahim.

'He's fine,' he assured the boy, sticking to Arabic. 'He'll sleep for a while, but he's okay.'

The occipital ridge, the region at the back of the head where the base of the skull meets the spine, is extremely vulnerable. In martial arts, striking a blow just below the occipital ridge was a commonly taught technique, and delivered correctly would cause an opponent to immediately blackout. Delivered incorrectly … he had never used the technique on a child before. Relieved he hadn't struck him too hard, he covered the naked boy's waist and legs with the boy's own *shalwar kameez*, before turning back to Ibrahim.

'My name is Hassan,' he said, thinking his old name more appropriate, 'and I'm here because I'm looking for a little boy who's been taken away from his mother. I'm not going to do anything bad to you and I'm not going to hurt you.'

Ibrahim's bronze cheeks glistened with the tears he'd shed, but now he seemed more wary than frightened.

'Mr Sulaiman said you've only been here for a few days …'

No response. He tried again.

'Who brought you here?'

No answer.

'Who brought you here, Ibrahim?'

Hesitation, then in a hushed whisper the boy answered, 'My father.'

He couldn't believe his ears, couldn't comprehend how any father could knowingly bring his son to an evil, depraved place like this.

Or sell him.

'Where's your father now?' he asked.

Tears welled in the boy's eyes again.

'I – I think he's dead. He – he came for me at school and brought me here and he – he had a big argument with Mr Mujahid. Mr Mujahid said my father owed him money, a lot of money, and they started fighting. I saw one of Mr Mujahid's men – he stabbed my father. My father fell down. He was bleeding a lot and – and I heard – I heard one of the men tell Mr Mujahid my father was dead ...'

He put his arm around the boy, hugged him closer. 'I'm sorry, Ibrahim. I'm really sorry.' He felt the boy's tears wet his shirt, as he comforted him. Then, when the boy wiped his eyes on his sleeve and looked up, he said, 'You said your father came for you when you were at school. Were you living with your mother?'

The boy shook his head. 'My mother died when I was little.'

He couldn't help feeling sympathy for the boy.

Been there, done that.

'Who was looking after you, before your father came for you?'

'My uncle.'

The boy's uncle, he learned, was married with three children of his own. Three girls. It became obvious, as he opened up about his uncle, aunt and cousins, Ibrahim had been happy and well cared for where he was, before his father suddenly appeared on the scene and stole him away – brought him here.

'Mr Mujahid,' the boy said, as fresh tears trickled down his cheeks, 'he told me he owns me now.'

'No one owns you, Ibrahim,' he said, softly yet firmly.

'My name – I'm not really called Ibrahim.'

'You're not?'

'I'm called Omar, but I – Mr Mujahid, he told me my new name is Ibrahim. He told me I have to pretend I'm eight, but I'm really ten.'

Ten made more sense than eight. Add a couple of years to Naabih's supposed age, and that would make him thirteen – about right. Clearly, when it came to child prostitution, younger was more lucrative. Having been fleeced twice by Sulaiman, he couldn't pretend he was surprised – just angry and sickened.

'One of my friends at school was called Omar,' he said, smiling as he put his arm around the boy again. This time, he felt the boy lean closer to him. 'It's a good, strong name – one you should be proud of.'

The boy didn't say anything.

He picked up the photograph of his son. 'Omar, if I don't find this little boy quickly and take him back to his mother, Mr Mujahid is going to hurt him.'

The boy didn't speak.

He squeezed the boy's shoulder gently. 'He was here, wasn't he?'

Omar nodded faintly. 'I saw him last night, but Mr Mujahid and Mr Sulaiman came for him this morning.'

Not for the first time, he silently wished he had arrived in Casablanca earlier, but he hadn't … there was something he wanted to know, but was scared to ask.

'While he was here, did he – did anyone hurt him?'

Omar nodded. 'The big boys teased him and made him cry.'

'That's all?'

Another nod.

Relieved his son hadn't been abused, he asked, 'Do you know where Mr Mujahid has taken him?'

'I – I heard him tell Mr Sulaiman to take him to his house.'

'To Mr Sulaiman's house?'

Omar corrected him. 'To Mr Mujahid's house.'

'Do you know where Mr Mujahid lives?'

Not surprisingly, the boy had no idea.

He spent a few more minutes talking to the Omar but, feeling he had drawn as much information as he could from the boy, he knew it was time for him to leave. But …

I can't just leave him here.

If he did, within a matter of weeks or months, Omar would be no better off than Naabih. Still, he hesitated, before asking, 'Do you know where your uncle lives.'

Omar nodded. 'Near the park.'

'The park?' He recalled seeing at least two or three green areas on the tourist map he had studied earlier, but at the time their names hadn't been important. Assuming, of course, the boy's uncle lived in Casablanca.

'*Parc de la Ligue Arabe.*'

'That's here, in Casablanca?'

The boy nodded.

'Do you know your uncle's address?'

The boy rattled it off.

'Okay, Omar,' he said, making the only decision he could live with, 'here's what we're going to do.'

Chapter 45

'Ready?'

The boy nodded. 'Ready.'

James sat on the edge of the bed, to make it easy for Omar to climb on his back. As the boy's arms circled his neck, he said, 'Remember, hold on tight, and don't look down.'

Before standing, he glanced to his right, where Naabih was still out cold. Only now, with strips torn from his own *shalwar kameez*, the boy's hands and legs were bound, he was gagged, and he had been secured to the foot of the bed – well out of reach of the panic button.

James had already opened the bedroom window, to recce the best route down. There was a drainage pipe, about three feet to the right of the window, but nothing else he could climb down. It was too dark to see, from where he was, if the drainage pipe was plastic or metal. If the circumstances were different, he would have simply lowered himself from the window ledge and risked dropping to the ground, but his chest had taken a battering and with a small child clinging to him, the drainage pipe was an easier, safer option.

He felt Omar's arms squeeze his neck tighter, as he climbed out of the window. A cool breeze caused a sudden chill to pass through him, as he edged along the window ledge. He stretched out his right hand toward the drainage pipe. He couldn't quite reach it. He stole another few inches of window ledge, and tried again. This time, just, his fingertips touched the near edge of the pipe.

As he leaned away from the window ledge, and toward the drainage pipe, he circled it with his fingers. Grime and what felt like rust flaked off. The pipe was metal, not plastic. That was a positive. Metal is stronger. He felt some give, as he tested how secure the pipe was, but not enough to concern him.

He was mistaken.

As soon as he transferred his and the boy's combined weight to the drainage pipe, he knew they were in trouble. Metal creaked ominously, and suddenly the bracket above his head screeched, as it was wrenched out of the wall.

He swore under his breath, as the pipe drifted away from the wall. The top end of the pipe had detached from the wall. Suspended fifteen feet above the ground, he slowly twisted his neck, glanced down. There was another bracket a few feet below him … he was horrified to realise, if the second bracket failed and he fell backward, he would probably land on top the boy.

I can't allow that to happen.

Omar started crying.

Ignoring the boy's distress, he tightened his grip on the pipe and held himself motionless, as he considered his options. If he tried to change position, or started to shimmy down the pipe, the movement might –

The pipe lurched another inch, as below him metal ground and strained against brick. No time to lose, he tried desperately to swing himself around the pipe – but, just as he'd feared, as soon as he shifted position the bracket below him tore out of the wall.

He plummeted to the ground.

Metal clanged noisily against metal, as the upper section of the drainage pipe crashed down on top of one of the large trash containers. Omar screamed in his ear and, as it came to a sudden halt two feet off the ground, the metal pipe slammed into his chest.

Fire blazed anew inside him.

The pipe recoiled and hit his chest again, and he wavered on the edge of a deep, black void as he fought to remain conscious. He must have blacked out for a second or two, because when he raised his head and opened his eyes, he was lying on the ground, with the bent drainage pipe having come to rest over his right shoulder.

Clutching his chest, where the fire burned fiercest, he was relieved to see Omar had been thrown clear. The boy was sitting just a few feet away from him, crying, but he didn't appear to be hurt.

Only too aware the sudden commotion must have been heard by someone inside the house, he reached up, used the drainage pipe to lever himself to his knees. He struggled to his feet. He was leant against the drainage pipe, trying to catch his breath and trying to come to terms with the crippling pain inside his chest, when the ground floor window directly ahead of him was suddenly illuminated.

He turned to the boy.

'Run, Omar,' he urged. 'I'll catch up with you …'

The back door flew open and the two heavies burst out.

'It's the American!'

'He's got one of our boys!'

James was in no fit state to run, even if he had wanted to. In his peripheral vision he noted Omar hadn't heeded his advice, and wasn't running, either.

'He's hurt!'

'Not as hurt as he is gonna be when we get our hands on him!'

The two heavies spoke Arabic, doubtless assuming 'the American' couldn't understand their exchange. He did, but he couldn't deny the heavies were right: he was hurt, the pain of the fall relived with each excruciating breath. He watched but he didn't move, as the two heavies moved into the alleyway, deliberately blocking his only escape route.

The heavy to his right was a bear of a man in every respect. At least six three, with a dense, black beard and huge, swarthy arms, the man even ambled like a bear. The bear's partner, to his left, was only a couple of inches shorter, but he was clean shaven, lighter skinned and leaner – and, he judged, the more dangerous opponent.

I'm going to have to fight.

Even before he completed the thought, a nine inch blade appeared in the bear's right hand, but it could have been worse. A lot worse. If either of the heavies was packing a firearm of any description, he might already be dead.

I have to end this quickly.

He was in no fit state to fight, not up close and dirty – and if the heavies got him on the ground …

'You make big mistake, American.' The bear grinned, as he waved the blade threateningly in front of him, making sure he saw it. 'Now I gut you like a dog!'

He waited, not moving as the two heavies began to close on him. On his own, in good health, he could have been up and over the wall behind him in a matter of seconds. But he wasn't in good health, and there was no way he was leaving without Omar. He took a deep breath, and another, as he tried to clear his mind and focus.

The bear was almost within striking distance when he made his move. Instead of backing off, as most people brandishing a blade would expect, he suddenly stepped forward on his left foot, and kicked sharply upward with his right. The topside of his foot connected with the bear's wrist, breaking it. The bear howled and the blade flew into the air.

Before the blade clattered harmlessly to the ground, showing no mercy, he twisted his hip, pivoted on his standing foot and snapped his kicking knee, sending his foot out sideways in a powerful roundhouse kick. His instep struck the bear's forearm, crushed it against his ample girth. Bone snapped and the bear screamed again.

He sensed, rather than heard, his second opponent closing on him from behind. No time to spin around, he glanced over his shoulder and leaned forward slightly as he executed a back kick, raising and bending his right leg, and kicking backward with the heel of his foot in one swift, fluid movement.

It was one of karate's most powerful kicks, and a strike to the stomach or groin would instantly incapacitate an opponent, but he'd rushed the move and his heel caught his opponent on the thigh – hard enough to stop him in his tracks, and knock him backward. Quickly, before his opponent recovered his balance, he spun around and used the power of his hips and legs to throw a reverse punch to the side of his opponent's head. His opponent hit the ground and didn't get up.

He turned back to his first opponent.

The bear, cradling his shattered arm against his chest, backed off as he stood with his left leg forward and his hands raised, poised and ready for action.

Then, suddenly, the bear turned and hurried back into the house.

He relaxed his stance, but he had only taken two steps toward Omar, when he collapsed to his knees. While he'd been fighting, he had blocked everything thing else out, but now … head down, face creased with agony as he grasped his fiery chest, he fought to hold on to consciousness.

I – we have to go.

The boys he'd been shown apart, he had no idea who else might be in the house, and he didn't want to find out. And reinforcements from the nightclub were only five minutes away. He placed his hands on his thighs, forced himself to his feet, staggered over to Omar and grasped the boy's hand.

He asked, 'Are you hurt?'

The boy shook his head.

'Great – let's get out of here.'

Chapter 46

'Are you a ninja?'

Despite his discomfort, the question brought a smile to James's face. 'Not exactly,' he answered, 'but I have been studying martial arts since I was little.'

He watched the red *petit taxi* they'd just stepped out of turn a corner, before he led Omar across what was, given it was past midnight, a surprisingly busy street, headed for the Peugeot 206 he'd hired. It was the second taxi he'd hailed in under ten minutes, in an effort to break their trail, should Sulaiman or anyone else attempt to follow them. Luckily, he had flagged down the first taxi – a shared *grands taxi* which already had two occupants – only a minute or so after he tangled with the two heavies, and as the taxi pulled up he told Omar, 'If anyone asks tell them you're my son.'

He regretted his statement before it even left his lips. It was a stupid, insensitive thing to say to a young boy who not so many days ago appeared to have witnessed his father's murder, but if he was upset or offended in any way Omar didn't show it. Quite the opposite. Not so long ago, the boy had been too frightened to even look at him. Now, Omar held his hand all the way to his car and chatted away like they had known each other for years.

'What does your uncle do?' he asked, after he'd fired the engine and pulled out into traffic.

'He's a teacher – he teaches at a big school.'

James had no knowledge of the education system in Morocco, but guessed Omar must still be at the equivalent of primary school. Having consulted his tourist map, and located *Parc de la Ligue Arabe*, he headed north. He assumed, once they got closer, Omar would be able to direct him to his uncle's home.

'Do you like school?'

'Sometimes I like it,' Omar answered. 'I like playing football and I like painting and I like playing with my friends, but I don't like writing and I don't like going to mosque, but my uncle makes me go.'

He smiled again. 'My father used to make me go to mosque, too.'

There was, he believed, a fine dividing line between culture and religion – and indoctrination. Of course, it was only natural Muslim parents should want their children to grow up adhering to Islamic teachings, but – he didn't want to risk promoting conflict between Omar and his uncle, and let the subject drop.

'Writing's very important, Omar,' he said. 'If you can't write or read properly, how are you going to learn about anything when you're older?'

'I'm a good reader,' said Omar, proudly. 'Auntie reads with me every night before I go to bed. I like reading, but I don't like writing.'

'That's no excuse for not trying,' he said. 'I wasn't very good at martial arts when I first started, but that didn't stop me from trying my best, and the harder I tried the more I improved.'

'My uncle always tells me to try my best.'

'Your uncle sound like a wise man – you should listen to him.'

'When I get big like you, I'm going to be a policeman like my Uncle Ahmed.'

He took his eye off the road, just long enough to glance at the boy. 'You have an uncle who's a policeman?'

Omar nodded. 'He catches bad men and puts then in prison.'

'Does he work here, in Casablanca?'

'Yes, he lives near us and I sleep at his house sometimes, and I like playing with my cousins. They're called Saeed and Shiraz, and my uncle Ahmed takes us to watch football sometimes, when he's not working. We support Raja, they're the best team!'

The boy chattered on, all the way to the front door of a second floor apartment.

'Nadia, Nadia – come quickly!'

James stood outside the apartment, smiling as he watched a bearded man in his late twenties scoop Omar up in his arms, and hug him tightly. The boy's uncle, he presumed, who Omar had told him was called Tariq.

A woman, a year or two younger and much shorter, with a pretty face and long black hair, came into view. Both Tariq and his wife were wearing what he guessed must be their night clothes. Nadia shrieked wildly when she spotted the boy in her husband's arms.

It was a happy reunion.

He waited until Omar's aunt claimed him and the boy's uncle turned to him. Not surprising, given his appearance, Tariq assumed he was Muslim.

'*Assalamu 'alaykum.*' Peace be upon you.

'*Wa alaikum assalam.*' And on you be peace.

They shook hands.

'Come in, my friend,' said Tariq, in Arabic, 'you are most welcome. You must come in and tell me everything. We have been so worried!

When his school contacted me and told me Omar's father had taken him, I feared we might never see him again.'

James slipped off his shoes, placed them on a wooden rack behind the door, and followed Tariq into a small square room that was austere by Western standards. Armless sofas against three walls, plain rugs on the floor, and in one corner there was a tall, single-stemmed *hookah*, for smoking flavoured tobacco after it has passed through water. There was one large picture on the wall, a photograph of hundreds of worshipers crammed around the *Ka'aba*, a black cuboid shaped building in the centre of the world's largest mosque, the Masjid al-Haram, in the holy city of Mecca. The picture was adorned with several verses, in green and gold, from the holy *Qur'an*. Omar and his aunt were nowhere to be seen but, although muted, he could still hear their excited chatter.

He knew it was the local custom to make small talk first, and drink tea – mint tea, most likely, before getting down to business. He couldn't afford that luxury so, at the risk of offending his host, he said, 'Please forgive me for being rude, but Omar told he has an uncle who works for the police.'

Tariq didn't hide his surprise. 'That would be Ahmed, my wife's brother,' he said. 'He is a detective with *La Sûreté Nationale*.' The National Police Force. 'Why do you ask?'

'I'd like to talk to him – now, if possible. I know it's late, but I wouldn't ask if it wasn't important.'

Tariq stared at him for a long moment, and nodded. Two minutes later, he was holding Tariq's mobile to his ear, talking to Ahmed. He kept it as concise as he could, and before he ended the call he made a request, and Ahmed promised he would see what he could do.

'Is it true?' asked Tariq, accepting his mobile back. 'Omar's father is dead?'

'According to Omar it is,' he said, nodding. Not knowing how close Tariq and the dead man had been, he added, 'I'm sorry.'

Tariq shook his head sadly. 'I will not mourn his passing.' They sat on adjacent sofas. 'He was my sister's husband, but he was a bad man – always drinking and gambling and chasing women ...'

James learned Omar's mother had died in childbirth when he was only three. The baby didn't survive, either, leaving Omar alone with a father who was better at getting into trouble than he was at caring for his son.

'Omar had been left alone for five days when we found him,' Tariq revealed. 'No one could tell us where his father was, and when he didn't come home we took Omar in and we have been raising him like he is our own son.'

Tariq left the room briefly, and returned carrying a tray with two glasses, a stainless steel teapot, a bowl of hard sugar cones, a sprig of fresh mint and a plate of sweet pastries on it. Omar, changed into a nightshirt, trailed his uncle into the room.

Tariq smiled. 'Omar would like to say something before he goes to bed.'

Grinning, the boy approached James. 'Thank you for rescuing me.'

'Thank you for telling me where my son is,' he replied, and he managed not to flinch too obviously when Omar threw his arms around him and squeezed his chest, as they hugged each other.

They wished each other goodnight, and before departing for bed Omar said, 'I hope you find your little boy before Mr Mujahid hurts him.'

'Thank you, Omar – so do I.'

Having been a soldier, James was used to waiting and he was good at it, but that didn't mean he enjoyed it. Sometimes he did, but mostly he didn't. He didn't care for mint tea, either, but he knew it would be impolite to refuse. He watched Tariq place several fresh mint leaves in each glass, before picking up the stainless steel teapot. The teapot had a long curved spout and Tariq poured the tea from a great height, filling the glasses in two stages, which resulted in froth on the tea.

He spooned a sugar cone into the glass Tariq passed him, and was pleasantly surprised when he sipped the mint tea. It was a little sweet for his palate, it would have been better without added sugar, but wonderfully refreshing. Tariq insisted he eat something as well, and he selected a pastry that reminded him of a misshapen doughnut, liberally sprinkled with sugar and oozing honey.

Now he made small talk, all the time hoping Ahmed would phone back with the information he needed, but he didn't. Ahmed called round in person instead.

Chapter 47

Ahmed pocketed his mobile, and sighed. 'My colleagues have raided the property where you found Omar – they were too late.'

James was disappointed to hear it, but not surprised. Clearly, it had taken him longer to get Omar home safely than it had for Sulaiman to transfer Naabih and the other boys to another, more secure location. A pity, but … he concentrated on following an unmarked police vehicle, headed for the affluent suburb of Aïn Diab, which ran along the Atlantic beachfront to the west of downtown Casablanca. There were two plain clothes officers in the lead vehicle, but Ahmed had elected to travel with him, so they could exchange information.

An older, male version of his sister, Ahmed was short and wiry, with a round, clean shaven face, silver rimmed glasses and short black hair. He was wearing a dark suit, light blue shirt and black shoes. No tie. No firearm, either, unless it was extremely well concealed.

After filling in some of the detail he had omitted in their telephone conversation, James said, 'Tell me about Mujahid.'

'His name is Muhammad Kamal Mujahid,' said Ahmed. 'He is forty-one, born and raised here in Casa. He has been on our radar for a number of years.'

'For?' The vehicle ahead turned left, and moments later he did the same.

'We believe he is a high level player in drug trafficking, money laundering, and of course prostitution – however, before tonight we were not aware of any involvement with child prostitution.'

'Has he ever been prosecuted?'

'Never,' replied Ahmed. 'He is an intelligent man, and very cautious. He is extremely wealthy and influential. To date, we have failed to compile enough evidence against him, to arrest him and bring him to trial.'

Something didn't feel right.

Why would a very cautious, intelligent man, who had managed to avoid arrest for however many years, risk taking a small boy he had acquired illegally to the luxury villa where he lived? Simple answer: he wouldn't. He was equally certain Omar hadn't lied to him, but the boy might have misheard or misunderstood what he'd overheard. But before he could query the point, Ahmed carried on.

'As well as the nightclub you visited, Mujahid owns two hotels, several restaurants and – ' He cursed loudly, and slapped his thigh. 'Turn around, turn around now – we're headed in the wrong direction!'

Ahmed's excitement was contagious.

'Mujahid owns a home – a children's home. It's one of the biggest private orphanages in the country. *That* is where we will find your son, I'm certain of it!'

Tyres squealed as James executed a U-turn.

The best place to hide a grain of sand is on a beach. James couldn't think of a better, more anonymous place to hide a stolen child than in an orphanage.

Luke's here, he's got to be here ...

The white-washed façade of the orphanage was dimly lit, and it reminded him of a nondescript, two storey hotel. It didn't look particular large, at least not from the outside, but Ahmed informed him it housed at least a hundred abandoned or orphaned children. No lights were evident inside the building. There was no visible security, either. No night guard, no CCTV. Ahmed reckoned, being a children's home, there was certain to be someone on night duty and he was correct. Ahmed asked his two colleagues to wait in their car then, seconds after he hammered on the front door, the frosted glass panel above the door suddenly lit up. A female voice asked, 'Who is it?'

'Police!' shouted Ahmed. 'Open the door!'

A woman in her mid-twenties, with shoulder length black hair and wearing a black shawl over a pale blue blouse, appeared. She only half-opened the door, but it was enough for Ahmed to thrust his police badge under her nose, and identify himself. The door opened wide, and James followed Ahmed inside. The woman glanced at him, no doubt assuming he must be police as well, but she didn't speak to him and, for the moment, he was happy to let Ahmed do the talking.

'What is this about?' asked the woman, understandably nervous given it was well after midnight.

'We have received a tip-off,' said Ahmed.

The woman looked even more worried. 'A tip-off?'

'Is there somewhere we can talk?'

'Of course.'

The woman led them to a medium sized office with magnolia walls. Two small windows. Several certificates and photographs of smiling children on the walls. Three desks, hiding under papers and files and two PCs. Three black leather swivel chairs. A row of four-drawer filing cabinets. Bookshelves. As the woman turned to face him, Ahmed said,

'We are here to check if there is any truth in certain allegations that have been made.'

'What allegations?'

James asked, 'Have you taken in any new children in the past few days?'

'I – I'm not sure.' The woman scratched her ear. 'I only work nights, so I don't really get to know the children that well. I – I could go wake Mrs Bouchtat, she's the Administrator and – '

'I assume written records are kept?' said Ahmed.

'Of course, but – '

'Show me.'

The woman located a lever-arch file, which she found on one of the desks, already opened. The records showed two children had arrived in the past few days, both boys. A seven year old called Yousef – and a five year old called Hakim.

That's him, that's got to be him ...

His son was four years and a half, not five, and he was called Luke, not Hakim. But a child as young as his son, even if he had been genuinely abandoned or orphaned, might not know how old he was. Not accurately. And even if he did, he thought it was a fair assumption Luke spoke only English. Not Arabic. Not French. So, his son probably wouldn't have understood a word anyone had said to him at the orphanage, and he would have been too confused and too scared to speak up.

It wouldn't be difficult, to falsify paperwork – fix a child's age and change his identity. That's what happened to Omar, and he was a lot older than Luke ... almost old enough to start earning his keep. This, he realised, is where Sulaiman should have brought Omar, and he probably still would have done, if he hadn't rescued the boy. Then, in another year or two ... how difficult would it be, when a boy or girl reached a certain age, to claim the child had run away, or been reclaimed by a relative, or been adopted – by a rich American couple, perhaps. So long as the paperwork was in good order, no one would question and no one would investigate, and no one would know that poor child's true fate.

'We have four dormitories,' the woman revealed, 'two for boys, one for girls and a mixed dormitory for the little ones. We have a lot more boys than girls.'

'What do you know about Hakim?' he asked.

'Only what it says here,' the woman answered, glancing down at the file on the desk in front of her. 'Apparently he was found abandoned – it doesn't say where or who brought him in.'

'I want to see him.'

The woman hesitated. 'He's asleep,' she said. 'All the children are, and – I really should go wake Mrs Bouchtat.'

'And so you shall,' said Ahmed, 'after we've seen the boy.'

Looking relieved the responsibility for whatever was happening wouldn't be on her shoulders for much longer, the woman agreed. 'He's on the mixed ward,' she said, leading the way out of the office.

Walking along a dimly lit corridor, close behind the woman with Ahmed trailing him, James felt his pulse racing and his heart pounding. He was excited, but he was scared, too, and his head buzzed with questions.

What if it isn't him?

What then?

What if it is him?

What then?

What if I don't recognise him?

All he had to go on was a holiday snapshot.

What if he looks at me and asks, 'Who are you?'

He hadn't told Ahmed he and his son had never met.

Will Ahmed allow me to take him?

He couldn't prove Luke was his son.

The woman led them down a flight on stone steps, and flicked a switch at the bottom, lighting up another corridor. 'We don't have enough beds for all the children,' she said, as they approached double doors painted brown. 'Some of the little ones have to double up.'

There was a room plan on the wall outside the dormitory, showing two rows of eleven beds. He spotted the name 'Hakim' before she stabbed the plan with her forefinger.

Eight beds along on the right.

'Here he is,' she said. 'He's sharing with Abdullah.'

There was a round window, about eighteen inches across, in each of the double doors at head height, and in the dormitory itself he could see night lights on each side, every two or three beds along. The woman switched off the light in the corridor, reached to open the dormitory doors, but Ahmed stopped her.

'We'll wait here.' He placed his hand on James's shoulder, and they exchanged knowing glances. Ahmed knew he must be nervous, but he had no idea how nervous.

The woman said, 'Please be quiet ...'

He didn't say anything.

Just pushed the double doors open – stepped into the dormitory.

This is it.

The moment of truth.

245

He allowed his eyes time to adjust to the darkness, before striding past the first twelve beds, without even glancing at the small children sleeping on them. He did glance at the seventh bed on his right.

Two little girls slept head to toe.

The children in the next bed were boys – again, sleeping head to toe. The face of the head nearest him belonged to a three or four year old, and the boy had a mop of curly black hair.

Not Luke.

The second boy wasn't significantly bigger, and he couldn't see him clearly … slowly, bracing himself against disappointment, he walked between two beds to get a closer look. The boy was sleeping on his back, with his head turned sideways … the instant he saw his face, he knew his search was over.

He swallowed a hard lump forming in his throat, and felt a magical welling of emotion building inside him as he knelt beside the bed. He raised his hand to touch his son's cheek – lowered it again without doing so. He'd wanted this moment so much, but now it was upon him he didn't seem to know what to do or how to react … tears filled his eyes, as he watched his son sleeping. He was a beautiful, beautiful child, and he looked so peaceful … he leaned down, kissed his son's forehead.

He hesitated then, gently, he lifted the sleeping boy out of bed and cradled him in his arms. He felt a sharp twinge inside his chest, but ignored it. His son didn't open his eyes, didn't wake. He kissed his son again, and whispered in his ear.

'Daddy's come to take you home.'

Chapter 48

Samantha woke suddenly.

Graphic images of James's naked, bullet-ridden corpse faded from her mind, and ... it was a bad dream, nothing more than a bad dream. But James *was* dead.

Realising where she was, and who was lying next to her, she snuggled closer. Alex was lying on his back. She put her hand on his firm, smooth chest, and impulsively leaned across and kissed him. She felt him stir, and he straightened his legs as he turned to face her, showed her the whites of his eyes. It was too dark to see his other features, even from a few inches away, but she sensed he was smiling.

'Sorry,' she whispered. 'I didn't mean to wake you.'

He kissed her lips. 'I'm not complaining.'

She smiled, too, as beneath the duvet he put his hand around her waist and drew her closer. Their bodies touched. He kissed her again, as she slowly moved her hand down his chest, and spread her fingers over his navel. Last night, she had been surprised to discover his head wasn't the only part of his anatomy he shaved. Now, as she moved her hand lower, she found he was deliciously warm and flaccid.

He moaned softly as she fondled him, and she could almost hear the rush of blood as he hardened. Her breasts pressed against his chest, and she could feel his heart beating fast, as their kisses became more passionate.

Breathing hard, she released him and withdrew her hand from between them, as his hands gripped her buttocks and crushed his body against hers. His erection pressed into her groin, and she groaned pleasurably as he rubbed against himself her vulva, over and over and over again.

The phone on the bedside cabinet rang.

She froze and so did he.

'It might be important.' His mouth was less than an inch away from hers.

Silently, reluctantly, she agreed with him.

She tore herself away from him, clambered over him and reached for the phone, which was still ringing urgently.

'Hello?' She was still short of breath.

'Sami, it's James.'

What!

It wasn't a great connection but his voice was unmistakable.

But – it can't be! That's impossible!

'Who is it?' asked Alex, placing his hand on her shoulder as he leaned closer.

Her mouth was so dry she couldn't speak.

He asked again. 'Who is it?'

'James …'

'No fuckin' way. It can't be – he's dead!'

That's what she believed as well, but …

The line had gone quiet.

It can't be – he's dead.

Silence.

Dread began to spread inside her like an incurable cancer, as she whispered, 'James …?'

'I'm here … I can call back, if this is a bad time.'

'No, of course not – I'm sorry, we thought – ' She stopped, realising she had said 'we' and not 'I'.

'I'm in Morocco, and I'm headed for Rabat-Salé Airport.' A brief pause. 'He's asleep, but I've got your son with me.'

Her heart exploded inside her ribcage. 'You mean – Luke's alive?'

She hardly dare believe what she was hearing.

'Alive and unharmed.'

'Don't forget to bring his passport.'

'James, I – '

He broke the connection.

Having pulled over to make the call, he was sitting in the Peugeot 206 he'd hired, with Samantha's son – *his* son – sleeping in the child seat behind him.

He wanted to scream.

It was the early hours of the morning in both Morocco and the UK, but he hadn't wanted to wait until the sun rose before he contacted Samantha, to break the news her son was safe and well and on his way home. He knew she would want to know immediately, as she had every right to … initially, when she picked up, he couldn't understand why she was so breathless if he'd just woken her. Then, in the background, he heard another voice – a male voice he recognised.

That's when the awful truth hit him.

He couldn't have felt worse, if he'd been on the wrong end of a vicious beating by a gang of racist thugs. He fought for air, bent forward and banged his head against the black steering wheel. His cracked ribs hurt like crazy. He closed his eyes but all he could see, in his imagination, is Samantha and Alex in bed together.

Tears stung his eyes.

He couldn't remember the last time he'd cried, before he set eyes on his son for the first time, and he didn't want to cry again now but he couldn't stop the tears. Angry with himself, he wiped the moisture away with his sleeve, but no sooner had he done so than another tear escaped, rolled down his cheek. The images of them making love screamed inside his head until he couldn't bear it any more.

He wanted to know – why?

Why? Why? WHY?

He wanted Samantha to know how much what happened three days ago, on board the *Amazon Dawn V*, meant to him. He wanted to get to know his son. He wanted to start seeing her again, tell her how much he wanted to be with her – how much he loved her.

But, in that moment, he knew he couldn't.

He fired the engine, resisted a desire to floor the accelerator only because there was a four year old boy sleeping behind him, blissfully unaware any chance they had of getting to know each other as father and son was gone.

I put my life on the line, I let Manny believe he'd killed me, so I could get our son back – and now I have, you're screwing the only real friend I've made since I was kicked out of the army.

Life, sometimes, was brutal.

He kept driving through the night … the pain inside his head, like the hurt racking his chest, became bearable but it didn't fade away. He soon lost all sense of time as headed toward Rabat, which he had chosen ahead of a return to Casablanca's Mohammed V International Airport on Ahmed's advice, to avoid trouble.

But now, trouble had slammed into him like a tank.

He drove on … he was halfway to the capital when his mobile rang. Answering it while driving, in the UK, would be a criminal offence. He had no idea what the law in Morocco had to say on the matter, but he did know who must be calling.

'James, it's – '

'Have you booked a flight?'

'Yes, I – there's no direct flight, so I'll be travelling via Paris. I – '

'What time are you scheduled to arrive?'

As soon as she told him, he ended the call, and slipped his mobile back in his pocket. He was in no mood for making small talk. No mood to listen to excuses. What had happened, had happened, and there wasn't a damned thing he or anyone else could do to change it.

His mobile rang again, twice in as many minutes, but he ignored it. Then, before she tried again, he turned his phone off.

Ten hours, eleven if was lucky – that's how long he'd got, before his son's mother touched down and reclaimed him. Earlier, he'd decided it wasn't his place to reveal his true identity to the boy, but now … it would be easy to place all the blame on Alex, but that would be harsh. But when he asked Alex to take care of Samantha, this is *not* what he had in mind.

They thought I was dead.

Samantha's reaction, when she answered his call, confirmed it.

Like she was hearing a ghost speak.

He couldn't remember his exact words but, not wanting Vaughan or Manny to know he had survived the latter's trigger happy assault, he recalled telling Captain Mendoza they thought he was dead, and that he would like to keep it that way. At the time, Mendoza hadn't given him any kind of assurance, but … no matter how he looked at it, he couldn't deny Samantha was sleeping with Alex for one very good reason: she wanted to.

Where does that leave me?

Chapter 49

'He's turned it off.'

Alex swore, and ran his hand back across his shaven head. 'I'm sorry, Sami.'

'It's not your fault,' she said. She'd had a quick shower while he was sitting on the bed with her laptop, booking her flight, and thrown on a pair of black Chino trousers and a black and peach blouse, but he was still naked.

'I guess,' he said, standing up and turning toward her, 'but I – Sami, can I ask you something?'

She couldn't stop herself, surreptitiously, from glancing down.

If you've got it, flaunt it.

He definitely had it, and he wasn't shy of flaunting it. He was, without question, an extremely fit, attractive man – very desirable. He was a wonderful lover, too.

And James isn't?

'Of course,' she answered, before she forgot his question. She tried not to let her nervousness show.

'You and James, I know you have some history,' he started, a little awkwardly, 'but – do you still have feelings for him?'

She found herself nodding. 'Of course I do, he's the father of one of my sons – but he doesn't have any claim on me, if that's what's bothering you.'

'I reckon he still has feelings for you,' he persisted. 'He's never said anything, but I've noticed the way he looks at you.'

He wasn't telling her anything she didn't already know.

She had noticed the way James looked at her, too, and the intimacy they'd shared in South America re-awakened so many happy memories, stirred emotions she thought she'd long since buried. But … she put her arms around Alex's waist, forced a smile.

'I spent the night with you – not James.'

'Yeah, I know – half of it, anyway,' he said, with a grin, 'but let's be honest, nothing would have happened between us, if we'd known James was alive.'

'You're probably right,' she conceded, 'but I thought he was dead – we both did. We can't change what's happened, or the fact that James knows, even if we want to.'

Silence.

She didn't know what to say.

She didn't say anything.

'I got hit when I wearing a flak jacket once,' he said, 'when I was serving in Iraq. I was sore for days afterwards. Let me tell you, James was taking a helluva risk, letting that fuckin' Nazi pump ten rounds into him. One head shot …' He shook his head slowly. 'Bye-bye, buddy.'

'But I don't understand,' she said, 'why would he want to fake his own death?'

'To buy some time,' he answered. 'We talked a lot about how he might do it, once he'd found out where Luke was being held. I'm guessing he forced the Nazi to talk, but he didn't let me in on what he was planning.' He shook his head again. 'He's one crazy fucker – I really believed he was a goner.'

She recalled, once again, the words James had spoken in her kitchen.

I'll find him and get him back for you, or I'll die trying.

Suddenly, she felt terrible – worse, knowing how much James must be hurting, physically as well as mentally.

He let Manny shoot him ten times.

Even with body armour for protection, that had to hurt. James had put his life on the line to rescue their son – a son he'd never even met.

And this is how I repay him.

Alex grinned. 'I wouldn't say no to a threesome.'

He said it jokingly, but his attempt at light-heartedness fell flat. His words did, however, remind her that he was bisexual.

'You like him, don't you?'

'Sure I do,' he answered, 'he's a likeable guy. He knows I'm bi, and he doesn't give a toss – we can joke about it and have fun. He's the only straight guy I've had that kinda relationship with.'

She sensed there was more to it than that. 'Do you fancy him?'

He hesitated, and scratched his groin. 'Yeah, I did, when we first met. But – okay, I admit it. I'd still be interested if he was, but he isn't and I respect that.'

She found his honesty refreshing, but …

'So what happens now,' he asked, placing his hands on her waist, 'when you get back with Luke?'

What indeed?

'I …' She faced at him, and sighed. 'Alex, I'd be lying if I said I knew the answer to that because I don't. Right now, I just want to see my son again, but beyond that …'

'Yeah, that's what I figured.' He didn't look surprised, but he did sound disappointed, by her response.

'I need to pack an overnight bag,' she said, breaking his hold on her. The earliest return flight he'd been able to book for her and Luke was early tomorrow morning. He'd asked about booking a seat for James as well and, after discussing it, they'd agreed it would be churlish not to.

'Anything I can do?' he asked.

'I can manage, thanks,' she said, not intending to pack any more than she could squeeze into her hand luggage. 'Why don't you go back to bed?'

He shook his head. 'No point, I won't be able to sleep – and I've got a flight to Tenerife to cancel.'

He did put a pair of white boxers on, but nothing else. He still looked great. Little more than an hour later, she was ready to leave.

'Are you sure you're going to be okay on your own with Josh?'

'Don't worry, I'll have him at school for ten to nine,' he said, 'and I won't forget what time to pick him up.'

She reminded him, as he accompanied her to the front door, to ring the DI they'd spoken to yesterday as well, to let him know Luke had been found safe and well. They embraced and kissed, and three hours later she was crossing the English Channel, on her way to Paris. Her connecting flight was only a few minutes late and, as the distance between her and Morocco's capital steadily decreased, so she felt her excitement growing, but she was increasingly nervous, too – and not a little scared.

How is James going to react?

She desperately wanted to see Luke again, give him a big hug and tell him how much she loved him ... she hadn't a clue what she was going to say to James. She owed him a huge debt of gratitude, but ...

Her flight from Paris to Rabat landed ten minutes late.

With no baggage to collect, she cleared customs ahead of most of her fellow travellers, and she hurried through the arrivals lounge. As soon as she exited, she looked this way and that, quickly scanning the myriad of faces of all waiting to greet or meet someone.

'Sami ...'

James!

She spun around, spotted him instantly, only eight or nine yards away. He was carrying their son but he put him down as, briefly, their eyes locked.

'Mummy!'

Luke spotted her. He started running, and she did, too. As they met, she scooped him up in her arms, and when he said 'Mummy' again she burst into tears. She hugged her son fiercely, tears streaming down her cheeks, and kissed him over and over again.

'Mummy, why are you crying?'

'Oh, sweetie,' she sobbed, laughing and crying at the same time, 'I'm crying because I'm so happy. I thought I'd lost you, I thought …' She kissed him again, and hugged him to her chest.

Then she remembered James.

Wiping her tears away with the back of her hand, she turned to where he had been standing, just a few moments ago. 'James, I …'

James was gone.

Chapter 50

Nine weeks later
London, England

James opened his eyes.

The nightmare faded, and as it did so he realised where he was: in a strange bed with a thirty-something woman he'd picked up last night.

Or did she pick me up?

Whatever.

He didn't think he'd had that much to drink, not compared to the night before or the night before that, but the deep, rhythmical bludgeoning in his head told a different story. Try as he might, he couldn't remember the woman's name. He did know she was the first woman he'd slept with in ... too long. But he didn't want to be around when she woke up. Quietly, he slipped out of bed, dressed and crept downstairs. He was on his way out the front door when he glanced at his wristwatch.

4:42.

He cursed aloud, but stepped outside anyway. It was a mild night, but a light drizzle was falling, that steadily became more persistent as he headed south. By the time he arrived back at his Bayswater apartment, over thirty-five minutes later, his jacket, shirt and trousers were dripping water. He stripped naked and fell on his own bed ... the next time he opened his eyes it was 10:17.

He would have turned over, and gone back to sleep, but his bladder was bursting. His head still pounded. He dragged himself to the bathroom, where he caught a glimpse of himself in the mirror. He hadn't shaved for ... too many weeks, and his black beard was thick and unkempt.

He hated it when, based on nothing more than first impressions, people assumed he was Muslim. But that is what the beard and his Asian appearance labelled him as. Maybe he would get around to shaving later today or tomorrow, or the day after ... he made himself a strong black coffee, stirred in a generous teaspoon of sugar. He fancied toast as well, until he noticed the profusion of wispy blue-green mould spots on the half loaf he had left out overnight, uncovered. After donning a pair of shorts, he took his coffee across to his sofa, set it down on a hexagonal occasional table, and picked up a thin wad of A4 sheets he'd printed out a couple days ago.

Who has parental responsibility?

He had only arrived back in the UK three days ago, but even when he was drinking too much and sleeping too much in cheap hotel rooms in Casablanca, he couldn't stop thinking about his son. He had assumed, as the boy's father, he must have some legal rights. An online search soon made it clear he didn't. Chances are, he wasn't even named on his son's birth certificate.

It's as if I don't exist.

Legally, he'd read, he had no parental responsibility at all for his son, and there were only two ways he could acquire it: by agreement with the mother or by court order.

He had no idea how Samantha might respond, if he raised the subject with her, and a court order was a non-starter. The court, apparently, would decide to accept or reject a father's application for parental responsibility based on three factors.

The degree of commitment shown by the father to his child.

The degree of attachment between father and child.

The father's reasons for applying for the order.

I have no chance.

Which left Samantha.

Is she still seeing Alex?

He didn't want to know, but part of him did.

He scratched his beard, held his head in his hands for a long moment; it didn't stop the banging. His ribs still ached, when he leaned forward or turned suddenly, but the bruising had faded. He reached for his coffee, took a sip. It was still too hot to drink.

The doorbell chimed.

James reflexively glanced toward the front door, but he wasn't expecting any visitors and he didn't get up. He ignored it, when the doorbell chimed again, and when whoever it was rapped on the door with a fist. Then, in a raised voice, his unseen visitor spoke.

'James, are you home?'

Alex!

He stared at the door, but he didn't shift off the sofa.

Alex knocked again. 'Come on, buddy. I know you're back …'

Go fuck yourself.

But even as the thought passed through his mind, the door handle moved, and as the door began to swing slowly inward he silently cursed himself, for neglecting to lock it when he'd gotten in last night. No, scratch that. He'd gotten in this morning, not last night.

Alex's shaven head appeared. 'Sorry, James – the door was open and I – can I come in?'

'You already are.'

Alex, dressed in a check shirt and blue denim jeans, appeared decidedly uncomfortable. 'Yeah, I – you okay?'

'Why shouldn't I be?'

'No reason, I – what's with the beard? You look like a fuckin' insurgent!'

He didn't say anything.

'Mind if I join you?'

He didn't say anything.

He indicated the other half of the sofa.

'I had a late night,' he said, suddenly feeling the need to justify why he was sitting in shorts, nursing a mug of black coffee. He hoped he didn't look as rough as he felt, but guessed he must do. Rougher, probably. 'I just got up.'

Alex sat down. 'Good night?'

'Not great.' He shook his head, and immediately regretted it. 'I don't even remember her name.'

Alex grinned. 'What, you went out and got laid, and you didn't think to invite me?'

He wasn't in the mood for levity.

Images that had haunted him filled his head again.

Bluntly, he asked, 'What's the score between you and Sami?'

'James, I – ' A pained expression replaced Alex's grin. 'What happened that night you called, to tell Sami you'd found Luke, I swear – I thought you were dead. We both did, and when you – when Sami got back from Morocco, her head was so far up her arse …'

He didn't say anything.

'Sami's been worried about you – we both have.'

He didn't say anything.

Where the fuck have you been, anyway?'

'Morocco.'

As soon as Samantha reclaimed her son, he'd driven back to Casablanca and checked into the first cheap hotel he found. An hour later, he was sitting in a chair, staring out of the window and nursing an empty bottle of red wine … the days and weeks that followed passed in a drunken blur. He rarely left his hotel room, and when he did … one night, he went to the waterfront, but the *Joie de Vie* was nowhere to be seen. Just as well, really, because if he had spotted any of the bastards who abducted his son ... he expected Ahmed to contact him, to ask for a written statement or to up-date him, but he didn't. He was thrown out of his hotel, booked into another ... he got into a fight at a seedy nightclub. Even now, he couldn't recall how things kicked off, but he did vaguely remember a woman was involved. He was arrested, and he spent six days and six nights in a Moroccan prison. Not a pleasant experience, especially once he sobered up. Then, with no explanation from anyone, he was driven to Mohammed V International Airport by two uniforms – and deported.

'I only got back a few days ago.'

'Yeah, I know.' Alex confessed he had bribed one of his neighbours, to give him a call when he returned home.

Silence.

He stared at Alex. 'You haven't answered my question ...'

'About?'

'You know what about.'

Alex did, and his body language told him what he wanted to know before Alex did.

'Me and Sami – we split up for a while, when she arrived back with Luke. I wanted to carry on seeing her, but she – she needed time, I guess. We didn't start seeing each other again until six weeks ago, and a week later ...'

He waited.

'... I moved in with her.'

'What do you want, Alex?'

'I ... ' Alex hesitated. 'Sami asked me to call by. She wants to see you. She didn't say why, but she said to tell you it's important. She wants to see you during the day, today if you can make it, while the kids are at school. I'm only guessing, but I think she might wanna talk to you about Luke.'

James didn't say anything.

And a week later ... I moved in with her.

He wasn't surprised to learn Alex and Samantha were still seeing each other, but to hear they were living together, and had been for five weeks ...

That makes him my son's step-father.

Luke was his son, not Alex's, but ...he was in no fit state to go see Samantha. Equally, this was an opportunity he couldn't afford to pass on, not if he wanted to play a meaningful role in his son's upbringing.

'Okay,' he agreed. 'Give me thirty.'

Standing in the bathroom, James took two headache tablets, before forcing himself to drink a half pint glass of water, and then another, in an attempt to rehydrate his body. He looked in the mirror, and hardly recognised the man staring back at him.

You look like a fuckin' insurgent!

Ten minutes later, his beard was gone. Initially, he left his moustache untouched, but most Muslim men who didn't have a beard did sport a moustache and he didn't want to appear Muslim if he could avoid it, so he shaved it off. He could use a haircut as well, but that was going to have to wait for another day. After a cold-hot-cold shower, he decided on smart-casual: light tan trousers, white shirt and a brown leather jacket.

Samantha was still living in the Henley-on-Thames she'd shared with her late husband. Alex, he noticed, was driving the professor's black Range Rover but he didn't say anything. Soon after they hit the A4, heading east, Alex asked how he had fooled 'the Nazi' into believing he was dead, and so he told him.

Alex grinned. 'You should have heard him, bragging about how he'd killed my Paki boyfriend – his words, not mine.'

A short silence.

'He won't be bothering you again.'

He glanced at Alex. 'He's dead?'

'Yeah, he got into an argument with a Glock and lost.'

He found a smile. 'What about Vaughan?'

'No idea – I didn't see him again, after he and the Nazi split.'

He fell silent, thinking Vaughan was intelligent enough and slippery enough to have made good his escape. Not good news, but then today wasn't turning into a good news day. He liked to think, one day, he would cross Vaughan's path again and when he did …

Alex said, 'I'm assuming it's the Nazi who told you where to find Luke?'

'He did,' he confirmed, 'but I arrived too late.'

Alex cocked his head. 'Too late …?'

He told him about Vaughan's deadline, and how he'd missed it by two days. 'The kidnappers were supposed to kill Luke, but instead they sold him.'

Alex whistled.

'They got two grand for him – US dollars.'

'That sucks – he's a kid, not a fuckin' slave!'

'What the bastards wanted him for was worse than slavery.'

Alex glanced at him, as if to ask 'what is worse than slavery?'

'Child prostitution,' he said, quietly.

Chapter 51

James tensed, as the Range Rover turned into the gravel driveway.

It was a large, detached red brick house with white bay windows and a white front door. Four, possibly five bedrooms, he reckoned. At least two bathrooms, with an en-suite for the master bedroom. There was a garage on the left, and he knew there was an impressive conservatory and a kitchen extension around the back, both of which led out into a garden half as big as a football pitch. Given its size and location, the property had to be worth at least a million.

Last time he visited it was dark and he'd sneaked around the back, climbed on the kitchen extension, and gained entrance through Joshua's bedroom window. Today, following Alex's lead, he took a more conventional route. But even before they reached the front door, he spotted a moving white blur through frosted, oval glass. Samantha, who must have been watching for their arrival, opened the door.

She stepped outside, smiled warmly as she threw her arms around Alex, and hugged and kissed him. 'Thank you, Alex.'

He kissed her back. 'Yeah, no worries.'

As the lovers parted, James noticed they held hands for a long, lingering moment. He found his voice. 'Hello, Sami.'

'James, I …' She turned to him, and he saw the uncertainty in her eyes as she took a pace forward and embraced him, hesitantly at first. As they hugged each other closer, he inhaled the alluring fragrance of her perfume. They held each other for a second or two and, as she relaxed her grip, her green eyes looked into his. 'I wasn't sure you'd come, I thought – you never gave me chance to thank you for getting Luke back.'

'I'm sorry, Sami. I …' He didn't know what else to say.

She was wearing a white, pleated skirt and a peach blouse, over which there was a fluffy, white cashmere cardigan that wasn't buttoned. Simple, yet elegant, and he noticed she'd had her hair styled. She looked stunning.

Coming into the house he detected the unmistakable whiff of fresh paint. Someone had been decorating – erasing physical vestiges of the late professor? He followed Samantha into a lounge that was nearly as large as his apartment, in terms of floor space. The walls were cream, the carpet beige, and the huge bay window filled the room with natural, diffused light. To his left, in a discreet alcove, there were a couple of free standing storage towers with clear, pull-out drawers filled with toys and games. Two satin blue three-seat sofas stood facing each other, with a third two-seat sofa across one end, forming a rectangle. An oval rug with blue and cream whirls filled the space between them, and two white round pedestal tables sat on it.

There were several paintings on the walls, landscapes mostly, including a beautiful tropical sunset. Pride of place, over the ornate white marble fireplace, was taken by a canvas mounted photograph of Luke and Joshua that must have been taken six to twelve months ago, but his eyes were drawn to a line of much smaller photographs lined up on the mantle. No professor, of course, but Alex featured on three of the snaps. One on his own, one with Samantha, and one crouched down between Luke and Joshua. Alex had an arm around both boys, and both boys had an arm around Alex. All three of them were grinning. It was a nice pose, but … he turned away.

Greetings over and done, he sensed Samantha's nervousness return. Hovering just inside the lounge, she asked, 'Can I get you anything to drink?'

'I wouldn't say no to a coffee,' said Alex.

She looked to him. 'James?'

He was tempted to ask for something stronger, but resisted. 'Coffee sounds good.'

Invited to do so, he made himself comfortable on one of the three-seat sofas. Alex sat on the edge of the opposite sofa, not directly across from him, and for a moment neither of them said anything. Then, to break the awkward silence and because he wanted to know, he asked, 'How's Luke doing?'

'He's doing good,' Alex replied. 'Sami said he was clingy when she got him back, and it took her a coupla weeks to get him settled in school again, but he's a resilient little guy and he's doing good now.'

Samantha returned, carrying a tray with three mugs, sugar, cream and a pot of coffee. One of the mugs was already filled with hot water, which had a green teabag floating in it. As she set it down one of the pedestal tables, he noticed a small brown envelope on the tray with a name handwritten on it: James.

'Nothing's been made public yet,' she said, sitting next to Alex, but facing and addressing him, 'but I'm hoping the authorities in Ecuador will formally attribute the discovery of the Metal Library to you and Alex, at the same time crediting my father's research.' Pouring steaming coffee into the two empty mugs, she continued. 'No firm decisions have been taken yet, but the local government is exploring the possibility of building a dedicated museum, to house some of the artifacts we found. Eventually, if they discover or can build a more accessible entrance, they're hoping to open up some of the underground complex to the public as well, to attract tourists to the region.'

She picked up the envelope.

'The Metal Library is a major find,' she said. 'It's as important and prestigious to Ecuador as Howard Carter's discovery of Tutankhamun's tomb was to Egypt.' She held out the envelope and, after a moment's hesitation, he accepted it. 'This is the government of Ecuador's way of saying thank you.'

The envelope wasn't sealed.

He slid out a cheque made payable to 'Mr James Harris', and noticed the payee was 'Ms S. Radcliffe', suggesting Samantha had reverted to using her maiden name. Understandable, given the circumstances.

The amount: £320,000.

He stared at the figure for a long moment, before he slid the cheque back in its envelope, held it out for Samantha. 'You need this more than I do.'

'That's exactly what I told her,' said Alex, 'when she gave me mine.'

He worked it out in his head. It wasn't difficult. Two times £320k is £640k – around $1 million, he guessed, at the current pound sterling/US dollar exchange rate.

Samantha smiled, but she made no move to accept the envelope back. 'I appreciate the gesture, James, but you're wrong. Richard didn't leave a will, so under intestacy law I'm going to inherit most of his estate. Even after I've paid death duty and other expenses, my solicitor estimates I should be worth at least five million – and that doesn't include this place.'

He guessed she was talking British pounds, not American dollars. Suddenly, £320k didn't seem as significant a sum as it had a few seconds ago.

'Keep the money, please – you and Alex are the ones who earned it, not me.'

What am I going to do with £320k?

He could drink himself around the world several times, if he wanted to. But he didn't want to. He spooned sugar into his coffee, but didn't touch the cream. 'Sami, I appreciate this, I really do, but … have you told Luke about me?'

She hesitated, before admitting no, she hadn't said anything to Luke. Nothing at all. Alex must have felt the temperature rising.

'I can take a hike, if the two of you want a bit of privacy?'

'No, Alex,' she said, placing her hand on his thigh. 'This concerns you as much as it does James. I want you to stay.'

He nodded acceptance.

James stared at Samantha.

How does this concern Alex?

But it did concern Alex. Of course it concerned Alex. How could it not concern Alex, when Alex was living under the same roof as his son and sleeping with his son's mother? And, if the snapshot on the mantle was any guide, Alex had already built up a pretty good relationship with Luke and Joshua.

'I want to see him,' he said. 'I wanted to tell him who I was in Morocco, but – it wasn't easy, spending time with him and not saying anything. I wanted to, but I didn't think it was my call and I still don't … I think it's time he found out who his father is.'

She looked deep into his eyes. 'I think so, too, James. I really do …'

'But?'

Why is there always a but?

'But … raising a child is a long time commitment,' she answered. 'I don't want to introduce Luke to you, let him get to know you, then have you disappear from his life after only a few weeks or months.'

He couldn't deny it was a valid point.

Suddenly he wished he was drinking something stronger than black coffee. 'So what are you saying – you don't want me to see him?'

'Of course not,' she replied, 'that wouldn't be fair on you and it wouldn't be fair on Luke. If it wasn't for you, I might never have seen him again. He has every right to know who his father his, and you have every right to see your son, but – I know I can't hold you to any guarantees you give, but I need to hear you're willing to make some kind of long term commitment to Luke.'

'I'm not planning on going anywhere,' he assured her.

She visibly relaxed. 'You've no idea how happy it makes me to hear you say that.'

'I mean it, Sami.' He hesitated, before asking, 'Am I named on Luke's birth certificate?'

'No, I – you weren't around at the time and I … even if I could have named you, I would have put you down as Mohammed Hassan – not James Harris.'

Funny, now she spelled it out it was blindingly obvious, but the fact he'd changed his name after he did a runner hadn't occurred to him once over the past couple days. He wanted to ask Samantha about parental responsibility, as well, but stopped himself. If he pushed too far, too soon, he risked hearing answers he didn't want to hear. No, if he wanted Samantha to grant him parental responsibility for his son, he was going to have to prove himself first. Earn the right. And he was determined to do just that.

263

Alex cleared his throat, and he and Samantha exchanged a knowing glance. 'James, there's something you need to know …'

What do I need to know?

Head down, avoiding meeting his gaze, Samantha was twirling her fingers around each other on her lap. A moment ago, she'd looked reasonably composed, but now …

It hit him like a sledgehammer.

She's pregnant!

'It's my fault,' she said, looking up. 'I – a few days after Alex moved in, Joshua came home from school and told me one of his friends had a new daddy, and he asked me if Alex was his new daddy? I asked him if he'd like that and he said he would, so …'

'We talked about it,' said Alex, taking up the story, 'and I kinda liked the idea of hearing him call me daddy.'

'Josh was delighted when we told him – he'd never had anyone he could call daddy before. Richard never allowed it, and … the thing is …'

She lowered her gaze again.

Alex wouldn't face him, either.

He didn't understand why – then, suddenly, he did.

'Luke,' he said, flatly.

'James, I – you've got to understand, at the time we had no idea where you were or when you'd be back, or even if we'd see you again. Last time you disappeared, you were gone for over five years …'

Rub it in, why don't you.

'I should have guessed Luke would copy his brother, but I didn't and – what was I supposed to tell him? That it was okay for Josh to call Alex daddy, but he couldn't?'

Silence.

He didn't know what to say.

He didn't say anything.

'James, no one is disputing Luke is your son – of course he is, but … this isn't a big issue, it really isn't. You'd be surprised how many kids these days have two dads.'

He repeated her words over in his head.

You'd be surprised how many kids these days have two dads.

He knew, for as long as Samantha and Alex stayed together, Alex was always going to be daddy number one.

That makes me daddy number two.

The realisation hurt, badly, but …

'There's something else I need to tell you,' she said, twirling her fingers again, more nervously than before. She glanced at Alex. 'Both of you …'

264

He waited.

Alex waited.

Then she dropped a bomb on them.

'I'm pregnant … one of you is the father.'